F
Gould

Gould, Judith.

The secret heiress.

DATE			

BAKER & TAYLOR

The Secret Heiress

Novels by Judith Gould

Sins
Love-Makers
Dazzle
Never Too Rich
Texas Born
Forever
Too Damn Rich
Second Love
Till the End of Time
Rhapsody
Time to Say Good-Bye
A Moment in Time
The Best Is Yet to Come
The Greek Villa
The Parisian Affair
Dreamboat

JUDITH GOULD

The
Secret Heiress

NEW AMERICAN LIBRARY

New American Library
Published by New American Library, a division of
Penguin Group (USA) Inc., 375 Hudson Street,
New York, New York 10014, USA
Penguin Group (Canada), 90 Eglinton Avenue East, Suite 700, Toronto,
Ontario M4P 2Y3, Canada (a division of Pearson Penguin Canada Inc.)
Penguin Books Ltd., 80 Strand, London WC2R 0RL, England
Penguin Ireland, 25 St. Stephen's Green, Dublin 2,
Ireland (a division of Penguin Books Ltd.)
Penguin Group (Australia), 250 Camberwell Road, Camberwell, Victoria 3124,
Australia (a division of Pearson Australia Group Pty. Ltd.)
Penguin Books India Pvt. Ltd., 11 Community Centre, Panchsheel Park,
New Delhi - 110 017, India
Penguin Group (NZ), cnr Airborne and Rosedale Roads, Albany,
Auckland 1310, New Zealand (a division of Pearson New Zealand Ltd.)
Penguin Books (South Africa) (Pty.) Ltd., 24 Sturdee Avenue,
Rosebank, Johannesburg 2196, South Africa

Penguin Books Ltd., Registered Offices:
80 Strand, London WC2R 0RL, England

First published by New American Library,
a division of Penguin Group (USA) Inc.

First Printing, October 2006
10   9   8   7   6   5   4   3   2   1

 REGISTERED TRADEMARK—MARCA REGISTRADA

LIBRARY OF CONGRESS CATALOGING-IN-PUBLICATION DATA:

Gould, Judith.
  The secret heiress/Judith Gould.
    p. cm.
  ISBN 0-451-21966-X
  1. Twins—Fiction. 2. Separation (Psychology)—Fiction. 3. Psychological
fiction.   I. Title.
  PS3557.O867S435 2006
  813'.54—dc22   2006010755

Set in Sabon
Designed by Ginger Legato

Printed in the United States of America

Fic.

PUBLISHER'S NOTE
This is a work of fiction. Names, characters, places, and incidents either are the product of the author's imagination or are used fictitiously, and any resemblance to actual persons, living or dead, business establishments, events, or locales is entirely coincidental.
   The publisher does not have any control over and does not assume any responsibility for author or third-party Web sites or their content.

To the one I love

And, after all, what is a lie? 'Tis but
The truth in masquerade.

Don Juan, CANTO XI
GEORGE NOEL GORDON
(LORD BYRON), 1788–1824

Prologue

❧

January 1994
On the island of Hydra, Greece

Wh
en she was suddenly awakened by her mother, she sat up in bed and rubbed her eyes with small fists. "What is it, Mama?" she asked in a sleepy voice.

"Don't ask questions now, Ariadne," her mother said sternly. "We must hurry."

"But what—?"

"No buts, Ariadne," Maria said, pulling the bedcovers off her daughter and shoving them aside. "You must get up now. Quickly."

Her mother had turned on the lamp at her bedside, and in its small pool of light Ariadne could see that her mother's eyes were red and swollen. She had been crying. "What's wrong, Mama?" she asked worriedly. "Why are you crying?"

Her father's voice came from out of the darkness at the doorway to the tiny bedroom. "Your mama is fine, Ariadne," he said. "Do as she says and hurry. We're going on a trip." She heard his footsteps as he marched back into the front room.

A trip? Ariadne wondered what he was talking about. Maybe it was for her birthday, she thought. Tomorrow she would be ten years old.

"Here," her mother said, gesturing to Sunday clothes she placed on the bed. "Put these on."

Ariadne pulled off her nightgown and dutifully began dressing, watching as her mother opened the drawers in the old pine chest and began emptying their contents into a small piece of luggage. Sweaters, shirts, underwear, socks—all of Ariadne's clothing in the drawers—went into the suitcase. Before she had tied the laces of her sneakers, her mother had taken the few things hanging in the battered armoire and placed them atop the clothing that already nearly filled the suitcase. Flipping the top down, she struggled with the zipper but finally managed to bring it all the way around.

When she was finished, she sat down on the bed and turned to Ariadne. In her hand was a long black scarf. She placed it on Ariadne's head, then wrapped its ends around her neck. It was so low on her forehead and high on her chin that it obscured everything but the child's eyes. Putting a hand on each of her daughter's shoulders, she gazed at Ariadne with an anguished expression, then slid her arms around her and hugged her tightly.

"You were a gift from God," she said in a sorrowful voice. "You know that, and you know that we have loved you more than anything in the world, don't you, Ariadne?"

"Yes, Mama," the child said, nodding her head. Ariadne knew that Mama and Papa weren't her real parents. They had told her many times that she had been given to them, but they never failed to tell her that they loved her all the more for that reason. They were unable to have children, Maria had confided, but God had given them Ariadne. About her birth parents they had always been vague.

Suddenly Maria drew back with a look of panic. She quickly unraveled Ariadne's scarf from around her neck and felt for the gold chain that was supposed to be there. She sighed with relief when her hand grasped it, and she pulled it out from beneath Ariadne's sweater.

Holding it in her palm, she gazed down at it reverently. It was a Byzantine gold cross, encrusted with small rubies and blue sapphires. Looking up into her daughter's eyes, she said, "You must never lose this, Ariadne. Promise me that."

Ariadne shook her head. "I won't, Mama."

Maria quickly tucked it back beneath the child's sweater, then arranged the scarf about her neck again. "Put your coat on."

Ariadne shrugged into the puffy parka that lay on the bed, and zipped it up.

"Let's go," Maria said, taking the child's hand in hers and picking up the suitcase with the other.

"Where?" Ariadne asked, hurrying to keep up with her mother's pace.

"Papa will tell you about it," Maria replied.

In the small front room of the cottage, Thrassos sat at the well-scrubbed wooden table in the middle of the room. At this table they ate all of their meals, Ariadne did her schoolwork, and her mother sewed. The hanging lamp over the table was lit, and in the pool of light it cast on the tabletop, Ariadne saw a bottle of ouzo—the pretty one with the ballerina on it—and a small glass of the clear liquid. Her papa hadn't put ice in it, so it hadn't become a milky cloud. As she watched, he hoisted the glass and downed its contents in one swallow. He set the glass back down on the table with a resounding bang, then rose to his feet.

"Are you ready?" he asked, glancing at her, then quickly averting his gaze.

"She's ready," Maria said.

"Let's go, then," he said. Taking the suitcase from his wife, he went to the front door and pulled it open.

Maria grabbed Ariadne and hugged her tightly. "I love you," she said, tears beginning to flow from her eyes. "Remember that, Ariadne. I love you. I love you more than anything in the world."

Ariadne found her mother's tears disturbing, but before she could ask her why she was crying or offer her mama consolation, Thrassos said, "Come on, Ariadne. We must hurry. Someone is waiting for us."

Her mother released her and pushed Ariadne toward the doorway, but Maria remained standing where she was, unwilling to take another step in that direction.

Thrassos took his daughter's hand and, without a backward glance toward his wife, led Ariadne out the doorway, slamming the door shut behind him.

The small walled-in yard in front of the cottage was lit by an old-fashioned lantern next to the door, and Ariadne saw that the ancient, gnarled fig tree cast eerie shadows on the wall. They quickly crossed the yard toward the gap in the wall that led out to a stony dirt path. The track, carved out over the years by donkeys, served as the only way to and from their remote cottage.

"Where are we going, Papa?" Ariadne asked again. But before Thrassos could answer, she heard a weird, frightening sound like nothing she'd ever heard before. It was coming from the top of the nearby hill. As her father hurriedly pulled her along beside him, steadily going uphill, the sound became louder and louder. Rounding a bend in the path, Ariadne saw that all the scrub and the wild sage and thyme were being blown nearly flat against the rocky ground by a powerful downwind.

She stopped short, pulling on her father's hand. "What is it, Papa?" she asked, her eyes wide with fright.

"A helicopter, Ariadne," he said. "We're going for a ride on it. It'll be fun. Now, come on."

She had little idea what a helicopter was, but she trusted her father. Ariadne let herself be guided on up the hill toward the awful sound and wind. Near the top, she saw the scary machine, illuminated by the powerful lights mounted on its exterior. It looked like a giant insect to Ariadne, and she clasped her father's hand in fear. The blades that turned above it were terrifying. She didn't want to go any farther. When she stopped, though, he ignored her protest, jerking her after him.

"There's no time to waste, Ariadne," he said in a no-nonsense voice.

When they drew near the helicopter, the dust thrown up by the rotors made a cloud around them. Thrassos bent down and hugged Ariadne close. "Cover your face with your hands," he yelled over the sound, "and stay next to me. We're going aboard now."

"I'm scared, Papa," she cried.

"There's nothing to be scared of if you stay next to me, Ariadne," he said. "We will hurry." He put an arm over her shoulders and propelled her alongside him, ducking his head. When they reached the steps, he rushed her up them and into the chopper. The two men sitting at the controls turned to look at them.

"Stash the suitcase in the net," the captain yelled, pointing aft, behind the two passenger seats. "Then buckle yourselves in." The copilot got out of his seat and pressed a button next to the cabin door opening. The steps automatically retracted into an upright position, bringing the cabin door with them.

"Sit," Thrassos said to Ariadne, and she slid into one of the small, upholstered seats. He quickly secured the suitcase in the net that was attached to the cabin's fuselage, then sat next to her. "Here," he said, grasping both ends of her seat belt, "be still while I tighten this." After he had secured her seat belt, he put on his own.

"Ready?" asked the captain.

Thrassos nodded.

The captain gave a thumbs-up signal and turned back to the controls. "We're taking off," he called.

Thrassos took Ariadne's hand and held it tightly. "This will be fun, Ariadne," he said, trying to reassure her.

"Where are we going, Papa?" she asked again.

"You'll see," he responded, smiling. "It's a surprise."

The helicopter slowly lifted into the air, and Ariadne gasped as it abruptly pitched forward. Her father put an arm around her shoulders and pulled her close.

When they were cruising at a steady speed, Ariadne ventured a look out the porthole next to her. At first she saw nothing but blackness, but in the distance she soon noticed small clumps of lights twinkling on various islands. Occasionally, larger areas of light indicated populous villages or towns.

They had been airborne for less than thirty minutes when she felt her eyes growing weary. The excitement of being wakened in the middle of the night and the ride in the helicopter proved exhausting. Ariadne fell into a deep sleep, her head against her father's chest.

When the ride was over, her father shook her awake. The helicopter was descending onto a concrete runway. She hadn't seen the enormous expanse of lights that illuminated Athens, a city of four million people. A big fuel truck and another aircraft were parked nearby, and in the distance she could see huge metal buildings of some kind.

After the pilot cut the engines, he turned in his seat to face them. "You can unbuckle now."

Thrassos removed Ariadne's seat belt as the copilot unlocked the cabin door. He stood back while Thrassos retrieved Ariadne's suitcase, then led her down the lowered steps.

"We'll be waiting," the captain called to him.

Thrassos led Ariadne toward the small jet a hundred feet away. She gazed at him in alarm, suddenly fully awake. "What now, Papa?"

"Another short ride," he replied. "A really nice one."

They reached the sleek Gulfstream V, and he guided her up the steps. His pace slowed as they neared the top. Once inside the jet, he set her suitcase down.

Ariadne gazed about the interior and was surprised to see that, in contrast with the helicopter, it was luxuriously appointed, with leather seats and thick carpeting. A man rose to his feet from one of the large seats and shook her father's hand. The stranger was dressed in an expensive-looking suit and a silk tie. His shoes shone with polish, and his hair was carefully cut. He smiled down at her, exhibiting perfect white teeth.

"You must be Ariadne?" he said in a mellifluous voice.

Ariadne looked up at him but didn't speak. His dark eyes gleamed frighteningly.

"I am Nikos," the man said. He extended a hand, but the child didn't take it. She suddenly clutched her father's arm with both hands.

"This is Ariadne," her father said. He bent down and kissed her. "I'm going to leave now," he said, "but you will have a very good time on this trip, Ariadne."

"Where are you going, Papa?" she asked anxiously.

"I'm going back to your mama," he said, "but you are going on an exciting trip. You must be a very good girl."

"But why?" she asked, panicked. "Aren't you coming, Papa?"

"Not on this one," he replied. "But it will be wonderful." Her father hugged her tightly and kissed her.

"I—I must g-go now." He relinquished his hold on her and gazed at the man with a pleading look that Ariadne had never seen before. "Please take good care of her."

"No need to worry," the man replied.

Ariadne lunged for her father, but he stepped out of reach. The other man grabbed her shoulder. "Papa?" she cried. "No, no! Papa!"

Her father hurried out the cabin door and then descended the steps quickly.

"Papa!" she cried after him. *"Papa!"* But he never turned around. In a few moments he had retreated to the helicopter that had brought them.

"Here, here, Ariadne," Nikos said. "Come and sit down."

Ariadne didn't move but stared up at him suspiciously. "No," she cried, her voice trembling with fear.

The man's dark eyes flashed with madness, and he clutched her arm in a viselike grip. He shoved her into a seat, slamming her against its back.

"*Papa!*" she wailed, tears running down her cheeks. "*Papa!*"

Chapter One

❧

January 2005

The landscape was Dantean in this part of Belarus. Smokestacks belched poisonous black clouds into the sky night and day, coating everything as far as the eye could see with a filthy residue. Animals had long since fled the area, having learned not to venture anywhere near the perimeter of the steel mill. What little vegetation that remained was blackened and dead, resembling nothing so much as Gorey's darkest wintry scenes. Over twenty thousand employees of the plant kept its outdated blast furnaces operating, and although they hated the conditions, they had to put food on the table. People joined in long lines to get work at the Belarus division of PPHL, Papadaki Private Holdings Limited.

The management complained to European headquarters in London, but their complaints fell on deaf ears. Thus, the fatal explosion that occurred came as no surprise. Sixty-two workers were killed in the blast, many of them incinerated to ash. Several hundred others were injured. Emergency crews swarmed to the plant to fight the fire caused by the explosion and cart off the dead and wounded.

"Let us in!" the crowd gathered outside screamed. Word had spread fast throughout the nearby town, and terrified relatives began to assemble at the high chain-link fencing that enclosed the steel mill. They shouted and begged with the armed gatekeepers to let them in. They wanted to know if husbands, fathers, brothers, or sons had been injured. But they were not allowed in, nor were they given any information concerning the explosion, the fatalities, or the wounded.

They began to protest, led by Anna Portnova, whose husband and son both worked at the steel mill. In desperation she attacked one of the guards with her fists, pounding his chest with all her might. In another moment the butt of his rifle slammed against her head. She was knocked to the ground unconscious, and blood began to stream from the wound at her temple.

The angry crowd was cowed by the guard's brutality, but they didn't disperse. A few carried Anna Portnova away in search of medical assistance, while the others kept up their chants, determined to get satisfaction of some sort from the company that ruled their lives. When the gates were opened and ambulances were waved inside, many of those waiting on the perimeter tried to sneak in, but they were caught and manhandled as if they were thieves rather than distraught relatives trying only to learn the truth.

Their pleas turned to a thunderous roar when they discovered that all of the plant's remaining furnaces were operating as usual. Just as no one was allowed in, no one was permitted to leave.

In the executive offices, Aleksandr Sokolov, the plant manager, paced the threadbare industrial carpeting in his office, waiting for someone in the London headquarters to pick up the telephone. When a secretary finally answered, Sokolov spoke to her in a rush. His heavily accented English rendered his frantic request virtually incomprehensible.

"Would you repeat that, sir?" the secretary asked. "I didn't quite understand you."

"This is Aleksandr Sokolov, the plant manager of PPHL in Belarus," he reiterated, more slowly this time. "We have had an explosion at the steel mill here, and I need to speak to Oliver Burdett immediately."

"I'm sorry, sir," the secretary said, "but Mr. Burdett is no longer with us."

Who is this idiot? Sokolov wondered. *And what does she mean? Did Burdett die? Was he fired?* He knew enough English to know that the phrase was ambiguous. "What do you mean, 'he's no longer with us'?" he asked, losing his patience. "I just spoke to him yesterday or the day before."

These Eastern European types! Violet Byatt thought, pursing her lips. *They're all animals!* This one was probably soused on vodka.

"I mean, sir," she said in a saccharine voice, "that Mr. Burdett is no longer with PPHL. He has been replaced." She brushed imaginary lint off the front of her pale blue twin set.

"Replaced?" Sokolov said. "You mean he's no longer the London manager?"

"That's precisely what I mean," she said.

"But—but who is his replacement?" Sokolov asked. "We have a dire situation here—a tragic situation—and we nearly have a riot on our hands. I need to speak to a manager at once."

"I'll have to transfer your call," Violet Byatt replied. "Please hold." *Let someone else deal with the drunken pig,* she thought.

"Who—?" But before Aleksandr Sokolov could ask who the new London manager of PPHL was, Violet Byatt put him on hold.

Aleksandr Sokolov listened anxiously to the *bleep-bleep* as she transferred his call. He dabbed the sweat on his brow with a handkerchief, wondering how much longer he could hold down his job under the present conditions. He had repeatedly warned Burdett that something like this would happen, but the corporation had no interest in his problems at the distant plant in Belarus. They were milking it for every penny they could get out of it, and damn the workers.

The pristine 265-foot megayacht *Nikoletta* had dropped anchor offshore the small but beautiful island of Barbados. Although she could have been docked at one of the piers, her owner, Nikoletta Papadaki, had been persuaded by the security detail that it was wiser to ferry guests to and from the yacht by helicopter and in its tenders and speedboats. That way the chance that a party crasher or other such undesirable would gain access to the yacht would be greatly reduced. Because of the guests, security was of paramount importance. Among them were a number of celebrities, several titled Europeans, several of the superrich, and even some of the ordinary rich. The jewelry worn by the women alone ran into the millions of dollars, and on the wrists of the men was a king's ransom in Patek Philippe, Breguet, and other watches of equally expensive provenance.

Nikoletta Papadaki had decided to have a prebirthday celebration. In another week she would turn twenty-one and ascend to the leadership of Papadaki Private Holdings Limited, as stipulated in her late father's will. She would now be the sole proprietress of one of the world's largest privately held corporations with worldwide interests. Only a partial list of her holdings included shipping, shipbuilding, and oil companies, oil refineries, mines of different kinds, various chemical companies, real estate, vast farming and livestock ranches, logging operations, hotels and resorts, even garment manufacturers and design firms. In short, there was hardly a continent or a business that PPHL didn't have a considerable finger in.

The Caribbean, Niki had decided, was the perfect place to celebrate her ascension. It was January, after all, and her host of rich, hedonistic friends, whether European or from the States, would be seeking the sun's solace during the dreary winter months. The South Americans she knew would think nothing of leaving their enclaves in Brazil or Argentina or their beach homes in Punta del Este to come to Barbados for a party.

One hundred and fifty of them had gathered, and they had all been ferried to her luxurious yacht, where they had dined on catered caviar, lobster, foie gras, and guinea hen. Now they were dancing the night away or enjoying more clandestine activities behind locked stateroom doors, fueled by the party's endless supply of Louis Roederer Cristal champagne or substances they'd brought themselves.

Niki was dancing to the band she'd brought in from Rio de Janeiro to play, to all appearances absorbed in her partner, but she was keeping an eye peeled for the sexiest man around. For later. She knew most of the men, of course, and had enjoyed dalliances with many of them. But being the connoisseur that she was, Niki wanted to make certain that tonight she bedded the most appealing man available.

"Don't you love them?" said Giovanni, a handsome, tanned Italian prince who'd come from Milan for the occasion.

"Who?" she asked, giving him the full attention of her huge dark eyes.

"The band, Niki," he said in an exasperated voice. "Have you already had that much champagne?"

"No," she said. "In fact, I'm just getting started. Anyway, who cares? The band's the best, Gianni," she replied, pressing her ample breasts against him lasciviously.

"Everything you do is the best," he replied, putting his hands on her round, firm buttocks.

Niki laughed raucously. "You're just horny, Gianni," she said. "You always are."

He smiled. "Who wouldn't be with you around, Niki?"

"Ha!" she said, poking his muscular chest with a lacquered fingernail. Gianni would do in a pinch, she thought, a tried-and-true lover. Yet she wanted to experience someone new tonight.

A hand lightly tapped Niki's shoulder, and she turned to see who it was. She frowned when she saw one of the yacht's stewards, a good-looking young blond whose name Niki couldn't remember. "What do you want?" she asked crossly. "Can't you see that I'm busy?"

"I'm very sorry, madam," he said, "but you have an important telephone call from London."

"Tell whoever it is to call back tomorrow," she said, refocusing her attention on Gianni.

"I'm sorry, madam," the young man persisted, "but the caller says it's an emergency."

Niki emitted a sigh of exasperation and reached for the cell phone he was carrying. "Give me that."

Before the young man could hand it to her, Niki snatched it out of his hand. "Hello?" she said, flipping a long tress of pale blond hair away from her eyes. Her manicured nails were varnished in a glittery gold, a touch she'd added to match the gold sequined gown John Galliano at Dior had designed especially for her bash.

At the other end of the line, Aleksandr Sokolov's surprise was shown in his voice. "Who is this?" he demanded.

"Who's *this*?" Niki fired back. "I was told this was an emergency, so whoever the hell you are, out with it. You're interrupting a party."

"This is Aleksandr Sokolov," he retorted. "I am the general manager of the PPHL plant in Belarus. I was trying to reach Mr. Oliver Burdett, the London manager of PPHL, and I was transferred to this number from the London office. Mr. Burdett has been replaced, I'm told. But I see that I've been connected to the wrong number."

"*Nyet*, Mr. Sokolov," Niki replied, mimicking his heavy Russian accent, "you've got the right number. This is Nikoletta Papadaki, and I'm the new chairman of PPHL worldwide. Now, what the hell do you want? I want to get back to my party."

Aleksandr Sokolov was momentarily speechless. "You have replaced Mr. Oliver Burdett?" he carefully inquired.

"You got it, Alek. Until I find a replacement for him, you answer to me. Now hurry up. Your time's running out."

"We have a crisis here at the Belarus steel mill," he said. "There has been an explosion. Sixty-two men were killed and many others injured. There are crowds at the gates—"

"Listen, Alek," Niki said. "You're the plant manager, right?"

"Yes, of course," he replied. "I told you that."

"Then *manage*," Niki snapped. "You're ruining my party."

"But—"

"But nothing. Don't ever bother me with crap like this again." She flipped the cell phone closed. "Idiot!" she said to no one in particular.

The steward appeared at her side immediately, his hand out for the cell phone.

"What's your name?" Niki asked, although she could clearly see it on the name tag he wore.

"Helmut, madam," he replied. "Helmut Schneider."

She ruffled his blond hair, then tapped his cheek lightly with the palm of her hand, as if warming up for a firm slap. "Well, Helmut, don't you ever interrupt me for something like that again or you're out of here."

"Yes, madam," he said sheepishly. "I was told it was an emer—"

"Never again!" Niki said.

He nodded. "Yes, madam. Of course."

He began backing away from her, and Niki turned back to Gianni.

"What was that all about?" he asked.

"Oh . . . business," she said. "At a damned steel mill in Belarus I bought."

"Belarus!" Gianni laughed, putting his arms around her. "How rude of them. The cretins have no manners. Bothering you with business at a time like this." He nuzzled her neck, his lips brushing against her flesh, and slid his hands over her ass again as they resumed dancing.

Niki tried to concentrate on the music, but she was too agitated by the interruption. She had to do something about it immediately. "Have you seen Adrian?"

He nodded to starboard. "He's over that way. Dancing with his sister."

Niki looked in the direction he'd indicated and saw Adrian and Honor dancing at the edge of the crowd. They were laughing about something. "I've got to have a talk with him," she said. "I'll see you later, Gianni."

"Aw, Niki," he complained, reaching out to grab her.

"Later," she repeated, already weaving her way through the throng of dancers to Adrian Single and his sister, ignoring the well-wishers who tried to engage her in conversation.

As she neared the pair, she noted how good-looking they were. Adrian, her forty-six-year-old godfather, was tall, dark, and handsome, and he was also suave and sophisticated and possessed of an acute business ability. Although he was much younger than her late father, he'd been his second-in-command and most trusted confidant and knew more about PPHL than anyone else. Honor Hurlstone, his widowed sister, was older than Adrian, but was still a beauty. When they saw Niki approach, they stopped dancing and turned to her with smiles.

"Are you having—?" Honor began.

"I need to talk to you," Niki said, her fiery eyes on Adrian.

"What's the matter?" he asked, letting go of Honor.

"I want you to fire the manager at the steel mill in Belarus," she said. "Fire him? But why?"

"I just got a telephone call from the idiot," Niki said, arms akimbo.

"What did he want?" Adrian Single asked, gazing at her with curiosity. His spoiled godchild's explosive nature alarmed him, and he could see that she appeared to have already had a lot to drink. Not a good sign.

"Who cares?" Niki retorted. "He's got a lot of nerve interrupting me during a party."

"But, Niki, he must not have known," Honor said, reaching out to stroke her arm.

Niki jerked her arm away, and her eyes flashed with fury. "Don't try to mother me, Honor."

Honor Hurlstone folded her hands together, and her features became an expressionless veil, giving away none of the turmoil that she felt. Niki was a complete mystery to her. She had been a virago since birth, and now that she had taken over the reins of her father's empire, Honor was dreading what effect the added power would have.

"Niki," Adrian said, smiling as if her demand were reasonable, "you know as well as I do that the man had no idea he was interrupting your party, and he wouldn't have called unless there was something extremely important going on. Now, what did he have to say?"

"Something about an explosion," she replied. "I don't really remember."

Honor gasped. "Oh, no!"

"Jesus," Adrian exclaimed. "Are you certain?"

Niki shrugged and plucked a glass of champagne from a passing waiter's tray. "I think so, but I'm not sure." She took a sip of the wine and gazed at him, her dark eyes taunting. "What I *am* sure about is that I want you to get rid of him." She started back toward Gianni, then turned to face Adrian again. "And *now*!"

Watching her weave her way among the dancers, stopping to chat and trilling laughter along the way, Honor felt a knot form in her stomach. "What are you going to do?" she asked Adrian, her dark eyes searching his.

"I'm going to call Sokolov and find out what the hell's going on first," he said, "then take it from there." He saw her worried expression. "Don't fret, Honor. It'll be okay."

"I'm not so sure," she replied.

He gave her arm a gentle squeeze. "I'll be back in a second," he said. "I need to hear myself think, so I'm going to make this call from my stateroom."

Honor nodded. "I'll be here." She sat down on an upholstered banquette and picked up the glass of champagne she'd left there. Niki's behavior concerned her greatly, and she couldn't throw off the feeling of impending doom that Niki's outburst had left her with. Nikos had been the only person who could ever control Niki, and even he had admitted defeat more often than victory. He'd admired his daughter's willfulness and even encouraged it. She was much like him, he'd often said, determined to get her way no matter what. Since his death, Niki had taken advice from no one, although she would sometimes listen to Adrian. Like her father, Adrian had been a constant presence in her life, somewhat like a benevolent uncle. But Honor wondered now whether Adrian would be able to help restrain Niki's more undesirable impulses. It was such a shame, Honor often thought, that Nikos and Larissa, his beautiful British wife, had divorced all those years ago and that Larissa had been killed in a car accident afterward. Perhaps Larissa might have had a beneficial influence on Niki, Honor idly mused, but somehow she doubted it. The girl had certainly never listened to *her*. On the contrary, she seemed determined to ignore every piece of advice Honor had ever tried to give her.

"Honor, darling! How are you?" A sleekly groomed and tanned woman near her age plopped down next to Honor, and they exchanged air kisses.

"Consuela," Honor enthused, "it's so good to see you. I didn't know whether you'd make it or not."

"Barely," her friend replied. "I'm getting a little old for all this." She waved a hand dramatically toward the dancing crowd.

"You'll never get too old," Honor said with a laugh. "Is Luigi with you?"

Consuela shook her head. "I gave the bastard the boot."

"What?"

Consuela nodded. "I decided that if he's going to live with me part of the year, then he's going to have to contribute something more than his cock to the household, you know?"

Honor laughed mirthfully.

"I discovered that he's seriously impoverished."

"But he's rich as Croesus," Honor protested.

"Poverty of *spirit,* darling," Consuela replied, lighting a cigarette.

Out of the corner of her eye, Honor caught a glimpse of Niki talking to Marella and Justin de Bord. She was standing between the two of them, an arm casually draped across Marella's shoulders, her lips close to Marella's ear as she imparted something to her old friend. But Honor also observed that Niki had a hand planted in one of Justin's rear trouser pockets. Her fingers were obviously very busy. The image was disturbing because Honor suddenly remembered the many spiteful and unkind words Niki had for Marella—behind her back—when she'd learned that her friend was going to be married to Justin. She wouldn't put it past Niki to try to cause trouble between the newlyweds.

"Men," Consuela said, interrupting her thoughts, "have been the bane and glory of my existence."

Honor laughed again. "Most of us could say the same, Consuela."

"You never seemed to have much trouble with old Jonathan."

"Well, it wasn't exactly a marriage made in heaven," Honor replied.

Adrian emerged from out of the crowd and beckoned with a hand for Honor to join him. "Have to run," she said to Consuela. "I'll catch up with you later."

She rose to her feet and went to Adrian, who led her forward. When they reached a deserted stretch of deck, he stopped and turned to her.

"Is it as bad as that, Adrian?" she asked. "You look very worried."

"It's worse than I thought," he said. "There's been an explosion at the steel mill, and a lot of people have been killed or injured." He paused, gritting his teeth. "And as if that's not horrible enough, there's a revolt going on at the plant. Relatives storming the gates and so on."

"Oh, my God," Honor said. "Those poor people. What are you going to do?"

"I'm leaving for there immediately," he said.

"But . . . do you have to do it?" she asked. "Can't you send someone to take care of it? That's Angelo's territory, after all."

He shook his head. "Angelo's got a bad case of the flu, remember? That's why he's not here. Besides, I don't want anybody else going," he said. "The situation is too volatile. I don't trust anybody else to handle it."

"I understand," she said. "You always were the best troubleshooter the company had." She heard the yacht's helicopter fire up its engines over the music of the band, then felt the downdraft created by the rotors.

"The helicopter's taking me to the airport," Adrian said. "I'll talk to you later, okay?"

She nodded her acquiescence. "Be careful," she said.

"I will," he replied. "I'd better hurry."

He rushed toward the stairway that took him to the top deck, where the helicopter pad was located. Moments later, Honor watched it rise into the air, then level off and head away from the yacht into the dying light.

In the owner's luxuriously appointed suite, Niki, with Justin's powerful arms about her, pressed the button that automatically closed the curtains. Then she pressed another one to dim the lights very low. She turned to him, and they kissed as if they were starved lovers, fueled by carnal desire, copious amounts of champagne, and a couple of lines of cocaine that

Justin had provided. Stealing Justin away from Marella made this occasion a triumph. From outside, the music of the Brazilian band intruded, but they paid no attention to it. As they kissed, he pushed her toward the silk-covered bed, finally toppling her onto it.

"Just a sec," Niki whispered, slipping out of the gold satin shoes she wore and dropping them to the floor. She scooted across the bed and lit two large candles on the built-in bedside cabinet, then pressed the button to turn the lights completely out. "That's better, isn't it?"

"You look good enough to eat in any light," Justin said in his low, raspy baritone. He grinned lasciviously. "And that's what I'm going to do."

He kicked off his loafers, then unbuckled his belt and let his trousers fall to the floor. He was wearing no underwear, and his fully engorged penis sprang out in front of him.

"Hmmm," Niki murmured, her dark eyes bright with lust. "Quick, help me out of this damn dress." She slid up on her knees with her back to Justin, and he unbuttoned and unzipped the dress. It slipped off her shoulders, and Niki turned to him, her breasts fully exposed. She wore no underwear, either.

Justin sucked in his breath and let it out. "Whew, babe," he said, putting a hand on each of her ample, rosy-nippled breasts and massaging them gently.

"That feels so good, Justin," Niki moaned with pleasure. She changed positions and squirmed out of her dress, tossing it carelessly to the floor, all the while enjoying his hands on her, his fingers thrumming her nipples. She sat on the edge of the bed, looking up at him coyly, and began flicking her tongue at his penis.

Justin groaned and eased himself into her mouth, and Niki laved him with her tongue. Her nipples had grown hard, and she was getting wet between her thighs. "Whoa," Justin gasped. "God, Niki. You're going to make me shoot." He pulled away from her, then lifted her under her arms, sliding her back onto the bed.

Niki spread her legs apart, anxious to feel him inside her, but Justin had other plans first. "I love that Brazilian wax job, babe," he said, running a finger up and down between her thighs. "That's so hot."

Niki mewled like a kitten, excited by the feel of his finger there, and shoved herself toward it.

But Justin quickly got onto his knees and raised her legs, placing one on each of his shoulders, then buried his face in her mound. She thought she would levitate with excitement when she felt his tongue inside her, licking and probing, licking and probing.

"Oh, my God. Justin . . . Justin," she moaned. "Oh, it feels so good. I can't stand it. . . . I'm . . . I'm . . ."

He abruptly stopped and eased her legs down onto the bed, spreading them wide. He mounted her, plunging into her with the force of a man possessed. He began driving himself in and out, in and out. All the while his mouth nuzzled her breasts, first one, then the other, his tongue licking, his teeth teasing her hard nipples.

Niki began to thrash from side to side, lost in a world of ecstatic lust. When she started contracting, she let out a cry. "Oh, God. Justin . . . Justin . . . oh, my God . . . I'm . . ." With another loud cry, she let herself go completely and began to spasm, overcome by wave after wave of breathtaking orgasm.

With a mighty thrust Justin drove himself into her and flooded her with his seed. His body tensed and jerked as he drained himself. Then he fell atop her, panting, his chest heaving against hers. "Fuck, Niki," he rasped. "That was so good."

"I know," she gasped, still catching her breath.

He gazed at her with eyes that glittered in the candlelight. "Was that okay?"

Niki laughed. "It was adequate," she said, running her hands up and down his back, finally bringing them to rest on his shoulders.

She kissed him, then gazed into his eyes. "But what about Marella? Is she going to freak out?"

He stretched out on the bed, pulling Niki alongside him. "What's Marella going to know?" He shrugged. "Besides, who cares if she does?"

"She's going to know something's going on if you're here all night," Niki said, "and if I know her, she won't like it."

"Yeah, she's like a nun," Justin said, laughing. "She doesn't like anything, including me. So I don't give a damn."

Neither do I, Niki thought. Marella was always too self-righteous for her taste. The only reason they'd been friends was that they'd been thrown together at the same schools and social events over the years.

He traced a finger around her nipples, then down her torso, encircling her navel, and letting it rest between her thighs. "I should have married you, babe," he said, "but then it wouldn't be as much fun, would it?"

"Hmmm." Niki brushed her hand across his testicles. "I like it better this way. I'm not ready to settle down like you and Marella."

"Marella may have settled down," Justin said, running his fingers up and down her mound, "but I don't have any intention of living that way. Not when somebody like you comes along."

Niki smiled. "My sentiments exactly," she said. "The world's a big candy store—why have just one piece?"

Justin began licking her neck and ears, his breath hot on her skin. "And you're the best piece of candy around, Niki," he whispered.

And you can have all you want, she thought, feeling his engorged manhood against her thigh. *The more I get, the less Marella can have.*

He mounted her again. "I want you to have a night you'll never forget," he said as he pushed himself inside her.

"I'm sure I won't, Justin," she cooed, already wet with excitement. "You're the perfect guest."

Chapter Two

❧

Ariadne slowly crossed the marble floors of the hushed museum, pausing now and then in front of a painting that especially appealed to her eye. She was familiar with the small but interesting collection of the Williams College museum. The building was a neoclassical structure of elegant proportions, and it contained a wealth of wonderful paintings and sculpture that spanned centuries of art. While she didn't claim to understand everything she saw—she was, after all, majoring in economics—she was learning how to appreciate beauty for its own sake. Having spent her teenage years buried at a boarding school and summer camp, spending only brief vacations with her foster parents in tiny, rural Roxbury, Connecticut, she hadn't been exposed to much art.

Through an arched doorway she stepped into another gallery and began a slow turn about the room. She felt the hair on the nape of her neck stand up, and became aware that someone was watching her. Shifting her gaze slightly, she caught sight of a man a few feet behind her at a diagonal. *Probably one of the guards,* she thought. But when she turned to have a better look, she instantly realized that the man wasn't a guard and that whoever he was, he was watching her. Quickly averting her eyes, she felt herself blush with embarrassment, and she stared hard at the painting on the wall in front of her. She was so nervous, she didn't really see it, but she tilted her head this way and that as if studying it closely.

He's the same guy I've caught watching me before. I'm sure of it. Hadn't she seen him looking at her in the student center dining hall several times? And she was certain that more than once when she'd been walking on campus, she'd seen him trailing along behind her. *Why would a guy who's so good-looking—so hot—be interested in me? I'm not a flashy dresser, and I don't even wear much makeup. What does he want?*

She tried to concentrate on the painting but couldn't. Her attention was focused on the stranger, whoever he was. He didn't look like the average student, she thought. For one thing, he was older. A graduate student? Possibly. Also, he looked more . . . what was it? she asked herself. Rugged and experienced. That was it. Somehow, he seemed more worldly than most students, as if he'd done a lot of things that had nothing to do with academics.

Nervously brushing a long strand of blond hair out of her eyes, she moved along a few feet to the next painting, pretending to study it as she had done with the last one. She failed to see more than a blur of colors. She was too agitated by the stranger's presence. *I wish Kurt was with me,* she thought. *Maybe if he saw my boyfriend, then he'd buzz off.* On the other hand, this guy didn't look like the type to be intimidated by another man. And Kurt, even though tall and athletic, was, she sensed, no match for this guy.

Moving a few more steps along, she caught movement out of the corner of her eye. The man was sitting down on one of the long padded benches in the center of the room and appeared to be eyeing one of the paintings. But she knew better. She'd seen him stare at her *again.* Suddenly Ariadne was angry. *I came here for a break,* she thought, *and this creep has ruined it.*

Without thinking about it, she abruptly marched to the bench and sat down a couple of feet from him, facing in the opposite direction. "Have you been following me?" she asked in a low voice.

He looked directly at her, and Ariadne held his gaze. His dark eyes sparkled with interest and humor, she thought, and his sensuous lips spread in a smile. "Following you?" he parroted.

"Yes," she said, her voice rising slightly. "I keep seeing you everywhere I go, and you're always staring at me."

He shook his head, and his dark, slightly long and curly hair shook with it. "I haven't been following you," he said, "but I have stared at you." He smiled again.

What? So he admitted it. Ariadne was momentarily speechless. "But . . . but why?"

"Because you're beautiful," he said. "I'm sorry if I've scared you, but I'm only doing what any red-blooded male would do." He shifted on the bench, and Ariadne sensed that beneath his clothing he was extremely well built. He was tall with broad shoulders and an impressive chest that tapered to a slim waist. She could see now that he was as she'd thought: very good-looking but in a ruggedly handsome way with dark hair and eyes. He wasn't perfectly groomed, nor did he appear to be a buffed, spray-tanned gym rat like so many of the big men about campus. No, the color in his face was more the result of spending a lot of time in the outdoors.

The man stuck out a hand. "My name's Matt," he said congenially. "Please accept my apology."

Ariadne looked down at the proffered hand, then up at him. His expression was so genuinely warm and inviting. She took his hand. "I'm Ariadne," she said. "I didn't mean to be rude, but I'm not used to being stared at. And I *have* seen you around a lot."

"I really am sorry," he said. He glanced about the room. "I guess part of it is that we have some of the same interests. I come to the museum a lot, and I've seen you here. Are you an art major?"

Ariadne shook her head. "Oh, no," she replied. "I'm studying economics."

He nodded. "But you like the museum?"

"Yes. It's soothing and peaceful, and a lot of the art is beautiful." She paused, then said, "What about you? Why do you come here? Are you an art major?"

He shook his head again. "Not exactly. I'm sort of a dabbler. I paint and sculpt. Sculpt mostly."

"You paint and sculpt, but you're not an art major?"

"No. I work part-time at the Clark Institute. I do a little restoration work."

"Oh, I go there a lot, too," she said, becoming enthusiastic. "I've seen the restoration center, but you're the first person I've met who works there." *He doesn't look like the type I imagined worked at a place like that,* she thought. Then she realized that she had no idea what that sort of person might look like. She'd never met an art restorer before. "It's funny," she said. "You look outdoorsy. Not like the type who stays cooped up doing whatever it is restorers do."

He laughed softly. "A lot of my work is probably not what you'd expect. I do spend time indoors. I clean paintings and analyze pigments and fill in the gaps where paint is missing. That kind of thing. But most of my time is spent welding and sanding and polishing. There's a lot of heavy lifting and dirty work with acetylene torches and chemicals."

A small group of women began circling the room, pointing at the paintings and speaking in self-important voices.

"That's interesting," Ariadne said as she watched the women discuss a provocative Paul Cadmus canvas. "I never gave much thought to that kind of work before."

"Well, why should you? You're in business. But enough about me. Tell me about yourself. Where're you from?"

"Would you like the short version or the long?" she asked.

"The long for sure," he replied, grinning.

"I was born in Greece and lived there awhile," Ariadne said, "but I grew up in Connecticut."

"Wow, Greece," he responded. "You're a long way from home."

"I only remember snippets," she said.

"Your parents moved to the States?"

Ariadne shook her head. "I lived with foster parents in Greece, then was brought to live with different foster parents here."

"That's unusual," he said. "Where in Connecticut?"

"A tiny place I'm sure you've never heard of," Ariadne said. "Roxbury."

"You're right," he said with a laugh. "I've never heard of it."

"Where're you from?"

"Oh . . . here and there," he replied—evasively, she thought. When he saw the puzzled expression on her face, he went on. "What I mean is, I've traveled quite a bit, but I grew up here in Massachusetts."

"Did your family move around a lot?"

"Not really, but work took me away."

"Oh? What kind of work?"

"Government."

What's that supposed to mean? she wondered, but before she could satisfy her curiosity, he grinned and said, "You've turned the tables on me. I was trying to find out about you."

A lady with salt-and-pepper hair gelled into spikes strolled past them, her long earrings jangling as she passed. She did a very quick sweep around the room and left as if there was nothing of interest to her.

After she was gone, Ariadne shrugged and said, "There's not much to know."

"That can't be true," he said, shifting on the bench slightly and gazing into her eyes.

He had moved only a mere three or four inches closer to Ariadne, but she felt a violation of personal space. She didn't move, however. She felt oddly at ease with this man—Matt, she reminded herself—but at the same time, he stirred feelings in her that were unfamiliar and unsettling. "I . . . I don't know what to say," she finally replied. "I'm just a simple girl from Connecticut."

"How do you like Williamstown?" he asked, apparently trying to make her feel comfortable.

"I like it. It's fun after being out in the sticks for so long. After Roxbury and boarding school, Williamstown seems almost like a city to me, and there're a lot of really nice people."

"I bet you've learned a lot," he said.

"I've still got a lot to learn," she said with a laugh. "I haven't had much exposure to the world. Most of the girls I went to school with were much more experienced and sophisticated than I am. They came from families with money, and they'd traveled and had great clothes and the latest *everything*."

"So you didn't come from a lot of money but went to a fancy boarding school?"

Ariadne nodded. "I was on a scholarship. I am here, too. My parents are comfortable enough, but didn't have enough money. Dad's a teacher, and my mom stayed at home."

"What does he teach?"

"Math and science. I guess that's what got me interested in business. He was always pushing me numberwise, if you know what I mean."

Matt nodded.

"But I think I took to math naturally," she added. "I guess it seemed like something I could control, even if I couldn't control anything else around me. I . . ." She paused and looked at him. "I'm rattling on like an idiot, aren't I? You must think—"

Matt touched her shoulder. "I think you're great."

Ariadne glimpsed the hand on her shoulder. It was long but wide and looked very powerful. His expression was one of intense interest. "You don't even really know me," she said in a low voice.

"No, but I'd like to get to know you better," Matt replied.

And I would like to get to know you better, too, Ariadne thought but refrained from saying. She found that she was very attracted to him—there was no mistaking that—but she didn't want to let him think she was desperate, either. "Why?" she asked.

"You're being disingenuous," he said. "You know very well."

"Maybe," she said teasingly.

They heard the loud thwack of sneakers on the floor, then an even louder squeak as someone came to an abrupt halt near the bench. Turning in unison with Matt to look at the intruder, Ariadne felt her face burn with embarrassment.

"Kurt," she said, quickly putting on a smile.

He shifted his gaze to Matt, looking at him with undisguised displeasure. He wrinkled his nose as if he smelled something particularly foul before looking back at Ariadne. "We're supposed to go to the movies, remember?" Long, muscular arms akimbo, his feet spread in a wide stance, Kurt looked every inch the threatening jock bully.

"Of course I remember," she replied, rising to her feet. "I just didn't realize what time it is."

"You were supposed to meet me out front five minutes ago," Kurt accused.

"I'm sorry," Ariadne said. She looked down at Matt. "It was nice to talk to you."

He nodded, a tight smile on his lips. "You, too," he replied.

"See you later."

Kurt sized up Matt again, then took Ariadne's hand in his, and they walked out of the room.

Matt watched them, Kurt's sneakers thwacking the floor as before. He was in sweats and a jacket, carrying a gym bag, and his blond hair was still damp from the shower. "Who's the . . . ?" Matt heard him begin before his voice faded as they went through the arched doorway.

What's she doing with a jerk like him? he wondered. *She deserves better than that.* He sat lost in thought for a few moments, then reconsidered. The guy was good-looking. No doubt about that. He was probably very smart, or he wouldn't have gotten into Williams. He was obviously an athlete of some kind. *Still,* he decided before getting up to leave, *the guy's an asshole, and Ariadne can do a lot better for herself.*

Chapter Three

❧

The stone castle crowned a rocky outcrop in Ayrshire, a massive gray testament to man's ability to conquer savage nature. It had endured for centuries both inclement weather and the many onslaughts of rival clansmen, as well as the repeated efforts by generations of owners to put their personal stamp on it. As old as it was, the ancient structure had been thoroughly updated by the present laird, who lived in a much more recent mansion on the estate. The castle was now the luxurious site of important international meetings, offering fishing and hunting in addition to the amenities necessary for conducting high-level business on its thousands of acres.

In a large conference room four senior executives of Papadaki Private Holdings Limited sat in leather-upholstered chairs around a long oak table. The walls that surrounded them were hung with the deer heads and antlers ubiquitous in such castles, interspersed with tapestries and hunting paintings. On the table were two large silver trays. On one of them several bottles of water, one sparkling, had been placed, along with an ice bucket and tongs, and crystal goblets. The other tray held a silver pot of fresh-brewed coffee, a bowl with sugar, and a creamer.

The presence of the four executives at the castle was unknown to anyone else within the company. Each of them had scheduled a trip elsewhere, then made a detour to this remote location, so as to meet in complete privacy. All four had been handpicked for their positions by Nikos Papadaki, their deceased leader. He had been a cynical man who trusted no one, but he had left these four individuals in charge.

Adrian Single sat at the head of the table, facing the three others. Adrian had been Nikos Papadaki's most trusted and highly valued executive. He was CEO and represented the North and South American holdings of PPHL. His handsome appearance often led opponents to underestimate his steely-minded negotiating abilities.

On his left sat Yves Carre, in charge of holdings in Africa, Western Europe, and Australia. French by birth, he spoke several languages. Tall, thin, and silver-haired, he was quiet, polite, and capable of great charm. He had an air about him of the continental art dealer or diplomat, but he could be as ruthless in the boardroom as any corporate-takeover shark.

Seated to Adrian's right were the two others. Angelo Coveri was now sixty-six years old and white-haired, his once-muscular frame bulked out with fat. He gave the appearance of a pugnacious dog, and he could be when the need arose. He was in charge of operations in Eastern Europe, including Russia and the various countries that had once comprised the former Soviet Union, and Asia.

Next to Coveri sat the sole woman, Cynthia Rosebury, known universally as Sugar. She was a formidable woman of middle age, who had broken the glass ceiling to become the chief financial officer of PPHL. She dressed fashionably, though not outrageously, forgoing women's boring business suits for feminine suits and dresses.

"Now, we've got the same problems in Indonesia that we've had in Belarus," Angelo Coveri was saying. "The steel mills are outdated and dangerous."

"Yes, Angelo," Sugar interjected, "but you have to remember that Nikoletta got them for nothing and the sellers are holding all their old debt. Nikos used to do that. It was one of his favorite tricks."

"That's true," Adrian pointed out, "but Nikos would never have neglected those mills, Sugar. She's created a dangerous brew of problems that threaten to tarnish the corporation."

"What's worse," Coveri said, "is this latest venture of hers."

"It's hair-raising," Adrian exclaimed.

"Disposing of toxic waste from Western countries by shipping it to Third World nations," Coveri said, shaking his head. "It's horrible. These countries can't afford to weigh the dangers in taking this waste. I'm telling you, it's going to be a disaster for us."

Yves Carre finally spoke up. "You may well be right, Angelo. There's a militant ecological group called Mother Earth's Children," he said. "They're singling out PPHL as one of their major targets."

"But this new venture is highly lucrative," Sugar pointed out. "It's making the company a bundle. I think the girl has some of her father in her, and he was a wily old fox if there ever was one."

"You may be right, Sugar," Adrian said, seeming to agree with her again. He looked off into the distance for a moment. "Sometimes I wonder if she's not so much wily as she is totally unscrupulous."

"Don't you think that's an exaggeration?" Sugar asked.

Before Adrian could respond, Angelo Coveri took a sip of water from the crystal goblet on the table, then cleared his throat. "I'm telling you this," he said, directing his gaze at Sugar. "Old Nikos would never in his life have dealt in toxic waste. That is a fact of which I am certain."

Sugar frowned and tapped the tabletop with manicured fingernails. "Maybe," she said, "but I'm not so sure, Angelo."

"Quite frankly," Yves Carre said, "I'm getting very nervous about the changes since she took over. All you have to do is check out the Internet to get an idea of the image PPHL is projecting. We're being accused of plundering natural resources. Refusing to modernize facilities and poisoning the environment." He looked around the table. "It's only beginning, but you know how word spreads on the Internet. And sooner or later, we're going to be vilified in the mainstream press because we're not dealing with any of these issues."

"Oh, come on. Do you really believe that?" Sugar asked, playing devil's advocate.

Yves nodded. "Absolutely," he replied. "The way the wind's blowing, Sugar, it would do us well to start addressing these issues right away. If Nikoletta is as intractable now as she has been in the last two years, then . . ." He gave a Gallic shrug.

"I think you're right," Angelo Coveri said. "Nikoletta, I'm sorry to say, is the root of the problem, and something's got to be done about her."

"We've got to discuss the best way of going about approaching Niki with this information," Adrian said. "I—"

A cell phone rang, and all four of the executives looked around the table, trying to decipher whose had rung. There was much patting of pockets before Adrian realized it was his.

"Excuse me," he said, flipping the phone open. Shifting his chair slightly away from the table, he said, "Hello?"

"Adrian?"

Adrian recognized the familiar voice at once. He rose to his feet and retreated to a far corner of the room for privacy. "I'm here," he said quietly.

"I've been doing as you ordered, but today she caught me."

"I see," he replied.

"Can you talk?" the man asked. "Did I catch you at a bad time?"

"Somewhat," Adrian replied, "but never mind. So what happened?"

"Nothing really. I didn't blow my cover. I just told her about what I supposedly do. She was so absorbed in it, I wish I did."

Adrian did not miss the interest in his caller's voice. "Well, you make sure you keep a better distance. I don't want it to happen again."

The caller sounded chastened. "Will do."

"You're not to allow this to go any further. Do you understand?"

"Yes, sir."

Adrian flipped the cell phone shut and slipped it into the pocket of his suit jacket, then returned to the table. "Sorry about that."

"Anything serious?" Sugar asked.

He shook his head. "No. Just an overenthusiastic assistant in New York," he replied with a smile. "Where were we?"

After another half hour or so of discussion, Adrian adjourned the meeting, and they left the conference room. As he walked down the long hallway toward his room, Adrian thought, *This wild child is going to be the death of me, and she might be the death of the entire company.*

He emitted a sigh. He was growing weary of intervening on Niki's behalf, fixing up the messes she made. He'd been behind her in the beginning, giving her the benefit of the doubt and the chance to grow with experience. Nikos had groomed her for years to lead the company, after all.

As Nikos had grown older, he'd never wavered from his belief that Niki must succeed him. In the beginning when Nikos had separated Niki and Ariadne, Adrian had thought that Nikos had lost his mind. He was convinced that Nikos had suffered one of his spells of madness. He thought Nikos would come to his senses and eventually change his mind. But he didn't. Nikos had always thought Niki was the daughter to be groomed to lead the company. Adrian and Nikos had argued about it many times over the years. Finally, Nikos himself had moved Ariadne to the United States just in case he'd made the wrong decision regarding Niki.

Adrian heaved another sigh. He had always thought he would eventually be able to talk Nikos into letting Ariadne claim her heritage, but that was not to be. Nikos had died without permitting it. *Maybe it's time to pay a visit to Ariadne and see if she can't replace her sister,* he thought. Of the twin sisters, he no longer had any question which one was the bad seed.

Chapter Four

❦

New York City

The photographer's studio was in an enormous eighth-floor loft in the Flatiron District, between Fifth Avenue and Avenue of the Americas. The dingy turn-of-the-century structure didn't give a hint that some of America's most compelling images were created within its confines. The loft of Greg Lichtenstein, the much-in-demand fashion photographer, was reached by a dark, creaky freight elevator that could hold twenty-five or thirty people with ease. Its spaciousness did little to dispel its cell-like creepiness, but when its door opened and newcomers stepped from the ancient bobbing car into Greg's loft, they were swept away by the futuristic atmosphere that greeted them.

In the spacious entry room thousands of square feet of flooring rescued from bowling alleys that were about to meet the wrecker's ball had been laid and several coats of polyurethane gave it a high gloss. The high walls and ceiling had all been painted in a photographer's white, and on them hung an assortment of Greg's most famous images, most of them published in high-fashion magazines all over the world. The reception room was lined with black leather-upholstered banquettes, where one could wait for an appointment in comfort, leafing through choice magazines placed on the black marble-topped end tables and coffee table. In the center of the room was the receptionist's desk, an enormous black marble slab on which an orchid sprouted dozens of white blossoms.

The receptionist complemented the environment, being totally clad in black down to her stiletto-heeled shoes. Even her straight, orange-dyed hair, cut near her shoulders in an even line repeated in the bangs across her forehead, fitted the picture. She commandeered the busy ultramodern Beo-Com multiline telephone with as much ease as she handled the keyboard accompanying the large flat-panel computer screen on the desk, even though she had long chocolate-colored fingernails that shone with new varnish.

When Bianca Coveri rushed into the reception area, she ignored the veneer of glamour in the reception area. Nor was she surprised to hear the loud hip-hop music playing on the studio's powerful stereo system. She had been here many times because she ran PPHL's garment subsidiaries. One of their expensive designer clothing labels was photographed here, and Bianca was frequently on hand to make certain that PPHL got what they wanted—and dearly paid for. Today's shoot was part of a multimillion-dollar ad blitz, and Bianca wanted to assure herself that every detail was as she wanted it. Today, she also had another reason for being here: she'd taken an interest in one of the models.

"Hey, Merilee," she said to the receptionist in a breathy voice. "I'm late. How long have they been shooting?" She unknotted the black cashmere scarf at her throat and left it dangling loose, then shrugged out of the black feathered-mink coat she was wearing and put it around her shoulders. She swept her shoulder-length jet-black hair back away from her face, then let it remain where it fell.

"They've barely started," the orange-haired woman replied, flapping a hand airily. "You know how it is, Bianca. High drama. Last-minute hysteria. Always."

"What kind of mood is Greg in today?" Bianca asked. Greg was a pro—of that there was no question—but he could be very temperamental. He was a perfectionist and expected the same level of participation from everyone involved, from the models to the hair stylists, makeup artists, and clothing stylists, down to the lowliest lighting assistant.

"No major dramas so far," Merilee said, "but, like I said, they're just getting started."

"I'd better get in there," Bianca said. "See you later." She hurried toward the tall ebonized double doors that led into the first studio, and opened one of them quietly, peeking inside to see what was happening.

Perhaps she could sneak in without distracting Greg or any of the models from their work, but it was not to be.

"Bianca, *cara*!" Greg gushed. He left his post at a tripod-mounted camera and greeted her at the door, his hair in wild Einsteinian disarray, his eyes bright with energy, his wiry body virtually throbbing with excitement. He came alive on a shoot, putting everything he had into it, then deflated like a balloon afterward. He gave her air kisses in the direction of both cheeks, and she returned them in kind. "You look divine as always, *cara*."

"Oh, thank you, Greg," she said. "Sorry I'm late, but you know what the damned traffic's like."

He waved her apology away. "Why don't you sit over there?" he said, pointing to an empty chair to his right. "Do you want something to drink? Hard? Soft?"

Bianca shook her head. "No, thank you, pussycat," she said. "I'll go sit and be a mouse."

"If you change your mind, tell Gretchen," he said, pointing to a blond-haired assistant. "She'll get it for you."

"Thanks." She patted his shoulder, then headed to the seat he had indicated. She sat down and crossed one long, slender leg over the other. Great expanses of white fabric hung from the ceiling all the way down the wall, then spread out onto the floor for thirty feet or more. Three male models stood in the middle of the white "ground," awaiting instructions from Greg. She was disappointed to see that Frans wasn't among them. Glancing around the studio, she didn't see him among the plethora of assistants and stylists.

Where could he be? she wondered nervously. Surely he'd come in today. Even if he was sick, she thought, he'd have dragged himself out of bed to get to this shoot. He was one of the hottest new male models in town, but he could ruin his reputation in an instant if word got around that he was late or didn't show up for scheduled shoots. She began nervously drumming her fingernails on the black alligator Dior handbag in her lap, then forced herself to stop.

The three models in the shooting area were attired in spring clothing that would be featured in one of the PPHL garment subsidiary's ad campaigns three months down the road. The outfits were nothing short of stunning, she decided, and not simply because the models were so good-looking. The stylists had done an artful job of dressing them with the clothing that the garment company had provided, and had added a few accessories of their own choosing. Mixing and matching, using a hat here, a pair of boots there, a belt or necklace, and so on.

Over the roar of the music, she heard Greg's voice. "Frans! Get your ass out here. *Now!*"

Bianca's stomach gave a lurch, and she looked toward Greg. His face was red with barely suppressed fury. She knew that it would turn a full-fledged purple before he let go and really lashed out, ruthlessly berating anyone who dared to hold up his shoot, no matter the reason. She hoped to God that Frans wasn't going to be a problem.

She had little time to worry about it. From a door that led into another part of the immense studio, Frans sauntered into the room, taking his time, dragging the shirt and jacket he was supposed to be wearing along behind him. Bianca felt her heart leap when she saw him. He had such a dazzling presence that she didn't think she would ever become accustomed to his extraordinary handsomeness. Each time she saw him she was shocked anew. He was over six feet tall, muscular but lean, so that every movement he made, even the slightest, was accompanied by the visible motion of a set of muscles. He was born with perfect proportions: wide shoulders, a long torso, narrow waist and hips, and long legs. His dirty-blond hair hung well below his neck, and his blue eyes were startling, mesmerizing even. She watched as he slid the shirt on, covering the tribal tattoos on one arm, then lazily tucked half of it into his trousers, deliberately leaving the other half out. Finally, he put his jacket on.

Greg began shouting instructions to the lighting assistants, then to the four models. The camera began to flash, over and over again, as the models moved about according to Greg's orders, and Bianca couldn't help but notice Frans's magnetism. He oozed a brooding sexiness through every pore, she thought, qualities that came across in the photographs of him. She'd often seen men and women who were stunningly good-looking in person but didn't photograph well. The camera, happily, loved Frans. Bianca thought part of his particular magic was that he didn't seem to give a damn about the appeal he had. It was as if he was totally unaware of his striking presence, and this, she thought, was a refreshing quality in a model. Most of them were hyperconscious of their beauty, and seemed to live for the attention it brought to them.

The shoot dragged on and on, but Bianca didn't move from her chair. She was absorbed in Frans's every movement, his every gesture, the sound of his German-accented English when he queried one of Greg's instructions, his laughter when he or one of the other models made a silly mistake. She was love struck—there were no two ways about it—and she couldn't get enough of him.

So what if I'm twice his age? she thought as she saw one of the makeup artists step in and carefully stroke blusher on one of the men's cheekbones. *He's a grown-up. Eighteen years old. That's old enough to know what you're doing, isn't it? Of course it is.* She knew that in her circle eyebrows would be raised when word got out that she was seeing a male model. But seeing an eighteen-year-old? It was like compounding a felony. She could hear it now. The vicious gossips that populated the worlds of fashion and business would crucify her, a thirty-six-year-old seemingly sane and responsible business executive, for robbing the cradle. Not only that, but dating a male model, a species that everyone knew was unreliable and unintelligent and therefore unpromising and undesirable as boyfriend, let alone husband, material.

Well, Bianca had decided, *let them talk.* She was concerned about the reaction of only one person and that was her father. Angelo Coveri would be apoplectic—of that there was no doubt. He would storm and rage, call her names, and invoke the memory of her saintly mother. But Bianca knew that her father would come around to her side in the end. Despite whatever his initial misgivings might be, Bianca knew her father better than anyone, and she knew that under his thick skin Angelo Coveri was a romantic. He would eventually give her his blessings when he realized that Bianca was in love.

She'd wondered if this was true, if she was really in love. She was obsessed with Frans, and she knew it. But was she in love with him? Yes, she'd decided. That, too. She was in love with his long dirty-blond tangle of hair, his penetrating blue gaze and sensual lips, his prominent nose and lean, muscular body. Even his tribal tattoos had become imprinted on her mind as erotic touchstones, and she loved nothing more than to lightly trace them with a fingernail. Even now, as she sat in the uncomfortable chair in the studio, Greg's shouted instructions and the loud music faded into the background, and she felt her pulse begin to race and a rush of electricity run through her body as she remembered the warmth of his flesh against her own, the distinctly masculine aroma that he exuded, enveloping her in its erotic potency, and the powerful yet tender way he made love to her.

Bianca was jerked out of her reverie when Frans sauntered off the white ground and directly toward her, his walk cockier than ever and his arrogant, brooding expression more pronounced than usual. When he reached her, he abruptly came to a halt and thrust his groin toward her obscenely. Followed by the flash of a thousand-watt smile, exposing his perfect white teeth. Then he blew her a kiss before striding back to the white fabric within camera range.

"Frans, you motherfucker!" Greg screamed at the top of his lungs, the veins in his throat extended with the effort.

Bianca immediately made a decision and rose to her feet. She quickly tiptoed to the door and left the studio, closing the door as silently as possible behind her. She was obviously too much of a distraction for Frans, and she'd better wait for him downstairs in the limo.

"Leaving already?" Merilee said, gazing up at her.

Bianca nodded, slipping into her coat.

"Greg getting a little too worked up for you?" Merilee said with a glint of mischief in her eye. "I could hear him screaming some of his sweeter profanities, even over the music."

Bianca shrugged and pushed the call button for the elevator. "I'm not in the mood to listen to it today," she replied. "Besides, it looks like it's going to be a great shoot."

"Okay," Merilee said. "See you later."

" 'Bye." Bianca sketched a wave in the air as the elevator arrived. On the way down, she checked her wristwatch. She was surprised that so much time had passed since she'd arrived, but she knew it might last another hour or so. Even longer. Frans had her cell number, so she would run some errands and swing back by for him when he was ready.

Nearly three hours later, Frans opened the limousine's door and slid onto the leather seat next to her. Wrapping an arm around her, he kissed her long and passionately, as if he had been starving for her. When he drew back at last and gazed into her eyes, his expression was that of a man deeply in love, Bianca thought.

"I've missed you," he said.

"I've missed you, too," she said. "So much."

They began kissing again, disregarding the chauffeur, who made an effort to ignore them by staring out the window. When they drew apart again, Bianca brushed the side of Frans's face with a hand. "I want to make a stop on the way to the apartment," she said. "Is that okay with you?"

"It won't take long, will it?"

She shook her head. "No. Just a few minutes. Besides, I think you'll enjoy it."

"What?"

"It's a surprise," she replied mysteriously. She turned toward the front of the limousine. "Azad?" she said to the driver. "Take us to the address I gave you before."

The handsome Kurdish driver nodded, and the big limousine began moving through the busy streets toward midtown. Frans took Bianca in his arms once again, peppering her face with kisses, his tongue darting out to flick at her ears and neck. When the car pulled over at the curb, Azad rushed out and opened the door on Bianca's side.

"Let's go," she said, drawing back from Frans.

"Okay," he said.

She exited the car with him following close behind her. On the sidewalk, Frans blinked at the heavy filigreed iron and glass door and the sign beside it. Harry Winston.

"What's this?" he asked, taking her arm. "The jewelry store?"

Bianca nodded. "Hmmm," she purred with a smile. She led the way, and before Frans could open the door, the uniformed doorman swung it wide for them. Bianca knew her way around the exclusive shop and went directly to the glass showcase where she would find what she wanted. Once there, she stared down into it, and Frans followed suit.

"It's all rings," he said.

"Yes, it is," she replied.

"May I help you, madam? Sir?" a middle-aged gentleman asked. The beautifully groomed and dressed Bianca seemed ill matched with Frans, a mass of tangled hair in an old surplus Russian-army greatcoat, leather jeans, and beat-up boots.

"I want to try on a couple of rings," Bianca said.

"Yes?" the salesman said. "If you'll point out which ones—"

"I love that. . . . Is it a canary?" She was pointing with one of her carefully lacquered fingernails.

"You have exquisite taste, madam," the salesman replied, removing the diamond ring from its velvet display case. "It is a canary yellow diamond, round cut, set in platinum."

"Whoa," Frans said. "That's some rock, Bianca."

"Some rock indeed," the salesman said with a smile. He held it out for Bianca to try on.

She slipped the ring on and held her hand steady, fingers splayed, then moved her hand from side to side, watching the diamond flash in the light. "How many carats is this?" she asked, her eyes remaining on the ring.

"Two," the salesman replied. "And perfect, I might add."

"What do you think?" Bianca asked Frans.

"It's hot," he said, smiling.

She returned his smile, then peered back into the glass display case. "May I see that one . . . there?" she said, tapping the glass. "The emerald-cut white one."

"Of course."

Bianca tried it on, then repeated the process with four more rings, consulting Frans each time. His responses were variations of his first one until she slipped on a perfect marquise-cut white diamond of five carats set in yellow gold. "Wow. Supercool zonker," Frans enthused. "Makes the rest look like river rocks."

"It is, isn't it?" She waved her hand back and forth, watching the marquise-cut white diamond flash its fire in the light. "It's less traditional than the others," she said, "but I love the cut and the yellow gold. And the size."

"Size matters," Frans said with a lewd laugh. "Even with diamonds."

Bianca punched his chest lightly. "Especially with diamonds," she said, "and this one is big."

"Five carats," the salesman said.

"You don't think it looks too . . . flashy?" she said.

"Oh, come on, Bianca," Frans said, "how can a diamond be too flashy?" He grabbed the hand on which she wore the ring and kissed it. "Flash is what you're after, babe. Why else bother?"

Bianca laughed lightly. "Oh, well. I'm Italian. I can get by with it, right?"

Frans put his arms around her and kissed her on the lips. "You bet you can," he said. "It looks just right on you."

Bianca looked at the salesman, and he nodded almost imperceptibly, a small smile on his lips. "Well . . . ," she began, "it does fit."

"That wouldn't be a problem, madam," the salesman said. "If it doesn't fit perfectly, we could size it for you, of course."

"No," she said. "It fits perfectly." She splayed her fingers again and glimpsed back up at Frans. He smiled, his sensuous lips spreading, and his intense blue eyes sparkled.

Her mind was suddenly made up. "I'll take it," she said.

The salesman nodded. "An excellent choice," he said. "It will only take me a moment to box it and get the GIA paperwork together. How do you wish to pay, if I may ask?"

Bianca retrieved her wallet from her pocketbook and slid out her American Express card. "Here," she said, handing the card to him.

He nodded and took the card. "I'll only be a moment."

"What paperwork?" Frans asked. "What's he talking about?"

"From the Gemological Institute of America," she replied. "You know, guaranteeing the weight and color. That kind of thing."

"Oh," Frans said. "So you'll know you didn't buy a fake or something."

She nodded. "Exactly."

The salesman returned with an envelope of paperwork, a velvet box for the ring, and the credit card receipt for her to sign. Bianca took the pen he offered, signed the receipt, and slipped her copy into her wallet.

"Do you want to put it in the box, madam?" the salesman asked.

"No," Bianca replied, smiling. "I'm wearing this zonker out of the store. I'll put the box in my pocketbook."

Frans led her to the door and back out onto the street. The limousine, which hadn't been able to idle at the curbside while they were in the shop, pulled over almost immediately. Azad started to jump out to open the door, but Frans waved him away. "Got it," he said, opening the door for Bianca. They slid onto the luxurious black leather, and Frans put an arm around her shoulders. "The ring looks beautiful on you," he said as the chauffeur pulled out into the traffic of Fifth Avenue.

"I'm glad you like it."

"It's nice," he said, "but you know you don't really need things like that to make you beautiful."

"But I need it for something else," she said, studying his face. It was adoring, his face. That was the best way to describe it, she thought. And it had been since they'd first met.

"Need it for something else?" He gazed at her quizzically. "What?"

"If I want to get married, then I need an engagement ring, don't I?"

"Get married!" he replied. "But—but . . . I mean . . ." His shoulders slumped, and his features turned glum.

"What?" she teased. She loved seeing his disappointment at her news.

He removed his arm from around her shoulder and stared into his lap. "I thought . . . I mean . . . I thought we had something, you know, going . . . and, well . . ." He gazed up at her with hurt eyes. "I can't believe you're suddenly springing something like this on me, Bianca."

Her heart melted, and she couldn't carry on her pretense any longer. "Oh, Frans," she said, "what I meant was that I want to marry *you*. If you'll have me. That's why I got the ring."

His blue eyes widened in astonishment. Then he smiled. "Are you serious?" he said in a whisper.

She nodded. "I've never been more serious about anything in my life."

Frans threw his arms around her and let out a shout of glee. "I can't believe it! You want to marry me. Frans. A nobody from nowhere."

"Whoa," Bianca said with a gasp. "You're about to smother me, sweetheart."

He relinquished his powerful hold of her and began dispensing kisses all over her face. Her eyes and forehead, her cheeks and nose, her chin. "I can't believe it," he said, then threw an arm into the air. "I want to tell the whole world. Bianca Coveri is really in love with me! Bianca Coveri wants to marry me!"

He took her into his arms again, more gently this time, and kissed her long and passionately. When he finally withdrew, he gazed into her eyes. "This is the happiest day of my life," he said. "When can we do it? Now?"

"Hold on, sexy," she said laughingly. "This is New York, so we have to get a marriage license first. We can't do that today because it's too late. Then, don't forget, we're flying down to St. Barth's later for that birthday party."

The light in his eyes momentarily dimmed. "I forgot," he said. "Why don't we skip the party, Bianca?"

"I can't do that, sweetie," she said. "It's for my boss, after all. Your boss, too, in a way, since you're modeling for a PPHL spread right now."

"Then when?"

"As soon as we get back," she said.

Frans was mollified by her response. "Promise?"

"I promise," Bianca said.

He kissed her again. "I can hardly wait."

"I know," she said, "but we have to." She glanced at him thoughtfully, then said, "In the meantime, let's keep this a secret. *Our* secret."

He looked puzzled. "But why? Don't you want everybody to know?"

She shook her head. "Not yet," she said. "First, I want to tell my father. I don't want it to be a surprise for him. You understand what I mean?"

Frans nodded. "Yes," he said. "I know that you treasure your father, and I think that's good."

"Yes," Bianca agreed. "He brought me up by himself, and I think I owe it to him." Then she added, "Plus, this is Niki's birthday, and I don't want to steal any of her thunder, you know?"

"I understand," he said. "She's the big boss, and it's her party."

"Exactly," Bianca said.

Azad pulled up in front of the Upper East Side high-rise. "Oh, we're home," she said.

"We can celebrate," Frans said, winking at her.

Bianca looked at her watch. "There's just enough time."

In the vast monochromatic expanse of Bianca's bedroom, Frans slid a Luther Vandross CD into the player and turned the volume down low. Bianca pushed a button built in to her bedside table, and hundreds of yards of beige silk draperies automatically slid across the floor-to-ceiling windows that composed two walls of the beautiful room. The views of Manhattan and Queens were spectacular from her aerie, but she preferred the insular protection of a womblike enclosure for their lovemaking.

Frans crossed the thick, soft carpeting to her, his sensuous lips framed in a smile. Encircling her with his arms, he drew her close. Bianca returned his kiss as she put her arms around him, running her hands up and down his long, muscular back and up into his tousled blond hair. His tongue delved between her lips and explored her with desire while his hands trailed down her back and cupped her firm, rounded cheeks, then pulled her against his hard, powerful body.

Bianca sighed with pleasure. She could already feel the swell in his leather jeans, and she held on to him tightly, as if to a lifeline. Frans began kissing and licking her ears, then traced a feathery pattern around her long, slender neck with his tongue. His hands moved up her spine, massaging her along the way before coming to rest on her breasts. He began caressing them through her clothing, and Bianca felt her body tremble with desire.

Frans drew back and gazed into her eyes. "Let me undress you," he whispered.

She let him slip the black cashmere sweater she wore over her head. Her black shoulder-length hair was a mess, but she didn't care. He drew her close and kissed the cleavage between her ample breasts while undoing the single hook that kept her black bra in place. When her breasts sprang free, Frans moaned with passion, first caressing them with his hands, then bending to them and kissing and licking each one. Bianca mewled with carnal delight when she felt his tongue on her nipples, thrumming them in turn, until they hardened with desire. She felt jolts of electric pleasure rush through her body, from her spine to her extremities.

Straightening up, Frans kissed her lips again, then went down on his knees and unzipped her high-heeled boots one at a time. After he freed her of her skirt, he remained on his knees and slid her panty hose off. He looked up into her eyes again while placing his hands on her buttocks, stroking them gently. When he buried his face between her thighs, Bianca cried out and held his head once more, her fingers intertwined with his long blond hair. She felt his lips kiss her, his tongue enter her, and the pleasure was exquisite.

"Frans," she whispered. "Oh, Frans . . . I . . . I . . . oh . . ."

He quickly stood up and wrapped his arms around her nakedness. "Oh, Bianca," he said, "I love you. I love you so much."

"And I love you," she rasped. "I love you, too."

He pulled off his heavy sweater in one swift motion, tossing it to the floor, then slipped his T-shirt over his head and flung it away. He kicked off his scuffed boots, pulled off his socks, and undid his belt. He shimmied out of his leather jeans, then stood before her naked. He was wearing no underwear.

Bianca sucked in her breath. His magnificent body never failed to enthrall her. His broad shoulders and powerfully muscled chest tapered down to a narrow waist with prominent abs and slim hips. He was fully engorged. He encircled her with his arms again, the tribal tattoos that decorated them flashing before her eyes as he drew her against his warm hardness.

"Let's get in bed," he whispered, licking her ear. "I can't wait another minute."

She nodded, and they lay down next to each other. "I want to make you so happy," he said.

"You do, Frans. Nobody's ever made me feel like you do."

He kissed her passionately as he eased himself atop her. Cupping her breasts in his hands, he ran his tongue down her torso, licking her, his breath hot like an erotic whisper on her flesh. She lifted her hips to meet him as he inevitably reached the mound between her thighs, where he delved between her lips with impassioned vigor, as if he could never get enough of her. Bianca cried out in ecstasy, and her body trembled, her erotic desire for Frans almost overwhelming.

He went up on his knees and gazed down into her eyes, a smile on his lips. "I love you," he rasped. "I love you." He leaned down and kissed her with renewed passion, slowly entering her, teasingly withholding the complete length and breadth of his manhood as long as possible.

Moaning with lust, Bianca thrust herself up against Frans, so anxious was she to have all of him, to savor all of him inside her. She threw her arms around his shoulders, drawing him closer, and Frans finally entered her completely. Bianca held on to him with all her might, never wanting to let him go. Frans began withdrawing slowly, then entering her again, panting with his carnal desire for her. Unable to restrain himself, he began moving with complete abandon, his lips on hers, kissing her voraciously, his hands on her buttocks, pushing her against him powerfully.

Bianca felt the first spasm of ecstasy, and she cried out. Her body took over, thrashing from side to side and up and down. Frans emitted a loud groan as he abruptly flooded her with his juices, his body momentarily rigid as he let loose again and again inside her until he had spent himself. In one swift movement he wrapped his arms around her, hugging her to him with all his might and smothering her face with kisses of gratitude. They both panted, their bodies heaving, their lust sated for the time being.

For a long time, they lay still, their bodies entwined as they caught their breath. They were covered with the sheen of sweat from their passion. Frans eased onto his side, bringing her with him, so that he remained inside her warmth. They gazed into each other's eyes and smiled simultaneously.

"That was so wonderful," he said softly. "You're so wonderful. No woman has ever made me this happy."

"I feel the same way," Bianca replied in a whispery rasp. "I feel so . . . complete, so fulfilled."

He kissed her and hugged her closer. "I'm enraptured," Frans said with a smile. "I think you've put a spell on me, and I don't want it broken. Ever."

Bianca could hardly believe this was happening. Fate, she thought, had brought them together. Two mismatched souls from thousands of miles apart, as different as night and day but somehow perfect together.

"I didn't know I could be so in love," she finally said. "You're not only the greatest-looking man I know, but you must be the greatest lover in the world."

"Only because of you," he said, stroking her face tenderly, then taking a breast in his hand and nibbling its rosy nipple.

Bianca could feel him stirring within her and let out a gasp. "Oh, my God," she said. "Oh . . . oh . . ."

He pulled her closer and began kissing her passionately, but Bianca pulled away after a moment. "We . . . we don't have time, Frans. The plane . . . the party."

He pulled her close again. "We have time," he said with a smile. He began kissing her passionately again, and Bianca gave herself up to the moment completely, to him, to the joy that they'd found together. For one of the few times in her life, she felt that she was completely alive.

We'll get to the plane on time, she thought, *and if we don't . . . ? This is worth it. This is worth anything.*

Chapter Five

✧

St. Barthélemy, the Leeward Islands

Paradise Rock, the entire seaside resort, had been taken over for Nikoletta Papadaki's birthday party. PPHL owned the resort, and it had always been totally booked for the months of January and February. But over the protests of several executives, Niki forced the manager to cancel all reservations that had been made for the week of her birthday. For her twenty-first-birthday party she was calling the shots, and nobody else was going to have a say.

"Poseidon's Orgy" was the theme engraved on the invitations that went out to guests from around the world, and they had been instructed to costume themselves appropriately. Around one of the swimming pools the international-society set talked, drank, and danced, more than a few of them dressed in "fish scale" bikinis or thongs and variations on sea-related costumes. A young heiress from France was attired in a revealing outfit consisting of cleverly placed seashells and little else, and her Argentinean boyfriend, not to be outdone, wore nothing but a cascade of Capiz shells artfully applied to the front of a thong. Like many of the other guests, they had devoted hours to ensure that their costumes were made and fitted in time.

For their enjoyment, mermaids and mermen—magnificently built young strippers who had been flown in for the party—swam, posed, and cavorted among synchronized fountains that leaped into the air. Blue and green lights accompanied the airy patterns created by the jets of water, adding to the dazzling display. In the background, the trance mixer DJ

Scary, who had come from Paris for the occasion, pumped out the music. It was a crowd he knew well, having played at parties around the globe for varying mixtures of the same set and their friends and hangers-on.

At a distance from the noise of the party three of the few older party guests stood in a group, chatting and drinking. Their faces wore smiles, but they weren't happy.

"Paradise Rock is almost unrecognizable," Angelo Coveri muttered after taking a sip of his red-wine spritzer. His gaze swept the scene. "The entire resort looks blue and green."

"As well it should," countered Sugar Rosebury dryly. "Especially considering the millions of company dollars that have been squandered."

"What are you three talking about?" Honor Hurlstone asked as she joined them. "You look like the three witches in *Macbeth* conjuring some sort of plot."

Sugar laughed, and the women exchanged air kisses. "You look heavenly," Sugar exclaimed. "I love your dress."

"Thank you," Honor said. "I thought it was appropriate. This embroidery looks like seaweed or something, doesn't it?"

"Hmm," Sugar said, fingering the delicate silk between her fingers. "And coral. It's absolutely gorgeous."

"So is yours," Honor said, "but then you're always dressed like a million dollars."

"You both look beautiful," Yves Carre said.

"Have you seen Adrian?" Angelo Coveri asked. Adrian Single was the New York CEO of PPHL and in charge of North and South American operations and had been Nikos Papadaki's most trusted ally. He was the glue that held together the board of the gigantic corporation, but perhaps most importantly, he had always been the only person who could influence Nikoletta since her father's death.

"He's right behind me," Honor replied.

Approaching them, Adrian took a glass of champagne off a passing waiter's tray. "Is everyone having a good time?" he asked.

"I think so," Honor said. "Certainly all of Niki's friends seem to be having a great time."

"It's a great party, Adrian," Sugar said, looking about. "It's beautiful. All the lights and candles. The fountains. Everything."

"You must be exhausted," Honor said, looking at him. "You've been in the air almost constantly for days. Belarus. New York to Scotland and back. Then here."

"I'm fine," he said with a smile. "I always catch a few winks in flight." In fact, what his sister had said was true. He was very tired, but not for the reasons she thought. He'd made a side trip up to the Berkshires in western Massachusetts, where Williams College was located.

Suddenly the air was rent with the blasts of trumpets.

As the music stopped, a large gilt platform, a canopied *lit,* held aloft by young muscle-bound men dressed in tiny gold thongs, appeared on the terrace at the far end of the pool. The trumpets blared again, as if announcing the arrival of a reigning queen. The crowd began applauding loudly and shouting the monarch's name:

"Niki! Niki! Niki!"

Surrounded by votive lights, Niki was draped atop the gilt platform on golden cushions. Her face was heavily made-up, and she wore a small, secretive smile, as if she alone held the keys to a kingdom. The trumpets sounded again, and the young men began to walk down the steps that led to the terrace surrounding the pool. Niki threw an arm aloft as if bestowing a blessing upon her loyal subjects. The crowd roared with approval, their shouts and claps growing more gleeful. Her bearers began slowly carrying her around the pool in order for all of her friends to get a close glimpse of her. Her diaphanous gold gown wafted in the breeze, and the diamonds that she wore in her hair, around her neck, and on her ears and wrists and fingers sparkled in the candlelight.

"My God," Honor murmured, gazing at Niki's outfit. Fluttery silk "fish scales" of gold clustered strategically at her crotch and nipples, but otherwise the diaphanous fabric left nothing to the imagination. "She's practically naked."

"But not quite," Adrian said, humoring her.

"She's dazzling," Yves Carre said appreciatively. "Absolutely dazzling."

"She's scandalous," Angelo Coveri muttered under his breath.

"Get over it, Angelo," Sugar said. "She's a beautiful young woman with a perfect body. Why not show it off? Besides, about ninety percent of this crowd sunbathes in the nude, so what's the big deal? She's wearing more now than most of the men and women here have worn all day on the beach."

From her perch above the crowd, Niki's smile widened from time to time when she passed a particularly close friend. She elegantly lowered one hand to allow a few of the more aggressive men to kiss it as the procession made its way around the pool. Suddenly she noticed Bianca Coveri and a man just ahead in the crowd. He must be her date, Niki reasoned, because one of his lean muscular arms was draped across her shoulders. Bianca, she knew, was not the type to get that cozy with someone she'd just met at a party. As her *lit* drew alongside Bianca and Frans, Niki stared at him openly.

My, my, she thought. *That long blond hair and those intense baby blues. And the body!* They'd obviously had a workout on the dance floor, because he'd stripped off his shirt and his muscular chest with its perfect pecs glistened with sweat. Her eyes traveled down to his outstanding abs and on down, beneath his navel, where she saw that he wore tight white pants that held promise.

Why, Bianca! she thought. *You've brought me the perfect birthday present.*

"You look ravishing, Niki," Bianca shouted above the noise of the crowd.

Niki's gaze shifted to Bianca, and she smiled widely. "Thank you, darling," she said, forming a kiss with her puckered red lips.

The *lit* moved on, and Bianca squeezed Frans's hand in hers. "That's the birthday girl," she said. "My boss."

"*She's* your boss?" Frans said with surprise.

"Yes. Stunning, isn't she?"

Frans hugged her to him. "Not half as beautiful as you are, Bianca."

Bianca felt that familiar frisson of excitement that these words caused, but before she could respond, a voice interrupted them.

"Bianca. How are you?" Adrian asked.

"Oh, hi," she said. "I saw you at a distance, but never got close enough to say hello."

Adrian's gaze shifted from her to Frans and back again. "I take it this is your date?"

Bianca nodded. "Adrian, I'd like you to meet Frans. Frans, Adrian Single. He's one of my bosses at PPHL."

Adrian and Frans shook hands. "I hope you're having a good time, Frans," he said.

"Oh, yes," Frans replied, casting Bianca an adoring glance. "I always have a good time with her."

"I see," Adrian said with a smile.

"Can you keep a secret?" Bianca asked him.

"You know I can," Adrian replied.

"Frans and I are engaged," she said.

"That's wonderful news, sweetheart," he said. He kissed her cheek, then clapped Frans on the back. "You're a lucky man."

"I know," Frans said, all smiles.

"I'm so happy for you both," Adrian said.

"I haven't told my father yet," Bianca said, "so please don't say anything, Adrian."

"You know I wouldn't do that. I'm sworn to secrecy, so I won't tell a soul. But I'll tell you what."

"What?" she asked.

He chuckled. "The way you two are acting, everybody's going to know, so you'd better tell him soon."

"Is it that obvious?" she said with a laugh.

Adrian nodded. "You can hardly keep your hands off each other."

Frans and Bianca laughed. "It's true," Frans said. "We're hopelessly in love."

"That's wonderful," Adrian said. He took a sip of his drink. "I'd better mingle, so I'll see you later."

Bianca hadn't planned on springing her news to her father tonight, but she felt emboldened by Adrian's reaction. He'd been genuinely pleased, she thought, and hadn't acted surprised at their difference in age. It hadn't seemed to matter at all.

"Why don't we go see my father?" Bianca said, turning to Frans. "I want to introduce you."

"Okay," Frans replied.

Bianca led the way through the crowd, twisting this way and that to where she'd last seen her father talking with Sugar. When they finally reached him, Angelo was sitting at a table, nursing a drink. At the sight of his daughter, he rose to his feet.

"Bianca, *cara*," he said, kissing each of her cheeks. "I wondered where you were."

"Dad," she said, "I want you to meet someone." She made the introductions and noticed the assessment her father's eagle eyes made of Frans. He was appalled by the young man's lack of a shirt, his sweat-drenched chest, low-rise pants, tribal tattoos, and long hair. She was thankful that Frans had a firm handshake, despite his casual, devil-may-care posture.

"It's a pleasure to meet you," Frans said enthusiastically.

"A pleasure to meet you, too," Angelo Coveri replied tightly.

"Frans, do you mind if I have a few words alone with my father?" Bianca asked.

"No, of course not," he said, grinning. "I'll take a stroll. See you at the bar inside?"

"Great," Bianca said.

When Frans was out of earshot, Angelo Coveri tapped the table with a demanding finger. "Who is he? Some of the Eurotrash Niki hangs around with?"

"No, no," Bianca said. *Oh, God,* she thought. *This is not going to be easy.* "Frans is one of the top models in New York. He's in a campaign the PPHL fashion division's launching."

"The same thing if you ask me," Angelo Coveri said. "Where's he from?"

"Germany."

"Eurotrash, just like I thought."

"Dad!" she exclaimed. "You don't even know him."

"I know enough already," he said harshly. "He's a *model,* for God's sake. No job for a man." He looked at her with hooded eyes. "And don't think I didn't see the way you were throwing yourself all over him."

"Father," Bianca said, stomping a stiletto heel on the stone terrace. "Will you give me a chance to say what I wanted to say?"

"Fire away," he said.

"Well . . . ," Bianca began, looking down at her elegant Manolo Blahnik shoes as if they could inspire her. Now she wondered how she could possibly tell her father what their plans were. His initial reaction to Frans was so negative that she doubted that she could accomplish anything, much less convince her father that she was taking a wise course of action. *I have to be honest with him,* she thought. *He knows me well enough to know when I'm holding back.*

Taking a deep breath, she gazed up into her father's eyes. "I'm in love with Frans," she said, "and we're engaged."

Bianca watched as he struggled to restrain himself from shouting at her. His face flushed, and he gritted his teeth. After a few moments he said too quietly, "If you like the sex, fine. Screw your brains out. But marry somebody like that? He's half your age, Bianca. It's absurd that you're even considering such a thing."

"Do I need to remind you that my mother was half your age when you married her?" Bianca retorted. "And she was still half your age when you got divorced."

"No," he said. "You don't have to remind me of a damn thing." He paused and took a sip of his drink. "I just don't want to see you make the same mistake. We're the only real family we have left, Bianca, you and I, and I hate to see you do something that's going to be a catastrophe."

Tears suddenly sprang into her eyes.

Angelo Coveri stared at his daughter for a moment. "Wipe your tears away," he said, "and go find your young German. We'll talk about this later. This is neither the time nor the place."

"Okay," she replied. She kissed his cheek and turned to go. "We'll talk about this later." She paused, then added, "But I've made up my mind."

He heaved a sigh. "So go. Find your horny Kraut."

When Niki saw Frans walking alone on the beach, she slipped off her shoes and danced down to the water's edge, where he was idly kicking at the incoming waves. Hearing her approach, he turned and smiled.

"Hi," he said.

"Hello," she said, returning his smile. "What's your name?"

"Frans," he replied, his attention back on the water.

"I'm Niki," she said.

"I know," he said with a laugh. "It's your birthday, and you are Bianca's boss."

"Yes," Niki replied, "I am." She slipped out of the diaphanous gown she was wearing and dropped it onto the sand. The gold fish scales that covered her nipples and crotch were intact, serving as the briefest of bikinis. "Why don't we take a swim?" she asked. "There's something I'd like to discuss with you."

If he found her costume alluring, he didn't let on. "Talk? About what?"

Niki picked up an air mattress that someone had left on the beach and shoved it out into the water, then followed it, walking in up to her waist. "Come on," she said. "We can swim out to look at the barge." She pointed to the long barge that would be used for the fireworks display, anchored fifty feet or so offshore. It was decorated with ten-foot scallop shells, behind which the fireworks crew hid.

"I don't have a bathing suit," Frans replied as an excuse. He swam in the nude all the time, but he didn't relish the idea of swimming naked with Bianca's boss.

"Oh, for God's sake," Niki said. "Who needs a bathing suit? Besides, aren't you wearing underpants?"

He nodded. "Yes."

"Then take off your trousers and swim in your underwear," Niki said. "I think you'll be glad you did."

"Why?" Frans asked.

"Because of the proposition I have for you," Niki said.

Frans didn't like the sound of that, but he realized that she was Bianca's boss, and he didn't want to make her angry. Finally, he said, "Okay, but I should get back to Bianca soon."

"This won't take long," Niki assured him. "Here, get on the air mattress, and I'll swim alongside."

Frans took off his trousers and left them on the beach, waded out to where she held the air mattress, then scooted up onto it and spread out lengthwise, staring up at the starlit sky.

"Perfect," Niki said, beginning to paddle with her feet. "You can relax while I tell you what I have in mind."

On the beach Adrian Single watched them from the sandy spot where he'd come and sat down with his drink. He had been taking a break from the party, but now he was intrigued with the scene being enacted before him. He could hear much of what Niki was saying and was certain that he knew what she was doing. *Poor Bianca,* he thought. *She's finally found someone she really loves, and Niki decides she wants him for herself.*

*   *   *

"Frans," Niki said, "I think you could do something better than modeling." After seeing him with Bianca, she had wasted no time in finding out who he was and what he did.

"Why do you say that?" he asked.

"It's a dead-end career," she replied. "No future after a certain age."

"I know that," he said, "but I'll get into something else."

"You could come to work for PPHL," Niki said, paddling with her feet as she held on to the air mattress. "We're always looking for men like you."

Frans grunted noncommittally.

"Just think," Niki enthused. "With salary and stock options, I could make you a millionaire within a year. Why, you'd never have to fly commercial again."

Frans laughed. "That's hard to believe."

"Believe me," Niki said, "I can make it possible." She stopped paddling and gave him a penetrating look. "Plus," she added, "you'd have *me*."

Her directness both startled him and put him off, but he laughed lightly again. How to respond to this egomaniac without insulting her? He had met plenty of beautiful, rich women like Niki who thought they could simply buy him. They thought everyone had a price. If Bianca weren't involved, he would tell Niki how boring her proposal was.

"I could even finance a major movie deal for you," Niki gushed. "With your looks you could be a real film star."

"I don't think I can act," Frans replied.

"Oh, that's not important," Niki assured him.

Onshore, Adrian looked at his watch. It was still over an hour and a half until the fireworks were due to go off, but he made a snap decision. Unclipping the cell phone on his belt, he pressed in the number for the crew foreman on the barge. *"Estrellas!"* he said in a low but firm voice, giving the signal for the fireworks to begin.

In less than a minute, roaring rockets zoomed into the sky and burst into brilliant displays of multicolored light. The light began to fill the night sky, and the crowd gathered at Paradise Rock began to applaud with delight.

*   *   *

"Goddamn it!" Nikoletta screeched as the spent remainders of the incendiaries began to shower down on both her and Frans. "The assholes are early!" She let go of the air mattress, all thoughts of Frans gone, and quickly began swimming back toward shore. Frans fought to contain his laughter while swatting at the hot cinders that continued to fall. He gave her a good head start before he slid off the air mattress and swam toward shore, deliberately aiming south of where Nikoletta was headed.

The showdown with Nikoletta was soon in coming. Adrian had quickly joined Sugar, Bianca, Angelo, and Honor, who had clustered on the pool terrace to watch the fireworks together.

"Where have you been?" Sugar asked him.

"I was in the men's room."

"What happened?" she asked. "The fireworks are early."

"I—" he started to answer, but Frans joined them, his hair dripping water, his white trousers wet from his soaked underwear beneath them.

"What happened to you?" Bianca asked, taking his arm. "Did you get thrown in the pool or something?"

"I took a quick swim," Frans replied with a grin.

"Maybe we should go to our room so you can dry off and change your clothes," Bianca suggested.

"I think that's a good idea," Frans said.

"We'll see you in a bit," Bianca said to her father.

Angelo Coveri nodded.

"She looks so happy," Sugar said.

"Here comes somebody who looks very unhappy," Angelo remarked darkly, extending his drink in the direction from which Nikoletta came.

Her hair, dripping diamonds and water, was plastered to her head. Nikoletta didn't seem to mind, however. Her gaze was focused on Adrian, and although the expression on her face was neutral, there was fire in her eyes.

She crossed her arms across her chest, pushing her golden fish-scale-encrusted nipples directly at him. "Why was the fireworks display early?" she snapped.

"I'm so sorry, Niki," he said. "I didn't realize my watch was off. Way off, as it turns out." He pretended to eye his watch as though it were to blame. "With all the traveling lately, somehow or other I reset it incorrectly when I went through all the different time zones."

"Niki, darling," Honor filled in smoothly for her brother, "aren't you going to say hello to your guests?"

Niki glared at Honor momentarily, then relented. "Hi, Sugar," she said. "Thanks so much for coming to the party."

"I wouldn't have missed it for the world, sweetheart," Sugar said. "It's everything a party should be."

"Yes," Angelo said. "A lovely party."

"Thanks," Niki said sourly.

She turned back to Adrian. "I don't want anything like this to ever happen again. An hour and a half off is a serious miscalculation, Adrian. What if this had been a business deal, huh? It might have made the difference between winning or losing."

"I realize that, Niki," he said, trying not to smile, "but it was an honest mistake. It won't happen again."

"Darling, he's passed through a thousand time zones in the last few days," Adrian's sister said in his defense. "From one continent to another. Surely you can understand."

"He travels like that nearly all the time, Honor," Niki said with an edge, "and if he can't do something as simple as turn his watch back, how am I to rely on him to conduct business on my behalf?"

"It won't happen—" Adrian began, but he didn't finish his sentence. At the edge of the terrace appeared a lean and muscular paparazzo with a beard. He was raising his camera with both hands. Yet Adrian spotted an unusual metal glint below the camera, of a round silver silencer. As Adrian watched, the camera lens shifted its aim, and he saw the paparazzo raise the revolver directly at Nikoletta.

Adrian instinctively gave Nikoletta a hard shove with his elbow, knocking her down onto the terrace. Grabbing one of the flaming tiki torches placed all around the pool terrace, he lunged at the man. The paparazzo stumbled backward as Adrian thrust the tiki torch into his stomach. Adrian threw down the torch and leaped on him, trying to wrest the revolver from the paparazzo's hand.

Suddenly a shot rent the air, and Honor saw blood splatter the stone terrace. She let out a bone-chilling scream, and Angelo stepped forward. Yet it was Adrian who rose to his feet and stood over the would-be assassin, placing a foot on each of the man's arms.

"Take this," he said, handing the gun to Angelo.

The assailant spit up at Adrian's face. "I missed this time," he snarled, "but next time we won't miss. What happens to me doesn't matter."

"Has somebody called security?" Adrian asked, trembling a bit now that the harrowing near miss was over.

"They're coming now," Angelo said.

While some of the partygoers had run into the clubhouse to escape the gunfire, others had gravitated to the scene. The PPHL security detail pushed their way through the crowd, shouting for them to move out of the way.

"Niki okay?" Adrian asked.

"I'm fine," she said at his side, scowling at the man who had tried to murder her. "But I hope he won't be."

"Don't you worry," Adrian said grimly. "We'll take care of him."

Honor put an arm around Niki's shoulder. "I think you need a drink," Honor said, still trying to calm her own frazzled nerves. "And maybe a change of clothes."

"I'll have a drink," Niki replied, shrugging off her arm. She shouted to the gathered crowd, "Spread the word, everyone. The party will continue as before. We won't let some two-bit holdup man or whatever he is ruin my party."

Shouts of glee greeted this announcement, and the music started again. The violence was over. Dancing, drinking, and loud conversation resumed as if nothing out of the ordinary had happened.

The PPHL security detail handcuffed the man and put leg-irons on him, then told him to get to his feet. Adrian began going through his pockets.

"Here's his passport," he said, holding it to the nearest light. *Kees Vanmeerendonk. Amsterdam, Netherlands,* he read, though he wasn't sure what to believe. It could well be a false passport. "Hang on to this," he said to one of the security force.

He continued searching the young man's pockets and pulled out a wallet. There was little of interest in it, a small amount of money. Then Adrian extracted a piece of paper. It was torn off a larger sheet and dirtied from handling. On it was a telephone number, handwritten and surrounded by asterisks.

Adrian took out his cell phone and dialed the number, but connections on the island were often atrocious and that was the case now. "Take him to the manager's office," he told the security detail, "around the back way, away from the guests. I want as few people to see him as possible."

Kees Vanmeerendonk was escorted away, held under the arms by two of the security operatives. Adrian turned to Honor. "I'll be back in a few minutes," he said. "I want to take care of this."

"Do you know anything about him?" Sugar asked.

Adrian shook his head. "Not at this point," he said.

"You want me to come with you, Adrian?" Angelo offered.

"No, Angelo," he replied. "Stay here with the ladies. I'll be back soon." He left, hurrying toward the clubhouse, the nearest building with a landline. He had a hunch that this telephone number might answer some of his questions.

In the clubhouse, he switched on the light in a storage room and dialed the telephone number scribbled on the dirty piece of paper.

He heard a machine click on, then: "Mother Earth's Children. We do whatever it takes to save the mother. Please leave a message."

Chapter Six

❦

St. Barthélemy, the Leeward Islands

Unknown to the revelers, an ambulance without a siren or flashing lights pulled into Paradise Rock, along with the local police. Because his wound was not mortal, the police took a preliminary statement from Kees Vanmeerendonk before he was taken to the hospital, and they promised him that they would obtain a more complete one at the hospital later.

"I don't give a damn what you do," Vanmeerendonk snarled. "I did it, and I'll try to do it again if I get a chance. And if I don't, then somebody else will."

Vanmeerendonk was unceremoniously hauled into the ambulance, still in handcuffs and leg-irons, and taken to the local hospital to be treated for his gunshot wound. He was fortunate that the bullet had merely grazed his side, creating only a raw, bloody gash.

At the local police station, Adrian gave his version of the struggle to Jean-Paul Daigre, who was nursing a large-ring cigar, alternately puffing on it, then rolling and gumming it with his lips and tongue.

"Zealots," Daigre commented, "whatever their cause or belief, can be very dangerous individuals, Mr. Single."

"You saw that silencer, and you know they don't sell them on street corners," Adrian remarked. "My point being, Inspector, that he's part of a highly organized terrorist group."

"I understand all this, Mr. Single," Daigre said, blowing a large plume of smoke toward the ceiling.

"And don't you agree, Detective," Adrian went on, "that it would be highly detrimental to St. Barth's image if word got out that a criminal like Kees Vanmeerendonk almost succeeded in murdering an heiress to a huge fortune?"

"Of course, Mr. Single," Daigre replied. "It would be very bad for the image of our island. We are known as a playground for the very rich, and we certainly don't want to scare them off."

"So then, you want to make certain that those people know that ecoterrorists like Vanmeerendonk are punished in the harshest possible way if apprehended."

"I don't think you need to worry about that, Mr. Single," Daigre said. "Right now Kees Vanmeerendonk is shackled to a hospital bed with twenty-four-hour armed guards stationed there, and as soon as we can move him to the jail, we will. It will only be a few days, the doctors say. After that, you have my word that he will be prosecuted to the fullest extent of the law. A man who has attempted murder on this island is not going to get off lightly—of that I can assure you." There was no mistaking the tone of harsh determination in Daigre's voice.

Adrian put out his hand. "I'm glad we understand each other."

When Adrian returned from the local police station, he found Niki in the resort manager's office, and they walked back to the party together. "You're a very lucky young lady," Adrian said. "You could've been killed."

"It's those filthy ecoterrorists," Niki snapped. "I'm sick and tired of them and their troublemaking."

"I think we're going to have to work on PPHL's image," Adrian suggested. "Get the word out that PPHL is an environmentally friendly organization. Which means that we're going to have to make a huge effort to clean up some of our recently acquired sites." He didn't have to remind her that she had negotiated the deals for those plants that were now getting them into hot water with environmental groups.

"I'm not giving in to terrorist scum," Nikoletta said.

"Don't you think it would be wise," Adrian said, "to make an effort to clean up our act?"

"Look, Adrian," she snapped. "I don't want to talk about this now, okay? It's my birthday, and I want to enjoy it."

"All right," he said. "I'm sorry this has interfered with it. I didn't mean—"

She stopped and turned to him. "Don't you think you've already done enough tonight? Setting off the fireworks display early?"

Adrian knew that it was useless to point out that he'd probably saved her life tonight, shoving her out of the way of an assassin's bullet. "Yes, the mistimed fireworks. That's the point I'm taking away from tonight."

Bianca lay entwined in Frans's arms, basking in the warmth of his body heat and the scent of their lovemaking. She felt his lips brush across her cheek.

"I love you, Bianca," he said solemnly. "More than you'll ever know."

She turned to him, a smile on her lips.

"We should celebrate," he said.

"What?"

"Our love, Bianca, of course." He grinned. "Let's have some champagne. Just the two of us. We don't need to go back to the party, do we?"

She slowly shook her head. "No. No, we don't."

Frans slipped his arm from around her and got out of bed. He padded to the minifridge and opened it, looking inside. "I can't believe it. There's no champagne. Not even a split."

"I guess we had the only one earlier before the party started," she replied, sitting up in bed. "I'll call room service." She dialed the room service number and let it ring repeatedly. "Damn. There's no answer."

"Probably because of the party," Frans said. "They must be swamped."

Bianca got out of bed and slipped a caftan over her head. "I'll go get some," she said. "I know they'll have plenty out at the clubhouse."

"You don't have to do that."

"I want to." She kissed him. "Why don't you hop into that big Jacuzzi like you wanted to?"

Frans grinned. "Only if you promise to hop in with me when you get back."

"It's a promise."

Frans kissed her and padded into the big bathroom, where he turned on the taps in the Jacuzzi. "I'm going to have it nice and full when you get back," he called out to her.

"I'll hurry," she said. She left the room and dashed along the beautifully lit path that led to the clubhouse. Loads of revelers were dancing, some of them making out on the dance floor. Most of the couches and chairs were occupied by couples involved in various stages of foreplay. The big bar was crowded with people engaged in drunken conversation, and raucous laughs punctuated the music. Waiters with trays of champagne passed, but she didn't take any. She wanted to get them a bottle.

She went to the bar and waited. When the bartender finally reached her, she said, "There's no champagne left in our minifridge, and I couldn't get room service. Could I get a bottle to take back, please?"

"Of course," he replied. "Hold on just a minute." He disappeared into a room behind the bar.

Bianca drummed her fingernails on the bar. She could hardly wait to get back.

"Bianca?"

She turned toward the voice. It was Honor Hurlstone with a friend. "Hi," she said. "Are you having fun?"

"Yes, darling," Honor said. "Do you know Consuela?"

"I'm sure we've met," Bianca said. "How are you?"

"Wonderful," Consuela replied, "and yes, we have met, Bianca. I believe it was at another party for Niki."

The women chatted at the bar for some time. The bartender returned and placed a bottle of champagne and two glasses on a tray. "If you can wait, I'll have someone take it to your cottage."

"Oh, no. That won't be necessary," Bianca replied.

"Shall I open it for you?"

She shook her head. "We can manage, thanks."

Consuela, who was telling them about her latest boyfriend, kept talk-

ing as if the bartender didn't exist. On and on she went, and Bianca grew
increasingly anxious to get away, but she wanted to be polite and wait for
the right opportunity. Honor finally came to her rescue.

"Oh, Bianca, darling!" she exclaimed. "Your boyfriend, Frans. I completely forgot. You must be dying to get back to him."

"Well, I find Consuela's story fascinating, but to be honest I would like
to get back to our cottage."

Consuela laid an arm heavy with glittering bangle bracelets on
Bianca's. "Rush to him, you divine creature!" she exclaimed. "How polite
you've been to listen to an old hag like me natter on. Go!"

Bianca laughed. "You're anything but an old hag, Consuela."

She left the clubhouse with the bottle in one hand and the two glasses
in the other, being careful on the path. When she reached the cottage, she
heard laughter as she pushed her way inside.

What on earth? she wondered.

The bathroom door was closed, and the laughter was definitely coming from there, that and the churn of the Jacuzzi.

She went to the bathroom door, which had been left open a crack, she
discovered. Pushing it open, she stepped into the room. For a moment, she
thought she would be sick. In the Jacuzzi, oblivious to her, Frans and Niki
were splashing each other, laughing as if they were children playing a
game. Only they weren't children. They were naked, and between splashes
they were giving each other playful little pinches.

Bianca's shock quickly turned to a white-hot rage.

Suddenly Frans saw her. "Bianca!" he cried excitedly. "Come and join
us. This is so much fun!"

Fun! Who is he kidding? She felt like battering his head with the champagne bottle.

"Niki gave me a drink with ecstasy in it, and it's so much fun!" Frans
grinned at her, deliriously happy.

Bianca glared at them, her body still trembling with rage.

"You bet it's fun." Niki giggled. "Come on in. There's some more ecstasy. Over there on the vanity."

Bianca threw the champagne bottle and glasses toward the tile shower.
The glasses shattered, but the bottle hit the wall and fell to the floor,
rolling back toward her.

"Oh, Bianca!" Niki cried. "Don't be a spoilsport!" She shoved her hands underwater and giggled wildly. "Frans has plenty for both of us!"

Bianca felt bile rise in her throat. She wanted to throw up, but she turned and ran from the cottage.

Chapter Seven

◈

Ariadne wrapped her striped woolen scarf around her neck several times and pulled her wool watch cap down over her ears, then turned the collar on her jacket up. *I probably look like Nanook of the North,* she thought, *but I don't care.* It was extremely cold and windy outside with snow on the ground, and she might have to wait awhile for the bus that would take her within easy walking distance of her dorm on the Williams campus. Set at last, she pushed on the big glass door and stepped out into the already darkening day. She hurried along under the covered walkway that led to the street.

When she reached the curb, she looked up at the late-afternoon sky. It was the same depressing, uniform gray that it had been when she'd come to the Clark Institute a couple of hours earlier. *There's going to be more snow,* she thought. Normally, she wouldn't mind it too much, and usually she thought the snow falling was beautiful. But today the biting wind and gray sky and descending darkness matched her mood.

What a lousy day, she thought, reaching the shelter where the bus stopped. She knew why her spirits were so low, but that didn't help make her feel any better. Kurt had called earlier in the week and asked her to go out to dinner tonight. Then he'd called back this morning and canceled. He couldn't turn down an invitation to go skiing with a bunch of buddies at a nearby ski resort, could he? She hadn't been asked—it was a bunch of guys, after all—but she was disappointed that she'd been brushed off, virtually at the last minute. *Why am I not surprised?* she wondered.

The first time she'd met Kurt in a class, she'd been drawn to him. He was very good-looking, tall and blond and well built, with a friendly manner and an easy smile. She'd soon discovered to her delight that he also possessed that rare combination of a very sharp intelligence along with his equally great looks. But after dating him for a few months, she'd begun to notice other, less attractive attributes as well. He was sometimes not only arrogant and rude but also self-involved and insensitive.

She'd gradually come to feel that she was a convenience to him. When he needed help on a difficult paper for a class, he asked her for assistance. When he needed a date for some function, he called her. When his buddies were all busy, and he didn't want to eat alone, he would ask her to join him. And, of course, when he wanted to get laid, he would try to sweet-talk her into being accommodating in that respect as well. She was "the greatest" or "the best," never "the greatest lover" or "the love of my life." *Love,* in fact, was a word they'd both avoided, as if its utterance would destroy their relationship.

Tonight—all weekend in fact—she'd turned out to be inconvenient for him. *Well,* she thought, *he can start calling somebody else because I've had it.*

While she was angry, she realized in all fairness that he had helped her as well. She'd been seen about campus with a hot-looking man, hadn't she? Nor did she have to fret about being alone when there was an important event on campus. She could always tell the girls in the dorm that, yes, she had a date for whatever special occasion was coming up. Kurt was there, physically, if not necessarily emotionally.

She sighed and watched her breath dissipate in the freezing air, and stamped her feet to keep them warm. There was still no sign of the bus, and she had just decided to go back and watch for it in the warmth of the museum when she heard the honk of a car's horn.

"Ariadne? Ariadne?"

An old, battered-looking black Jeep stopped at the walkway, and a man was leaning out the driver's window. Who on earth? She didn't know anybody with a Jeep like that, did she?

"It's Matt," the voice called. "Remember me?"

Matt? He was smiling, and she could see his perfect white teeth from where she stood. She walked toward him. "How are you?" she asked.

"Fine, but you look like you're freezing."

"That's because I am," she replied with a laugh. "I've been waiting for the bus to take me back to the dorm."

"Want a lift? I'll be glad to take you."

"Well . . ." She hesitated a moment, then thought, *Why not?* "Sure, if it's not too much trouble."

"Hop in," he said. He leaned across and pushed open the door on the passenger side.

Ariadne slipped gladly into the Jeep's warmth. "Oh, this feels so good," she said, pulling the door closed. "It's really freezing out."

"It looks like more snow, too," he said cheerfully, disengaging the hand brake and putting the Jeep in gear. "Say, do you mind if I stop at my studio to pick something up? It won't take a minute."

"Of course not," Ariadne replied, suddenly curious to see what his studio looked like.

"It's just over there," Matt said, pointing with a finger.

He stepped on the gas and drove into the parking lot, pulling into a space near the long brick building. "Why don't you run in with me?" Matt asked. "I think you'd find it interesting."

"I'd love to," she said.

Matt shut off the engine, hopped out of the Jeep, and went around to her side and opened the door.

"Thank you," Ariadne said, surprised by his manners. Nobody bothered nowadays with such old-fashioned courtesies.

The sidewalks had been salted, and their boots crunched on the crystals and melting snow. Inside, he led her down a long hallway. Ariadne wrinkled her nose at the intense smell. Although she could hear the hum of extractor fans, the air was filled with the odor of linseed oil and turpentine, mixed with other smells she couldn't identify.

"Most of this area is studio space where paintings get cleaned, sometimes relined," he said. "Depends on what's needed. They'll also get touchups or even repainting in some cases."

Where doors had been left open, Ariadne peered into large rooms with skylights. She saw people bent over paintings, intent on their work. In most cases, they wore gloves in which they held small cotton balls, dampened with some kind of solution. They lightly brushed the cotton back and forth across small sections of canvas. The natural light was supplemented by high-intensity lamps with magnifiers built in, and the restorers peered through the magnifiers as they worked, closely evaluating the effects the cleaning solution was having on the canvas.

Down the hall, Matt took out a key and unlocked a door. "Here we are." Ariadne followed him into the studio space, glancing around with fascination. It looked much like the others, except for the shelves that contained statuary composed of a variety of materials. She recognized marble, granite, bronze, and terra-cotta. On a long worktable, an army of tools was laid out with military precision. Stacks of various woods and wood veneers, cardboard, fiberboard, and paper of various colors and weights were placed neatly in rows along one side.

Matt crossed to a corner and picked up a small box. He tossed Styrofoam peanuts from a garbage bag into it. From a shelf he picked up a small structure made of wood and placed it in the box.

"What is that?" Ariadne asked.

"It's a maquette," he replied.

"A maquette?"

He nodded. "Yes. A model for a sculpture that I'm making." He looked at her and shrugged. "Nearly all sculptors make them. They're miniature versions of what you want to make. Like an architect's model of a building."

"May I see it?"

"Sure," he said. He took the maquette out of the box and held it up.

The small three-dimensional structure was about six inches tall, wide, and deep, made of thin wood that had been cut and glued with precision. "It's unbelievable," she said. "It must take incredible patience."

Matt groaned good-naturedly. "It does."

"So it's a model of a sculpture that you want to make?"

"Exactly. It's a model for a piece that I'm working on now. It's the third step . . . no, the fourth step in the process."

"So many? What are the others?"

"First, imagining it in my mind's eye. Second, drawing a two-dimensional model. Then, making the maquette."

"It's beautiful," she said.

"Thanks," Matt said. "It's taken a lot of work. I've been gluing and regluing and shaving the wood, reshaping it, trying to get it to look the way I imagined it." He placed it back in the box, tossed a few more peanuts in, then closed the lid. Using a large tape dispenser, he sealed the box in one fluid motion.

"Ready to go?" he asked.

"Yes," Ariadne said, although she would have liked to explore the studio further.

Matt locked the door behind them, and they returned to the Jeep. He placed the small box in the backseat, then started the engine and backed out of the parking space.

"That was fascinating," Ariadne said. "I had no idea of what actually goes on in there."

"You only saw a little bit," Matt said. "It's a very busy place. There are experts who teach students, and there's always more work than they can handle. People send art from all over the world here to have it repaired or restored."

"So that's what you're doing with all of the statues and things I saw in your studio?"

"Yes. Soldering, welding, gluing, carving. You name it. Repairing cracks, making parts to replace missing pieces. All sorts of things." He drove through the parking lot and around the Clark Institute to the main road, stopping at the red light. A light snow had begun to fall. Matt turned and looked at Ariadne. "So, it's the weekend. You have big plans for tonight?"

"Well . . . no," Ariadne confessed.

The light changed, and Matt took a left. "You don't?" he asked. "I know I'm being nosy, but I—"

"No. It's okay," Ariadne said. "I had plans tonight, but they got canceled."

"So you were looking forward to . . . whatever it was?"

"Yes and no," she said.

He glanced at her with a puzzled expression. "That makes perfect sense," he said with a laugh.

"I know it sounds lame," Ariadne sighed. *I might as well tell him the truth,* she thought, even if he was almost a stranger. "I was invited out for my birthday, but my date called and canceled."

"It's your birthday?" Matt said.

She nodded.

"Then we've got to celebrate." He slowed behind a dump truck loaded with gravel. "What do you say? You can't go back to the dorm and stay in tonight."

"Oh, I don't know. . . ." Ariadne hesitated. "I didn't mean to get you involved in something that—"

"You didn't," he broke in. "I asked, didn't I? Besides, it gives me a good excuse to go out, too." He glanced at her and smiled. "See? It's best all around, isn't it? So you can't refuse."

"I . . ." Ariadne didn't know what to say, but she did know that she liked the idea of going out with Matt. "Okay," she said at last.

"Terrific," Matt said. "Now, what if I drop you off at the dorm? I've got to shower and change. Then I can pick you up. Say, in two hours? How's that?"

"That's fine." She realized she didn't know what he had in mind. "Where are we going? I just need to know what to wear."

"To a good restaurant I know," he said. "Not real fancy but nice."

"Okay." Two hours would allow her enough time to change into something a little more . . . attractive and inviting.

They drove south on Route 7 through the still-falling snow. The two-lane road was practically empty of traffic, and the snow seemed to close all around the warm, cozy interior of the Jeep. When they reached Great Barrington, Matt headed for Railroad Avenue. "I'll try to park close to the restaurant," he said, "so you won't freeze on the way inside."

"I'll be fine," Ariadne said. "I'm used to it."

He parked in a municipal lot, then opened the door for her.

The restaurant was only a short walk, and he took her arm when they went inside. He'd called to make reservations, and it was a good thing. The room was crowded with diners, as he'd suspected it would be on a Friday night.

"Do you want to hang up your coat?"

"Yes," Ariadne said. He helped her out of it, then hung it up after she'd shoved her long woolen neck scarf and watch cap in the pockets. When he took off his own, Ariadne could see that he wore an expensive sport jacket with a tasteful silk tie. The restaurant was abuzz with conversation but not too loud, and she could hear soft music in the background.

"Welcome to Verdura," the maître d' said. He took Matt's name, then led them to a table in the center of the big dining room. They ordered drinks, Ariadne a chardonnay and Matt a pinot grigio. He looked at her appreciatively across the table. Her long blond hair shone in the candlelight, and her big dark eyes appeared at ease as she took in the room. The pumpkin-colored cowl-necked sweater she wore was perfect with her slightly olive-complected skin, he thought.

"You look beautiful," he said.

"Thank you," she said, slightly embarrassed. In the past she'd been told that she was pretty, though she didn't put a lot of effort into it. "And you look great in your tie and all," she replied.

"It's the light," he quipped.

The waiter brought their drinks and set them down.

Ariadne smiled. "The lighting *is* beautiful," she replied. "All of the candles and the fireplace. The pictures on the walls." She was curious about how he could afford to bring her to such an expensive restaurant. Regardless of what his position was at the Clark, this must be a splurge.

"I'm glad you like it." He lifted his wineglass. "Happy birthday, Ariadne."

She lifted hers and touched his. "Thank you." She took a sip of the wine. "This is very good."

"So is mine," Matt said, swirling the liquid in the glass.

"These people don't look like the college crowd," she said, her eyes scanning the room again. The majority of the women were beautifully dressed and coiffed, and the men wore suits or sport jackets. *It's like a sea of expensive cashmere,* she thought, idly fingering the sweater she wore, a Christmas gift from her parents.

"A lot of the crowd is from New York City," he said. "People with weekend houses up here. This time of year, they come up to ski."

"It sounds like a pretty good life to me." Ariadne smiled. "In northwestern Connecticut, where I grew up, there are a lot of New York City people. Some of them very rich and a few even famous. Weekenders. But I didn't know any of them. In fact, I hardly ever even *saw* any of them. They only socialize with each other in their big houses. They eat in the few really expensive restaurants the locals can't afford, if they go out, and shop in little specialty places."

"It's pretty much the same around here, I think," Matt said, taking a sip of his wine.

"It's odd. They come up here to get away from it all, and end up seeing the same people they see in the city."

Matt nodded. "Birds of a feather."

"It's fun to be one of those birds tonight," Ariadne said mischievously, "and I really appreciate your bringing me here."

"It's your birthday," he said, shrugging. "It's the least I could do. Now, are you ready to have a look at the menu? They have northern Italian cuisine here."

They opened their large menus, and Ariadne quickly noted the column of prices. They were quite high, as she'd suspected they would be, and she wondered again if this was a big splurge for Matt. She decided she should be careful about what she ordered for his sake.

Matt closed his menu and set it down.

"You've already decided?" she asked.

He nodded. "No doubt in my mind. What about you? What appeals to you on this special day?"

"I'm not sure. . . ." Ariadne's voice trailed off as she continued to study the menu.

Matt watched her intently, certain that she was going to choose the least expensive items on the menu. "What if I order for us both?" he asked.

Ariadne looked quizzically at him.

"It's done a lot in Europe," he said, spreading his hands in a defensive gesture. "But maybe you think it's sexist, huh?"

Ariadne didn't hesitate a moment. "I think it *could* be, but I don't think in this case it is. In fact, I think it's a great idea."

"Good. I think you'll really like it."

The waiter appeared, and they listened as he reeled off the list of specials.

"Thanks," Matt said. "I think we'll pass on the specials tonight. We'll have the endive and baby arugula salad with the white-truffle-infused olive oil, goat cheese, and walnuts to start, and the chateaubriand for two." He looked at Ariadne. "How do you like your meat?"

"Rare or medium rare usually," she said.

"Rare," he said.

"Very good."

"And a bottle of the Barbera d'Asti Bersano."

"An excellent choice," the waiter said.

"Are you an oenophile?" Ariadne asked when he left.

"Not really," Matt replied. "Like everything else in life, it seems the more I learn about wine, the more I discover I don't know."

"I know what you mean," she said. "That's what I've found out in my studies. The further I go, the more I find out that I don't know."

"Do you enjoy your college work?"

"Oh, yes," Ariadne said. "I guess it's what suits me best. I'm naturally drawn to business and finance. I love studying the different markets and trading, the ins and outs of buyouts and takeovers, management techniques, all kinds of things like that."

"I'm impressed," he said. "You're one of the few women I've ever met who really enjoy that sort of thing. I bet your classes are mostly men."

"You'd be surprised," Ariadne said. "There are a lot of women in economics now, and a lot of women going on to work on MBAs."

"Do you know what you want to do when you graduate?"

"I'm not totally certain, but I think I want to go into corporate business management. The trading floors—nearly all of them—are dominated by men. Besides, I'm interested more in the big picture. You know, the direction companies are heading in. Strategic planning. That kind of thing."

"Wow," he said. "I really am impressed. It's great to hear somebody who has enthusiasm for what they're doing."

"What you're doing is really creative," Ariadne said. "I can't even imagine being able to draw or paint or sculpt. It's a whole different world, and I find it daunting."

"But you obviously find it interesting," he said. "The first time we talked, you were at the college museum. Then today I ran into you by chance at the Clark Institute. You must love soaking up art."

"Hmmm . . . yes," she said dreamily. "There's so much beauty. It takes me outside myself into another world."

"Do you have any favorites at the Clark?"

"Oh, yes. The Sargent painting of the lady with the big hat. I should know the name of it. . . ."

"I know the one," he said. "A lot of people think it's the best painting in the museum."

"Really? I didn't know that." She took a sip of her wine, then set the glass down. "What made you decide to be a sculptor?" she asked.

"I hope to be a sculptor someday," he said. "In the meantime I have to make a living. But to answer your question, I guess it's just like with you. I naturally gravitated toward drawing and sculpture. When I was a little kid, I was always drawing. Making models, too. You know, from kits. Later on, I started carving. It was just an urge that I can't really explain."

"Did you study art in school?"

"Yes, among other things."

"And you decided to come back to school?"

"Something like that," he said evasively.

"So you've been working?"

"Yes, that, too." He shifted in his seat somewhat uncomfortably, Ariadne thought. "But let's not talk about me," he continued after a moment. "I'm pretty boring."

With his dark eyes and sensuous lips, he smiled at her. She remembered how she'd thought that he looked like a man who spent a lot of time outdoors, and her initial impression was confirmed. He was somewhat sun- and windburned, and his slightly curly dark hair, even now in the restaurant, looked as if it had been disturbed by the wind.

"I don't think you're boring at all," she said.

"That's nice of you to say."

The waiter served their appetizers. Ariadne looked down at her plate and sighed with pleasure. The salad had been elegantly arranged and looked very appetizing. They began eating with relish.

"The truffle flavor is delicious," Ariadne said. "So . . . earthy."

"I love it, too," Matt said.

They talked about food as they ate, discovering that they were both adventurous eaters, willing to try almost anything. When the chateaubriand was served, Ariadne almost swooned over its buttery texture and the cognac sauce drizzled over it.

"This is so wonderful," she said. She took a sip of the deep garnet wine. "This will be a birthday dinner to remember."

"I'm glad," Matt said, very pleased. "What were you planning to do, by the way?"

She frowned at the thought of Kurt. "Oh, someone had asked me out to celebrate, but then canceled to go skiing instead."

"On your birthday?" Matt looked at her incredulously. The culprit must be the arrogant jerk he'd seen pick her up at the college museum.

She nodded. "Pretty dismal, isn't it?" she said with a light laugh.

He sensed that despite her laughter she was hurt. Who wouldn't be? "I hope you didn't think of this . . . *person* . . . as a close friend."

Any number of obscenities could have been substituted for *person,* the way he'd said the word, Ariadne thought. "Well, actually, I was beginning to suspect that this . . . *person* . . . as you say—" She smiled, letting him know that she appreciated the way he'd used the word. "Anyway, this jerk wasn't a real friend, and this was all the proof that I needed. So I'm not going to see him again."

"Good for you," Matt said. He looked at her thoughtfully. "Will you miss him? I mean, were you emotionally involved?"

"Kurt's just not very mature, and he's a long way from wanting to commit to anybody."

"And you do?"

"I—I don't know," she said, startled by his directness. "I guess that's a fair question since I just said he wasn't, but I don't really know. I suppose, if the right person came along." She paused, nervously fingering her napkin. "But that hasn't happened. I've never been . . . well . . . that involved with anyone."

"You've never been in love?"

Ariadne gazed into his eyes. "No. Have you?"

He reared back in his seat. "I thought I was a couple of times. A long time ago. But I think it was more of a case of being in lust. Both times."

They both laughed.

"Aha! So you've played around a lot," she said teasingly.

"Not really," he replied. He reached over and gently squeezed her hand. "I do know I'm glad I took you out for your birthday."

Ariadne relished the feel of his hand on hers, and she stole a glance at them. His was sunburned, with its long masculine fingers, and hers, so pale and slender and delicate.

The waiter appeared. "Would you like to see the dessert menus?"

Matt looked at her questioningly. "How about it, birthday girl?"

"Oh . . . I shouldn't. Really."

Matt studied the dessert menu for a moment. "Why don't you bring us some of the chocolate mousse cake? We'll split it. And two espressos."

"Very good."

"You are a very bad boy and a psychic," Ariadne said.

"Why?"

"Bad because of all those calories you're tempting me with, and a psychic because you know that I'm a closet chocoholic."

"The calories won't hurt you, and since you're a chocoholic, you need your fix. So I'm really a saint."

After they shared the cake and Matt paid the check, they rose from the table to leave. He helped her into her coat, and put his on while Ariadne wrapped her scarf around her neck and pulled her watch cap on.

When they stepped outside, they were surprised to see that a foot of snow had fallen and it was still snowing, much more heavily than on the drive down. Matt took her arm, and they walked slowly along the sidewalk. In places it had been cleared, but long stretches were deep with snow.

At the corner, they were about to turn toward the parking lot when Ariadne slipped on a patch of ice. "Oooooh!" she shrieked, then laughed as Matt grabbed her before she fell. He held her arms with his hands, steadying her, and drew her closer to him. They stood face-to-face, and Ariadne's smile abruptly fell away when she saw the unmistakable longing in his eyes. She held his gaze, hoping that he recognized the willingness she felt.

Matt leaned down and hesitated a moment, then kissed her on the lips, slipping his arms around her and hugging her against him gently. She returned his kiss, tentatively at first, then with more passion as she relaxed in his embrace. Her mind whirled with conflicting feelings, with doubts and questions, but there was no confusion about what she wanted at this moment: him.

From down the street came the sound of applause and loud whistling.

Matt drew back, and they both turned toward the noise. A group of teenagers pulling sleds was watching them.

"Wee-uuuuw!" one of them called. "Go to it, man!"

Matt looked down at Ariadne, and they both laughed. "I didn't realize we had an audience," he said softly.

"Neither did I."

He put an arm around her shoulder and squeezed it reassuringly. Together they walked out of the splash of light spilling from the streetlamp and on toward the parking lot.

Chapter Eight

ℤ

Lake Como, Italy

Angelo Coveri's villa rose from the shoreline in ocher neoclassical splendor above the verdant growth of lovingly tended gardens. Up its walls climbed a variety of vines, and roses scented the air nearly year-round. Below was a boathouse, built along the same neoclassical architectural lines of the villa. Its roof served as a terrace overlooking the lake, and Angelo's two boats were housed beneath.

The stately villa had been the site for many a festive occasion, most of them centered around Bianca's growing up. Today was an exception, however, as Adrian discovered after he drove up the well-raked pea gravel drive to the house and brought his Aston Martin sports car to a stop. He fully expected Bianca to rush out of the house and greet him, or perhaps Angelo.

He started up the marble steps to the grand entrance hall, but the front door opened before he reached it and Giulia, the housekeeper for many years, came down the steps toward him.

"Ciao! Mr. Single," she exclaimed, happily smiling. "So good to see you."

They exchanged kisses on each cheek in the continental manner, and she held him at arm's length, looking him up and down. "Still, you are the most handsome man," she said.

"And you, Giulia, are *bellissima*. The most beautiful woman in all of Italia. Maybe the most beautiful woman in all the world."

"Ah," she said, "you flatter me, you naughty young man." She shook a finger at him. "Come in, come in," she said, waving her hand toward the door.

Following her up the steps, he asked, "Is Angelo here?"

"Ah, yes," she said. "Thanks be to God."

"Why?" he asked. "Is something wrong?"

They reached the door and went into the magnificent marble entrance hall. Giulia put a finger to her lips. "I say nothing. I know nothing. Understand?"

"Yes," he said, but he wondered why Giulia was so closemouthed. She was virtually family, and was privy to all the family secrets.

"Follow me," she said. "They are in the gray salon."

Their footsteps echoed in the marble hallway as she led him to the main reception chamber, a room built of many gray marbles, decorated with early Roman and Greek statues and busts. He could hear voices as they approached the room, and when they reached the door, he saw Bianca standing at a desk, scribbling on a piece of paper. A courier was waiting at her side.

"Here we are," Giulia said in a whisper. She tapped Adrian on the back. "I will leave you to her and see you later."

Adrian nodded and smiled.

"I think that does it," Bianca said. She handed the courier a padded envelope that appeared to contain a small box.

"*Grazie,* signorina," the courier replied. He sketched a salute and, nodding at Adrian and Giulia, left the room.

"Oh, Adrian," Bianca cried. "I'm so glad to see you." She threw her arms around him, hugging him tightly to her. He saw that there were tears in her eyes.

"What's wrong?" he asked.

Across the room, he heard the rattle of a newspaper and saw Angelo pushing himself up out of an armchair. "Adrian," he said. "Good to see you."

"Good to see you, Angelo," he replied. He turned his attention back to Bianca. "Now, what's with you?" He thought he knew the source of her woe, but he wanted to let her tell him.

"Oh . . . ," she began in a murmur, "I'm . . . I'm returning my engagement ring to Harry Winston."

"Oh, no," he said, hugging her and stroking her back. "Don't you think that's premature?"

"No," she replied, shaking her head. "It's a lost cause."

"Are you sure about that?" Adrian asked.

"Yes," she said, pulling away from him. "Niki's seen to that."

"Come," Angelo said. "Have a seat, Adrian."

"Oh, I'm sorry," Bianca said. "I'm so . . . so preoccupied that I'm afraid I'm not a very good hostess."

"Don't worry about it," Adrian said to her. They crossed the room and sat with Angelo near the French doors that led out onto a terrace overlooking the lake.

"Would you like something to drink?" Bianca asked. "Coffee, anything?"

"No, thank you," Adrian said. He watched as she wiped her eyes with a Kleenex. "Are you sure about this, Bianca?"

"Oh, yes," she said. "I've never been more certain of anything in my life." Her voice rose in volume as she became angry. "It's that damned Niki," she railed. "She's nothing but a tramp. A common whore! If she wants to steal Frans from me, and he falls for her, so be it." She glared at Adrian with a tormented but furious face. "I hate her. And I hate him," she cried. "I hate them both!"

Adrian was relieved to see that she was angry. He knew that she was far from recovering from the loss of Frans—if their affair was really over—but it was better to be angry than to wallow in a pit of despair over him. "You have every reason to," he said. "What happened is terrible, but don't you think that Frans deserves a break?"

"A break!" She looked at him as if he were crazy.

"He's brokenhearted, Bianca," Adrian said. "I really believe that. You've got to remember the circumstances. He didn't—"

"Oh, damn it!" Bianca cried. "If only we hadn't gone to that damned birthday party together. Once we were there, I knew she had her eye on him, but I never imagined . . ." Her voice became choked, and Adrian took one of her hands in his.

"I had a long talk with him, and Frans is . . . well, he's really beside himself over this whole thing."

"Are you sure about that?" she asked.

Angelo, who had remained silent during their exchange, cleared his voice. "It's better this way," he said quietly. "It breaks my heart to see you suffer, Bianca, but if Niki could so easily seduce this young man, then he wasn't worthy of you." His voice suddenly became harsh. "You would be a prize for any man, and if he chose to throw you away, then he's stupid and—"

"Oh, Dad," she said, "I love you and appreciate what you have to say, but it really doesn't help any."

Angelo sprang to his feet. "If that's the way you feel, Bianca—that I'm not really any help—then I'll go out for a walk. You and Adrian can hash this out." He headed for one of the open French doors and exited in a huff.

"Damn!" Bianca swore.

"Let him cool his heels," Adrian advised. "He'll be back in a few minutes."

"See what a mess that prick has caused? He and that bitch!"

"Don't you think you could at least talk to him?" Adrian asked. "He's really going crazy not being able to see you." While most people thought the relationship was completely inappropriate, Adrian found that he liked Frans, and he truly believed that the young man was deeply in love with Bianca.

"Oh, no," she retorted. "I couldn't . . . I couldn't stand the thought of him even touching me after being with that . . . that bitch."

"Frans didn't know that Niki put ecstasy in his drink, Bianca. You know Frans doesn't do drugs."

"I know that," she replied, "but that doesn't excuse his behavior."

"He hardly knew what he was doing," Adrian said, "and I believe him when he says nothing like that would ever happen again."

Bianca gazed into his eyes. "Why did he let her into the cottage to begin with?" she asked.

"She's your boss," Adrian replied. "She told him she wanted to talk to him about a job opportunity, and he was worried that he might get you into trouble if he didn't let her in. She even brought the doctored drinks with her."

"Yeah, right," Bianca said sarcastically. "That's so lame."

"Come on," Adrian went on soothingly. "Won't you at least see him? Hear what he has to say?"

Bianca looked away from him. She wanted nothing more than to see Frans, to talk to him, to touch him, to feel his arms about her, but she wasn't ready yet. She didn't know if she would *ever* be ready.

The three young tourists were attractive, well dressed, and already well tanned when they drove up to the Sunset Hotel in Gustavia, the small town of several hundred inhabitants that is the capital of St. Barth's. They climbed out of their rented Suzuki Samurai and retrieved a minimal amount of luggage from the car's backseat and storage compartment, then registered at the hotel.

Outdoorsy types, the man at the reception desk thought. With their lean, tanned bodies, they weren't office drones enjoying their first foray into the sun this winter. Their reservations were in order, and he checked them in quickly, wishing them a wonderful stay on St. Barth's.

"Thank you. I'm certain it will be," the young lady, Viv, as the young men called her, said in a British accent as she took the arm of one of the young men.

Upstairs in their room, the trio unpacked the few belongings they'd brought, showered, and left the hotel.

In their rented Samurai they drove straight to the little hospital. Viv checked to make certain the revolver she'd put in her tote bag was still there. She slipped a long bright red wig and two blond ones out of the tote, tossing a blond one to Doug in the backseat and handing the other one to Tyler. She put the long red one on, adjusting it slightly in the rearview mirror. Satisfied, she put on a pair of large-framed sunglasses.

"All set?" she asked the young men.

Tyler pulled his revolver out of the waistband of his trousers, where he'd placed it against his spine. "Just about," he said, putting it in a side pocket of his sport jacket. He donned the curly blond wig and the sunglasses he had put in his sport jacket. "How's this?"

"Great," she said. "We'll all look ridiculous, but that's beside the point. We'll be harder to ID."

Doug patted his sport jacket, where his revolver was placed in the inside pocket over his heart. "I'm ready."

The trio went through the hospital's front door into the deserted lobby. A lone nurse sat at the reception desk, where she did double duty, admitting patients—usually minor scrapes from moped accidents—and watching over the few patients the small hospital normally cared for.

"Could I help you?" she asked. When she looked up at the trio, she laughed. "Party tonight?"

Viv slipped the revolver out of her straw tote and pointed it at the nurse. "Who else is on duty tonight?" she asked, ignoring the nurse's comment.

"What the—?"

"Shut up," Viv hissed between her teeth. "Now, be a good girl and take us to Kees Vanmeerendonk's room."

"But there's—"

"Just shut up and do it," Viv said.

The nurse eyed the revolver in fear, then slowly rose to her feet. "This way," she said, indicating a single wide door that led off the lobby. They followed her through the door into a hallway that stretched right and left. "Down here," she said nervously, walking to the right.

Several doors down the short hallway, the trio saw a uniformed policeman slumped in a chair, sleeping soundly, his chin resting on his chest, his cap in his lap. "You take care of him," Viv whispered, poking Tyler's arm.

They waited while Tyler went ahead, creeping up on the sleeping policeman. He lifted the revolver, holding it by the barrel, then brought the grip down hard on the policeman's head. There was a loud thwack as it made contact, and the policeman slumped forward.

The nurse started to cry out, but Viv shoved the small barrel of her revolver against her back. "Shut up."

Tyler grabbed the policeman before he fell out of the chair, and with Doug's help propped him back up. They slid the chair out from the wall slightly and pulled the policeman's legs forward in the seat so that he appeared to be merely asleep, his head back against the wall, his mouth open. Doug put the man's cap on his head, the bill down over his eyes, resting against his nose. If someone from emergency ventured this way, nothing would look amiss.

Viv pressed the revolver against the nurse's back as the terrified woman opened the door to the room. Once inside, Viv turned to Doug. "Watch her." She nodded toward the nurse. Of the four beds in the large room, only one was occupied. Kees lay asleep, one arm handcuffed to a metal bed rail and one foot cuffed to another.

Viv turned to the nurse. "The cop have the keys?" she asked.

The nurse nodded.

"Get it," Viv said to Tyler.

He opened the door and peeked up and down the hallway. No one in sight. He went to the policeman and immediately saw the key chain dangling off his canvas web belt. He unsnapped the key chain and took it back into the room, searching as he went for a handcuff key.

"Here we go," he said, spotting the key at once, it being much smaller and more oddly shaped than the others.

Kees's eyes opened, then widened in surprise when he saw them gathered around the bed. His lips spread in a smile, but he didn't say anything.

Tyler unlocked the handcuff on his wrist first, and Kees rubbed it vigorously with his other hand while Tyler unlocked the cuff on his ankle. He sat up in the bed and threw off the sheet as he swung his legs over the side of the bed.

"Here," Viv said. She tossed him a pair of cargo pants, a T-shirt, and flip-flops. "Put these on."

Kees untied the hospital gown he wore and tossed it onto the bed. He stood naked except for the large white bandage covering the wound on his left side.

"Jeez, mate," Doug said. "Looks nasty."

"It's nothing," Kees said as he quickly began to dress. Finally slipping into the flip-flops, he said, "Ready."

"Let's get out of here," Viv said.

"What about—?"

"Shut up," Viv hissed again. "You're coming with us." She held the revolver at the nurse's back, nudging her forward with it.

Tyler opened the door and checked the hallway. The policeman was still out, to all appearances sleeping peacefully. "All clear."

They rushed down the hall to the lobby door. Tyler opened it and checked out the small lobby. "Okay," he said.

Shoving the nurse in front of them, they went through the door leading outside. "To the parking area," Viv said, letting the nurse lead the way. It had been mere minutes since they had first entered the building.

In the parking area, Viv looked at her wristwatch. "It ought to be here any second."

"Wh-where are we going?" the nurse asked, her eyes widened in terror.

"None of your business," Viv replied.

In the distance, they heard the unmistakable *thwack-thwack* of a helicopter's rotors. "There we are, mates," Doug said. "Our ride outta here."

The sound grew louder, and they could see the powerful lights of the approaching craft. Viv stood at the nurse's side, the revolver still at her back, but it was concealed from any passing traffic.

The noise of the helicopter became deafeningly loud, and they felt the downdraft from the rotors as it hovered directly overhead. "Hang on to your hats," Viv said, referring to their wigs, as she placed her free hand atop her head.

The helicopter bobbed in midair for a moment, then slowly descended to the parking lot. Its door slid open, and a man inside yelled, "Hurry up. Let's get out of here."

"Go on," Viv said to Tyler and Doug.

They raced to the chopper and were virtually lifted inside by the man just inside the door. "Now, go see to your patients like a good girl," Viv said to the nurse. She shoved her away, and the nurse stumbled but didn't fall. Viv ran to the helicopter and was lifted inside.

The door slid shut, and the chopper began ascending into the air, already heading east, away from St. Barth's and away from St. Maarten, where it had been commandeered from the Dutch side of the island. Twenty minutes later, in international waters, the helicopter landed on the helipad of *Earth Mother*, Mother Earth's Children's converted research vessel that the organization used to attain maximum publicity for its maritime activities.

The ship's doctor, a young German, examined Kees to make certain his wound was healing properly. "Ah, *ja,*" he said, a gleam in his eyes. "You're almost ready for the next fight."

Earth Mother cruised off into the night at top speed.

Chapter Nine

᠎᠎

Nikoletta tossed her leather-bound notepad on her desk and went into the private rooms that adjoined her office. The bathroom was spacious, sheathed in sparkling onyx, and the dressing room, reached through double doors, was paneled in pale Russian birch. The rooms had all the features of such spaces in the most luxuriously appointed homes, but she proudly told everyone who commented upon them that for her they were an absolute necessity. She often began work early in the morning and worked until late at night, leaving for parties or business engagements directly from her office.

She checked her makeup in the mirror over the double sinks, applied a fresh coat of Crystal Tiger lipstick, then washed her hands. Leaving the bathroom, she went through her office and into her private dining room. The table had been set for three with starched white linen, heavy Buccellati sterling, Flora Danica china, and St. Louis crystal. A small arrangement of creamy white gardenias adorned the middle of the table, their heady scent perfuming the room. Nikoletta wrinkled her nose in disgust.

"Christian," she called angrily.

Her office butler immediately appeared from a jib door that hid the butler's pantry. "Yes?" he asked imperturbably.

"Get rid of those damned gardenias," she said. "How many times do I have to tell you that I don't want flowers with heavy scent on the table? They interfere with the aroma of the food."

"They were sent by one of your guests," he replied, "so I thought it would be appropriate to use them."

"Well, you were wrong," she snapped. "Get them out of here."

Christian, whose face had turned a bright red, quickly picked up the bowl of gardenias and whisked them out of sight.

She heard the telephone on her desk bleat and went to answer it. "Yes, Maria," she said, knowing that it was her secretary. She sat down behind her desk.

"Bianca Coveri is here," Maria replied.

"Send her in," Nikoletta said.

The door to her office opened, and Bianca stepped warily into the room. Her appearance was strikingly elegant as usual, but Nikoletta didn't miss the cautious demeanor. It contrasted significantly with the Bianca who normally swept into the office with authority and confidence.

"Hi," Nikoletta said. "Why don't you have a seat." She indicated one of the chairs facing her desk.

"You told me that Heidi Lyons was going to be here." The statement was almost an accusation.

"She is," Nikoletta replied, "but I wanted a few minutes with you alone to discuss a private issue."

"Then why don't you get to the point, Niki?" Bianca said.

"Okay," Nikoletta said, folding her hands on the desktop and looking Bianca in the eye. "First, I want to get the obvious out of the way. The business with Frans wasn't meant to be sexual, whether you choose to believe me or not. I went there to discuss job possibilities with him."

"Oh, right," Bianca said sarcastically.

"I don't expect you to believe me," Nikoletta said, "but it's the truth. He's good-looking and personable and could be an asset to the company. Plus he was *your* friend. I figured that if you kept company with him, then he had to have something on the ball besides his looks." She paused and gazed at Bianca with a gleam in her eye. "Meaning brains, Bianca. I know you don't suffer fools gladly."

"I'm flattered," Bianca said, "but that still doesn't account for what happened."

"No, but I'm getting there. I'd asked one of the waiters to make drinks for us. The three of us. I'd already had a little too much to drink, and I didn't even notice the pills he'd put on the tray with the drinks. Frans saw those after we'd already started drinking. And I had no idea that the drinks had been spiked. I guess he thought he was doing me a favor, but he didn't know me. You know that I'm not the type to use drugs. How the hell would I do my job?"

Bianca knew that this was probably true. Nikoletta might get a little drunk sometimes, but she'd never heard anything connecting her with drug use. "Go on," she said.

"What happened is all a blur," Nikoletta went on. "I had no intention of having sex with Frans, and we didn't have any. We were too busy laughing."

"So what's the point?" Bianca asked.

"I'm offering you a promotion," Nikoletta said. "A huge promotion, with a corresponding increase in salary. It would be a new position in the company. International vice president and director of Ethics and Goodwill."

Bianca blurted a laugh. "*You* are suddenly interested in ethics and goodwill?"

Nikoletta nodded. "Yes. Nobody on the board seems to think that I've been listening, but they're wrong. I can see that today's business climate is really changing, and we have to change with it."

Bianca didn't know what to believe. Was it possible that Niki—the Niki she'd known so many years—could actually be changing her mind?

"Anyway, that's where you come in," Nikoletta went on. "I'd like your help. You'd be sort of a roving ambassadress of goodwill and ethics for PPHL. Helping find solutions to the problems at various facilities. Reporting back to me what the conditions are."

"I have to admit that I can hardly believe what I'm hearing," Bianca said.

"I guess what's changed me—at least a large part of it—is that I was nearly killed by that ecoterrorist," Nikoletta said in a small voice. She looked at Bianca with her huge, dark eyes. Bianca thought she saw tears about to spill. *Is that possible?* she asked herself. *Niki tearful?*

"The guy who tried to murder me in St. Barth's escaped," Nikoletta continued, "and it makes me furious. And now that he's on the loose, he'll probably try again. If he doesn't, another one will. So part of this move is for my own self-protection."

Bianca's mind was reeling. She'd reluctantly come to Nikoletta's office.

In the back of her mind there still lurked the urge to tell Niki off. But now Nikoletta had stunned her with an enticing opportunity. Under ordinary circumstances, she'd jump at the chance.

Her reverie was interrupted by Nikoletta. "So, what are your thoughts about it?"

"I agree with you about the changes needed," Bianca responded, "and the job sounds like it's made for me." She paused and looked down at her manicured fingernails. "But I'll have to think about it."

"Fine," Nikoletta said. The telephone on her desk bleated, and Nikoletta picked up the receiver. "Yes?" She listened for a moment. "Send her straight in, Maria." She gazed at Bianca. "Heidi's here. I think you'll be fascinated to hear what she has to say. She knows a lot about what would lie within the scope of this position, and the possibilities are intriguing."

I'm already intrigued, Bianca thought. "Okay," she said.

Maria held the door open for Heidi, and she came into the room sketching a wave in the air. "Hi, Niki."

"Hi. Heidi Lyons, meet Bianca Coveri."

They shook hands. "I've heard a lot about you since I've been here," Heidi said.

Nikoletta watched as Heidi sat down in the chair next to Bianca's. They were both very intelligent, even brilliant, she thought, but they were opposites in other ways. Bianca's perfect grooming, fashionable clothing, and well-toned body didn't necessarily give the impression that she was a high-powered businesswoman. Heidi was another story. She had frizzy, unkempt hair and ugly eyeglasses, and wore an unfashionable gray suit and practical, scuffed black shoes with low heels. Yet behind those ugly spectacles were steely eyes that never missed a thing. She wasn't yet thirty, but had proved her worth time and again.

"I've wanted you and Bianca to meet for some time. I'm hoping that Bianca will be our new troubleshooter. The job I described to you, Heidi."

"From what I've heard about you," Heidi said, looking at Bianca, "you're perfect for the job."

"Why don't we go on into the dining room?" Nikoletta said. "I think Christian's ready for us."

She ushered them into the next room and went to her customary chair. From it a dramatic view of Manhattan spread out below. Christian had already appeared and pulled her chair out for her. After she was seated, he performed the same service for Bianca and Heidi.

"This is lovely," Heidi said.

"Yes," Bianca agreed. "It's really beautiful, and so much nicer than going to a restaurant."

"Shall I serve the wine?" Christian asked, looking at Nikoletta.

She nodded, and he began pouring. "I hope you like a chardonnay," she said to Heidi. "As Bianca knows, we only serve wines from our own vineyards, and this is one of them."

"That's fine with me," Heidi said brightly.

"What do you do here at PPHL?" Bianca asked Heidi.

"I'm a futures trader for one of PPHL's food subsidiaries," Heidi said.

"Heidi scored a major coup speculating on cocoa futures."

"Oh, how's that?" Bianca asked with interest.

"Buying two percent of the world production," Nikoletta said, "then selling it at its seventeen-year high. She made PPHL tens of millions of dollars."

"That's very impressive," Bianca said. "Congratulations."

"Thank you," Heidi said.

Christian returned with a large tray that he set on a buffet and began serving bowls of a salad, beginning with Nikoletta.

"That looks delicious," Bianca said.

"It's a curried lobster salad," Nikoletta said. "I had Christian call a friend of mine in Paris to get the recipe. I stayed at their château one weekend and loved this."

"Oh, I've never seen so much lobster in my life," Heidi said, ogling the salad with relish.

"Well, *salut*," Nikoletta said, holding her wineglass up for a toast.

They clinked glasses and began eating, Nikoletta picking at the food carefully. She was a perpetual Atkins dieter, although she was model thin. After a few small bites, she gazed over at Bianca.

"What do you know about chocolate?" she asked.

"Only that it's fattening," Bianca said, "and that I eat too much because I love it so much."

Heidi and Nikoletta smiled. "I love it, too," Heidi confessed.

"And what about the so-called Cocoa Belt? Do you know anything about that?" Nikoletta asked.

Bianca looked at her with questioning eyes. "Absolutely nothing," she said.

"Why don't you fill her in, Heidi?" Nikoletta said.

"Well," Heidi began, putting down her fork and warming to the subject, "most of the world's cocoa for chocolate production is grown in West Africa. Especially in Mali and Burkina Faso and Ivory Coast. In 1999, the World Bank and the International Monetary Fund put pressure on Ivory Coast to stop fixed pricing."

"So that freed up the cocoa market?" Bianca guessed.

Heidi nodded. "Yes," she said. "Not that the cocoa farmers were any better off afterward. No trickle-down economics there. Plus, the International Labour Organization, a UN agency, singled out Ivory Coast for child labor abuses. They estimate that around two hundred thousand children work in hazardous conditions there."

"That's . . . that's so overwhelming I can hardly conceive of it," Bianca said.

"Well, it's true," Heidi said. She took a sip of wine, then continued. "The major chocolate manufacturers have said they'll try to certify that all their products are free of abusive child labor practices."

"And . . . ?" Bianca said. "Let me guess. The government in Ivory Coast won't help implement the plan?"

"It's a little more complicated than that," Nikoletta interjected after a nibble of salad. She explained that fighting between government and rebel forces had interrupted the UN's global campaign against child labor abuse.

"In other words," Bianca said, "it's a war zone."

"Well, let's just say that Ivory Coast has its share of civil strife," Nikoletta replied. "Most of those African countries do, you know."

"So where would I fit in the picture?" Bianca asked, although she was forming an answer to the question even as she spoke.

"Well, if you took the job . . . ," Nikoletta began, gazing at Bianca shrewdly, "this would be your first assignment. I know that you've been working very hard over the years to help put an end to child labor abuse in the garment industry—"

"—where it's *still* epidemic!" Bianca burst out passionately.

"Maybe so. But it's people like you in the industry who have made headway," Nikoletta said, emphasizing the point with her fork.

"Nikoletta and some of the other people here have told me about some of your work in the area," Heidi chimed in, "and I think all the good you've done is wonderful."

"I like to think so," Bianca said. She couldn't help but feel flattered by their appreciation for her efforts in the garment industry, but she added doubtfully, "It seems like a losing battle sometimes, Niki."

Nikoletta shook her head. "No, Bianca," she said, "you can't think that way. It's an *ongoing* battle. And you know what I think?"

"What?" Bianca asked.

"I think that if anybody can try and convince these planters and farmers in Ivory Coast to change their ways, it's you. You've had some experience in this area. Besides, you've got the kind of . . . well, it's charisma, really . . . that Adrian has. You can talk to people. Common people. And you can convince these planters that they should be sending their children to school instead of out into the fields with machetes."

Nikoletta took another nibble of her salad. She knew that she had dangled irresistible bait for Bianca, and she enjoyed waiting to see her take it. Hook, line, and sinker. She knew that this was just the kind of social injustice that Bianca was so passionate about. Her bait was taken more quickly than she'd anticipated.

"There's no way I can say no to this," Bianca said excitedly, setting down her wineglass. "It's just the sort of thing I love getting involved in, and if the job entails this kind of assignment, you've got me, Niki."

"You're sure about that?"

"I'm absolutely positive," Bianca said enthusiastically.

"You know that it could be dangerous," Nikoletta responded. She quickly added, "Of course, you won't be going alone. You'll have a local guide by the name of . . ."

"Moctar Yanou," Heidi supplied. "I've been working on this for weeks," she said to Bianca. "It's such a challenge."

"Plus you'll be escorted by hired guards." Nikoletta paused and looked at Bianca. "I know you're excited, Bianca," she said, "but you're really certain you want to take on something like this? Maybe you should think about it like you said. I want to make it perfectly clear that I'm not ordering you to do this."

Bianca shook her head emphatically. "No, no," she replied. "I *must* go, Niki. Just don't tell my father where I am until I get back." She laughed. "You know him. He would blow a fuse."

Nikoletta laughed. "I know," she said. *Believe me,* she thought, *telling Angelo is the last thing in the world I would do.*

"When would I leave?" Bianca asked.

"Heidi is going to give you a detailed briefing," Nikoletta replied. "Then we'll take it from there. Probably within a week? What do you think, Heidi?"

"I can just tell," Heidi said, gazing at Bianca with admiration, "you'll soak in all the information I've got for you in no time. Plus, of course I've got everything on a laptop that you can take with you."

"Sounds good to me," Bianca said.

"Excellent," Nikoletta said, touching Bianca's arm with her hand. "I knew this new position was for you."

She folded her napkin and placed it on the left side of her plate. "Well," she said, "do you two want to go ahead and get started? I've got a busy schedule today." Before Christian came forward to help pull her chair away from the table, she twisted it sideways and rose to her feet. Bianca and Heidi quickly followed suit.

Nikoletta placed a hand gently on Bianca's shoulder. "If I don't get a chance to see you again before you leave," she said, staring into her eyes, "just remember that you can back out of this if you want to. And if you go through with it, you've got all of PPHL's support behind you."

"I won't back out," Bianca said.

"Well, I'll see you later, then," Nikoletta said.

Christian ushered the guests out of the dining room. "This way," he said, indicating a door that led directly back out into the hallway, so that they wouldn't have to go through Nikoletta's office.

Nikoletta watched them leave, then went back to her office. She sat down at her desk, opened a drawer, and took out the latest issue of *L'Uomo Vogue,* the Italian men's fashion magazine. On the cover, intense blue eyes staring directly into the camera as if he was taunting it, was Frans. His long dirty-blond hair was a wild mass framing his handsome face, with its prominent cheekbones, aquiline nose, and sensuous lips. She smoothed her hand over the cover and smiled. "Bye-bye, Bianca," she whispered. "And hel-*lo*, Frans . . ."

At three o'clock, Nikoletta called her secretary, Maria. "Tell Anthony to be downstairs waiting for me in fifteen minutes," she said. "I'm leaving early."

"Yes, Ms. Papadaki," Maria replied.

Nikoletta hung up the telephone, then placed some paperwork in her briefcase and snapped it shut. Going into the bathroom, she checked her makeup and washed her hands, then dabbed her neck with perfume. Flipping off the light, she went out and picked up her briefcase and took the elevator downstairs to meet Anthony.

"We're going to West Forty-second Street and Twelfth Avenue," she told him.

Anthony, the behemoth who served as her driver and personal bodyguard, swung the limousine out into the traffic. He knew where they were going without more specific instructions. Weaving in and out of the heavy traffic, he reached the construction site in a short time.

"Wait for me here," Nikoletta told him. Before her rose an extravagantly designed, three-sided titanium-and-green-tinted skyscraper. Swelling with pride as her gaze traveled its height, Nikoletta felt a surge of pleasure rush through her. The huge billboards in front proclaimed the building as the soon-to-be-completed PPHL International Headquarters.

"Nikoletta!" a man called to her.

Rik Persoons, the world-famous innovative Belgian architect, hurried toward her.

"Hi, Rik," Nikoletta said.

"Shall we go up?" he asked, holding out a construction helmet stenciled with PAPADAKI.

"Yes," she said, anxious to see the progress.

He led her to the steel girders framing the main entrance, and they began a tour that took them down into the basement and subbasements, then back up through the building to its seventieth story.

"As you can see," Rik told her, "we're still ahead of schedule. Work is proceeding around the clock, and I mean twenty-four hours a day, seven days a week."

Nikoletta's eyes gleamed with a pride that bordered on megalomania. She had surveyed every nook and cranny of the building's top three floors. Not even the ductwork had escaped her attention. These three highest floors would be the heart of her empire as well as her new home. The triplex apartment for her was going to be the largest, most expensive apartment in New York City.

No one . . . no one . . ., Nikoletta thought, surveying the vast expanse of the seventieth floor, *has ever had it so good.*

Seventy stories above street level, fierce gusts of wind sweeping down the Hudson River buffeted her, but she didn't notice. She was completely absorbed by the dreams of glory the site inspired. *This is* my *building,* she thought. *My half-a-billion-dollar baby.*

"It will be the most fantastic apartment in the world," Rik said over the wind.

Nikoletta frowned. "Yes, but it could've been even more spectacular. Those ridiculous zoning boards and community associations! They work overtime to impede progress."

"I know," Rik said. "Still it will be the most sought-after apartment in New York. Hands down." He felt as if he was always trying to humor this impossibly difficult woman half his age. She had wanted the building to be the tallest in the world—120 stories high—and to rule her empire from a roost at the top. Unfortunately, New York City's community groups and the zoning board put a stop to that.

"Yes, but look at Shanghai," Nikoletta said peevishly, "and Singapore. You don't have any of that nonsense there, do you? There the sky's the limit."

"Yes, but what can you do?"

Nikoletta turned away from him, gazing out across the Hudson River to New Jersey. Then, shifting on her feet, she made a complete circle, taking in the views from every direction. South, past where the World Trade Center used to rise, over to New Jersey and then Staten Island. East, all the way past Manhattan and Queens and Brooklyn to Long Island. North, beyond Manhattan and the Bronx to Westchester County.

Eventually, she told herself, Manhattan would be like Shanghai and Singapore. The sky would be the limit, here as there. She would see to it. *Oh, yes,* she thought. *This is great, but it's not good enough.*

Chapter Ten

The dirt road leading up to the cabin in the Berkshires was treacherous. Even though the snow had been plowed and they had his Jeep, Matt took the curves slowly. "Four-wheel drive won't help on ice," he told Ariadne. "Nothing much will help on ice."

"Is it much farther?" she asked, gazing out at the skeletal trees that lined both sides of the road.

He glanced at her and grinned. "Are we there yet?" he said. "I think you're anxious to get off this road."

"No, I'm used to it," she said. "Remember, I live in northwestern Connecticut."

"It's just around the next curve. Less than a mile."

"It's really beautiful up here," Ariadne said. "Pristine. It's almost as if it's untouched. Like real wilderness."

"That's not quite the case," Matt said, maneuvering the Jeep around a hairpin curve. "There're ski resorts nearby and summerhouses here and there, but it's still fairly isolated and unspoiled." He pointed ahead, to the left. "There's the road that leads up to my place." He slowed down and made the turn, downshifting for the steep incline.

The road was little more than a path cut through the forest. In places, the branches of tall trees intertwined above it, giving it the appearance of a tunnel. At the top of the hill, they came to a small clearing and Matt's cabin.

"Oh, this is spectacular," Ariadne said enthusiastically. "It looks enchanted. Like something from a fairy tale."

"I hoped you'd like it," Matt said. "It's small and simple, but I love the place."

The driveway formed a circle in front of the cabin, and in what would be its grassy center come spring stood a large steel sculpture, a contemporary piece that was all angles jutting out into the surrounding space.

"Did you do the sculpture?" Ariadne asked.

Matt nodded. "It's my fallen star."

"It's beautiful," she said admiringly. "And I love the idea that a star fell directly in front of the cabin in the ideal spot for it."

He chuckled. "A very happy accident."

Matt got out of the Jeep, then went around and opened Ariadne's door. "Be careful," he said. "There are some icy patches, and I know you have a tendency to slip."

She gave him a mock frown. "You've only seen me slip on ice once."

He led her up the steps onto the porch and unlocked the door. They both wiped and stomped snow off their boots. "My humble abode," Matt said, ushering her inside and switching on a light.

Ariadne glanced around the very big room with a huge stone fireplace. Off to the right, a counter separated off the kitchen. Subdued winter light poured in through a huge central skylight. "This is so great," she said.

A stack of kindling had already been laid in the stone fireplace, and Matt crumpled some newspapers to stuff under it. In another minute the wood was ablaze, crackling and snapping. Warmth began to fill the large room.

"I'm going to go out and get some more firewood," Matt said. "I haven't replenished the baskets in here or the log holder on the porch, and I think we ought to have a roaring fire, don't you?"

"That would make it even more perfect than it already is," she said.

"Make yourself comfortable. It'll only take me a few minutes outside. Then I'll make us something hot to drink."

Ariadne shrugged out of her parka, and he hung it on one of the coat hooks near the front door. "You want me to help you bring in wood?"

"No, I can handle it," he said. "Take a tour of the place, and if you want, put some water in the kettle. It's on the stove. Some hot tea would warm us up."

"Will do," she said.

"I won't be too long," he said. "If you hear something like thunder on the porch, it's just me dumping logs to stack." He headed back outside.

Ariadne went to the kitchen and put the kettle on. Afterward, she began exploring the cabin. *He did suggest it,* she thought as she began to roam. A large, comfortable sofa was placed in front of the fireplace, with big over-stuffed chairs on either side. Atop a coffee table were several maquettes. A small dining table was positioned under windows on a far wall, and built-in bookcases lined either side of the fireplace. They were overflowing with all kinds of books, she noticed, from art to fiction to nonfiction, with a lot of history and political works. A staircase at one end of the room led up to a big balcony and what looked like other rooms. She wandered into a small hallway that led to a bathroom and a cozy, inviting bedroom.

Retracing her steps to the living room, she noticed a big ax leaning against the wall near the front door. Its blade glistened as if it had recently been sharpened. Ariadne laughed to herself. *Matt is not a serial killer. He's a perfectly sane and wonderful man who chops wood!* She climbed the stairs that led up to the balcony, wondering what she would find.

The balcony walls were lined with bookcases, punctuated with two doorways, and against the balustrade overlooking the living room there was a big desk. On it were stacks of paper and other supplies, pencil and pen holders and such, all of it neatly arranged. A computer hummed. Lots of people never turned theirs off, she knew, although she usually shut down hers. Curious, she touched the mouse, and the big, flat-screen monitor came to life.

The computer was in Outlook Express, and an e-mail was highlighted. Sitting in the desk chair, she glanced at the e-mail. She wanted to know more about Matt, but she felt guilty at the same time. Mail was personal, after all. *Well, it can't be too personal,* she reasoned. *Not if he left it on the computer like this.*

She saw that the e-mail was from an "A.Single." *What an odd name,* she thought. Or *was* it a name? It could be a cute way to signify a single person, couldn't it? Like a name someone might use in a chat room, she thought with a twinge of jealousy. She quickly perused the e-mail, but it didn't make any sense to her. It was almost as if it read in code. A.Single wanted an update on "her." If Matt had done what he'd asked about "her." "Her," frustratingly, was never identified by name.

The message was signed "Adrian." That was the *A* in *A.Single,* she thought, but it posed another mystery. Was Adrian a man or a woman? The name could be either.

At a resounding thunk from the front porch, Ariadne nearly jumped out of her skin. She laughed to herself nervously. *It's only Matt dumping firewood,* she thought, *just like he warned me that he would.* But she decided it was time that she quit snooping. She didn't relish the idea of being caught reading his e-mail. She got to her feet, eyeing the two doorways surrounded by bookcases.

She went to the first one and opened it. Inside was another bedroom, this one quite large and definitely Matt's. Although it was neat like the rest of the cabin, it was more lived-in than the bedroom downstairs. A large skylight opened directly over the bed with a blind that could be open or closed to shut out the light. Against the wall opposite the foot of the bed was a flat-screen television and CD-DVD player on a stand. Near it was a fireplace. A sculpture—entwined lengths of brushed steel—dominated a corner. Books were piled on one of the bedside cabinets and on the floor next to it. Several framed drawings dotted the walls, and she circled the room, looking at them. *They're drawings for his sculptures,* she thought. *Part of the preliminary planning he told me about.* They were very well-done, art in their own right as far as she was concerned. She passed a big dresser decorated with another few maquettes, and checked out the bathroom. It had a large Jacuzzi as well as a walk-in shower and a big vanity with sink. On one wall was another sculpture, this one of geometric shapes—circles, squares, parallelograms, and so on—finished in a glossy white. It made her think of a Léger.

Ariadne went back out onto the balcony, looking down at the big living room. The cabin was truly beautiful, she thought. It was not decorated to be "cute" or "country" or to look like a mountain lodge, as so many of these places were. She'd seen a few that belonged to the families of friends from boarding school or college. Here, there were no stuffed trophies. No deer heads, pheasants, or fish. No bearskin rugs on the floor or Native American blankets on the walls or beds. The decor was restrained, modern, and clean, with a decidedly masculine air about it. The only knick-knacks were Matt's maquettes and sculptures.

She heard another loud thunk on the porch and went down the stairs to the living room and saw that the tea water was boiling furiously. She switched it off and started looking for tea bags in the cabinets. Matt came in the front door, his arms loaded with firewood.

"Hey," he said, smiling.

"That's great," she said. "Where're the tea bags?"

"In the cabinet just to your right," he said. He went to the big basket by the stone fireplace and neatly stacked wood in it, then placed some in the fireplace. From the kitchen, Ariadne watched as the fire started to dance high with flames.

"What kind of tea would you like?" she asked.

"The green tea, please."

He went to the front door and took off his boots, placing them on a mat to dry off, then hung his parka on a hook. He put a CD in the player. Soft music soon filled the room. "What is that?" Ariadne asked.

"It's a DJ compilation," he said. "All kinds of things that have been rearranged and tinkered with. This is one of the Café del Mar CDs. Do you like it?"

"It's great. I've never heard it before."

"There are a bunch of them out there now," he said.

He joined her in the kitchen. "Now for the crowning touch." He opened a cabinet and took out a bottle of brandy. "How about a dollop? It'll get your heart beating, as my dad used to say."

"Why not?" she said.

He poured a small measure in each cup of tea, then handed her a mug. "Let's go sit. I could use a breather after carrying all that wood. Normally I keep the basket in here and the stack on the porch replenished, but I've been so busy lately I let it go."

They sat on the big oversize couch in front of the fireplace, and Matt put his feet up on the coffee table. The fire was roaring, and its warmth felt wonderful. Dusk was rapidly descending, and light in the room was growing dim. Matt reached over and switched a lamp on, turning the dimmer down, so that it gave off a soft, low light. "Are you comfortable?" he asked. "You can put your feet up."

"I'm fine. This feels so good," she said. She sipped the tea. "And the brandy helps."

"Good. The brandy and fire should warm you up, and if they're not enough, use one of the throws." The arms at either end of the sofa were draped with big wool throws.

"I feel great," she assured him.

"Did you have a look around?" he asked.

"Yes, and I love this place. Really love it. It's homey, but not cute, you know?"

"Thank God," he said with a laugh. "I'm not crazy about cute."

"I'm not, either," she replied. "I love your sculptures and maquettes. Oh, and your drawings, too. They look so . . . *right* here."

"Thanks," Matt said somewhat sheepishly.

Ariadne was curious about the odd e-mail and wanted to ask him about it, but wasn't certain about how to approach the subject. Finally, she said, "I was looking at your computer, and it came on when I hit the mouse."

"It was just asleep," he said. "I never shut it down."

"There was this strange e-mail on it," Ariadne went on. "I guess I'm terrible, but I looked at it."

She thought she saw him tense slightly. "What was it?" he asked.

"Something from somebody named Adrian," she said. "It was all about a woman or girl. All this stuff about 'her.' It was so odd that I—"

"Ah, it was nothing," Matt said. "Nothing important anyway."

Ariadne sensed that he was embarrassed, and she was sorry that she'd brought it up. "I didn't mean to pry," she said apologetically. "I—"

"Don't worry about it," Matt said, reaching over and patting her shoulder. "Please. It's not anything personal or important at all. He's a friend of mine and makes silly games out of all his e-mails."

Ariadne's curiosity wasn't satisfied by his response. She wondered what the message was really about. It had been composed so that anyone reading it other than Matt—herself for instance—wouldn't be able to decipher its meaning. She remembered the first time they'd met, Matt had said something about having worked for the government in the past.

And now, seeing the way he lived made her all the more curious. He'd taken her to an expensive restaurant in Great Barrington. He had this cabin in the mountains, and a place like this did not come cheap. Where did the money come from? she wondered. Doing restoration work at the Clark didn't provide for this sort of lifestyle, did it?

"What are you thinking about?" he asked, blowing steam off his tea.

"Oh . . . nothing really," she said. "The tea and brandy and the fire are just making me a little dreamy, I guess."

Matt slid next to her on the couch and slipped an arm around her shoulders. "Do you mind sharing your dreams with me?"

Ariadne felt her heart leap, and a frisson of excitement ran through her body. She remembered when he had kissed her near the restaurant, the feeling of his sensuous lips on hers. She inhaled his distinctly masculine aroma, a compelling and erotic scent that was all him. "My mind was just wandering," she replied vaguely. "I was just thinking about your house. How beautiful and comfortable it is."

"I'm so glad you like it," he said softly. He began stroking her back, and Ariadne could feel his breath on her neck. The urge to reach out to him was irresistible. She set her tea down on the coffee table, then relaxed on the couch, letting her head rest against the cushions.

Matt leaned over and kissed her lips gently, and Ariadne emitted a sigh of pleasure, kissing him back, her lips hungry for him. Matt parted her lips with his tongue and began exploring with more passion, then put his arms around her, drawing her closer to him. Ariadne ran her hands up and down his back, feeling its muscular strength through the flannel shirt he wore. Their breathing grew more rapid as they kissed deeper and harder, their tongues meeting and parting, again and again.

She felt his warm hand slip beneath her sweater and stroke her back, then move to her breasts, where he began gently caressing her, his fingers searching out her exposed cleavage. He found the clasp that held her bra in place, between the two cups, and undid it. "Hmmm," he breathed as his hand swept softly over her freed breasts, tenderly touching her nipples, which were fast hardening.

Ariadne moaned with desire, anxious to feel his bare flesh against her flesh. The outside world and its concerns had seemingly vanished, leaving only the two of them and their desire for each other. She felt him draw back gradually, reluctantly removing his hand from her breasts and his mouth from hers.

"Let's go upstairs," he said softly.

She nodded silently, and when he stood and offered her a hand, she took it. He pulled her to her feet and led her up the stairs to his bedroom. Picking up a remote, he hit a button, and the fireplace blazed, casting a lovely light into the darkened room. Turning to her, he helped her slip her sweater over her head, then removed the bra that dangled from her shoulders.

"You're so beautiful, Ariadne," he said. "So beautiful." The firelight danced on her body, and he could hardly take his eyes off her as he quickly unbuttoned and removed his shirt, then slid his T-shirt over his head.

Ariadne drank in his broad muscular shoulders and robust chest, with its thatch of dark hair between his pecs. His torso tapered down to abs that, unsurprisingly, were well-defined.

He put his powerful arms around her, drawing her close, and she relished the feel of his hard masculinity against her softness. He began kissing and licking her ears, then slowly moved down to her neck, passionately kissing its length before running his tongue over it as if he couldn't get enough of her. His hands found her breasts, and he cupped them gently before leaning down and kissing each of them. Ariadne moaned as his tongue began delicately flicking her rosy nipples, teasing her mercilessly, her passion for him mounting.

He paused and drew back again. He looked into her eyes and smiled. "Here," he said. "Sit on the bed." He led her there, then took off her thick socks, her jeans, and finally her panties. When she was completely naked, he drew in his breath sharply, his eyes running up and down her body. Leaning over, he placed a kiss on the blond thatch between her thighs. He stood up then, and quickly took off the rest of his clothes. When he was completely naked, he stood in front of her, his manhood fully engorged. Ariadne reached out and took it in her hand, and Matt swooned with desire, tilting his head back, letting her caress him.

Then abruptly, he took her hand in his and removed it. "You're driving me crazy," he said.

Ariadne smiled triumphantly, pleased to see her effect on him.

"Let's spread out," he said. He pulled the pillows out from the cover and piled one of top of the other. Ariadne lay on her back, her head propped up slightly on the pillows. Matt got on the bed, getting onto his knees between her legs. Gazing down at her, his eyes explored her pale flesh with relish. "You are so beautiful," he said again, "and I want you so much."

Leaning over, he kissed her breasts, first one, then the other, teasing her nipples with his tongue again. Ariadne felt a damp readiness between her thighs. "Matt, oh, Matt . . . ," she whimpered. "I want you, too. Oh, yes. I want you." His tongue trailed down to her navel, circled it, then moved on down to her golden pubis. He kissed it and licked it, then sought out her wet lips and licked them tenderly before finally entering her with his tongue.

Ariadne cried out with erotic delight and put her hands on his head, her fingers stroking his dark curly hair. Pushing herself against him, she moaned and groaned with a newfound pleasure. No one had ever given her such joy, and she had until this moment doubted that such a feeling of utter carnal bliss existed. Matt's tongue delved and explored vigorously, as if he'd found a treasure that he could never let go of. When he gradually withdrew, Ariadne rasped, "Please, please. I want you."

He mounted her, his mouth on hers, kissing her with wild abandon. Then he slowly entered her, and Ariadne cried out again. Her passion was such that she thought she would have an orgasm at any moment, and as he began to fill her with his manhood, she threw her arms around him tightly, holding him against her with all her might. She never wanted this to end. Never. She had never felt anything like it before, and she knew that it was because she wanted him—Matt—like she had never wanted any other man.

He began thrusting in and out, his speed increasing, and they moved in a wild erotic rhythm, giving in to their desires completely, letting go of any inhibitions that they might have had. Ariadne felt her muscles begin to contract, and she cried as she felt her body orgasm, overwhelming her with its power. Matt let out a loud bellow, and she could feel his cock spasm inside her, again and again, as he exploded, his body heaving against hers, pumping mightily as he emptied himself.

"Oh, my God," he rasped breathlessly. "Oh, my God, Ariadne." He wrapped her in his arms and lowered himself against her, his body, like her own, slick with a sheen of perspiration. He laughed breathily. "Thank . . . *you* . . . I have never . . . come like that. Not . . . in my life." He kissed her, gasping for breath as she was, then squeezed her tightly and lay still atop her.

She stroked his back as she caught her breath, listening to his pants, inhaling the erotic scent of their sex, her body sated, her mind still whirling with a sense of fulfillment and satisfaction that she'd never experienced. *No,* she thought. *Not like this.*

When at last he could speak, Matt whispered, "You . . . you are the greatest. I feel like the luckiest man alive. I've wanted you since the first time I saw you, but I never had any idea it would be like this."

"I didn't, either," she said. "And I've never experienced anything like it."

He kissed her tenderly. "I don't want to move," he said. "Ever."

She laughed softly. "We'll have to sometime, won't we?"

He leaned back and looked into her eyes. "Next week maybe?"

She hugged him to her. "Too soon," she murmured.

He was supposed to take her back to the dorm Saturday evening so she could study, but Saturday turned into Sunday. It was finally Monday morning when they got back in the Jeep and headed toward Williamstown.

Chapter Eleven

※

The streets in the meatpacking district, once a no-man's-land in downtown Manhattan, were crowded with hip trendsetters on their way to restaurants and bars in the now-fashionable part of town. When Bianca emerged from the company limo, Frans was waiting for her on the sidewalk in front of Pastis, the chic bistro where she'd asked to meet.

"Hey, beautiful," he greeted her, putting his arms around her and kissing her with passion.

"Wow!" she said with a laugh. "It's good to see you, too."

The restaurant was crowded and noisy, but a table in a corner had been reserved for them, as Bianca had requested. They sat side by side at the small table, and he took one of her hands in his and kissed her. She wanted to give him her news in a public venue, where it was unlikely he would make a fuss.

The waiter appeared. "Anything to drink?"

Bianca ordered a glass of chardonnay.

"You, sir?"

Frans looked up at the waiter and smiled. "Water," he said.

"Still or carbonated?"

"Tap," Frans said.

The waiter smiled and left.

"Oh, you're being so good," Bianca said.

"I have to be," Frans replied. "You know that. I don't dare gain an ounce of weight with all these photo shoots lined up, so it's water and tuna

in water nearly all the time. Besides"—he looked at her and smiled sadly—
"I want to stay as clearheaded as possible."

Bianca stroked his cheek with a hand. "You're always clearheaded,"
she said, "if a little too trusting."

"I know. I still can't believe how *evil* some people are."

He didn't even want to say Nikoletta's name, Bianca thought. After
she had finally called him at Adrian's urging, she'd discovered that he
was truly heartbroken. Their reunion had been swift, and every day had
been a joy since then, but they were keeping their relationship very
quiet. When Frans moved in with her, she didn't tell a soul, not even her
father.

"How did the shoot go today?" she asked.

"It went really well," he replied. "How was your day?"

"Okay," Bianca said, "but I'm about to OD on new information."

"What do you mean?"

"I've been given a big new assignment," she said. "It's the first one
with this new position."

"What is it?" Frans asked with interest. "You look excited about it."

"I am," Bianca replied. "It's the opportunity of a lifetime. One of
those assignments that could make a lot of difference in people's lives. At
least that's what I hope."

"What—?"

The waiter reappeared with their drinks and placed them on the table.
"Are you ready to order?" he asked.

"I'll take the steak," Bianca said, pointing to the one she wanted on
the menu. "Rare. And the fries."

"That's all?" the waiter asked.

Bianca nodded.

"I'll have the same steak, also rare," Frans said, "and a salad with
nothing but greens. Olive oil on the side."

The waiter nodded and took their menus away.

"Now," Frans said, putting an arm around her shoulders, "tell me
about this assignment of yours."

"Well . . . ," Bianca said, clearing her throat, "I'm going to Ivory
Coast to work with—"

Frans removed his arm from around her shoulders and sat up straight in his chair. "Ivory Coast!" he exclaimed. "Isn't that where they're having that civil war?"

"Wait a minute," Bianca said defensively, clutching his hand in hers. "Don't get too excited about it. I will have guards, Frans. Armed guards. I will be well protected. And—"

"I'm telling you, it's very dangerous there, Bianca. It's the craziest thing I've ever heard of. I mean, what would you be doing there anyway?"

"Calm down," she said. "The company produces cocoa for chocolate there, and what I would be doing is trying to convince the farmers and planters to let their children go to school rather than work."

"What?" he said in bewilderment.

"I would be trying to stop the use of child labor. Don't you see how this could help those children?"

Frans nodded. "I understand that," he said, "and I know it's a worthy cause. But, Bianca, what if something happens to you there?"

She grasped his hand again. "Nothing's going to happen to me, darling."

"I—I couldn't go on living without you," he declared miserably. "I mean it. When I thought I had lost you, I didn't want to live anymore, Bianca. I really didn't."

"I know that," she said, stroking his hand. "And I don't know what I would do without you, either, but this is something that I feel like I have to do, Frans. Surely you can understand that."

He nodded. "Yes, of course, but it still scares me."

"You are so sweet," she said. She reached down into the small shopping bag she'd brought in with her. "I brought each of us a present."

"Oh, come on," he protested. "You didn't have to do that, Bianca."

"Oh, yes, I did," she replied. "Look, these are to help put your mind at ease." She handed him one of the two small packages. "Go ahead and open it."

Frans unwrapped his package and looked down at the present, then looked up at her. "Why did you get this? You know I already have a Palm Pilot."

"Yes," she said, "but you don't have one in platinum or with your initials on it." She finished unwrapping hers and pressed some keys. "Besides, your old one is way outdated."

"Well, it is outdated, but I hardly ever use it—"

"What I figured was," she interjected, "we'd vow not to use these for anything except communicating with each other."

"I like that idea," Frans said, more enthusiastic. "In fact, I love that idea."

"And they're already activated," Bianca declared. "Look."

Frans watched her for a moment, then fiddled with his until he retrieved the message she'd just sent: *I love you.*

"Whoa!" He grinned. "Hey, this is pretty cool!" He kissed her. "But you shouldn't have done this."

"But I did," Bianca said. "Just remember." She gazed into his eyes. "They're not for anything except personal communication between *us.* Promise?"

Frans was silent while he tapped out a message.

Bianca retrieved it: *Cross my heart.* She looked up and smiled. "See? Now it doesn't matter if I'm stuck in Timbuktu. We can send messages back and forth."

Frans gazed at her adoringly. "You really are too much," he said. "You know that?"

"Yep." She grinned. "I probably am."

"I mean, you're, like, totally *crazed,* Bianca." He hugged her tightly.

"I'm totally crazed about *you,*" she emphasized. "I can hardly wait to get home with you and rip your shirt right off of you."

"And I can't wait for you to do it," he replied.

Bianca drew back from him and tapped out a message.

Frans looked down and retrieved it: *Then why are we sitting here? What do you say we skip dinner and go have great sex?* He looked up at her. "I would love to," he said.

Chapter Twelve

∞

Adrian Single and two security men rushed into a waiting car at the airport in Lima, Peru, taking them to the site of a toxic-waste plant several miles south of the city. The security men, Jeff Austin and Bill Cawley, were dressed as he was—dark suit, tie, and highly polished shoes—but they were highly trained guards armed with automatic revolvers. Adrian didn't know what to expect when they arrived.

As they neared the plant, he found himself repulsed by the devastation of the landscape. There didn't appear to be a living plant or animal as far as the eye could see.

Jeff said, "It's a damn lunar landscape."

Adrian nodded in agreement, his gaze riveted to the nightmarish atmosphere outside his window.

"Je-sus!" Bill cried. "Look at that!"

"What is it?" Adrian asked.

"Over there," Bill said, pointing a finger on his side of the car. "A dog with its paws wrapped up in rags. What the hell?"

Adrian saw a skinny dog limping toward them, all four of its paws swathed in rags tied in place with cord. Then he saw three more dogs, straggling along behind it. They, too, had their feet wrapped.

"What's that all about?" Jeff asked.

"The earth is poisoned. They can't walk on it without burning their feet," Hector, the driver, said.

"What? Are you kidding me?" Bill said.

"No." Hector shook his head. "Nobody can walk barefoot around here. The closer you get to the plant, the worse it gets."

Adrian felt a sour splash in his stomach. The landscape, the dogs—the entire scenario was repellent. He had known from the beginning that the toxic-waste facility might pose problems to the environment, and for that reason he'd discouraged Nikoletta from pursuing the purchase. When she went ahead and bought it anyway, he had read reports from the plant manager regarding environmental hazards, and he'd thought they were hyperbolic. When he'd consulted with Nikoletta about the matter, she'd claimed to have personally talked to government regulators in Peru and resolved any issues relating to the environment. Now he wondered how honest she'd been with him or what kind of bribes she paid Peruvian regulators.

As the car approached the facility, automobiles and trucks lined both sides of the road, and a steady trickle of demonstrators, mostly men, but even women and children among them, came and went from the plant's gates. The closer the car got, the slower it had to move as the trickle became a crowd. Finally, the car had to come to a crawl. The road was clogged with demonstrators.

A woman, screaming loudly, her eyes blazing with fury, rushed toward the car. She held a baby aloft and shoved its feet and then its hands toward the window next to which Adrian sat. He couldn't understand a word the woman was screeching, but he could clearly see what appeared to be burns on the baby's hands and feet.

"Damn," Jeff said, "that's disgusting."

As the car reached the gates, Adrian noticed Mother Earth's Children activists among the demonstrators. The militants were hard to miss with their familiar green armbands centered by an upraised black fist. *Oh, no,* he thought. *This could mean real trouble.* Some of them were teenagers, but others were well into their twenties and thirties and even older, as evidenced by their hair. They wore everything from dreadlocks to shaved heads to green-tinted Mohawks to white hair pulled back into buns. Mother Earth's Children wouldn't listen to reason, and they would make negotiating a lot more difficult.

Directly in front of the car, the gates into the facility were blocked by demonstrators, but the driver persevered, laying on the horn, and finally the tide parted, allowing the guards to open the gates and let them through. Plant workers on the inside had joined the demonstration, and the route to the office building was lined with an unruly mob, shaking their fists at the car and throwing stones.

"Hang on," Hector said, and he stomped on the gas pedal. The car jumped the curb that separated the parking area from the concrete apron in front of the office building, and the driver headed straight for the glass doors that led inside. Just before reaching them, he spun the wheel to the left, fishtailing the rear end around so that the passenger side of the car was no more than a few feet from the doors. On the opposite side of the glass, they saw two armed guards, weapons drawn.

"Close as I can get," the driver said.

"Very good," Adrian said, already opening his door. "Could you come with us to translate? Just as far as inside the doors?"

Hector shrugged. "Sure, why not?" he said, as if the dangers presented by the mob didn't frighten him in the least.

"Ready, guys?" Adrian asked, looking toward both Jeff and Bill.

"You bet, boss," Jeff said. He slipped his revolver out of its holster. Bill already had his out, and his hand was ready to shove his door open.

"Let's go," Adrian said, pushing his door open at the same time.

The men leaped out of the car at the same time and rushed to the doors to the office building, but the guards shook their heads, refusing to open them.

Hector yelled at them in Spanish, and after the guards exchanged a few words, they unlocked one of the doors and opened it a couple of inches. Adrian grabbed it and slipped inside, closely followed by the other men. One of the guards locked the door behind them.

"Tell me what this is all about," Adrian said to one of the guards.

The man stared at him uncomprehendingly.

Hector repeated the question in Spanish and listened to the guard's reply. "No raises and the working conditions," he said. "Also, because word has leaked out that there's a shipment of uranium about to arrive."

"Where do they have Nikoletta?" Adrian asked.

Again, Hector spoke to the guards. "In the plant manager's office on the third floor."

"Let's go," Adrian said, leading the way to the elevator. "Hector, please be ready to leave."

The men crowded into the small elevator car and went up to the top floor of the building. When they exited, they found a small knot of nearly hysterical secretaries and several men in suits.

"Where's the boss?" Adrian asked.

One of the secretaries pointed down the hallway, and Adrian led the way to an open door. Inside the large office, Nikoletta sat at a large desk with two executives. They were surrounded by a crowd of men in soiled work clothes, who wheeled around and glared at Adrian and his bodyguards.

"Adrian!" Nikoletta shouted, jumping out of the chair and rushing toward him. "I thought you'd never get here."

He hugged her, even though he was furious with her. She'd called him to come to her rescue after being taken hostage at the plant. He glanced about the office. "Senor Mori." He nodded to the plant manager, whom he'd met only very briefly once.

"Mr. Single," Mori said. "Like I told Ms. Papadaki, I'm very sorry about this disturbance. We had no—"

"Forget it," Adrian said. "It's not your fault, Senor Mori." He addressed the workers. "Who's your leader?"

When there was no response, Senor Mori pointed to an older man dressed in a filthy uniform. "This man," he said. "Luis Perez."

Perez stepped forward, his chin lifted proudly.

"Do you speak English?" Adrian asked.

Perez knew enough to shake his head no.

"Senor Mori," Adrian said, "would you kindly translate for me?"

"Of course," the man replied.

"I want to know what the workers' demands are," Adrian said, "and their reasons for them." He had an idea of what to expect, but he didn't want to make idle promises. A situation this serious demanded a serious negotiation.

From outside, they could hear the increasingly raucous crowd. Adrian was momentarily stunned to hear chanting in English begin to blare from speakers. "Burn down the office building. Burn it down." Over and over, the crowd of demonstrators shouted the chant. Mother Earth's Children, he thought grimly.

"The men are demanding safer working conditions," Senor Mori said, translating for Luis Perez, "and a cleanup of the entire facility and surrounding area. That is number one."

Adrian nodded. "Go ahead," he said.

"The recent explosion," Mori continued to translate. "It would not have happened if the equipment was upgraded."

"I understand," Adrian said.

"Add to that the way the men were treated when it happened." Mori shrugged, speaking for himself. "What do you expect? The plant was not shut down as requested. Instead, workers were locked in so they couldn't leave."

"What else?" Adrian asked.

"Better pay," Mori said. "No one has had a raise in four years. The men thought that would change when PPHL bought the facility, but conditions have only gotten worse. The men complain they are being treated like animals."

"You don't—" Nikoletta began, but Adrian gave her hand a hard squeeze.

"Let Senor Mori finish," he said sternly.

Nikoletta frowned but kept silent.

"Burn down the office building! Burn it down!" The chants grew louder and louder.

"Do you have a PA system?" Adrian asked. "One that works outside?"

"What is this, *PA system*?" Mori asked.

One of the men quickly translated for Senor Mori.

Mori shook his head. "No. But we do have bullhorns like they're using outside."

"Where are they?" Adrian asked.

Mori exchanged a few words in Spanish with one of the executives who sat near him. "They're in a storage closet on the ground floor. I can send someone for them."

"Good. Do that," Adrian said.

Mori issued the order to the executive, and the young man reluctantly rose to his feet and left the room.

"Do you have access to the roof from up here?" Adrian asked.

"Yes," Senor Mori said, "but why?"

"Because I want to speak to the demonstrators, and that's the best place I can think of," Adrian replied. "They'll be able to hear me inside and outside the gates."

"If you can ever shut them up," Nikoletta said.

Adrian squeezed her hand again. "I think we can get them to listen," he said. "Will you come with me and my men, Senor Perez? And you, Senor Mori?" he asked. "The men will recognize Senor Perez as one of their own, and he can translate for me. Of course, you're highly recognizable, Senor Mori, and maybe if you're there, along with Senor Perez, they'll believe what I have to say."

Mori nodded. "Of course," he replied, "but do you think that's a good idea? Someone in the crowd could be armed. We don't know for sure."

"We'll have to take that chance," Adrian said.

The young executive returned holding two large yellow bullhorns, one in each hand.

Adrian took the bullhorns and handed one to Senor Perez. "Ready?" he asked.

Perez nodded.

"Follow me," Senor Mori said.

Adrian turned to Nikoletta. "You sit down here and don't say one word," he told her in a threatening voice. "Not a single word."

She nodded, but offered him one of her sourest expressions.

He gestured to Jeff and Bill, and the three of them followed Senor Mori and Luis Perez out of the room. They went down the hallway, and the plant manager opened a steel door that led to a flight of stairs. They rushed up the staircase, at the top of which was another steel door. This one was locked, and Mori extricated a large key chain from his trouser pocket, selected a key, and unlocked it.

The flat roof spread out before them. It was fifty feet to the nearest edge, marked by a three-foot-high wall.

"I'm turned around," Adrian said. "Which way is the front?"

Mori pointed. "That way."

Following his directions, Jeff and Bill were the first out on the roof, Jeff going right and Bill left, their revolvers drawn. When they saw that the roof itself was devoid of demonstrators, they motioned for the others to come on out. Adrian came first, followed by Mori and Perez. Adrian walked straight to the edge of the roof and looked out over the crowd.

"Burn down the office building! Burn it down!" The chant was much louder now that they were outside.

Adrian had no way of knowing exactly how many Mother Earth's Children demonstrators were among the plant workers and their families, but he guessed no more than a few dozen. Still, they had a worthy cause here, and he could kick himself for not intervening in Niki's management of the facility before. But now was not the time to think about that, he told himself.

He put the bullhorn to his mouth, pressed the ON button, and cleared his throat. *"Señores y señoras,"* he shouted, the bullhorn amplifying his voice. When the crowd saw him, there was a sudden hush, before the chants began again, louder than ever.

Leaning out over the wall, Adrian shouted into the bullhorn again. *"Señores y senoras, por favor. Atención."*

Mori and Perez had drawn up to his side. "Senor Mori," Adrian said, "would you translate what I say for Senor Perez, then tell him to repeat it to the demonstrators?"

Mori nodded and spoke briefly to Perez in Spanish.

Adrian lifted his bullhorn again. "First," he shouted, "I want to thank you for being here today to express your displeasure with the terrible explosion that has occurred at this plant."

The chanting began to die out as Adrian spoke, and when Perez began speaking, complete quiet fell over the crowd. They would listen to their leader.

"Second," Adrian continued, "I personally want to promise you that we are going to radically improve the working conditions at this plant for everyone."

He waited for Mori to translate, then listed the points he wanted to cover, allowing Mori time to translate between each point. When he reached his final point, and it was translated—that there would be across-the-board raises to everyone at the plant regardless of their length of employment and that the rest of the week would be a paid holiday—a roar of approval went up from the crowd.

A number of the Mother Earth's Children militants had attempted to drown out Adrian and Senor Perez from time to time, but the crowd had silenced them. Adrian was gratified by their response and fully intended on carrying out every promise he'd made to them.

Senor Mori turned to him with a serious expression. "I hope you meant what you said."

"Every word," Adrian said. "I don't make idle promises, Senor Mori."

He turned to Senor Perez and offered the man his hand. At first Perez, his dark face with its Incan features still drawn, refused to take it. Then he took it in his iron clasp and shook it vigorously. "Amigo," he said in Quechuan-accented Spanish.

"Amigo," Adrian repeated with a smile. Perez's features finally relaxed and a semblance of a smile appeared on his lips.

When they reached the office, Nikoletta turned away from the window, where she had been staring out at the crowd. She looked at Adrian questioningly, her arms folded across her chest. "Am I free to go now?"

"Yes," Adrian said. "I think the situation is defused for the time being." He glanced at Senor Mori. "Do you think I can take Ms. Papadaki out of here safely now?" he asked.

Mori's eyes shifted to Perez, and he spoke a few words. Perez nodded solemnly, then spoke to two of his men, who immediately hustled out of the office to the elevators.

"I don't think you'll have any problem leaving now," Senor Mori said, "but if you'll give these men a couple of minutes, they will speak to the people outside and clear the way."

"May I go to the restroom?" Nikoletta asked him in a haughty voice.

"Of course, Ms. Papadaki," he replied. "The closest one is down the hallway to your left. Shall I have one of the secretaries show you the way?"

"I think I can find it by myself," Nikoletta said with a snarl. She strode out of the room on her stiletto heels.

"I want to thank you for your help and cooperation," Adrian said to Mori and Perez, "and I want you to know I will personally do everything in my power to see to it that conditions here change very quickly. I won't pretend that it's going to be overnight, but I'll get my people on it right away."

"Thank you," Senor Mori said. Then he translated for Senor Perez.

Gazing at Adrian with a serious expression, Perez said, "I believe you, Senor Single, and I will do what is in my power to keep the workers peacefully at their jobs in the meantime."

So he speaks English, after all, Adrian thought. *"Gracias,"* he said.

Perez's men returned to the office, and Nikoletta glided into the room behind them, going to Adrian's side.

"We'll be going now," Adrian said, turning to look at Bill and Jeff, who stepped forward at the ready.

They went down in the elevator and stopped at the glass doors leading outside. The crowd of demonstrators was still milling about, although the chanting had ended.

"You ready?" Adrian asked Nikoletta.

"Yes," she said nervously, seeing the crowd.

Bill shoved the door open, and he and Jeff went outside first, their hands on their revolvers. Jeff stood to the side, while Bill shielded Adrian and Nikoletta. They hastened to the car, but before they could get inside, a woman rushed from the crowd directly at Nikoletta. Before anyone realized what was happening, the woman, who was wearing huge industrial rubber gloves, shoved a dead piglet in Nikoletta's face. The woman began shouting in Spanish.

Nikoletta stopped and screamed, throwing her hands up to her face. Jeff quickly shoved the woman away, and she stumbled backward and fell.

"Go, go, go!" he shouted as Adrian pulled Nikoletta toward the car.

They got inside, and Hector shifted into drive and swung the car around toward the driveway, kicking up gravel as he gunned the engine. The crowd parted when they saw the car roaring toward them, and when the gates swung open, Hector picked up speed. Demonstrators rushed out of the car's path, seeing that Hector wasn't going to slow down.

When they'd left the plant behind, Adrian squeezed Nikoletta's hand. "Are you all right?" he asked.

"I've been better," she said. "That horrible old woman with that . . . that whatever it was didn't help."

"What was that woman yelling?" Adrian asked Hector.

"The one with the piglet?"

"Yes," Adrian said.

"She says half its skin burned off just from lying on the ground."

Adrian shook his head, trying to clear it of the gruesome image.

"She had some nerve," Nikoletta said.

"Look," Adrian said sharply, "you're lucky to get out of this alive, Niki."

She responded furiously. "And you are a traitor."

"A traitor? And how did you come to that decision?"

"Promising the workers changes," she spit. "You stabbed me in the back."

"I got you out of there alive!" he exclaimed.

"There're going to be changes, all right," Niki said darkly, looking straight ahead, "but they won't be for the better."

"Niki," Adrian reminded her, "do you honestly believe that making things worse for those people is going to get you anywhere?"

"None of this would have happened," Nikoletta replied, ignoring his remark, "if somebody hadn't tipped off those crazies from Mother Earth's Children. And I mean somebody in the highest ranks of PPHL's management." She gazed at Adrian with flinty eyes. "How else would they have known I was coming on a surprise inspection? Only the top echelon knew. Even management in Peru had purposely been left out of the loop."

"I think you may be getting paranoid," Adrian said. "The workers were already upset about the accident. The strike would have happened whether you were here or not."

Nikoletta shook her head adamantly. "No," she said. "They'd been told I was coming and were prepared. What happened wasn't spontaneous. They were too organized, and you know it."

"Right or wrong," he said, "conditions at that plant have to be improved, Niki. There's no question about that."

As if he had said nothing of any importance, Nikoletta didn't respond to him, but began rifling in her handbag. Finally, she said, "I wouldn't be so sure about that. Those people treated me like an animal. Why should they expect better?" She found the bottle of perfume she'd been searching for and lavishly sprayed about her neck and arms. "Pigs," she said with disgust. "They're pigs."

Chapter Thirteen

❧

Nikoletta's town house was situated in Chelsea on the best end of Cheyne Walk, amid a garden that could exist only in a city like London and only for a person as rich as Nikoletta. Adrian arrived directly from the airport. After the fiasco in Peru, he had made the stopover reluctantly, but he had just learned of Bianca's trip to Africa and he had to confront Niki directly about this dangerous assignment.

Charles, Nikoletta's butler, answered the door. Normally as imperturbable a man as could be imagined, he could hardly conceal how flustered he was by Adrian's unannounced appearance at the grand black lacquered door. He hemmed and hawed, then finally disappeared into the house "to see if madam" was in residence.

Adrian was amused by Charles's consternation, but at the same time felt sorry for the older man. He could well imagine the iron hand with which Niki ruled the household, not to mention her outbursts and temper tantrums.

In the entry foyer, Adrian couldn't help but notice the monumental baroque gilt mirror over a marble-topped console of a similar over-the-top design. The better to see herself on the way out, he thought, knowing Niki's habit of checking herself any chance she got. When she had been younger, he'd thought this habit a cute one. A little girl primping, miming the actions of an older woman. But as she'd grown older, he realized that she had fallen in love with the image that she saw reflected.

His musing was interrupted by Charles, who returned on virtually silent feet and startled him when he cleared his throat. "I'm terribly sorry, sir, to have kept you waiting," he said formally. "Awful to've kept you standing here like this."

"Don't give it a thought, Charles," Adrian said.

"Please," Charles said stiffly, "follow me." He shook his head slightly. "An awful state of affairs. Terribly rude to've kept you waiting."

Charles began climbing the gracefully spiraling stairs that led to the upper floors, and Adrian stayed a couple of steps below him, keeping his pace slow so as not to overtake the older man.

On the second floor, Charles ushered him down a hallway to a large door surrounded by heavy carved molding. He tapped on the door lightly with his knuckles.

"Come in," Niki's voice called from within.

Charles opened the door a small distance. "It's Mr. Adrian Single, madam."

"Yes, Charles," came the petulant reply. "You just told me that. Send him on in."

Charles turned to Adrian. "Please, sir," he said unnecessarily. "Madam says to go on in."

"Thank you, Charles," he said.

The butler nodded and went back down the hallway, muttering under his breath as he went.

Adrian was barely a foot inside the bedroom before he stopped abruptly, taking in the scene that greeted his eyes. Nikoletta was spread out naked on her grandly draped, canopied bed. Between her long, tanned legs, a young Jamaican, he supposed, in dreadlocks was on his knees. His hands were massaging Nikoletta's breasts. Shifting his eyes from her, Adrian gazed at the two younger men—underage by all appearances and Jamaican, he assumed—who were also on the bed. One was on a pillow near Nikoletta's head, and the other was on the bed's far side, his hands in her thighs. Looking back at Nikoletta, Adrian saw that her face was flushed bright red and was beaded with sweat, which also trickled down her chest.

She's high on drugs, he thought. She hadn't even noticed him yet, and when she finally looked his way, her eyes looked vacant, if not dead.

Adrian quickly turned back to the door, pulling it nearly closed behind him, and called to Charles, who was making slow progress down the hallway. "Charles," he said. "Could you hold on a minute, please?"

The butler turned and nodded. "Of course, sir."

Adrian went back into the bedroom and took his wallet out of a trouser pocket. From it, he removed several hundred pounds, then went to the bed. He gave the boy on the pillow several of the notes.

"What's this for?" the boy asked excitedly.

"It's time to leave," Adrian said. "Get dressed and go. And be quick about it."

On the other side of the bed, he repeated the offer with the other boy. "Hurry," he told him. "The butler's waiting to escort you and your friend to the door." The boy snatched the money and began dressing with alacrity.

When both boys were dressed, Adrian took them down the hallway. "Charles," he said, "please see them to my car downstairs. Tell the driver to take them home, wherever that is. Okay?"

"Certainly, sir," the butler said. His eyes shifted to the waiting boys. "Follow me, young gentlemen," he said archly. "You are to be driven home by a chauffeur."

Adrian went back to Nikoletta's bedroom. She and the Jamaican were still in bed together, although he was now atop her, slowly making love to her, pumping in and out, as they both groaned in lustful bliss.

Adrian turned his back to the scene, although neither Nikoletta nor the Jamaican seemed bothered by his presence in the least. "Nikoletta, please ask your friend to leave," Adrian said to her. "We need to talk."

"I don't want him to leave, Adrian," she rasped. "No way." She laughed. "You don't want to leave, do you, Timothy?"

Her speech was quick, too quick, Adrian thought. Cocaine-fueled perhaps.

"No way," he said, continuing to make love to her. "No way will I leave now."

"See? It's settled, Adrian," Nikoletta said. "Two against one. You lose."

Adrian was both embarrassed and angry. He was no prude. Far from it, in fact. But Nikoletta shouldn't be subjecting him to this humiliation. When their lovemaking continued, he finally took a deep breath and asked point-blank, "Did you send Bianca Coveri to Ivory Coast? Angelo is extremely distressed about it, and I'm certainly not happy about it myself. Did you do this so you would have Frans all to yourself?"

From the bed came a laugh, muffled at first, then louder. "I did no such thing," she scoffed. "That's ridiculous. Does it look like I need Frans? If you don't believe me, just give Bianca a call. Why are you wasting your time coming here? For God's sake, she's got her mobile with her. All you have to do is give her a phone call."

"I've tried her and haven't gotten an answer," Adrian responded.

"Then try her again," Nikoletta said impatiently. Timothy had dismounted and was fondling and licking her breasts.

Disgusted, Adrian took his cell phone out and speed-dialed Bianca's number. He received a message that said the person being called was out of range.

"She's out of range," Adrian said worriedly.

"Well . . . ," Nikoletta said, "try her again later, Adrian." She sat up in bed and stroked Timothy's dreadlocks. "And when you get hold of her, why don't you ask her whether or not I warned her it was dangerous to go? Bianca's a big girl, Adrian. You might remind Angelo of that fact." She sighed with exasperation. "And think about it, will you? I *need* Bianca. This job is extremely important. Do you think I'm going to cut off my nose to spite my face?"

"No, Niki," he replied. "That's one thing I would never think of you."

"I didn't think so," she replied, "but you and the rest of the board have made it clear that you think that I've made some unwise decisions regarding the company."

"We certainly haven't agreed with some of your decisions," Adrian admitted.

"Well, as you can see, I'm preoccupied, and I'm in no mood to discuss this nonsense now," Nikoletta said. "So why don't you buzz off, Adrian?"

"Of course," he replied. "Be glad to go."

Bianca was simultaneously exhausted and exhilarated. She'd flown into Abidjan from Paris, and Moctar Yanou and two security guards had been there to meet her. The flights had been long and tiring, and she had thought that Mr. Yanou, a tall, thin, and very gracious man, would suggest that she rest in an Abidjan hotel before venturing out. He'd met her with a surprise, however.

"We are going down the coast," he told her in French-accented English. "It's about a three-hour drive to the place you're going to be staying. The guards and I will be staying with you."

"I see," Bianca said. "I thought I would be staying here in Abidjan and making trips into the field from here."

"I think you will find that you like it down in the Sassandra region near Dagbego," Mr. Yanou said. "There is a very nice place where I've booked us. I hope you don't mind."

"No, of course not," Bianca said. "They assured me that you are the best guide in all of Ivory Coast."

Mr. Yanou bowed his head slightly. "Thank you," he said, smiling. "This place is also very near to the cocoa plantations and the smaller farms that you're going to be visiting."

"So it's very convenient," Bianca said. "That's great."

He nodded. "Also relatively safe," he said, holding up one long, thin finger to make his point. "These people have been in business for quite some time, and they've had the cooperation of both the government and rebel forces. Besides, we are headed south, and most of the rebel strongholds are in the north. The Sassandra region is government controlled. So"—he spread his hands wide in a gesture that assured her all was well—"I hope that you can see that you are in capable hands."

"I don't have any doubts," Bianca said.

They'd hopped into the waiting Toyota Land Cruiser, an ancient, beat-up vehicle that proved to be the perfect transportation on the dusty, rutted roads that led down the coast to Dagbego.

Bianca, tired as she was, came wide-awake on the journey, entranced by the beauty of the landscape. Through the coconut palms and other vegetation, she caught glimpses of the Atlantic to the west. When they reached the place they were to stay, she was stunned. In a country of dire poverty the resort bordered on the luxurious, with lovely rooms, a swimming pool, an attractive restaurant, impeccable service, a very useful conference room with Internet, an extraordinarily beautiful lagoon, and a private white-sand beach lined with stately coconut palms.

She and Moctar Yanou dined in the restaurant, while the guards went elsewhere. Bianca was stunned again. The cuisine was classic French along with local specialties. She followed Mr. Yanou's suggestions and had braised chicken piled with onions and tomatoes, followed by *aloco,* a ripe banana fried in palm oil and spiced with steamed onions and chili. They washed the delicious food down with a bottle of *Bangui,* a palm wine made nearby. In the background, lively regional music played on the sound system.

"It is music of the Dan," Moctar Yanou told her. "They are one of the indigenous peoples and very musical. There are also Senufo. . . ." He paused. "But we'll get into that tomorrow. You'll be meeting people from different ethnic groups. I think you'll find it very interesting. We have a small percentage of Christians and Muslims, but Ivory Coast is predominantly made up of people who've retained their native customs. Ancestral worship and all sorts of magic."

"It sounds fascinating," Bianca said. Although she already knew a lot of what he was talking about from her briefings at PPHL, she didn't want to steal his thunder, so she feigned ignorance of the country. "I can hardly wait."

"We will leave in the morning about seven a.m.," he told her, "so you will want to get a good night's sleep. I want to show you the lay of the land tomorrow and introduce you to a few of our cocoa farmers. You'll be seeing everything from huge plantations to small farm plots. There are also a lot of pineapple and coffee growers and citrus plantations in this area, but we'll be concentrating on the cocoa growers, of course. Part of the time we'll be on quads, so dress very informally in lightweight slacks or jeans."

"What're quads?" she asked.

"Oh, I believe you call them . . . what is it? Recreational vehicles. Something of the sort. Small vehicles with four wheels. They can get almost anywhere. Places the Land Cruiser can't reach."

"It's that rugged?"

"In places." He nodded. "The guards will be going everywhere with us, so you needn't worry about your safety."

Sitting in the restaurant of the resort, Bianca couldn't conceive that anyone would need a guard for anything. "I'm not worried about it," she said.

"Good. I'll meet you in the dining room at, say, six thirty?"

"Fine," Bianca said.

He walked her to her room, then went on to his own. Bianca quickly undressed, showered, and got ready for bed. She was so excited, she was

afraid that sleep would elude her, but she had hardly pulled the sheet over
her before her eyes began to droop. When she got the wake-up call at six
a.m., she groaned and rubbed the sleep out of her eyes, but was dressed
and ready to leave in mere minutes.

After breakfast, she and Moctar Yanou met the guards in the parking
lot. They took off in the Land Cruiser and traveled inland, due east, toward the plantations that stretched across the vast plateau as far as the eye
could see. The roads here, as everywhere, were a dusty red clay. In small
villages she saw little, unadorned houses built of concrete blocks alongside
wooden structures, sometimes with the boards laced together with a reed-
like material. Tall women wrapped in traditional ethnic fabrics walked
down the roadsides with baskets balanced atop their heads. Some of them
were loaded down with produce, while others were piled high with laundry. The women were erect, tall, and lean, and their walk was elegant,
Bianca thought.

Inevitably, she caught sight of small children, most of them dirty and
poorly clothed, sometimes accompanying their mothers, often playing
with one another unattended. She knew that some of these children should
be in school, but she consoled herself with the fact that at least they
weren't yet working on the cocoa plantations. Her job was going to be a
highly challenging one—of that, there was little doubt. The parents of
these children were uneducated and poor. Convincing them that their children needed to be in school rather than helping to support their families
was a daunting task. Trying to convince the landowners, many of whom
were educated, that they shouldn't use the children for cheap labor was
going to be equally difficult.

They passed through another small village and reached an area where
cocoa grew on both sides of the roads as far as the eye could see. "We're
going to stop at a large cocoa plantation," Moctar Yanou told her. "I want
you to see a big operation first."

"Do they use child labor?" Bianca asked.

"Yes," he said. "That's one of the reasons I want to stop here first.
You can have a firsthand view of the situation. But there's another reason
as well. The owner of this operation is a very influential man in all of the
Sassandra region. Very rich and powerful. He is also, I believe, somewhat
less rigid than some of the other owners. If you can get him to listen to

you, then other owners will listen to you, too." He looked at her with a smile. "There's yet another consideration."

"What?"

"I don't want to offend you, but I believe he might be susceptible to your feminine charms," Moctar Yanou said.

Bianca laughed merrily. "Using the oldest ammunition there is, huh?"

"Precisely," Yanou said.

They soon reached the simple gates of a cocoa plantation. The Land Cruiser came to a stop, and Moctar Yanou got out. The guards, who were riding on the roof with their automatic weapons, hopped off.

"The owner knows we're coming," Moctar told Bianca. "He has provided some quads. Said they would be inside the gates and down the road a little way. We'll walk from here, then tour the operation on the quads."

He opened one of the gates—they weren't locked—and let her in. The foursome walked down the road for about a quarter of a mile before they spied the quads sitting on the side of the road.

A boy of eleven or twelve was sitting on one, waiting for them. He hurried to Moctar Yanou, thrusting keys into his hand. Yanou said something to the boy in a strange tongue, and the boy mounted one of the quads, standing on a steel rod that ran across the quad behind the seats.

"I thought the owner might be here to meet us, but apparently he couldn't make it," Yanou said. "We'll see if we can catch him after we've finished the tour."

He handed the guards a set of keys and pointed to the quad the boy wasn't standing on. They got seated and fired it up, and Yanou led Bianca to the other one, indicating that she take a seat. He sat down beside her, turned and said a few words to the boy, then started the engine and put the quad in gear. "Hold on tight," he said to Bianca.

They led the way down the road, the guards bringing up the rear. They traveled for a quarter hour without seeing another human being, a building, or farm equipment of any kind. Cocoa grew everywhere. They reached a sharp bend in the road, and Yanou slowed down considerably. "These things are known to tip over," he told Bianca. She turned to check that the boy was holding on tightly. His knuckles were white from the effort. She assumed he knew the drill. He'd probably been doing this most of his life, she thought.

Around the bend another straight stretch of road unrolled. "We'll soon reach an area where they're working," Yanou told her. He sped up on the straight stretch, the quads throwing up a terrific ducktail of dust. On they went, until they reached a hairpin curve. Yanou slowed down again, and Bianca and the boy held on tight.

They had just rounded the bend when they saw an olive drab truck with a big bed of wooden slats coming their way. The bed was covered with an olive drab canvas, lashed to the bed with rope. The engine noise of the quad behind them became faint. Bianca turned in her seat and saw that the guards had let off on the gas and were making a turn in the road. As she watched, they gunned the engine and headed straight into the cocoa fields.

She turned back around. "What the—?" The truck was approaching them now, no more than twenty feet away. It stopped and a group of men in camouflage jumped out of the back of the truck, their weapons drawn.

She heard a scream behind her. The boy had jumped off the still-moving quad and was rolling in the road. *Jesus!* she thought. *What the hell's going on?*

"Moctar," she shouted. "What the hell's—?"

"Oh, my God. R-rebels," he stammered, giving the quad gas. The four-wheeler lurched forward, almost throwing Bianca off, and as she watched, Moctar's head suddenly turned into an exploding watermelon. Or that was what she imagined. The reality was too much to comprehend. Then she heard the deafening reports of the men's weapons, and her body began to jerk as bullet after bullet tore into her. She bounced off the side of the quad and hit the road. Making claws of her hands, she tried to crawl toward the boy, but she saw his body pirouetting down the road in a spastic dance as it was pummeled with round after round of ammunition. When he fell at last, Bianca heard a scream. She didn't realize it was her own. Then she shut her eyes, never to open them again.

Chapter Fourteen

≈

"You come highly recommended, Mr. Atkins," Nikoletta said to the man seated in her office. "More than a few of my friends mentioned your name. I gather you've done a lot of work in both personal and corporate security?"

The man merely nodded. He didn't need to list his record of achievements for her. He'd worked for many of the rich international set in several world capitals, and the word spread among them about his talents, just as it did about the best personal trainers and hairdressers. Only the very rich could afford him, and they used him for everything from the simplest tasks, such as following a philandering husband or wife to obtain proof of an adulterous affair, to more complex tasks such as discovering the culprit within a multinational corporation who was leaking vital information to competitors.

"I've gotten together a folder of information about the man for you," Nikoletta said. "There's nothing in it you couldn't have found out yourself, but I thought it might save you time."

"Could I have a look?" he asked.

Nikoletta pushed the folder across her desk toward him. She watched as he began flipping through it. "Most of the information came from either the personnel or publicity department at PPHL," she said. "I don't have anything about him that isn't more or less a matter of public record."

Mr. Atkins didn't acknowledge her remark, but kept scanning pages.

Nikoletta observed him without interrupting. What an odd man he was, she thought. When he'd arrived at her house in London, she'd been somewhat surprised when Charles had shown him into the office. She didn't know what she'd been expecting, but it certainly wasn't this ordinary-looking man. But, she supposed, it was his ordinariness that made him ideal for what he did.

He closed the file. "Is there anything specific that you want to know about this man?"

"No. Nothing specific," she replied. "But I want to know anything—and I mean *anything*—you can come up with that I can use against him. Dig up all the dirt on him that you possibly can."

"Do you suspect him of anything in particular?" Atkins asked.

Nikoletta shook her head. "No, but I have a feeling that he's working against me behind my back. He's on the board of PPHL, as you can see from the file, and I'm interested in getting him *off* the board. Because of the way my father left things, I have to have a good reason to get rid of him. So anything you can come up with that I can use to discredit him with the rest of the board would be very useful." She paused, then asked, "What do you think? I know you haven't had time to study his file, but for what it's worth, do you think you can get something on him?"

Atkins grunted. "Almost everybody's got a skeleton in his closet, Ms. Papadaki. Or has a secret vice of some kind. And I'm betting your Mr. Adrian Single is no different. If he hires hookers or likes little girls or little boys or goes on the occasional drug binge or talks to your competitors—no matter what it is—I'll find out about it."

"Very good, Mr. Atkins," she said. Her eyes gleamed with intensity as she went on. "I've got to get something on him, and you've got carte blanche. He travels a lot, so it's not going to be easy to keep up with him, but I don't care how much it costs or what it takes. Dig up some dirt on the son of a bitch."

"Not a problem," Atkins said confidently. "We'll exchange cell numbers, and I'll take a retainer. Then I'll get busy on it right away."

"Excellent," Nikoletta said. Adrian Single had been like a surrogate father to her, but those days were over. She would never forgive him for his betrayal in Peru. He'd made promises to the workers there in direct violation of her policies. He was a traitor, and he was going to pay.

At first Adrian thought he was dreaming, but as the telephone at his bedside continued to ring, penetrating the layers of his consciousness, he realized that the sound was not part of a dream but only a few feet from his pillow. Blindly reaching toward the lamp, he turned on the switch and peered at the clock. Two a.m.

It couldn't be good news, he thought, picking up the receiver. "Hello," he said, still half-asleep.

"Adrian, it's Yves."

"What's going on?" Adrian asked, sitting up in bed, struggling to fully awaken from a deep sleep.

"I have very bad news to report, I'm afraid," Yves said. "There's been a rebel attack in the Sassandra region, near Dagbego."

"Where?" he asked.

"Near Dagbego. It's in Ivory Coast," Yves said. "It's been under government control, but apparently New Forces, the rebel group, has made inroads and—"

Adrian bolted wide-awake, his body flooded with a rush of adrenaline. "Don't tell me," he said, interrupting Yves.

"I wish I didn't have to," Yves said. In his distress, his English, which normally was barely accented, was heavily laden with French. "It's . . . it's Bianca. I'm afraid she was killed in a massacre."

Adrian felt his stomach knot, and bile began to rise in his throat. "Does Angelo know?" he asked, fighting back the nauseous taste in his mouth.

"No, not yet," Yves replied. "I'm on my way to Milano now. I would appreciate it if you'd meet me in the office there."

"I'll fly over at once," Adrian said, already getting out of bed.

"Oh," Yves added, "I would have Sugar Rosebury come with you. She has a very good . . . ah . . . stabilizing effect on Angelo. And God knows we'll need it. Even with the three of us breaking the news to Angelo, he'll be beside himself."

"What about Nikoletta?" Adrian asked, wondering if she'd been called with the news yet.

Yves barked a laugh. "I say let the dragon sleep while she can. Angelo's not going to take this lying down, you know."

"Not a chance of that," Adrian replied.

"I think keeping Niki out of the loop for the time being is the best policy."

"You're right about that," Adrian agreed. "I'll meet you in Milan and bring Sugar with me. We'll stay in touch by cell phone."

"Very well," Yves said.

Adrian replaced the receiver in its cradle. He would have to call Sugar immediately and tell her to fly to Italy. The thought made him feel sick to his stomach. *Bianca gone,* he thought. *Dead.* It seemed impossible. She had been so vibrant and beautiful and good. She'd had everything in the world given to her, but she was one of those who wanted to give back selflessly. She'd never taken anything for granted.

His thoughts turned to Nikoletta. This was her doing. Of that, there was no doubt. Her recklessness had reached a truly dangerous point, resulting in Bianca's death. *I'm afraid it's time to finally do something about Niki,* he thought as he picked up the receiver to dial Sugar. *Niki's completely out of control.*

The helicopter descended onto the helipad situated on the vast lawn of the Coveri estate on Lake Como. From its windows, Sugar, Yves, and Adrian had a view of the beautiful lake and the stunning residences that dotted its shores. Directly beneath them, the well-tended grass was blown almost flat to the ground by the downdraft of the chopper's powerful rotors. After it landed and the rotors were switched off, the threesome walked together toward the Coveri villa, dreading what lay ahead.

Giulia came toward them from the villa's main entrance, a worried expression on her face. The unexpected arrival did not bode well. "Adrian?" she called to him, in a strained voice. "I mean, you are all very welcome, of course, but . . . ?"

"Giulia," Sugar said, rushing forward to greet her, kissing her on both cheeks. She put an arm around the old woman's shoulder and took one of her hands in hers. "We must talk," she said, guiding her back toward the house.

On the steps stood Angelo Coveri, smartly dressed in a sport jacket, an open-neck checked shirt with paisley ascot, trousers, and suede driving shoes. He had heard the helicopter, and the grim expressions of the approaching visitors told him everything he needed to know. The blood drained from his face. He silently turned and went back inside.

Adrian caught sight of him. "I'll meet you there," he said to Yves, and went ahead, pausing briefly at Giulia's side, gently patting her heaving shoulders. Tears streamed down her face, but she was silent. "Give me a moment alone with Angelo, okay?"

Adrian rushed on inside. The house was still as a tomb, he thought as he walked to Angelo's library, where he was usually to be found. Reaching the doorway, he gazed in and saw Angelo slumped in the well-worn leather chair he normally occupied. He was staring unseeingly out the French doors.

Adrian walked quietly toward Angelo. Putting a hand on the back of the chair, he said softly, "We need to talk."

Angelo didn't appear to have heard him. He continued staring dully out the window, unmoving and mute.

Adrian pulled a small chair next to Angelo's and put a hand on the old man's shoulder. "Angelo," he repeated, "we need to talk."

Finally, Angelo turned his face slightly toward Adrian. "What is it you have to say, Adrian?" he asked sotto voce.

"There's been news about . . . Bianca," Adrian began. He cleared his throat before continuing. "She's been killed in an attack in Africa, Angelo."

Angelo's face, already pale, grew rigid as a death mask. He gripped the arms of the leather chair with his hands, the veins standing out in bold relief. His jaw began to quiver uncontrollably.

Adrian took a deep breath and expelled it noisily. *What can I say?* he wondered, groping for words. *What in the world can I do that will ease his pain?* But he knew that there was nothing he could say that would make this any easier for Angelo. His daughter had been the only life he'd ever had outside of his work for PPHL.

Adrian hadn't removed the hand he'd placed on Angelo's shoulder, and now as he saw tears roll down the man's cheeks, he stroked his shoulder gently.

Behind him, Adrian heard Yves enter the room. Sugar, her arms around a weeping Giulia, followed him in. They sat on a love seat nearby. Sugar saw the pallor of Angelo's face, then looked with alarm at Adrian. He signaled her with a finger to his lips, but Sugar ignored him.

"Angelo, darling," she said soothingly. "We know this is terrible for you, but we're here for you. If you need anything, anything at all, you just say the word."

Angelo didn't look at her, nor did he respond. After a few more moments of silence, he took a crisp white handkerchief from his trouser pocket and dabbed the tears on his cheeks. Then, as if possessed by a demonic spirit, his face turned crimson with rage, and he threw Adrian's arm from his shoulder with terrific force.

"Get your goddamned hand off me!" he shouted. "Don't you touch me!"

Adrian quickly stood up and moved away from Angelo, standing near the French doors. "Angelo—" he began.

"How dare you show your face here?" Angelo roared. "How dare you?" He thrust an accusatory finger in Adrian's direction. "*You.* You who disregarded my fears for Bianca's safety. *You* who mimicked Niki, saying she would be safe with the guards. You . . . you fucking *Judas*!"

Adrian stood in shamed silence listening to his old friend's rebukes, knowing that there was little he could say in his defense. He had known of the risks that Bianca was taking. There was no doubt about that. But he'd also known that she insisted on taking them and that there was no stopping her.

When he didn't immediately respond to Angelo, the old man roared like an animal and leaped to his feet. Without warning, he launched himself at Adrian and began pummeling him with his fists, beating his chest with all his might.

Adrian stood his ground, allowing Angelo to hammer away at him, refusing to fight back. *If it helps him,* he thought, *he can beat on me till kingdom come.*

Sugar and Yves rose to their feet and grabbed Angelo's arms, trying to make him stop. "Angelo!" Sugar cried. "Stop! Stop at once. You're only going to hurt yourself, and this isn't going to solve any problems."

As suddenly as he'd started, Angelo ceased pummeling Adrian and slipped from Yves's and Sugar's grasps. He collapsed on the floor at their feet. Giulia let out a cry of alarm and rushed to him, kneeling down on the floor beside him. "Angelo!" she cried. "Oh, Angelo! What have you done to yourself?"

He lay silent, his chest heaving with exertion, his face still red with rage. Then he shoved Giulia away with an arm and lifted his head from the floor. Holding Adrian's gaze, he said, "I swear by Almighty God that

I am going to kill you. And when I've accomplished that, I'm going to kill that bitch Nikoletta."

Giulia sucked in her breath and began crying again. She shook her head from side to side in anguish while the others stared at Angelo.

He began sobbing and cried out, "My Bianca was worth a hundred Nikolettas! A thousand Nikolettas!" His head slumped to the floor again, and he wept quietly, his strength almost spent.

Sugar caught Adrian's eye and nodded imperceptibly, signaling that perhaps it was for the best if he left.

"When you're ready to talk about this, Angelo—" Adrian began, but he wasn't allowed to finish.

"Out! Get *out!*"

Adrian had no choice but to obey. He went down the hallway disconsolately and out the entrance to the helicopter. He hoped that Angelo would have a change of heart. He'd loved Bianca like a favorite cousin, and her death had been a terrible blow to him, too. Angelo surely knew that.

Nikoletta was another story. He heaved a sigh. *The time has come to implement my plan,* he thought with rising dread. *I've held off too long already. Bianca's death is proof of that.* When the telephone call had come from Yves, he'd known it was time. For years he'd prepared for something like this, and he saw no choice but to move forward.

Chapter Fifteen

~

London, England

Darkness had fallen, and the tour boats with their guides and camera-toting tourists had stopped running for the night. Only a few late strollers walked along the promenade. Along the picturesque canals of Little Venice the colorfully painted live-aboard barges decorated with flowerpots and laundry lines seemed to be apparitions with glowing windows.

Just across the pool from Browning's Island, draped with its willows, the windows of one single-wide, permanently moored barge glowed in the dark like others, but anyone passing by along the promenade would find it impossible to peer in past the drawn curtains. Nor could anyone eavesdrop. The windows and doors aboard this barge had been carefully locked, and only indistinct shadows could be seen moving about behind the cheerful print of the curtain fabric.

Inside the barge, the moderately successful young sculptor who owned it was playing host to a gathering of acquaintances. His wife, a designer of Web sites, sat quietly breast-feeding their baby. Their guests were nine bohemian types, all young men and women with faces that radiated ideological righteousness.

The group were all environmental activists who belonged to this particular English cell of Mother Earth's Children. Like the other cells in various countries, this one was kept separate from others for anti-infiltration purposes. The nine members of the cell invited to gather on the barge considered themselves especially honored. On board was a thirteenth person—a heroic guest of honor—on whom all eyes were riveted.

Kees Vanmeerendonk was recovered from the gunshot wound he had suffered while scuffling with Adrian Single on St. Barth's, and his eyes burned with the feverish intensity of a revolutionary. Compared with the photographs in Interpol's files, Kees was totally unrecognizable. The slender, dark-haired and bearded would-be assassin had purposely gained weight, shaved off his beard and hair, and assumed the guise of a skinhead, wearing the familiar uniform of bleachers—skintight bleached jeans—held up by suspenders, along with a Fred Perry shirt and twenty-hole boots that laced up to his knees. His gaze, that of a true believer, was the only physical characteristic that was familiar to those who knew him.

"Is it really necessary to resort to violence?" asked the newest member of the cell, a gaunt-faced young woman who sported a buzz cut, denim overalls, and Doc Martens.

Before the guest of honor could answer her question, she continued. "Wouldn't peaceful activism like Martin Luther King's, or nonviolent, headline-grabbing confrontations like Greenpeace's serve us equally as well?"

Kees Vanmeerendonk shook his hairless head. "The answer is no," he said adamantly. "Especially where PPHL is concerned. Under Nikoletta Papadaki, PPHL has joined the five privately owned top polluters in the world. And privately owned polluters are the most dangerous because they don't have to answer to stockholders."

His eyes took on a fiery intensity, and he used a finger to stress his point, saying, "Nikoletta Papadaki is the symbol of all that is wrong with this planet. The damage that she alone is doing to mother earth will take thousands, maybe even millions, of years to repair. She is guilty of trying to kill the planet that sustains us, and the only way to send out our message so that it is truly heard is to make an example of her. She's left us no choice."

He paused briefly for dramatic effect before continuing. "She has to die."

Kees looked around the small circle. "Any other questions?"

There were none.

He nodded with satisfaction. "In the meantime, don't let up the pressure. Continue with the demonstrations. And remember, the more violent and newsworthy they are, the more the world will be aware of the continuing transgressions against nature."

After another fifteen minutes or so of conversation, the host thanked Kees with the effusiveness reserved for heroes, and Kees slipped out into the night alone, his destination unknown to the other cell members. The gaunt-faced young woman quickly rushed out after him, ignoring the protests of her hosts. She spotted him, already in the distance, and ran to catch up with him.

Over a period of another hour, the remaining guests left the barge at intervals, each one alone.

The activity had been so furtive that not even the residents of the neighboring barges were aware that a meeting had taken place. They knew little of the young sculptor and his wife, but they would all agree that he seemed a talented young father and she a wonderful mother to their adorable baby.

Chapter Sixteen

∾

They were still miles from the city when Ariadne got her first glimpse of Manhattan's skyscrapers. "It's breathtaking," she said enthusiastically, squeezing Matt's shoulder. "Pictures don't do it justice. Oh, look, Matt! You can see the Empire State Building."

Matt grinned. "I can't believe you've never been into the city."

"I know. It's crazy, especially since it's so close. I wanted to come in so much, but my parents always warned against it. You know, they think it's a big bad place where people get murdered in the streets."

"A lot of the people in the country are like that," he said.

"Most of the locals around Roxbury have never been, and they don't have any desire to."

They drove in on the East Side, and Matt parked the Jeep in a garage. "How about if we start with a walk?" he asked, pocketing the parking ticket. "That's the best way to see things."

"I'd love that," Ariadne said. She was so excited that she thought she could walk all day.

Holding hands with her, he led her across town from Third Avenue to Madison, and they began walking downtown. "Oh, my," Ariadne said as they strolled past the designer boutiques. "I've never seen so many beautiful clothes in one place in my life."

Matt put an arm around her shoulders. "It is nice, isn't it?"

After several blocks, he led her across to Fifth Avenue, and they changed direction and began walking uptown. "You can get a different perspective," he said.

Ariadne loved strolling along Central Park, gawking at the apartment buildings across the avenue, with their white-gloved doormen, then turning to look into the verdancy of the park itself. "The people who live along here have a fantastic view," she said.

They reached the Metropolitan Museum of Art and sat on the steps for a while, enjoying the sunshine while taking a breather. "We can go in if you want to," Matt offered, "or save the museum for another time."

"Let's save it," she said. "It's so wonderful outside today." Besides, she thought, she liked the idea of coming into the city with him again.

They watched a mime's performance and a juggler before reversing direction and heading down the avenue. She enjoyed window-shopping at the big department and specialty stores and strolling through the Art Deco wonder of Rockefeller Center. Afterward, they peeked into the silent grandeur of St. Patrick's Cathedral.

"Are you getting tired?" Matt asked solicitously.

She shook her head. "No. Not even close," she said. "This is all too exciting to get tired."

They walked on, finally reaching Thirty-fourth Street and the destination Matt had in mind. Looking up, Ariadne turned to him. "I don't believe it," she said. "You want to go to the top of the Empire State Building? It has to be the most touristy thing we could possibly do."

He nodded. "Guilty on both counts," he said. "But it's something everyone should do whether it's touristy or not."

The crowds waiting to get in were large, but they didn't have to wait too long. They took the high-speed elevator to the floor where the observation platform was located and stepped outside. The wind was powerful and whipped Ariadne's long hair about her face. She gathered it up and quickly put it in a ponytail, then, holding Matt's hand, went as close to the edge as she could.

"This is really awesome," she said. "Unbelievable."

Initially, they looked north. Matt pointed out landmarks in Manhattan and beyond, up past Central Park to the Bronx and Westchester County. Taking their time, they walked west, where they looked across the Hudson River to New Jersey, then south to Staten Island and more New Jersey. Finally, they made their way to the east side, and gazed out across Queens to Long Island.

She was mesmerized by the views all the way around. "I'm so glad we did this," she said. "This must be one of the greatest vantage points in the entire world."

He squeezed her hand in his. "I'm glad you like it," he said. "I haven't been up here myself for many years. I'd forgotten how impressive it is."

Other tourists bumped against them, talking animatedly. Matt leaned down and kissed her cheek, and she looked up with shining eyes. "Thank you for this," she said.

When they got back down on the street, he hailed a taxi and gave the driver an address in SoHo. There, at a small French bistro on Spring Street, they had a late lunch, gorging on steak and *pommes frites*, washing it down with a good red wine, then enjoying a *tarte tatin*, all the while observing the street life of the neighborhood. Afterward, they walked off some of the lunch, window-shopping in the trendy environs.

"Nearly everybody is so well put together," Ariadne said. "What I mean is, everybody seems to have a look."

"There's definitely a passion for fashion," Matt said.

She smiled at his rhyme. "That's one way to put it."

"I think we have time for one more thing," he said, looking at his wristwatch.

"What's that?"

"You'll see."

He hailed a taxi, and they shot back uptown on the West Side Highway. Near Forty-second Street, the driver came to a screeching halt. Matt paid the fare, and they got out of the cab.

"Where *are* we going?" she asked. She saw bicyclists whizzing by and joggers running in a cordoned-off area across the street, and beyond that there was a ticket booth for the Circle Line, where a long queue of tourists waited.

A new tower was nearing completion, and the sun struck it, turning the entire western side of the sleek silvery mass a blazing fiery column.

"Just imagine the fantastic views the people will have in that building," Ariadne said. Her gaze traveled to the top of the skyscraper. "It's really beautiful, isn't it?"

"Yes," Matt said nervously. "It's quite a building."

She read the large sign in front. "Papadaki. A Greek name, just like mine. I've heard of the company."

*   *   *

Her driver pulled over in front of a loft building on the far western fringes of Chelsea. What had once been a neighborhood of garages and warehouses had metamorphosed into an area of art galleries, many of them driven out of SoHo by the skyrocketing rents and the popularity of the neighborhood that, ironically, they'd helped make so desirable. The same trend was repeating itself in Chelsea, but this building didn't look very promising. Nevertheless, Nikoletta was not daunted. She knew that some of New York's most stylish lofts were housed in buildings that looked much like this one.

The driver opened the door, and she stepped out of the car. "I don't know how long I'll be," she said. "I'll call you on the cell when I'm heading down, so don't stray too far."

The behemoth, who also served as a bodyguard, tipped his hat. "I'll be here."

The day was windy, and grit and litter were blowing up off the sidewalks. Ignoring the debris, Nikoletta went to the entry door and looked at the brass panel of buzzers. When she saw the one for number 7, she noticed that there was no name in the slot provided.

How like Frans, she thought. *He's hiding out, licking his wounds. Well, he can't hide from me.*

She'd tracked him down after Bianca's death. New York might be a big town, but the task had been a breeze for Nikoletta. Angelo Coveri, she'd learned, had ordered Frans out of Bianca's apartment the day he had been informed of her death. When she'd heard about it, she'd called Frans and generously offered him the use of one of PPHL's corporate apartments, but Frans had refused, angrily shouting at her on the telephone and hanging up. He'd disappeared, or so he thought, moving back into his old Chelsea loft. But Nikoletta had easily gotten that address from his agent. After all, PPHL provided the agent with a great deal of work, using models who were signed with her for innumerable advertising campaigns.

Nikoletta had contacted him again, allowing a few days for grief. He would be especially vulnerable in his sorrow, wouldn't he? But Frans had refused to see her. He still blamed her for Bianca's death. To Nikoletta's surprise, he'd actually been in love with Bianca. Well, Nikoletta had thought, he'd get over it. But even when she'd invited him for a cruise aboard her yacht after the upcoming film festival in Cannes, he'd refused. Dangling the powerful movie producers and directors who would be there as bait hadn't worked in Frans's case, either. More shouts and another hang up. He certainly wasn't like most models, who'd jump at such an opportunity.

She pressed the buzzer for his loft and waited for a response. No one answered, so she pressed it again, longer this time. Still there was no response. She pressed the button again, this time leaving her finger on it for a good thirty seconds. No one could stand the unbearable noise for that long.

She heard the familiar static from the speaker as he pressed the response button in his loft. *Aha!* she thought. *He's answering.*

"Who is it?" the irritated voice asked.

"Please give me just a second," Nikoletta said. "I've got plans for Bianca's memorial, and I have to discuss them with you."

That should do the trick, she thought.

Frans didn't respond immediately, and only the sound of static buzzed for a while. Finally he muttered, "I don't want to see you."

"But Bianca's memorial!" she cried. "She loved you, Frans, and I thought you loved her. You're the only one who can help."

There was silence again, then, "What memorial?"

"Something very special, Frans. Something to honor Bianca's memory. Forever."

She could practically hear his mental gears turning in the ensuing silence. Then the speaker came to life again. "Only a few minutes," he muttered.

The buzzer sounded, releasing the locked lobby door. Nikoletta quickly shoved through and rushed to the elevator, pressing the UP button. When the elevator stopped on seven and the doors slid open, she stepped out into his loft.

Frans, who was sprawled on a big leather sofa in the living area staring off into space, didn't bother getting up. He didn't even look in her direction.

The loft wasn't the typically vast, luxuriously furnished space of the lofts belonging to Niki's friends. It was large, but was barely furnished at all. Besides the sofa on which Frans lay there were two chairs that might have come from the street, a coffee table made from shipping pallets, and a flat-screen plasma television along with a CD player/radio that were placed on a long board propped up by concrete blocks. The dining area was empty, but there were two stools at a kitchen counter. There was no art on the walls, no plants, nothing much to make the place feel like a home, unless the sneakers, boots, jeans, underwear, and various garments strewn about were considered a homey touch. She could only imagine what a mess the bedroom must be.

She started to cross to the sofa, her heels click-clacking loudly on the hardwood floor. She stopped near one of the empty chairs, waiting for him to acknowledge her. On the splintery pallet that served as a coffee table, she noticed an overflowing ashtray, a pack of Marlboro cigarettes, a lighter, a half-empty bottle of Stolichnaya vodka, and a smudged glass.

"I really hate to bother you, Frans," she said. "I know you're in pain, but I need your advice about the fund I'm planning in memory of Bianca."

He finally focused on her. "Why would *you* do anything for Bianca?" he asked. His voice was subdued but hostile. "To appease your guilt?"

"I . . ." Nikoletta's voice trailed off. She had to tell Frans what he wanted to hear, regardless of her own feelings. "I guess you're right," she said. "If I hadn't created that assignment, Bianca wouldn't have taken it, would she? I realize that now. Once she found out about the assignment, there was no stopping her. I told her over and over how dangerous it was and so did other people at the company. But she wouldn't listen to me or anyone else."

Nikoletta began pacing, nervously wringing her hands. "I could kill myself," she said in an anguished voice. "I've never felt so awful about anything in my life. If only I could have stopped her." She paused and made a choking sound, hanging her head, her face turned away from Frans. "She was my friend, and I loved her so much."

She heard the leather upholstery on the couch creak and knew that Frans was changing positions. Maybe she was getting his attention, she thought. "After what happened in St. Barth's, I would have done anything to make it up to Bianca, to make her happy again. I hated losing her as a friend and seeing her relationship with you end. That was the worst thing, the absolute worst." Nikoletta sniffed as if holding back tears. "One reason I created the new job was to try to make it up to her. I was so . . . so devastated."

"You should've been devastated," Frans said, the couch creaking again.

"I know. . . . I *know*," Nikoletta said in a whispery voice. "I—I've made a mess of everything in the last few months, and now I've *lost* her. Lost her forever." She extracted a handy Kleenex from her little clutch and blew her nose, still turned away from Frans. "That's one reason I want to start this memorial. I—I was mortified when Angelo had a private funeral for Bianca. He barred me from it, and I don't blame him. He blames me for her death. Everyone does. But I did everything I could short of firing Bianca to keep her from going on that assignment." In an exasperated voice, she added, "She was just so headstrong. So independent. That was one of the things I loved about her, but it made it impossible to get through to her. To make her change her mind."

She turned to face Frans with tears in her eyes. She saw that he was sitting up now, his elbows on his knees, his head in his hands. *He's such a hunk,* she thought. *Even now, tormented as he is.* "I don't expect you to forgive me," she said. "Not ever. But I'm begging you to help me with a memorial for her. I can't work. I can't do anything. I can barely function," she went on, "and I think that doing something in her memory will help."

Frans saw the tears on her cheeks, the anguish in her expression. "I— I can't work, either," he murmured. "I've canceled all of my photo shoots. There's no way I can smile for the camera."

"I'm so sorry," she said. "I know that nothing . . . and nobody . . . can replace Bianca in your heart, but maybe helping with the memorial will give you some relief." She wanted to sit down beside him and put her arms around him, to feel that incredible body next to her own, but she restrained the urge, knowing that would be the worst thing she could do.

Frans looked up, his intense gaze on her. "What do you want to do?"

"I'm not sure," she said. "For once, even I'm at a loss. I know I want to establish a memorial fund in her name. Like a foundation. But I don't want to do it without your suggestions. You knew her better than anyone else."

Frans shrugged his powerful shoulders. "I don't know." He poured a small measure of Stolichnaya in the glass and took a sip, then set the glass down. "I never thought about it, but it is a good idea."

Nikoletta felt a surge of excitement course through her. He had taken the bait. *Give him time,* she reminded herself. *With time, he will be mine and no one else's.* "Bianca was interested in making a difference in the world," she said thoughtfully, "so I think it should be something along those lines. You know, something that would help the poor or disadvantaged."

"That's what she was trying to do when she went on that awful assignment," Frans snapped.

"Yes, I know," Nikoletta said soothingly, "but as awful as it may have been, you have to remember that she was doing what she felt she had to do, Frans. She was so brave, so courageous. . . ." Her voice broke, and she turned away from him again. After a few moments she said, "Anyway, something along those lines would be a fitting memorial, I think. Something that would help underprivileged children."

"Yes," Frans said softly. He drained the glass of vodka, then poured some more in the glass. "I think . . . I think that Bianca would like something that would help children."

"And you can help me decide exactly what and how to administer it," Nikoletta said. "I'll make the initial contribution, of course." She turned to face him. "At least a million dollars or so. But . . . oh, never mind. I know what a strain this must put on you, and I don't want to add to your troubles right now."

"Thank you, Niki," he said. He drank more vodka.

"It's the least I can do, Frans." She could see that the vodka was loosening him up, but she didn't want to push her luck. "Maybe one day when you're feeling up to it, we can discuss it. I know I want to keep my name out of it entirely, at least as far as the public is concerned. We'll put your name on it if that's okay with you."

"What do you mean?" he asked, looking up at her.

"You know. When it's announced in the press, and we start to solicit donations," Nikoletta said. "We'll say that it's you who's doing it for Bianca, and leave me out of it. I think that way we can raise a lot more money. You and Bianca were a couple in love, and you're doing this in her memory. You see what I mean? People will like that. On the other hand, they see me as a monster."

Frans stared at her thoughtfully, then nodded. "Thank you, Niki," he said again, his voice a whisper.

Nikoletta felt a dampness between her thighs. Oh, God, how she wanted him. All raw nerves and pent-up anger and sorrow. But she knew she would blow it if she made a move. She backed away with a hint of a smile on her lips.

"No, I have to thank you, Frans," she said. "Now, I'd better get going. I'm just so happy that you let me tell you about it. I can never undo what was done, but I want to do everything I can to atone for it."

She started toward the elevator, then turned back around. "You have my numbers, so when you feel like it—not before—let's get going on this."

"Okay, Niki," he said.

She went to the elevator and pressed the CALL button, aware of his eyes on her back. *I have to get out of here fast,* she thought. *Another minute and I'll be all over him.* The elevator arrived, and the doors slid open. She stepped in, then let the doors close without waving good-bye. *I'll be seeing him again very soon.*

Chapter Seventeen

Dutchess County, New York

It was dark by the time Matt turned onto the Taconic State Parkway. Ariadne had nodded off. The long walks and the excitement of the day had exhausted her. He was grateful, but at the same time he dreaded what was soon to come. Millbrook was only an hour or so away. He only hoped that she would forgive him when she found out what was going on. She would feel betrayed by him and with good reason.

They had reached Dutchess County when she awoke. Covering her yawn with a hand, she glanced at him in the near darkness of the Jeep. "Was I asleep long?"

"Not too long."

"Poor you," Ariadne said. She leaned over and kissed his cheek. "Driving all the way down, showing me all over the city, then driving back while I nod off. It's not fair."

He forced a smile through gritted teeth. "I'm fine," he lied.

"Where are we?"

"We're in Dutchess County, in New York," he said evasively.

"B-but why? I mean, is this some special way back?" She looked at him with curiosity, studying his features in the light reflected from the dashboard of the Jeep.

"Because . . . well, because . . ." He glanced at her, then shifted his gaze back to the road. "There's something I've got to explain to you, Ariadne. I'm afraid that you're going to hate me but—"

She laughed uneasily. "I couldn't possibly hate you, Matt."

"You might change your mind," he said.

His dark tone of voice put Ariadne on alert, and her smile faded away. "What is it?"

The sign for the exit appeared on the right. "We're going to be stopping in Millbrook," he said. "At a friend's house." The exit came up, and he slowed down as he drove the Jeep downhill off the parkway.

"What friend?" she asked suspiciously as he stopped at the end of the exit ramp.

He gave the Jeep gas and sped off to the right unnecessarily fast.

"Matt, tell me what's going on," she said. "You're acting . . . well, you're not acting like yourself."

"Everything will be explained to you once we get there," he said. "There are some people who want to meet you. I'm not sure how much they want me to tell you. They don't know that we've become . . . involved."

She was completely baffled. "You're not making any sense, Matt. What people want to meet me?" She gave an exasperated sigh. "Why are you being so mysterious suddenly?"

"Ariadne, I want you to know that no matter what happens . . . I . . . the way I feel about you, well . . . I've never felt that way about anyone else."

Ariadne wanted to reach over and kiss him. His words sounded so heartfelt, and she believed him. Her quickening pulse attested to that. At the same time, she was completely confused by whatever it was that he *wasn't* telling her. He was clearly keeping something from her, and that didn't make sense.

"Matt, you're not leveling with me," she finally said, staring straight ahead. "I don't know what it is that you're afraid to tell me, but I don't like you playing with my feelings like this."

"I'm not . . . or I don't mean to," he said guiltily. A deer appeared in the Jeep's headlights. It was directly in his path, staring at the approaching lights.

"Oh, my God," Ariadne cried, seeing it at the same time.

Matt slammed on the brakes and turned the steering wheel toward the shoulder of the road. Ariadne braced herself against the dashboard. The deer stared in their direction a moment longer, then leaped off the road and into the woods.

"Jesus," Matt said, turning to look at Ariadne. "We could've been killed. Are you okay?"

She nodded. "I'm fine, but I would've hated to die not knowing what it is you're not telling me."

Matt pulled back onto the road. "I was hired to spy on you," he said very low.

"Spy . . . on . . . me?" she replied in a stunned voice. She stared at him, her eyes wide. "But why on earth would anybody want to spy on me? That's the craziest thing I've ever heard of." A ripple of fear made her stiffen. She was supposed to be going back to the lovely campus at Williams College, but instead they were headed to a mysterious hideout in the woods. *What's going on?* she wondered anxiously.

The road to the house was just ahead on the left, and Matt flipped on his blinker. After he'd made the turn, he said, "I don't know all of the details myself, but the man who hired me is a big honcho at PPHL."

"What's that?" she asked.

"Papadaki Private Holdings Limited," he said. "It's a huge multinational corporation into all kinds of things. Shipping and so on."

"Oh, right. I know of the company, of course, but not much about it. It's privately held."

Matt nodded. "Hold on a second." He brought the Jeep to a stop before a stone pillar with an intercom. Ariadne watched as he pushed a button on the intercom.

"Who is it?" a disembodied voice asked.

"It's Matt," he said.

Wide iron gates swung slowly open, and Matt pulled through them. There was the crunch of pea gravel under the tires, and in the headlights Ariadne could see that the drive was lined with tall pines and hemlocks.

"Before we go another foot, I want you to finish what you were saying," Ariadne said determinedly.

Matt didn't look at her. "It seems that you may be a Papadaki."

"What? But I'm Ariadne Megas. I—"

"I know you're originally from Greece," Matt said. "You were adopted by a couple there named Megas before you were brought to this country. I know that you were brought here and raised by another couple from the time you were ten years old. I know that Adrian Single, the man who owns this estate, is going to explain everything to you." He paused and took a deep breath. "And I also know that, no matter what you think of me after tonight, I—I think I'm in love with you."

Despite the many questions that swirled in her mind, she felt a jolt of electric excitement rush up her spine. *He thinks he loves me.* His proclamation of love overwhelmed everything else, at least for the moment.

Matt reached for her hand and took it in his. "Please remember that," he said. "I mean it. From the bottom of my heart."

They kept driving until light spilling from the windows of a big colonial house bathed the driveway in its glow, and Matt pulled the Jeep to a stop. Ariadne saw the front door open, and a man step out onto the front porch. Although there were lit lanterns at either side of the door, she could see only that he was tall and slender and appeared to be middle-aged. "Is that the man you said would explain everything to me?"

"Yes," Matt replied. "That's Adrian Single." He switched off the engine and turned to her. "It'll be okay, Ariadne. I promise you. You'll be safe here. This man is your friend."

"I don't even *know* this man!" she exclaimed. She was both afraid and angry and suddenly felt on the verge of tears, but she held them back. Whatever this was all about, she thought, she would get it over with, then insist that Matt take her back to Williamstown.

He squeezed her hand again. "Let's go in. You'll see."

Ariadne stepped out of the Jeep and let him lead her toward the porch. The air was perfumed with the scent of the pine trees, normally a comforting fragrance, but it did not soothe her now. The man stared at her for a moment as if he'd seen a ghost. Then his face broke out into a smile. "Ariadne," he said, recovering his composure. "I'm Adrian Single, and I'm very happy to meet you." He extended his hand, and she shook it firmly.

"I'm happy to meet you, too, Mr. Single," she said, and then only half jokingly added, "At least I think I am." She was certain she had seen him before—he was a very handsome man, tall, with dark hair and a sophisticated air—but couldn't quite place him. "Matt hasn't told me what this is all about."

"That's my fault, I'm afraid," Adrian said. "Come in, and I'll explain everything."

He held the door wide for her, and Ariadne stepped into the large entrance hall. She quickly took in its black-and-white checkerboard marble floor, the elegant spiral staircase, and the pale pumpkin-colored walls. They were hung with paintings, some of which were landscapes.

"If you'll come with me," Adrian said, "I have some friends I want you to meet."

In the well-lit hallway, Ariadne was suddenly certain where she'd met Adrian Single, but she didn't say anything. She let him guide her through a large living room and into a book-lined library. Three strangers were sitting on leather couches, conversing among themselves, and they stood up as she walked into the room.

"This is Ariadne, everyone," he said, "and Ariadne, I want you to meet Sugar Rosebury, Yves Carre, and Angelo Coveri."

Ariadne shook hands and exchanged greetings with the three strangers, noting how they stared at her the same way Adrian had.

"The resemblance is eerie, isn't it?" Sugar said to no one in particular.

"Uncannily so," Angelo replied uneasily. "If not for the haircut, and I didn't know better—"

Yves smiled thinly. "I know. You would swear she was her sister."

My sister? Ariadne thought, more puzzled than ever. *What are they talking about? And who, exactly, are they anyway?*

Sugar suddenly hugged Ariadne. "Oh, sweetheart, we're embarrassing you, aren't we? Treating you like some sort of laboratory specimen. I'm so sorry. I hope you'll forgive us."

"Why don't we all get comfortable?" Adrian said. As everyone took a seat, Sugar guided Ariadne to an overstuffed leather chair and sat on its big arm, close to Ariadne as if to protect her.

"Quite frankly, I don't know what to think," Ariadne said. "Nobody's given me a clue about what's going on here yet." She looked back through the doorway for Matt. His presence would make her feel a little safer. "Where's Matt?" she asked in alarm.

"I'm right here," Matt said, coming in through another doorway. He stood behind one of the couches, facing in her direction.

"I think I'm owed an explanation," Ariadne said warily.

"This is Matt Foster, as you know," Adrian said, indicating Matt with a gesture.

"I'm quite aware of that," Ariadne said with a hint of sarcasm.

"Matt's been in my employ for some time," Adrian said. "Expressly to keep an eye on you."

Ariadne stared at Matt with a sinking feeling, momentarily speechless. *So all that attention he lavished on me was merely because he was being paid,* she thought. *How stupid of me to have been taken in by him.*

"I don't understand," she said, tearing her eyes away from the man she'd thought she'd known. "Why would you keep watch over me?"

"What the hell is going on here?" Sugar asked.

"I'll explain," Adrian said. "I've been trying to keep watch on you over the years because I'm partially responsible for bringing you to this country."

"So you helped take me from the only home I knew and brought me here to strangers with no explanation."

"Yes, I helped Nikos," he said, "but I thought in the long run it was the best thing for you. Then several months ago, I decided it was time to find out if you were prepared for the role we have in mind. So that's why I instructed Matt to keep a close eye on you."

"I see," she broke in, the calmness of her words belying the agitation that she felt. She was almost overwhelmed by the sense of betrayal she was experiencing.

"Ariadne," Adrian said, "we don't want to alarm you, but if word somehow got out that you're alive, you might be in great danger. We think it's best to have someone around all the time. A personal bodyguard. So while you're here and perhaps later when we take you into the city—if our plan works out—you will be seeing Matt. You can trust him with your life."

Ariadne didn't know whether to laugh or cry. *Trust him with my life?* she thought. *I wouldn't trust him with my pocketbook, not now.*

"Let me get this straight," Sugar said to Adrian. "This young man"— she pointed at Matt—"and Ariadne have met?"

Adrian nodded. "She and Matt met in Williamstown while he was watching her."

"You've got a lot of explaining to do," Sugar said.

"Indeed, you do," Angelo added. Some of the hostility he'd shown Adrian after Bianca's death flared again, although they'd mended the relationship at her funeral. As grief-stricken as he was, he had come to realize that Adrian didn't know about Bianca's new job until it was too late.

"It's time," Adrian said. He paused and gazed around the room. "I've been reluctant to tell you all of this before because I was afraid that word might leak out somehow."

"So you don't trust us?" Angelo said.

"I do," Adrian said, "but I thought until it was absolutely necessary I would keep my secret."

"So you really don't trust us," Sugar said tartly.

"It doesn't matter anymore," Adrian said. "I'm telling you everything now. It was so long ago it seems unreal now, as if it happened in a fairy tale, not in this life."

Adrian shifted in his chair. His eyes took on a faraway look as his mind cast backward in time. "It started in January of 1984," he said. "It was a terrible night. I vividly remember how the waves and wind lashed the cabin cruiser that took me to the Papadakis' villa in the Peloponnese."

There's that name again, Ariadne thought.

"Planes and helicopters couldn't land because of the storm, and the roads had been washed out in places, but Nikos Papadaki had called me there, demanding that I come immediately.

"Anyway, Larissa had given birth," he went on. "To twin girls."

Everyone in the room abruptly turned to Ariadne, but she was making an effort to keep her face devoid of expression, despite her intense interest in the story.

"Nikos came rushing out onto the terrace and shoved a bundle at me." He paused and looked at Ariadne. "It was you, Ariadne. The second born of the twins."

"So I have a twin sister?" she said, astounded.

"Yes," Adrian said. "And Nikos and Larissa Papadaki were your real parents."

Ariadne started to ask another question, but he quickly picked up the thread of his story and continued. She decided to hear him out before asking anything else.

" 'Take this child,' Nikos ordered me. 'Leave it somewhere with strangers who don't know who she is. Tell my wife nothing. Nor anyone else. *Nothing!*' He'd reached into a trouser pocket and pulled something out. 'See that the child receives this. It is her mother's.' "

"He thrust a small jewel-encrusted Byzantine cross on a gold chain into my hand," Adrian said.

Ariadne felt for the chain around her neck and pulled it out. A cross, just as he'd described, dangled from the end of it. "It was this, wasn't it?"

Adrian looked at the small cross she held in her hand. With a touch of awe he said, "So you still have it after all these years."

"My mama in Greece made sure I took it when I was brought to America," Ariadne said. "It's all I have left of them except for memories."

"And it belonged to your real mother," Adrian said. "Larissa Papadaki."

Ariadne fingered the small cross before finally letting it hang loose around her neck again.

"I'd received many strange commands from Nikos over the years," Adrian went on. "He would have bouts of . . . madness. I don't know what else to call them. Normally, I didn't question him, but I truly found myself flustered when this happened. As Sugar and Angelo know, Nikos could be . . . well, terrifying. His rages were legendary, but this was one time I couldn't simply follow orders without knowing what was happening.

"I asked him why the child was being taken away," Adrian continued. "Why must she disappear?

" 'Twin heiresses are a curse!' Nikos bellowed at me.

"That night, I thought Nikos was demented. I could see the zeal of the village peasant in Nikos's eyes. And something else as well: fear. I knew it was useless to argue with him then. He didn't even want to touch the baby that he had given me."

Ariadne swallowed. He was obviously referring to her. She was the baby her own father had been afraid to touch.

"I asked Nikos how he could possibly be certain which baby was which. How could he possibly know that one of them was evil? He just roared he'd used his own judgment, and that everything he'd slaved for and built would—poof!—disappear into thin air if he didn't get rid of you."

Adrian paused again, and cleared his throat. "As I've said, there was no use arguing with him when he was having one of his spells. He pulled me over to the cliff side of the terrace and pointed down to the cabin cruiser I'd come on. I'll never forget it. 'Now go! Take that cursed creature and get it out of my sight!'

"I asked him where, and he said he didn't know or even want to know. He said he'd set up a generous allowance for the baby's care for me to administer. Said it could be a hovel for all he cared, so long as no one, above all you, Ariadne, ever learned your true identity. Then, in typical Nikos fashion, he made me swear to it. I figured I could argue with him when he came back to his senses. And I did. For years and years. But he was always convinced that he'd made the right decision. He truly believed in the curse."

Adrian sighed wearily. "I had never disobeyed him, so I swore to him that I would do as he said." He paused and looked at Ariadne. "I took you down the steep path to the boat. I remember I stopped on the path at one point because your blanket was soaked, so I took off my jacket and covered you with that, too. Anyway, I set off with you in the boat."

Adrian drew a deep breath, coughing to clear his throat. "Within a week, I located a middle-aged couple on Hydra," he said. "They lived on the almost-uninhabited part of the island, as far away from the town as you could get. They were childless and thrilled to accept Ariadne—*you*—into their home as their daughter. I sent them a monthly stipend over the years, from the fund that Nikos had set up."

"But then why was I taken away from them?" Ariadne asked.

Adrian drew himself up straight, like a responsible executive. "I'd argued with Nikos over the years about whether or not he'd made the right decision, and I finally convinced him that you should be brought here. I knew that if you remained with the Megas family on Hydra, you would never be prepared to take control of PPHL if it ever came to that. You wouldn't be properly educated." His voice took on more passion as he continued. "I also thought you should be able to claim your birthright. You've always been Nikos's heir as much as Niki is. Believe it or not, Ariadne, I was trying to do what was best for you. I even convinced Nikos to go get you himself. I thought he might have a change of heart if he saw you. But he didn't. He was still afraid."

There was so much information to digest all at once, Ariadne didn't know what was best for her. "It sounds like something out of a Greek tragedy," she murmured.

"What do you know about the Greek tragedies, young lady?" Angelo asked her, not unkindly.

Before Ariadne could respond, Adrian said, "I assure you that I arranged for the best education possible for Ariadne at one of the best boarding schools in the Northeast, and then she got into Williams College." He addressed Ariadne as he added, "You're not going there on scholarship, by the way. Your father set up a very generous bank account for me to use for your care."

Ariadne didn't appear to be listening. A faraway look had come into her eyes. "So . . . I have a sister," she murmured reflectively. "I can't believe that I never knew."

"Yes. An identical twin," Adrian replied.

"And a real mother and father?"

"Both unfortunately dead now," Adrian said. "Your mother, Larissa, died in a car crash after your parents divorced, and Nikos, your father, died a few years ago of heart disease."

Ariadne was overwhelmed by all this information. Finally, she said, "And my sister really is an identical twin?"

"Yes," Sugar said, "but Niki is a very . . . difficult sort."

"She's a monster, in my opinion," Angelo said harshly. "I don't think you're anything like her. You certainly don't seem to be."

There was a long silence while Ariadne digested all she'd been told. The pieces of the puzzle that had been her past were beginning to fall into place at last.

"Now I understand why my father came to Greece for me," she said. "Why I was brought to Connecticut, and now why you had Matt bring me here. Nikos Papadaki, my real father, made the wrong choice, didn't he? Mr. Coveri said that my sister's a monster. You hope to replace my twin sister with me. You want us to trade places. That is it, isn't it?"

Adrian wasn't surprised by her quick grasp of the situation. He inclined his head, acknowledging the truth of what she'd said.

"And what about her? What is her name . . . Niki?"

"Nikoletta," Sugar said, "but nearly everyone calls her Niki."

"Does Niki desire to be replaced?"

Adrian heaved a sigh. "I imagine not."

Sugar snorted in laughter. "You might as well be completely honest,

Adrian. Like hell would Niki want to trade places." She turned to Ariadne. "Sorry to have to tell you this, sweetheart, but your sister is the worst kind of megalomaniac," Sugar said. "Sometimes I think she's inherited Nikos's madness."

"Worse, she's like a disease," Yves added, "leaving poison everywhere she goes. She's bought some of the most notorious toxic-waste companies on the planet."

Adrian did not mince words. "Well, I think Nikos—mad or not—was right about one thing. One twin *was* born good and the other bad. The only problem is, it seems your father picked the wrong sister."

Solemnly Ariadne asked Sugar, "And you believe this to be true, also?"

Sugar nodded. "I do. I've given her the benefit of the doubt, but Niki's history has proven it over and over again."

"And you?" Ariadne inquired of Angelo. "Do you also believe this to be true?"

"With all my heart," he replied heavily. "Your sister as good as murdered my only child, my daughter. And why? Because Nikoletta wanted the young man my daughter loved. She wanted him as a toy for herself."

"So you see our dilemma," Yves cut in. "We feel we must honor your father's wishes and do everything we can to keep his empire intact. We cannot continue to let Nikoletta destroy everything. As long as she's in power, there's nothing we can do to stop her. That's why we've come to you, Ariadne."

Ariadne took a deep breath. "I . . . I was raised simply. First on the island, then by my foster parents in Connecticut . . . in a sheltered environment, and now I find myself thrust into . . . *this*. It's . . ." She lifted her hands and then let them drop. "It's overwhelming."

"We're asking you to make a decision," Adrian added. "Whether or not you are willing to take Niki's place is not a decision to be taken lightly. But ultimately the decision has to be yours, Ariadne. We can't force you. Consider us your counselors, if you will, much as we're supposed to be to Niki. But that's our only role."

"I don't know what to say," Ariadne said.

"We must also warn you that Nikoletta is a formidable enemy," Adrian said. "That's one of the reasons we've kept you a secret from her."

"So she doesn't know I exist?"

Adrian shook his head. "No. When Nikos died, she inherited immense power and wealth. International prominence. She wouldn't want to share any of it with you or anyone else. Do you see?"

"But she possesses all of these things now," Ariadne said.

"Of course she does," Sugar said, "but her ambition knows no bounds. You must believe us when we tell you that she would not want to share *anything* with you. She would most likely hate you for even existing." She took one of Ariadne's hands in hers. "You've never known anyone like her because of your upbringing, Ariadne. For Niki, the world is not enough. What Adrian and the others say is true. Niki would never share anything. Not since the day she was born."

"Believe it or not," Ariadne said, "I have met some fairly wicked people. Even in the boarding school and at college. Terrible gossips and backbiters. Girls who are jealous or greedy. Even really nasty teachers."

"I doubt that any of them are capable of the cruelty your twin is," Angelo Coveri said.

"And what if I went public?" Ariadne ventured. She saw Adrian Single turn ashen, and Sugar Rosebury gasped.

Adrian steepled his hands. "First, you would be risking your life," he said. "And make no mistake about that." He thumped his hand on his chair for emphasis. "Second, you wouldn't be able to help us save your father's legacy from destruction. Not only saving his legacy, Ariadne, but saving the *lives* of people who live in those parts of the world where Nikoletta is now doing business."

Ariadne listened intently as Adrian explained the ways in which Nikoletta had changed PPHL and the directions in which she was taking the company. In great detail he described the environmental and human costs of her policies.

Angelo supplied added emphasis. "We can bring it to an end, though. Think about it. If you were to become Nikoletta . . ."

Ariadne sat in stunned silence. She'd already realized that they wanted her to change places with her sister, but when the momentous proposition fully registered upon her consciousness, she said, "You mean . . . I would no longer be Ariadne? I would have to shed my true self?"

"Only in a sense," Angelo said with a nod. "Your essential nature will never change, I'm sure. But to all outward appearances you would become Nikoletta Papadaki, and there would be no going back."

"But why not?"

"Because for Ariadne to become Nikoletta," Adrian interjected, "Nikoletta would have to disappear, just as you yourself once did."

Ariadne felt a chill run up her spine. To do something like this to her sister was repugnant, but at the same time, if what they said about her was true, she would have the opportunity to help make the world a better place. Plus, for all these years her true parentage and inheritance had been stolen from her. Now she would have a chance to regain what was rightfully hers.

It was a dizzying prospect, and it almost made her physically ill. *I have so much to think about. What they are offering me is a new identity, a new life entirely. A life of adventure and excitement. Of incredible opportunities.*

Or would I be exchanging my simple, uncomplicated life for a gilded cage?

Chapter Eighteen

❧

New York City

Steaming water spilled from a gold swan's head into the large onyx bathtub in Nikoletta's master bathroom. Nelly, her personal maid, poured in three capfuls—no more, no less—of a foaming mineral muscle soak of sea salts and aloe vera. She tested the water with her hand to make certain that it was the temperature Nikoletta liked. Nelly didn't want to think about the possible repercussions otherwise. Nikoletta might turn on her like a virago, giving her a tongue-lashing of epic proportions and threatening to fire her, or she might brush it off with a flick of a wrist. Nelly never knew what to expect.

Nikoletta came into the bathroom, her body sheathed in the sheen of sweat. She had just spent an hour with her personal trainer, a young Russian with chiseled features who had guided her through a grueling workout. "Is my bath ready, Nelly?"

"Just about, ma'am," Nelly said. "Another inch or so of water, and it will be."

One of the cell phones on the onyx vanity bleated, and Nikoletta looked over at them. It was the one with her most private number. "You can go, Nelly," she said. "I'll take care of the rest."

"Yes, ma'am," Nelly said. She left the bathroom in a rush, knowing that Nikoletta would want privacy. She always did when that particular cell phone rang.

"Hello," Nikoletta said, stepping into the steaming bathtub.

"I have some information for you, Ms. Papadaki," the man's voice said.

Nikoletta quickly twirled the tap shut to reduce the noise and settled back in the bubble-filled tub to hear what he had to say. "What is it?"

"I've been following Single," he said, "and he came up to his estate in Dutchess County this afternoon."

"That's hardly news," Nikoletta replied derisively. "He goes there nearly every weekend." She stroked one leg with a sponge.

"I know that," the man said, "but this is different. There's been a whole lot of activity at the Single estate tonight."

Nikoletta's ears perked up, and she dropped the sponge. "What kind of activity?"

"It's very interesting," the man drawled. He enjoyed toying with Nikoletta, drawing out the suspense. He'd never worked for anyone as unpleasant as Nikoletta Papadaki, and he'd worked for some real monsters.

"What?" she demanded. "What's interesting?" The man was beginning to get on her nerves. "Get to the point."

"I haven't been inside," he said. "The area around the compound is fenced, you know. Quite a security system this Single has."

Nikoletta tapped her foot against the bottom of the tub. "I said, get to the point."

"I'm getting there," the man said. "I hid the car close by, and I've been watching the place from across the road with binoculars. Remember those pictures you gave me of the big shots at PPHL?"

"Yes, of course," Nikoletta said, exasperated. She began brushing the sponge up and down her other leg, using quick, unnecessarily firm strokes.

"First I saw this woman, Sugar Rosebury, drive in. She had that old man with her, ah, Angelo Coveri."

"Really?" Nikoletta said excitedly. Why were Sugar and Angelo going to visit Adrian in the country? she wondered. She knew that normally Adrian didn't mingle much with the other PPHL people outside the corporate schedule.

"Yes," the man said. "They arrived about two hours ago. They were buzzed in, then went to the main house. Single himself came to the door. I saw them go inside, and they've been inside all this time."

Nikoletta dropped the sponge again. The man certainly had her full attention now.

"They'd been there about fifteen minutes," the man went on, "when I saw another car pull up to the gates. That turned out to be your Frenchman . . . Yves Carre. Then another car pulled in. Say, twenty or thirty minutes after Carre. Neither one of the people in the car matched any of the pictures of PPHL people you gave me. In fact, they don't match anybody in my files."

"What did they look like?" Nikoletta asked.

"A man about thirty years old, tall, well built, dark hair. That's all I could tell about him when Single let them in the house." He paused and cleared his throat. "The woman, she was early twenties, I'd guess. Long blond hair. Tall, slender. I didn't get a good look at her when they went in. The guy with her was in the way."

"You're sure they don't match any of the pictures you have?" she asked.

"Pretty certain," the man said.

Who on earth? she wondered again. The PI's information was very exciting, but it presented two intriguing questions. Why would the board be gathering at Adrian's place in the country? And why would a young couple be joining them? She had to know. A secret meeting of the board was suspicious in and of itself.

"I want you to get in there," Nikoletta said.

"Shouldn't be a problem," the PI said. "I told you the place is fenced and gated, but—"

"I don't give a damn," Nikoletta blurted. "I want you *in* there. *Now.* I've got to know what's going on and who those other people are."

"I could . . ." His voice trailed off as if he was lost in thought.

"Just *do* it," Nikoletta said. "There'll be a bonus in it for you if you do."

"I'll get in there. No problem."

"I want you to call me back," Nikoletta told him. "I want to know everything you can tell me about what's going on, and see if there's anybody there who might've gotten there before you did."

"Will do," he said.

"And I'm especially interested in this young couple," she said. "See if you can get a better look. Better yet, get a picture."

"Leave it to me."

"And I'll want to know when they leave," Nikoletta went on. "Don't leave there until after they do, no matter what time it is. If they should spend the night, you do the same."

"Agreed."

Nikoletta hit the END button and placed the cell phone on the wide onyx shelf that surrounded the bathtub. *What the hell is Adrian Single up to?* she asked herself. She'd suspected him of working against her for a long time, and now she was certain of it. The board meeting behind her back at his place? They were going to be sorry. All of them.

But the young couple? Nikoletta frowned. They were a mystery, and Nikoletta despised a mystery. She would have to wait up for the PI to call her back.

Chapter Nineteen

༄

Dutchess County, New York

The day was sunny and warm, and its allure was irresistible for Ariadne. She had sat reading in the beautifully manicured formal gardens with their parterres of clipped box, weeping cherry trees, and blooming perennials, and then took a walk along the paths with herbaceous borders that had just come to colorful life. The fields and woods beyond beckoned to her, especially after several days of being in the confines of Adrian Single's home, where she was seldom left alone.

Now that she was outdoors on his beautiful country estate, she felt like a bird set free from its cage, and the sensation was both exhilarating and a little frightening. She roamed among the tall grasses and into the peaceful woodland and completely lost track of time, not allowing any fears she had to keep her from enjoying the bucolic afternoon. On a huge fallen hemlock tree that provided a natural bench she sat down, inhaling the heady scent of the trees and the mosses and ferns that covered the woodland ground. Except for the occasional birdsong and rustling of squirrels, it was quiet and peaceful.

Suddenly her ears pricked up, and she felt a chill creep up her neck. She was sure she heard the distinctive sound of breaking undergrowth. Someone was approaching her in the forest.

She went rigid when she heard the crunch of a shoe or boot. She was prepared to take flight when Matt Foster appeared from around a thicket of pine and hemlock trees.

She expelled a breath of relief, although she still felt a flutter in her chest.

"I—I'm sorry," he said apologetically. "I hope I didn't scare you."

"I—I . . . well, actually you did," she said, her eyes admiring his tall, lean, and powerful-looking physique. His dark eyes and slightly curly black hair appealed to her, too, and she loved his hesitant smile. She longed to reach out and hold him, despite his having deceived her, but she wouldn't allow herself to do that.

"I *am* sorry," he said sincerely. "The growth here is pretty thick, and I couldn't see around that thicket back there. I didn't see you sit down."

"You've been . . . following me?" she asked.

He nodded. "It's my job," he said. "You know that."

"I guess so," Ariadne said. She couldn't help but smile. "It's okay. It's just a little . . . unnerving to know I'm being watched. Have you been watching me long?"

"Ever since you got here," he said sheepishly.

"So you mean today? All day? Even while I was in the garden? Then on this long walk?"

"I mean since the night I brought you here," he said. "From a distance. From the time you get up in the morning till the time you go to bed."

"How do you manage that?" she asked. "Aren't you staying in the guesthouse?"

He cocked his head. "Yes, but I have my trade secrets."

"Oh-ho," she said, "so I'm not supposed to know about the peephole in my bedroom wall?"

"It's nothing like that, I can assure you, Ariadne," he replied with a hint of indignation.

"I was only joking," she countered. "Believe me, I'm still angry about being deceived, even if it was for a good cause, but for some reason I don't think you're the type to have a peephole in my bedroom."

"I appreciate that," he replied. "I didn't mean that I watch *you* every second that you're awake, but I do secure the perimeter of the estate for your safety. During the day I check out every visitor, whether it's FedEx or a nursery delivery. Anyone like that coming onto the property. At night I use night-vision binoculars and such to make certain that no one has trespassed. Simple safety measures like that."

"Do you really think that's necessary, Matt?"

"Adrian and the others think so, and they know better than I do," he replied. "I have to say that what I've learned about your sister leads me to believe that they're right. You need protection."

Ariadne shuddered at the idea of looming danger. "I guess this job must be very boring for you."

He shrugged. "It's . . . different."

"I hope you don't mind my long walks," Ariadne said. "I really enjoy getting out."

"I know you do," Matt said. Then his face became grave. "But I can't really imagine what you're going through. Finding out the truth about who you are and all."

Ariadne's gaze lingered on him, and she saw once again what had appealed to her so much. The dark, liquid look of his eyes, the depth of them, and the strong set of his square jaw. His hair was so black, his nose so straight, and his lips so—dare she think it?—sensual. His masculinity was immensely alluring and a little frightening.

"Do you mind if I sit down?" he asked.

"Oh . . . no, not at all," Ariadne replied. She laughed lightly. "I should probably say no, but it's a big tree and there's plenty of room."

"Thanks," he said. He sat down and spread his arms wide, placing his hands on the log and crossing his feet and swinging them slightly. "You must still be very angry with me."

"Actually, I . . . I guess I am," she replied.

"I hope you'll forgive me," Matt said. "I didn't mean any harm."

"Well, I guess you didn't," she said, staring into her lap. She looked up and about. "It's so peaceful and quiet here," she said, changing the subject.

"Until I came along?" His smile revealed even white teeth.

"It's okay," she said.

Matt gazed at her longingly. "I think you're amazing, Ariadne. The way you've handled all this information you've been given. A lot of people would be mental cases if they'd been through what you have."

"Maybe I am," Ariadne said. "I'm still so confused and . . . oh, I don't know. Just mixed-up about it all."

"Of course you are," he said. "That's natural. I think you're handling it all amazingly well."

"Thank you, Matt." His words seemed genuine, and she found her anger difficult to maintain.

"You're very strong," he said. "I can see that already."

She looked at him seriously. "Do you really think so?"

He nodded. "Oh, yes. And I admire that very much."

She blushed slightly. "You know so much about me," she said. "In fact, you know almost as much about me as I do myself, since you were there to hear everything."

He nodded again. "Yes. I hope that doesn't bother you."

"I don't know," she said honestly. She sighed, then gazed directly at him. "Maybe it does a little because I know so little about you."

"I really don't think you want to hear about me," he said. "We've already talked about me a lot."

"Oh, cloak-and-dagger stuff," she said lightly. "Up at your cabin, you told me you'd worked for the CIA, and I've read about it. But I don't really know much about it."

"You don't want to know more than you already do," he said.

The expression on his face was troubled, and Ariadne realized that she had hit upon a sensitive subject. Still, she wanted to know everything she could about him. "Why wouldn't I want to know?" she asked.

"Let's just say that my work for them was very unpleasant. Worse. It was like living in a kind of hell." He gazed into her eyes. "Why don't we talk about it another time?"

"Of course," she said, realizing that he really found his CIA work in the past a painful subject. As angry as she'd been, she wished more than ever that she could reach out to him. She wanted to feel his powerful arms about her again, to feel his flesh against hers, to inhale his masculine scent. But she couldn't allow that to happen again. She couldn't bring herself to trust him again. Not after what had happened.

If only I could turn back the clock, she thought, *and things could be the way they were before he brought me to this place. Before I discovered that he'd deceived me.*

In the library, Angelo paced back and forth in front of the fireplace, a cell phone at his ear. Although he was making an effort to speak sotto voce, the conversation was a heated one, and his reddened face and extravagant gestures contradicted the volume of his voice.

At the far end of the large room, Adrian went to one of the French doors that led to the terrace. "She's been gone for hours," he said to Sugar quietly so as not to interfere with Angelo's conversation. He parted the draperies and looked out the window. "What if she doesn't come back?"

"O ye of little faith," Sugar said lightly. "Why don't you settle down and relax? Look at the newspaper or something. We've got to give the poor thing a little time to spread her wings, Adrian. Don't you see? Besides, I don't think Matt Foster is going to let her out of his sight."

"Well, no. He certainly won't, and he does come with impeccable credentials," Adrian said. "I just don't like it that she's been gone for so long without telling us."

Angelo flipped his cell phone shut with a loud metallic click. "Goddamn it!" he cursed.

"What's wrong?" Adrian asked.

"Everything and more." He turned to face Adrian and Sugar. "That was Nikoletta. The new PPHL International Headquarters is having its official grand opening in eight weeks. Eight weeks. Nikoletta's already complaining about all the media attention, the publicity blitz, the parties, the photographs needed for the new ad campaign. She never fails to amaze me. She seeks out publicity for all kinds of nonsense, but she's suddenly complaining about this."

"She's micromanaging," Sugar said. "This is a huge affair, and she's trying to keep her finger on every little thing. That's the problem. If she delegated more of the detail work instead of insisting on being consulted about everything, she wouldn't be having this problem. The trouble is, she trusts almost no one."

Adrian was tapping his watch. "You know what? With so many things going on at once, that might be the perfect time to make the switch. If Ariadne is willing."

Angelo shook his head. "It's much too soon. Ariadne isn't ready to face the public, especially not on this kind of scale. For God's sake, the girl has been so sheltered. She's not prepared to imitate Nikoletta Papadaki. She doesn't have her gestures and nuances. All those things that could be dead giveaways. She doesn't even have her accent, and that's going to take some work. And what about Nikoletta's clothes? Do they fit her? And what about the photos and videos we've gotten together? Ariadne has only begun to look at them, and she certainly hasn't begun to really absorb them. She wouldn't even be able to recognize Nikoletta's friends. There are a thousand and one things to work out."

"Aren't you forgetting a little something?" Sugar interrupted.

"Like what?" Angelo groused.

"Like not putting the cart before the horse. Ariadne still hasn't agreed to be a part of this scheme."

Angelo sighed glumly and nodded. "You're right. It's a big decision for her, and we dare not rush her into making it. It has to be her choice, or it won't work."

"A nice sentiment, Angelo," Sugar replied, "but we haven't got time now. She's going to have to make up her mind *today*." She brushed errant hair away from her face. "And if she says yes, then she's going to have to work double time. But you know what?"

"What?"

"She can do it. I'm sure of it. Ariadne's sharp, a quick study. She's attending Williams College, for God's sake. Underneath that unsophisticated exterior we see, I suspect, there's a brilliant mind at work."

"Thank God!" Adrian exclaimed in relief as he peered out the window again. "I see her coming."

Sugar rolled her eyes. "What did I tell you? You have to have a little faith."

Later that day, Ariadne sat in the library alone, shuffling through a stack of magazines, when she found a *Paris Match*. Staring at the cover, she let out a groan, and let the magazine drop as if she'd been defeated.

Sugar, who walked into the room at that moment, came over and sat down beside her. "What is it, darling?"

Ariadne pointed a finger at the floor. Staring up at them was a glamorous cover shot of Nikoletta Papadaki.

"It's me . . . and yet it isn't me!"

"Only on the surface," Sugar said. She gestured at the magazine cover with disgust. "Believe me, she may be your twin, but Nikoletta is totally unlike you, Ariadne. We've told you before, but I can't emphasize it enough. She has no heart and no soul, and no sense whatsoever of right and wrong. *Zilch*. It's amazing. It actually stuns me when I encounter it." Tapping a hand on the coffee table for emphasis, she added, "Someone who can live without a conscience."

She looked into Ariadne's eyes. "Think about it. *Without a conscience*." Sugar sighed. "Nikoletta actually believes the entire world revolves around her. And you know something? In many ways, it does. At least the part of the world she encounters." Sugar rose to her feet. "Why do you think we're so desperate to replace her? And why do you think you have to say yes?" Without waiting for an answer, she excused herself and left the library.

For a long time Ariadne stared at the *Paris Match* cover. Finally, with trembling hands, she picked it up and turned to the cover article inside.

It consisted mostly of glamorous photographs of Nikoletta interspersed with some more serious shots to illustrate the text's message. On one page was Nikoletta swirling and laughing on a ballroom floor, wearing a gown that exposed a generous portion of her ample breasts and the full length of one shapely leg. On the page opposite was a grim picture of a toxic-waste dump. Ariadne flipped the page. Once again Nikoletta was glamorously posed, entertaining friends at her various apartments and country houses around the world. Opposite the spread was a black-and-white aerial photograph of a huge steel plant that belched smoke into the air. The picture had been taken in Belarus, the copy noted.

Ariadne was repulsed, but she flipped the page yet again. Nikoletta was posed in her pinks, riding to the hounds, and opposite that, again in stark black-and-white, big-eyed children, some with injuries covered in filthy-looking bandages, were depicted working in deplorable factories. Then a series of small photos of Nikoletta hobnobbing with high society, leaders in government and industry, and movie stars.

Ariadne put the magazine down. She had seen countless images of her sister at this point and listened to the horror stories that Sugar and the others had told her. But the photographs and scant copy in this magazine summed everything up in a very powerful manner. The article was a sobering indictment, and the full import of what Sugar, Adrian, Angelo, and Yves had been telling her finally struck home as it hadn't before.

She forced herself to pick the magazine up again and flipped to the next page. It was a montage of old photographs of Nikoletta at various stages in her life. In one she was shown coming down the boarding ramp of a yacht, followed by her parents.

Her parents. My *parents.*

Ariadne studied the picture closely, then placed the magazine on top of the stack on the floor. She sat there for a long time lost in thought, considering her alternatives. Later—much later—she heard someone stirring about in the kitchen.

She was close to a decision, but she had one more important question she had to ask.

The next day Ariadne asked Sugar to tell Adrian, Yves, and Angelo that she wished to speak to all of them in the library. Now, gathered there, they all suspected that the young woman had decided what to do, but they had no idea what that decision would be.

"I have never had riches, nor have I exercised power," Ariadne began slowly. "And I can't say that I hunger for either."

"Yes, but just think, Ariadne," Adrian interrupted, "you have a one-in-a-billion chance to become richer and more powerful than many world leaders. This is your opportunity to have those things you've never had before."

"Adrian, I think that you've failed to understand what Ariadne is all about," Sugar said, exasperation evident in her voice. "In fact, you missed the point of what she just said. She doesn't hunger for riches or power. What she's trying to say is that she needs a valid reason to replace Niki. Something more than money and power."

Adrian stiffened. "I was merely pointing out the facts."

"And what happens to Nikoletta if I should trade places with her?" Ariadne asked hesitantly. "She certainly doesn't sound like the passive type. How would you take her out of the picture? I mean, she is my twin sister, after all."

"Our best choice, Ariadne . . . our *only* choice as we see it, is to have you, posing as Niki, commit her sister, Ariadne, to a private clinic. One where escape is impossible." Adrian paused, choosing his words carefully. He knew that their solution would horrify Ariadne, and he wanted to soften the blow as much as possible.

"There are a number of places where wealthy people park their relatives," he went on. "The clinics are enormously expensive, as you can imagine, and they are quite luxurious, like the best resorts."

"What kind of people are in these places?" Ariadne inquired.

"Sometimes they're mentally ill, or troubled in some way or other," Adrian replied. "Friends of mine have a lovely daughter who suffers from manic depression, and so far doctors haven't been able to control it with drugs or anything else. When she goes into a deep depression, they check her into one of these clinics to protect her from herself until her mood swings back up. There are all sorts of situations."

"And Nikoletta? What would the clinic be told?"

"That Niki—or Ariadne, in this case—has been kept a family secret because of her psychotic states, but that unfortunately the Papadaki family can no longer take care of her at home because she's become so dangerous to herself and others. She would be extremely well taken care of, but held incommunicado and unable to stir up trouble. The staff, which is accustomed to delusional behavior, would ignore all of her attempts at bribery and ascribe any tales she might tell as fiction."

Ariadne looked mortified.

"I know, I know," Sugar commiserated, stroking Ariadne's back. "It's not a pleasant solution, but it's the only viable one."

"So I'm to imprison her."

"There's no use pretending," Sugar replied. "That's more or less what it amounts to."

The ensuing silence was long and drawn out. Finally Ariadne spoke. "You've given me a lot to think about, and I need to search deep within my soul and think this through. I'm going outside to take a walk, if you don't mind, and I'll talk to you later."

Chapter Twenty

❧

Ariadne ventured out into the fields and on into the woodland. Without seeking it out, she wound up at the same clearing where she had been before, where the huge hemlock had fallen, providing a perch for her to sit down and think. Shafts of light that were filtered through the trees angled across the clearing, making it look like the interior of a church.

Sitting on the moss- and lichen-speckled tree, she drew her feet up and leaned back against the natural rest created by the curve of the tree's uprooted base. Staring up into the treetops, she tried to focus on the awful choice that she faced. *It's all so complicated,* she thought, *and there is no simple solution.* The ethereal quiet of the woodland was interrupted by the crunch of someone's boots on the path, and Ariadne jerked up, although she knew at once that it must be ever-watchful Matt.

He stopped in his tracks when he saw her, his expression tentative. Once again, she was struck by his physical appeal, the fit body that his clothes seemed barely able to contain.

"I should've known that you would stop here," he said guiltily. "I've disturbed you again." He had hoped that she would stop here and had deliberately stumbled across her, but he didn't want to tell her that.

Ariadne heard the guilt in his voice. "It's . . . all right," she said.

"I'll leave you alone," he offered.

"You're here, aren't you?" she said in a matter-of-fact voice. After a pause, she added, "Actually, I could use somebody to talk to." As angry as she'd been with Matt, she was glad he was here. In her loneliness and confusion, he was a comforting presence.

"Are you sure?" he asked, tentatively taking another step in her direction.

She nodded. "Yes. I'm positive."

Matt heaved himself up onto the tree and sat down. "I've missed being with you," he said. "I've missed you more than you'll ever know."

"But you *have* been here," she replied in a slightly tart tone. "We've both been here."

"You know what I mean, Ariadne," he said impatiently. "I want it to be like it was before."

She looked into his eyes and saw the truth that they expressed, then gazed down into her lap. Their familiarity had been an easy one, and besides, she was as drawn to him as ever. "I . . . I wish it could be like it was before, too, but it's all so complicated."

He nodded. "You're in a real fix."

"Do you mind telling me what you think?" she asked.

"I think that most people in your situation wouldn't hesitate to take them up on their offer. After all, Nikoletta Papadaki is very rich and powerful. She can have anything in the world that she wants, and that means that you could have all the same things." He began kicking the trunk with his heel. "I don't think most people would even see this as a dilemma. They would go straight for the power and money without giving it a second thought. But you're different, and you're in a real moral dilemma."

"Yes," she admitted. "At least that's the way I feel."

"On the other hand," Matt said, looking down at his clasped hands, "think about the good you could do if you did take Nikoletta's place. What you could do for the world would be immense. There's no question about that. As it is, she's a destroyer, and she'll stop at nothing to get richer and richer and more and more powerful." His kicking had become more insistent. "You could change that, Ariadne. In one fell swoop. You could do so much good for the world through the company instead of handling things the way your sister is. But remember, you have to follow your own heart, Ariadne." He paused and reached over and touched the hand she had placed on the tree. "You have a good heart. Listen to what it's telling you."

Ariadne remembered the last time they had touched. Now, as then, she felt excitement course through her body, and she wanted him again. Despite what had happened, she discovered that she wanted him more than ever.

"I—I will," she said, looking down at their hands.

He followed her gaze and gently squeezed her hand in his. "I hope that you can find it in your heart to forgive me, Ariadne. I meant it when I said that I care for you, regardless of what's happened, and now I feel more strongly than ever, if that's possible."

He scooted next to her, and she immediately felt a kind of power emanating from his close presence. That and his masculine scent created a stirring within her that she couldn't deny.

"I haven't been able to get you out of my mind," he continued, "and being here with you has been . . . well, it's been a real trial."

"A trial?"

He nodded. "Because I've wanted you so much."

"I . . . well . . . I thought about you, too."

He smiled, and she thought it was one of the most wonderful smiles she'd ever seen. She felt her heart begin to race.

Matt put an arm around her shoulders and hugged her. "Please forgive me," he said softly. He leaned toward her and brushed her cheek with his lips.

Ariadne had never felt so desired as she felt now, and the stirring deep down inside her overcame any hesitation she had. Matt embraced her, expelling a rush of breath that was a mixture of relief and desire. He kissed her lips with a moan and pulled her closer. She put her arms around him and returned his kiss, giving in to her yearning.

"I've wanted this so much," Matt whispered. "I've wanted you and missed you so much." He brushed his lips across her forehead and down her cheeks, then kissed and licked her ears and throat.

"I've missed you, too," she said softly. Then she added, "And I forgive you, Matt."

With a new urgency he kissed her deeply, his tongue exploring the depths of her sweet mouth, while his hands ran slowly up and down her spine.

She relished his arms about her and his kisses as never before, and the erotic flames of desire that he had stirred to life in the past were rekindled, reawakening the dormant sensuousness in her loins. "I want you," she whispered. "I want you so much."

He embraced her, then withdrew slightly and looked into her eyes. "I want you, too. Here and now. I can't wait." He took her hand and slid off the fallen tree. Ariadne slipped down and let him guide her into the thick of the woods. He stopped when they reached a small glade where the ground was thick with ferns sprouting from the moss-covered earth. Turning to her, he put his arms around her again and held her close, kissing her tenderly and deeply.

Ariadne sighed with desire, returning his kisses, her arms on his broad shoulders. Matt moaned and pulled her closer. She could feel his urgency pressed hard against her through his khakis, and her breath caught in her throat as she remembered the erotic pleasure their love-making had brought her. Gently, Matt drew her down with him until they were both on their knees among the ferns, their lips still joined in a kiss, their arms still about each other. He ran his hands up and down her back, then massaged her rounded buttocks before pressing her firmly against his engorged manhood. Ariadne slid a hand between them and lightly stroked his hardness. Matt moaned again, kissing her more deeply, then licking and kissing her ears and neck, one of his hands exploring her ample breasts through the soft cotton shift she was wearing.

Ariadne swooned with desire as she felt her nipples harden against his touch. Drawing back, she whispered in a breathy voice, "Ooooh, Matt. Please. I want you. I want you . . . now."

He gently laid her on the ground and lay beside her, gazing into her eyes as he placed a hand between her thighs and began tenderly stroking the mound there. Ariadne reached down and pressed his hardness again. Matt gasped, then slid his hand under her loose shift, inexorably trailing up her thighs to the cleft between them. The thong she wore was damp with her desire for him, and he slipped his hand inside it and began caressing her swollen lips. Ariadne mewled with passion, and her body trembled with excitement.

He kissed her again as he drew her thong down, Ariadne shifting to help him take it off completely. He quickly unzipped his trousers, pulling them down with his briefs at the same time. His manhood sprang free, and Ariadne encircled it with her hand. Matt sucked in his breath, but let her delicately stroke him. "Oh, my God. I can't wait any longer," he rasped.

Drawing her shift up to expose her golden mound, he gently mounted her, letting Ariadne guide him to her.

As he entered her, she swooned with pleasure and spread her legs wide to receive him. Matt moved slowly at first, savoring the exquisite sensation of his cock inside her, but he couldn't hold back long. He had ached for this moment, and in his fervent desire for her he began to rapidly move in and out, finally thrusting with all his might.

Ariadne cried out in ecstasy. The joy was almost too much to bear. She felt engulfed by him—physically and emotionally—yet pushed against his mighty groin for more, her own yearning as powerful as his. In only moments she felt the first wave of orgasm overcome her, and she began thrashing beneath him, throwing her head from side to side.

"Matt . . . oh, Matt . . . ," she cried. Her hands dug into his back as she held him to her as tightly as possible.

Her joy urged him on, and he pumped against her with abandon, unable to control his desire for satisfaction. With a mighty heave, he emitted a gasp and thrust himself inside her as far as possible, his body bucking against hers as he flooded her with his juices. He collapsed atop her, panting as if he were a long-distance runner, but his mouth covered hers, kissing her lustily and deeply.

"Ariadne . . . ," he rasped. "You're so . . . wonderful." He hugged her as if he would never let her go, his powerful chest heaving against hers as he caught his breath.

On the mossy ground they lay together, the dappled light on their spent bodies. When he eased off her at last, he brought her with him, and they lay face-to-face on their sides. He kissed her brow and eyes, her nose and cheeks, her lips and chin, all with the greatest tenderness, as if she were a delicate porcelain doll that might break. He gazed into her dark eyes, a smile on his sensuous lips. "I . . . I'm so . . . so thankful for you," he whispered. "I've missed this—you—so much in the last few days. We've been here together but not together."

She held his gaze. "I've missed you, too, Matt."

He hugged her again. "And I'm so happy that you understand now. That I really do have feelings for you."

Ariadne nodded but remained silent. She was wary of stating her own powerful feelings for him, even though she believed him and trusted him.

Perhaps she was being irrational, she thought, but she was afraid of putting a jinx on what they had together.

Matt brushed her lips with his. "And you've really forgiven me?"

She nodded again. "How could I not?"

He kissed her again. "Oh, Ariadne, you are so wonderful," he said with puppyish exuberance, squeezing her to him.

She smiled. "You are, too, Matt."

Matt slowly brushed a hand up and down her back and kissed her lips passionately, his tongue delving into her mouth. She ran a hand through his tousled hair, then across his broad, muscular shoulders. His lips moved to her neck, and she threw her head back as his tongue licked her. She could feel him inside her, swelling with hardness again, and she moaned with pleasure as they began making love again. They savored each other slowly, as if in their own world, a place without demands and constraints and time itself.

The man had been watching them ever since they had sat quietly talking on the fallen tree. He had seen them make love the first time, and now he observed them begin coupling yet again. *Bloody hell*, he thought. *She's a fucking nympho. Who the hell is she?* He reluctantly glanced down at his watch. He could hardly wait to call his boss with the news, but he realized that he had to be patient. He didn't dare make a sound. Not now. The risk of being caught was too great, and at this point that would in all likelihood entail a very messy scene. The guy could be a real bruiser, he thought. Tall and muscular, fit as they come. He didn't want to tangle with the son of a bitch. He would have to wait until they were finished with the old in-and-out and went back to the house.

Then he would get on his cell phone and call his boss. *Have I got news for her,* he thought, wondering how she was going to take it. He smiled at the mere idea of reporting this piece of news to her. The nympho on the ground, humping only a few feet away from where he was hidden, looked remarkably like his boss. He didn't know the significance of this, but he was certain that it meant something. What's more, he was sure that his boss would think so, too. *Hell,* he thought, *my description of her might provide her identity: the boss might know who the nympho is when she finds out that she looks just like her.*

He smiled again. *Bet there's going to be a bonus in this for me.*

*   *   *

A couple of days later, Ariadne asked everyone to gather in the library. It was time to give them her decision. Sugar was startled by the transformation in the young woman's mien. She was rosy-cheeked, and there was a glow of happiness about her that seemed to come from within.

Ariadne clasped her hands in her lap and quietly said, "I've made up my mind."

Adrian, Yves, Sugar, and Angelo waited silently, knowing better than to push for her answer at this point.

"Everything inside me tells me not to go through with this masquerade. Pulling off an undertaking of such magnitude is surely near impossible. There are too many things that can go wrong."

She paused and sighed, then continued. "I weighed all the reasons for deciding against it, and compared them with various things Nikoletta has done or is planning to do." She smiled humorlessly. "Although my father robbed me of my identity, I am, for better or worse, his daughter by blood. And morally, I think that I have no choice but to do what is best for the common good."

There was an almost palpable feeling of relief in the room, but no one voiced a word of congratulation.

Ariadne raised her chin with dignity and pride. "So. Now that we have that out of the way, when do we begin?" she asked, breaking the silence.

"There is no time like the present," Adrian replied, smiling with relief, "especially since time is the one luxury we can't afford. The grand opening of the new PPHL headquarters is in seven and a half weeks."

Seven and a half weeks? Ariadne thought. *That's how long I have to transform myself into a totally new person.*

She suddenly felt queasy.

A flurry of e-mail and cell phone messages from Nikoletta stirred Adrian, Sugar, Yves, and Angelo into action. They had thus far managed to escape Nikoletta's radar, but now they had to resume their duties at PPHL. They decided to take turns teaching Ariadne how to transform herself into a convincing Nikoletta. Angelo would be her first instructor. Adrian, Yves, and Sugar left with hurried good-byes, leaving Ariadne in Angelo's firm, capable hands.

"You know that I hold Nikoletta responsible for the death of my daughter," he told her, "and you are the only person who can make up for it."

Ariadne immediately felt the weight of an awesome responsibility on her shoulders. "I will do my best to succeed," she said.

"I know that," he said gently, "but if our endeavor fails, I hope you won't feel that it's your fault. We're asking an awful lot of you. Now, then, to begin with I'm going to show you video clips of Nikoletta. There's a mountain of material, so I suggest that you make yourself comfortable before we get started."

Angelo began feeding the videos into the player. After hours of watching them, broken up by time to eat together and discuss them, Ariadne was dumbfounded. While only a small record of her own life existed, her twin sister seemed to have had almost every hour documented. The sheer number of videos was dizzying.

Ariadne watched endless footage of Nikoletta at parties, fund-raisers, and sporting events. Winter bobsled runs and ski slaloms at fancy resorts, romps on water skis and Jet Skis in warm waters the world over, and horseback rides and sports car rallies—all of the videos reminded Ariadne that she had never participated in any of these activities, much less expertly as Nikoletta did. She watched hordes of friends and acquaintances as they greeted her sister, air-kissing, hugging, shaking hands, often using pet nicknames. Many of them were celebrities, even film stars, whom Angelo needlessly pointed out, giving the faces names. Ariadne had no problem learning who they all were, since she had seen so many of them on TV, in the movies, or in magazines or newspapers. She thought that she had even seen Nikoletta in magazines, but she couldn't be certain. She'd never gotten the kind of magazines that featured pictures of celebrities, but she had the feeling that Nikoletta was familiar and not just because they were twins.

Oddly, no one had ever pointed out that she looked like Nikoletta, but Ariadne attributed that to several factors. For the first ten years of her life, she had lived in a very remote spot on a Greek island, a part of the island where tourists never ventured and there were no stores that sold magazines or tabloids. There was no village at all where her foster family lived, and even on the rare occasions when they went into the town on Hydra, she was still a child. No one would have thought to compare her to the daughter of very wealthy Greeks who lived primarily in Paris, London, and New York. At that time, Nikoletta, a child also, would seldom have appeared in magazines or newspapers.

When Ariadne was taken to Connecticut, she lived in a tiny hamlet with foster parents who never bought the kind of magazines and newspapers in which Nikoletta would have appeared. Even at boarding school, they were rarely if ever available. Besides, Ariadne reasoned, Nikoletta always wore a lot of makeup, her hair was styled and lightened, and she was never seen in anything but designer clothing, even if a bikini. Ariadne had hardly ever worn any makeup and had never even been in a beauty salon. Her foster mother cut her hair, and it had never been styled. As for clothes, jeans and hand-me-down sweaters and T-shirts and inexpensive sneakers had been her uniform. When she'd entered Williams College, she'd been able to buy some clothes, but they were primarily the gym clothes that nearly everyone wore on a daily basis. She did have a few nicer things now, but nothing that Nikoletta would be caught dead in.

The old expression "Clothes make the man" came to mind, and Ariadne thought that in this case it applied. Only here, it was the clothing and a whole lot more that made the *woman*. Nikoletta's grooming, her daily use of makeup, and her expensive haircuts and styles, along with the costly designer clothing that made up her wardrobe, made her look very different from her twin. Strip all that away, Ariadne thought, and Nikoletta would look just like her. Performing the reverse procedure would turn Ariadne into Nikoletta, or one of the Nikolettas.

For what amazed Ariadne more than anything else was that there seemed to be many Nikolettas, all rolled up into one person: Nikoletta the party girl was joined by Nikoletta the fashion statement, the businesswoman, the philanthropist, the seductress, the publicity hound, the hostess, and the sportswoman. And Ariadne had a strong sense of Nikoletta the bitch, a presence that somehow seemed to pervade all the other images.

Ariadne felt like a voyeur watching the videos, but in a strange way, she felt that she was watching herself. No, not herself, she thought. Nikoletta was truly different in every way. She didn't walk; she strutted as though she owned the world. She gestured extravagantly. She smoked on occasion, something Ariadne didn't even want to try. She cursed like a sailor in a number of languages.

The longer Ariadne watched the videos, the heavier was the sinking feeling that came over her. *I was right,* she thought. *Pulling off this charade is impossible.*

After hours of viewing Nikoletta, overload began to set in, and even after she turned the television set off, images of her twin sister swam in front of her eyes. During a lunch break, Ariadne and Angelo had lunch on trays.

Ariadne picked up her fork but put it back down.

"What's wrong?" Angelo asked.

Ariadne shook her head. "I . . . I'm just not hungry," she replied. The truth was, she thought food might make her sick.

"Are you beginning to panic?" Angelo asked.

"I do feel overwhelmed," she replied. "I feel as if my entire life has been an awful joke based on lies, and it seems that's what my future's going to be, too."

"I won't try to humor you," Angelo said. "This is going to be extremely tough. You can see now that your sister is a complicated and brilliant young woman. But you have what she has plus something else. Something she doesn't have."

Ariadne looked at him in amazement. "That person I've been watching could run circles around me. She is so accomplished and beautiful and savvy. I can't even imagine being compared with her."

"Ariadne, don't forget that you're twins. You, too, are beautiful, and you're extremely bright. And you have heart, something your sister doesn't have." He touched her tenderly. "You can do this, Ariadne. I know you can. For yourself, for us, for my poor Bianca and the others who've suffered—and still are—because of her."

She felt tears forming in her eyes. "I'll try," she promised.

"Now, pick up that fork, young lady," he said. "You're going to need energy."

Chapter Twenty-one

❧

East Hampton, Long Island

Summoned to Nikoletta's shingled "cottage"—a sprawling estate with indoor and outdoor swimming pools and tennis courts—tucked behind the dunes by the ocean, Sugar arrived by helicopter from New York City as dusk was falling. As the helicopter neared the mansion, she could see that the circular driveway was lined with trucks and vans, and two huge party tents had been erected on the lawn, along with outdoor dance floors and a stage. Potted tropical trees and flowers and miles of strung lights were everywhere.

I wonder what the occasion is, she thought. Nearly always apprised of Nikoletta's big parties and often invited, she knew nothing about this one. As the helicopter began to descend to the helipad, she noticed that the vans and trucks were being loaded, and the party planner's work was being dismantled. *Has there already been a party?* she wondered. That was unlikely because she would have read about it in the papers or already had a phone call from a friend. *What's going on?*

After the helicopter landed, she was immediately whisked to the house by one of the retinue of plainclothes security men who guarded Nikoletta and her various homes at all times. In the house, the servants were all virtually on tiptoe, and Sugar received a subdued reception.

"What's going on?" she asked Percy, the requisite British butler.

"Madam is on a rampage," he whispered.

"So what else is new?" Sugar responded.

Percy smirked and looked suspiciously around before speaking. "It's Frans," he whispered, a hand hiding his mouth as if someone who could read lips might be spying. "The young man. He refused to cooperate with her birthday party plans for him."

"Oh, I see," Sugar said sotto voce. "No wonder she's furious."

"She planned the 'surprise' for him anyway, but he still refused to make an appearance, so you can imagine. Invitations had gone out, guests RSVP'd, the orchestra was hired, the DJ. The caterers have been here all day—everything was set up!—and still Frans said no."

"Small wonder she's throwing a fit. She must be pulling her hair out."

"Very good guess," Percy intimated, rolling his eyes. "She said to send you straight up to her suite when you arrive. Shall I take you up?"

"I can handle this," Sugar said, flapping a hand. "I'm used to her fits."

"Good luck."

Sugar hurried up the gracefully curving stairwell and down the hallway to Nikoletta's suite. Knocking on the door, she took a deep breath to prepare herself for the unpleasant encounter.

The door was snapped open and thrown back, and Nikoletta in all her fury stood there prepared to screech at whoever was disturbing her. "What—?" she began, then saw that it was Sugar. "Where the hell have you been?" she said, her voice low and menacing. "I've had you called and called and left messages everywhere for you. Don't you even answer your e-mail anymore?"

Sugar, an old hand at dealing with Nikoletta, smiled. "And a good evening to you, too," she replied calmly. "Aren't you going to ask me in?"

Nikoletta sullenly stepped back to allow her into the room.

"As for my whereabouts, I was at a spa." She turned her face this way and that. "What do you think? Refreshed, no?"

"If you want to know the truth, I can't tell a bit of difference," Nikoletta said. "At least no positive improvement."

Sugar shrugged, unfazed by her nasty, spoiled boss. She had developed a Teflon shield as far as the younger woman's barbs were concerned, and even if she had been to a spa, she wouldn't have expected a different answer.

"Although it *might* become a better evening if someone like you could talk some sense into Frans," Nikoletta added hopefully.

"*Me?*" Sugar pointed a beautifully manicured nail at her chest and suppressed a laugh. "What's the problem, darling? And why do you think I could help solve it?" She didn't want Nikoletta to know that Percy had told her anything.

"Don't act like you don't know a thing or two about men, Sugar," Nikoletta said. "With all of your marriages and affairs, you must know something. You even have them chasing after you now. And at your *age*." She said *age* as if it were the filthiest word in the English language.

Sugar patted her hair in a girlish manner. She enjoyed playing with this vicious beast sometimes, although she had to be very careful. She knew she could go only so far. "Well, maybe I have picked up a thing or two along the way," she said. "That's one advantage of age, Niki, darling. It gives you more time to play with more men."

"Anyway, I've planned this big birthday party for Frans, and he refuses to cooperate. It's like everything else I've tried to do for him. I've tried to introduce him to major producers and directors, but he won't show up. He hasn't even been modeling. And now with this party! He won't even leave his room."

"So he's here?"

"Yes, I finally managed to coax him out from the city, but he didn't know I was going to go ahead and have the party. When he got here and saw what was going on, he locked himself up and won't speak to me, except to say no."

"Oh, dear," Sugar said in a semblance of empathy.

"He might listen to you," Nikoletta said. "He'll listen to anyone but me."

The reason he might listen to me, Sugar thought, *is because he knows I genuinely loved Bianca and have grieved for her. Unlike you, Nikoletta.*

"And to think of all the trouble and expense I went through!" Nikoletta went on. "Jesus Christ, you'd think Bianca died only yesterday. And it's been . . . what? Who remembers? Long enough."

Perhaps for Frans it seems as if it were yesterday, Sugar thought. *After all, he was in love with Bianca.* "We all grieve in different ways and for different lengths of time," Sugar murmured. "I remember that when old Rosebury died it came as a real shock. It took me quite a while to get over it."

"Well, Frans will be grieving, all right, when he runs out of money!" Nikoletta hissed. She flopped into a chair.

Sugar remained uncharacteristically silent, arming herself to listen to Nikoletta's woes.

"I know what you're thinking," Nikoletta said. "Why don't I just get over him? Just kick him out and be done with him."

"I wasn't actually," Sugar said, "but—"

"Maybe you'd understand better if you saw the way he's *hung*."

"I'm sure I can use my imagination in that department," Sugar said with a dry laugh.

"Like a *horse*!" Nikoletta said smugly.

Sugar cleared her throat. "That's great, Niki, but it's not everything. Maybe it would be better if Frans pushed off. He's making you unhappy, and he's certainly not happy, so what's to be gained by pursuing him?"

"I just told you," Nikoletta snapped.

"Oh, I forgot," Sugar said blithely. "Of course. *That.* Well, boy toys aren't always cooperative, I guess, so you're going to have to decide whether or not to put up with it. If I were you, I'd just find myself a gigolo that's hung like Frans and put him on the payroll. The world's full of them. Ask any rich woman from Palm Beach to Portofino."

Ignoring Sugar, Nikoletta said, "Go to his room, and see if he'll talk to you."

"I'll see what I can do," Sugar said, rising to her feet. "Which room?"

"On down the hallway on the left. The closest one."

Sugar immediately left and went to Frans's door. She knocked on it softly and called his name. "Frans, darling. It's Sugar. May I have a word with you, please?"

She heard no response, but waited at the door patiently. Finally, she knocked again. "Frans? Please, darling. Just a word. I won't even come in."

Sugar heard a soft click as he unlocked the door. He stood in the opening looking at her sheepishly. Sugar discovered that she had not grown immune to his rare physical handsomeness. He truly was a beauty to behold, troubled though he was.

"Darling, I know you're still grieving for Bianca," Sugar said, "so I'll only keep you for a minute."

Frans made a barely detectable nod of his head.

"You won't make an appearance at this party, will you?" Sugar asked.

He shook his long, blond-streaked mane. "No," he said in a whisper.

"Okay," she said. "Then I'll tell Nikoletta that is your final word."

"Thanks, Sugar," he said. "You're . . . a . . . friend."

"I hope so," she replied. "If you need anything, let me know. I'll be leaving soon, but you've got my number in Manhattan."

He nodded. "Thanks," he repeated.

She kissed his cheek. "Take care, darling." She had lots of advice for him—like *Get the hell out of Nikoletta's life for your own sake*—but this was neither the time nor the place to give it.

He softly shut and locked the door, and Sugar went back to Nikoletta's room, preparing what she would say.

"Well?" Nikoletta asked, gazing up at her.

"He's simply not up to a party, Nikoletta," she said. "I think he ought to consider seeing a therapist. I think he's deeply depressed. If I were you, I wouldn't put any pressure on him."

"Why? Do you think he's going to wig out on me or something?"

"I certainly think it's possible," Sugar replied. "And I don't think one party is worth it. What it might do to him, I mean. If you could get him out of that room, that is."

"Damn," Nikoletta swore. "I don't want him getting all mental on me. I hate that."

"Then maybe the best policy right now is to leave him alone," Sugar said, "because something like that might happen."

Nikoletta sighed heavily. "I hate this. Hate it, hate it, *hate* it."

"Maybe he'll pull out of it soon," Sugar offered. "Maybe with plenty of rest and no pressure."

"All right," Nikoletta said at last, gritting her teeth.

"There's something I need to talk to you about if you don't mind," Sugar said carefully, hoping that the change in subject would not upset Nikoletta.

"What?"

"I ran into Eviana Chen from *Vogue*. You know how they have that '*Vogue* Index Checklist' feature in the back pages of every issue? Using various celebrities as inspiration and then picking out what new 'in' things that celebrity might buy to suit her style—dresses, bags, candles, shoes, whatever?"

"I take it you're going somewhere with this?" Nikoletta growled. "Not just testing my patience with idle chitchat?"

Sugar ignored her barbed comment. "Do you have any idea how hard it is to make that 'checklist,' even if you're a bona fide movie star? And you'd better be a sensational cover-girl star at that. Anyway, the instant I saw Eviana, I had a lightbulb moment. Instead of going through our publicity department, I cornered her and out-and-out volunteered you and got a verbal commitment. Can you believe it? On the spot!" She smiled triumphantly.

But if she had expected a reaction from Nikoletta, none was forthcoming. Sugar was not to be deterred.

"Best of all," she crooned, "is that they have plenty of file photos of you, so you don't need to do a thing. Not even pose. But they will need some display stuff. Not for actual use in taking pictures, but to get a real feeling for the Nikoletta Papadaki style. All that means is, an editor and a stylist will have to go through your closets, borrow a few items, then put together an entirely 'new' wardrobe based on *le style* Papadaki. What do you think?"

"I hate other people touching my clothes!"

"Oh, for heaven's sake, Niki. It's not as if they're going to *wear* them. They're only going to hang them on a garment rack. Besides," Sugar went on, going in for the kill, "would you rather they chose Halle Berry or Kate Hudson or Sarah Jessica Parker? Remember, it's not only free publicity— it's the cachet."

Nikoletta emitted a sigh of boredom. "Okay, okay," she conceded, but added ominously, "It better not interfere with my schedule."

"It won't," Sugar promised quickly.

"They'll have to go through my closets in the city. I only keep seasonal stuff out here. And I want you there in person when they choose things. I expect you to keep an inventory of every item taken out of the house. We are clear on that, aren't we?"

"Crystal clear."

"Then I suppose I'll let Percy know," Nikoletta said.

"You won't regret it," Sugar said, knowing full well that if all went according to plan, this would be one decision that Nikoletta would regret for the rest of her life. She flashed one of her biggest smiles. "I'll let you know when *Vogue* plans to run the column."

Nikoletta Papadaki is beginning to piss me off, the PI thought. Unbelievably, he hadn't been able to get hold of her. Clients like her were usually chewing on their fingernails waiting for his calls and were in the habit of leaving messages for him at all hours of the night and day regardless of his instructions otherwise. But this woman had him stumped.

What the hell is she up to? he wondered. She was young and beautiful and, he suspected, the type who might disappear briefly for a little bit of off-the-record self-indulgence. *Gone on a bender? Holed up screwing her brains out?* He had no idea, but it was highly unusual for a woman in her position to suddenly make herself unavailable, especially considering the circumstances.

He'd tried every number he had for her, starting with her most private cell number, but hadn't reached her. He'd left messages everywhere, on voice mail and with various assistants—even a couple of butlers—without getting a response from her for days. But now his caller ID indicated that the elusive Ms. Papadaki was on the other end of the line, trying to get hold of him.

"I've been trying to reach you," he said, answering his cell on the third ring.

"I've been busy," Nikoletta responded petulantly. "What have you got for me?"

"It's not easy spying on the activity at this place. I'll tell you that," the PI responded.

"You're not getting paid for 'easy,'" Nikoletta said.

"I'm not complaining," he huffed. "I'm just making an observation."

"What's the problem?"

"They have a live-in security man at this place twenty-four hours a day," the PI said. "He's all over the place. Patrols the grounds. Constantly checks the house and outbuildings. Very unusual, don't you think?"

Why would Adrian have a security man at all? Nikoletta wondered. *Much less 24-7?* "It *is* unusual," she agreed.

"Anyway, this guy makes it difficult to nose around, if you know what I mean."

Nikoletta expelled an impatient breath. "You've been leaving messages all over the place and ringing all my numbers off the hook, and that's all you've got to report to me?"

The PI chortled. "Not exactly," he replied. "The security guy can't be watching out for the place when he's screwing some dame."

Nikoletta's ears perked up. *This might be interesting,* she thought. "You're sure about that?"

"Saw it with my own eyes," he said. "But that's not all."

"What else?" Nikoletta asked.

"The dame he's balling?" The PI paused dramatically.

"Yes?"

"She looks just like you."

"What?" Nikoletta cried. "Are you kidding me?"

"No way. I've seen her up close and personal, you might say." He chortled lewdly again. "And believe me, she could pass for you."

Nikoletta began anxiously brushing hair away from her face, trying to get her mind around this piece of news. *A look-alike? What in the world is Adrian up to?* she thought. "Anything else?"

"That's it for now," he said.

Nikoletta suddenly wanted to hurry him off the phone because she had a lot to think about. "Good work," she conceded. "Check back in with me, tomorrow at the latest, unless you've got something before then."

"If I can get hold of you."

Nikoletta ignored the barb. "You'll be able to get me," she said mildly, already lost in thought.

"Okay, but—" he began, but she'd already hung up.

Nikoletta sat with her chin in her hands, staring off into space for a long time. She could understand Adrian's having a security man at his estate in the country. After all, he had a lot of valuable paintings and antiques in the house. Plus, she thought, some of the horses in the stables had set him back a big chunk of change. Anyway, lots of people in the country had live-in help who doubled as security. But this was different, she decided. This guy patrolled the grounds. He was constantly checking out the house and outbuildings, according to the PI. *And* he was making it with some chick who looked like her.

Nikoletta swiveled around in her chair restlessly. *What the hell is Adrian up to?* She idly picked a pencil up and began tapping it against the top of her desk.

There could be only one answer, she decided. This woman had been brought in to serve as an impostor. She tapped the pencil against her desk with more force. *That's it. He's found somebody that he can use to replace me.* She reached for the telephone. *I'm going to give the son of a bitch a call right now and confront him with what I know.* She picked up the receiver and started to press in his number, then abruptly replaced it in its cradle.

Her lips slowly formed a smile. *I can do better than that,* she thought. *I'll plan a surprise of my own for Adrian.*

Chapter Twenty-two

❧

"*B*asta!" Angelo cursed. "No, no, no! Stop." Generally a patient man, he was at his wit's end. For days now he had been playing Professor Higgins to Ariadne's Eliza Doolittle. *To no avail,* he thought.

Ariadne was no actress. As hard as she struggled to imitate Nikoletta's movements and accent from watching the videos, she had thus far failed to deliver anything approaching the real thing.

"You have to *be* Nikoletta!" Angelo beseeched her. "Don't you see? You must *think* like Nikoletta. You must truly step into her shoes and fill them. You must *become* her."

Ariadne collapsed wearily on a sofa. "I'm trying," she groaned, raking her hands through her hair. "It's just . . . she and I are so different."

"Remember, Ariadne. You own the world! It's yours and anything in it that you want. That's the key to Nikoletta. The way she thinks. There's nothing that you can't have. Nothing that you can't do."

Ariadne's eyes brightened. She knew this about her sister, of course. She had seen that in the videos. But Angelo's words concisely summed up the attitude.

"You can see it in her strut," Angelo went on. "The way she carries herself."

"I think I need a pair of stiletto-heeled shoes," Ariadne half joked.

"You're on to something there," Angelo agreed eagerly. "And you will have them soon. Now, then. Up you go. Let me see you walk across the room, then turn and walk back toward me. When you reach me, give me an order as if I were your secretary."

Ariadne pushed herself up off the sofa. *Here we go again,* she thought, wondering why she had ever agreed to such a proposition.

She did better this time, but from his pursed lips she could tell she still wasn't close. "Let's move on," he said brusquely.

There were many more tasks as well: conquering her sister's signature, which required endless practice so it would not only pass muster but seem effortless; learning her speech patterns and her difficult accent, which was a mixture of American English and British, with a touch of Swiss German and Greek.

"Don't worry so much," Angelo told her. "We can always pretend you're suffering from a hoarse throat for a while. It won't work for a long period of time, but it'll help us out temporarily."

One morning Angelo had arrived with flash cards. On them were photographs of Nikoletta's household staff and her "five hundred closest friends," as Angelo cynically called them, along with acquaintances, including identities, nicknames, and their relationships to Nikoletta. Ariadne must be able to recall all of this information in an instant. She also had to recognize business friends and foes, top company managers, heads of state and government employees, even hairdressers, manicurists, masseuses, pilots, copilots, and stewards—a few of whom served more than drinks and meals aboard the Papadaki fleet of corporate jets, Ariadne was appalled to learn. In short, everyone with whom Nikoletta dealt on a regular basis had a flash card.

And there was more. Much more.

Nikoletta's table manners, for instance. They ranged from the exquisite to the barbarian, depending upon her mercurial moods. "The most important thing to remember is that she knows exactly what is correct, no matter how complicated the table setting. How she chooses to behave is something else," Angelo told her. Ariadne had to familiarize herself with her favorite wines and champagnes, plus distinguish between the vintages. She must learn to hold her liquor and smoke cigarettes without choking, as much as she despised them.

"When you don't know what to do, be rude," Angelo advised.

All of which went entirely against Ariadne's grain.

The lessons never seemed to end. The videos ran day and night, until Ariadne thought she would scream if she saw another image of her twin sister. When her throat was sore from repeating words and phrases and coughing on cigarettes, or her eyes stung from smoke or blurred from flash cards or videos, there were dance lessons. Mock business negotiations. Compilations of gossip columns to peruse in order to learn about the latest scandals and rumors about the flash-card people.

Everything in the environment, Ariadne discovered, had been calculated to be a lesson of one kind or another. The art books and piles of auction catalogs. Even the foods she was served. Apparently Nikoletta could subsist on nothing more than caviar, foie gras, sushi, and very rare red meat. She had liked meat but virtually raw? She was repulsed.

"I'm sorry," Angelo told her, "but you have to stop making those faces."

Oddly, after several days Ariadne found that she was beginning to like most of the foods Nikoletta subsisted on.

She took the unheralded arrival of Adrian Single as an opportunity to relax and be herself.

No such luck, she discovered. "Hello, Nikoletta," he greeted her.

Ariadne's natural response was to look around to see where Nikoletta was. After a moment she realized her mistake.

"I'm sorry," she said sheepishly.

"Remember," he said, not unkindly, "Ariadne no longer exists. Only Nikoletta." He grinned wryly. "Anyway, you two, rejoice! I know it's not Christmas, but I've brought you a real treat."

He began unwrapping the package, and Ariadne felt her heart sink. He had brought architectural plans of Nikoletta's various apartments, houses, estates, and offices, plus glossy pages torn from shelter magazines featuring the same.

I should have known, she thought. *More work.*

"It's imperative that you know your way around the rooms," Adrian explained. "Otherwise, you'll arouse suspicion among the staff."

Ariadne couldn't help groaning. "More to learn! I'm already living, talking, thinking, and dreaming in Nikoletta's world!" she exclaimed. "Don't I deserve a break?"

"I know this is very difficult for you, Ariadne," Adrian commiserated, "but that's a luxury we can't afford."

"Well, the hell with it all!" she exploded. "I'm going upstairs and don't expect me to come down again until tomorrow! And don't bother getting up early, either. I intend to sleep *late*." She sniffed.

"Now, go," she added, unaware that she was gesturing grandly. "Amuse yourselves with someone else."

With that said, Ariadne swept out of the room toward the staircase and went up to her room.

A long silence ensued as Angelo and Adrian stared after her and then at each other.

"My God!" Adrian whispered. He clutched Angelo by the arms. "Angelo! Did you see what I just saw?"

"I'm afraid so."

"Afraid? Why are you afraid? I can hardly *believe* it! Congratulations are in order. You're definitely making progress."

Angelo shook his head ruefully. "What we've just witnessed isn't progress, I'm afraid. It's a poor, sweet girl we're driving to the end of her rope."

Adrian begged to differ. "I don't think so, Angelo. That was a scene worthy of Nikoletta herself. She was *exactly* like Nikoletta. It's bizarre."

"I've grown truly fond of Ariadne," Angelo murmured. "It's a shame to create a monster out of that lovely creature."

Adrian sighed. "We have a duty to fulfill. Whatever works, my friend. Whatever works." He paused, then added, "But I think you can rest assured that regardless of how well Ariadne learns to impersonate Niki, she is incapable of *becoming* Niki. Ariadne was born with a truly good nature, I believe, and we can't take that away from her."

"I hope to God you're right," Angelo said.

Frans was getting dressed, but his movements were mechanical. He gave it no thought, but simply grabbed whatever came to hand. Ironically, with no intention whatsoever, he ended up looking extremely fashionable, since his wardrobe was filled with designer clothing that had been given to him on photo shoots. His white shirt with tiny black square appliqués was half-buttoned, but at least his black-and-white paisley Versace pants were zipped shut. Around his neck was a necklace of turquoise chunks and flat silver disks, a gift from Nikoletta—in memory of Bianca, she'd told him—that he hadn't bothered to take off since he'd returned from East Hampton, and on his feet were worn black lizard pointed-toe cowboy boots, the first thing he'd tripped over when he went into the room.

He didn't look at himself in the cheval mirror that was in the closet, nor did he check himself out in the walls of mirror in the bathroom. Instead he flopped down on the living room couch to wait for the buzzer to sound. Nikoletta was sending a car and driver around to pick him up.

"Dress is casual," she'd told him on the telephone, which he took to mean it would be just the two of them, along with a few discreet servants on hand.

He was really not in the mood to go out. Without Bianca, life still had not regained its shine. Everything was devoid of meaning for him. Without her, there seemed to be no reason to go on, even though he knew that wasn't true. He *must* get out, *must* focus his mind on the *living*. He knew he had fallen into a pit of despair. But he was finding it very difficult to pull himself out of that pit.

The buzzer rang, and Frans got up off the couch to answer it. He told the driver he would be right down. He backtracked to the sofa to grab the white sport jacket he'd tossed there and snatched the bottle of Stolichnaya vodka off the coffee table. He took a few gulps, then screwed the lid back on, grabbed his keys, and left the loft.

In the backseat of Nikoletta's limo, he slumped across the red calfskin seat, slid open the built-in bar, and continued to drink during the ride uptown, having one vodka after another from one of the cut-crystal decanters. Before he reached Nikoletta's, he was smashed.

Uptown, Nikoletta Papadaki was in a good mood for various reasons. Frans's imminent arrival excited her, of course, and another mood elevator for her was the private spa in her apartment. She was presently being pampered with a chakra-balancing massage while soft Japanese koto music played in the background and a manicurist worked on her nails and a pedicurist her feet. The nail color of the day was Gumdrop. Nikoletta didn't have to go to the mountain; the mountain came to her. She had no desire to mix with the hoi polloi that frequented even Manhattan's most luxurious spas.

All in all, life could be worse, she mused, telling her masseuses and the manicurist and pedicurist to get a move on. She had to get ready and wanted plenty of time. After all, she wanted to be appropriately seductive for Frans.

Nikoletta personally greeted him at the door, wearing a sexy pale gold silk chemise trimmed in frothy lace. After she'd kissed his cheek, she wagged a finger at him. "Someone's been hitting the bottle."

"So?" he retorted. "Maybe I have a good reason."

Nikoletta stepped aside to let him in and sized him up through half-lowered lids. Actually, he'd never looked quite as attractive, perhaps because he looked as if he had just gotten out of bed after a particularly hot romp. With his face flushed, hair disheveled, clothes somewhat wrinkled if fashionable, he didn't look the perfect model. She was curious as to what kind of drunk he was: the obnoxious type who was unmanageable or the type she could wrap around her little finger. She'd certainly known more than her share of both varieties.

Frans slumped onto a down-filled sofa in the living room while she poured each of them a glass of champagne. Handing him a glass, she curled up decoratively beside him. "Now, why don't you tell Niki what's wrong, hmmm?" She trailed a finger along his thigh.

Frans gulped down the contents of his glass. "Nothing new," he said without looking at her. "I just . . . well, I miss Bianca."

"Of course you do," Nikoletta cooed. "You really loved her, and she loved you." She took a long sip of her champagne.

He smiled grimly. "A lot of good it's done us."

"I know you're being ironic," she said, "but it's true. A love like that is rare, Frans. Few people ever experience it, and as hard as it may be for you to realize now, you were very lucky to have had it at all."

Frans looked directly at her for the first time. Although his normally intense blue eyes showed the effects of his copious alcohol consumption, his expression was pensive. He didn't say anything, however, but remained silent, thinking about what she'd said.

Nikoletta picked up their glasses and went to the drinks table. *I have his attention now,* she thought with a sense of triumph. She poured refills for them both. She returned to the sofa and settled down beside him, handing him his drink.

"You know what's really crazy?" Frans said as he took the champagne.

"What?"

He gave a bitter laugh. "What's *really* crazy"—he drained his glass in one swallow, then set the flute down on the coffee table with a bang—"is that I'm still in love with her. Yet here I am. With you."

"I wouldn't call that crazy, Frans," Nikoletta responded mildly. "It's only natural. We all need friends who can console us after tragic events. I think it makes perfect sense." She gently brushed his hair aside and ran a finger down his face, then kissed his cheek chastely. Her manner was that of a close sister.

"Friends, yeah," Frans murmured. "But what I'm doing here with you, I don't know, Niki. I just don't know." He turned and gazed at her beautiful sad eyes and lush, sensuous lips, her lovely swan neck and perfect breasts, which were barely contained by the low-cut gold and lace sheath she wore.

"We've both suffered so much, Frans," she whispered as if she might burst into tears at any moment. She reached toward him, letting her hand brush against his partially exposed chest and settle on his thigh, as if seeking support. "I think . . . well, I think that Bianca, being the loving and generous person that she was, would be happy that we could help each other."

"Maybe," Frans said. He saw Nikoletta's bereft expression and heard the anguish in her voice, and his heart went out to her. She missed Bianca, too. He slid an arm around her shoulders. "You're probably right, Niki."

Nikoletta brushed her hand against his thigh, then began stroking it lightly. "I think—no, I *know*—that she would want you to be happy, Frans." Her voice was choked with emotion. She laid her head against his chest. "She was so loving that she wouldn't want it any other way."

Frans could smell her intoxicating scent and feel her heat against his body. "Yes," he murmured in agreement. "That's . . . that's the way she was."

Nikoletta's lips brushed against his chest tenderly, her tongue lightly flicking a nipple. Then she rested her lips there as if content to feel his muscular chest against them. She heard him suck in his breath and moved her hand from his thigh to the top of his low-cut trousers, and began stroking his hard abs. After a while she slowly shifted her hand, gradually slipping it beneath his trousers. She let it remain there, softly caressing him, but not venturing any farther. Not yet.

Frans's chest heaved as his breathing quickened, and he leaned over and kissed the crown of her head. He felt Nikoletta shiver at his touch, and he lifted her face to his and began kissing her. Suddenly he felt desire suffuse his being, as if he needed Nikoletta desperately, as if she had lit a spark of fire in him and he was coming back to life.

Her hand slipped around him, fully engorged now and straining against his trousers.

Frans emitted a moan of pleasure. "Why don't we go upstairs?" he murmured.

"Hmmm," she whispered.

Dinner was completely forgotten as they had sex in her bedroom. Afterward, they slept entwined in each other's arms, before awakening and making love again and again. Forgotten, for the meantime at least, was the ghost of Bianca and the harsh realities of the world beyond the walls of her bedroom. By morning, Nikoletta was certain that Frans was hers.

Chapter Twenty-three

⤜⤛

Dutchess County, New York

Ariadne awoke early and went down to breakfast feeling sheepish. She was ashamed for her outburst of the previous day. Adrian Single and Angelo Coveri were already seated at the breakfast table, drinking coffee in the sunlight that streamed through the east-facing windows.

"I want to apologize for my out—" she began.

"No, no, never apologize for your behavior," Adrian broke in. "And even then, make it sound as though you don't mean it."

"But good manners—"

Adrian shook his head. "Nikoletta never worries about manners."

"I wasn't speaking for Nikoletta," Ariadne said, feeling misinterpreted, "but of course I know what you mean."

"Of course," Adrian said, "but you were perfectly in character for Nikoletta, and that's very gratifying to see. As far as that sort of thing goes, remember, it's like Angelo has told you. She knows all the rules, but obeys them only when she chooses to do so. There's no way of gauging how she'll react in any particular situation. She's that mercurial, but it's exactly this utter unpredictability of hers that works in our favor."

"How so?" Ariadne asked as she sat down and poured herself some coffee.

He smiled. "Easy. Say you happen to make a mistake. Well, you just ignore it as though you're above it all or else make a joke of it—at someone else's expense, of course."

Ariadne lowered her eyes. "This is so not me."

"I'm glad it's not. Believe me, we all are. But don't worry. You'll get the hang of it soon enough. Also, bit by bit, over a stretch of time, you can taper off with some of the shrewishness, as if you're mellowing. It might be because you're maturing or because you're in love and more generous and kind to others because of it."

Ariadne blushed. "I don't know—"

"That's just an example, Ariadne," Adrian said. "Who knows what might cause a change in someone like Nikoletta? It happens to people all the time. But that sort of change in Nikoletta's character has to be done rather slowly, with careful calculation. Whatever you do, do not, and I repeat, *not,* make the fatal mistake of being too nice and too forgiving too fast. That would raise red flags immediately. Also, I, er—" He coughed. "I don't know whether anyone's let you in on a bit of information about Nikoletta that is important. . . ."

"Yes?"

"Well, you see, Nikoletta is a bit of a nymphomaniac," Adrian said. "Perhaps not clinically. I mean, a psychiatrist might not label her as one technically. Let's just say she's a sexual compulsive."

"She . . . *what*?"

"She's a sexual compulsive. Very active sexually."

"I know what it means," Ariadne snapped as if she'd been insulted. "But I didn't know that it applied to my twin sister."

"There!" Angelo clapped his hands together. "You've done it again. You were Nikoletta. Exactly like Nikoletta."

Adrian smiled. "You certainly were," he agreed.

"Great," Ariadne said, her hands on her hips, staring at Adrian. "But can we get back to Nikoletta's nymphomania? I find it a little disconcerting at this stage that I haven't been told this before."

"Yes, I'm afraid Nikoletta is rather like a vampire. She's constantly on the prowl for new conquests to conquer and then discard. She seems especially challenged by men she can't possess."

"Oh, dear," Ariadne said, thinking of Matt. Her hands fluttered nervously. "I don't have that much sexual experience. I'm what you would call a one-man woman, I guess."

Angelo shut his eyes. "What idiots we are," he hissed. "We didn't take this aspect of Nikoletta's behavior into account." He turned to Ariadne. "I'm so sorry, Ariadne. Please, forgive us. We should've given this a lot more thought."

"Astounding, isn't it, that we could overlook something this crucial?" Adrian said. "Even Sugar didn't bring it up."

Ariadne gazed at Adrian, then Angelo. "Look," she said, her voice determined, "we're going to have to figure something out, guys, because I'm *not* going to be screwing one man after another. In fact, I'm not going to be screwing around with anybody but"—she caught herself before she used Matt's name—"well, whoever I want to."

"You don't share Niki's views," Adrian said, chuckling, "but you *sounded* like Niki. Bravo!"

"Great, but what do we do about it?" she asked.

"We'll figure out a way around that." Adrian smiled reassuringly. "You won't actually have to sacrifice yourself for this cause."

"I'm not about to 'sacrifice' myself, as you put it," Ariadne snapped, "so get that through your head. The first thing I'm going to do as Nikoletta is find the love of my life."

The two men exchanged glances. That didn't sound like Niki. "I guess it could happen," Adrian said hesitantly.

"It is going to happen," Ariadne snapped, "or you can find yourself another girl."

Nikoletta's cell phone rang, and she picked it up. Checking her caller ID, she saw that it was the PI. She was anxious to hear any news he had and quickly pressed the TALK button. "Yes?"

"I don't know exactly what these people are up to," he said, "but it's very odd, to say the least."

"Why? What's going on?" Nikoletta asked.

"I managed to get a good view into one of the rooms at the back of the house today," he said. "The library, I'd guess they call it. It opens out onto a big slate terrace."

"I know exactly the room you're talking about," Nikoletta replied. "And it's the library. So what did you see?"

"The TV set—it's one of those large-screen plasma jobs—is on nearly all the time," the PI said. "I'd see the light from it, flickering at all hours. Anyway, at first I thought they were television junkies or something. Watching the damn thing all the time. I didn't pay much attention to it. I mean, what was on the TV. You know, I concentrated on the people in the room."

"I see," Nikoletta said impatiently. *What's this nonsense leading up to?* "So, what's the point?"

"The point is, I got a good view of what was on the TV. Something, I might add, that a lot of men who call themselves pros in my field would've not seen."

Jesus! Nikoletta thought. *The jerk wants me to pat him on the back all the time.* "And?"

"And what I saw was a little shocking," he replied. "It's all video footage of you. That's what they've got running in there night and day."

"Me?" Nikoletta felt the hairs on the back of her neck stand up. The mere thought that Adrian and the others were watching videos of her gave her the creeps. It was such an invasion of her privacy.

Anger welled up in her and threatened to explode in a vile, pustulous mass, but before she could respond to the PI, he went on.

"But that's not all," he said. "Seems to me like they're training her. You know. Making her practice walking like you. She'll walk back and forth across the room, again and again."

"You actually saw that?"

"I've got very good binoculars, don't forget."

Her entire body trembled with fury. She wanted to lash out, to tear and scratch, to *kill*.

"You *shit*!" she screeched.

"Look, I'm just the messenger," he said calmly. "I'm doing this for you."

In her rage, Nikoletta's mind raced in a dozen different directions at once, and she found it difficult to concentrate. It was time for action, she thought. Yes. Time to put a stop to this . . . *whatever* the hell it was. This *plot*! They were definitely training a look-alike to replace her—that much was obvious.

"Anything else?" she finally asked him.

"That sums it up," he said. "I think you get the picture."

"I get the picture, all right," she said. Then in a hurried voice, she added, "I'll talk to you later." She flipped her cell phone shut without waiting for a reply.

After she had calmed down, she sat immobile in the chair for a long time. The board of advisers, she finally decided, could be taken care of. She would have to hire the best legal team to get around her father's will, but she would eventually be able to effect a boardroom purge, getting rid of every single one of them. In the meantime, she would make their lives a living hell. If they thought they could play hardball with her, they had failed to comprehend the extent to which she could respond in kind.

As for the impostor, she was another story. Whoever she was. She presented a different kind of danger altogether. The thought that such a person even existed—someone the board thought could actually impersonate her!—horrified Nikoletta.

She unlocked a drawer in her desk where she kept an ostrich-skin address book that contained her most private telephone numbers. No one else had access to these numbers or even knew about them. Flipping through it, she quickly found the name and number she needed. Nikoletta had met the man only once a couple of years previously. The introduction had been provided by an international arms dealer of her acquaintance in the south of France, where he often entertained at his villa in the hills above the Côte d'Azur. Yemal, the arms dealer, had taken her for a stroll at one of his legendary parties. Just the two of them, champagne glasses in hand, had chatted about business. In the privacy of a classic lavender knot garden, they came upon a man sitting alone, nursing a glass of club soda. Yemal had airily introduced him as the world's greatest gun for hire, indicating that only a handful of people knew of his existence or could afford him. The man, in turn, had slipped her a business card on which was printed only a cell phone number.

If anybody can take out this impostor, Nikoletta thought with satisfaction, *he can.*

But before she called him, she had to make one other call. She wanted the PI off the case. He had become a potential hazard, since he was spying on Adrian's house in the country. Assuming the impostor stayed there for the next few days, the PI had to be out of the way. *I'll call him first,* she thought, *and then pay him for services rendered. After he's gone, I'll call the assassin. He'll take care of the imposter. Whoever she is, she won't be a threat for long.*

After dinner Ariadne went outside for a brief walk. She meandered around the garden and wandered over toward the swimming pool. There were no lights on in the pool house or outside around the pool, but a blue-tinted light shone from within the pool itself. As she idly stepped onto the blue-stone terrace that surrounded it, she gazed into the pool's lit depths and saw Matt swimming underwater. His motions were powerful and propelled him with a fluid grace from one end of the pool to the other in only a few strokes.

When he surfaced at the deep end, he shook his head, flinging water off his hair. He looked up at her with surprise, then smiled widely. "Are you coming in?"

"No," she said. "I was just taking a walk and saw the light, so I thought I'd have a look."

"Why don't you? It's really warm. They run the heater nearly all the time."

"I don't think so," Ariadne said.

"Aw, come on," Matt coaxed as he pushed himself up onto the terrace with his arms.

Ariadne noticed the ease with which he got out of the water and the way his biceps and triceps flexed. When he stood up, she saw that he wore a very brief blue swimsuit that clung to him. He looked so handsome, she thought. So strong and masculine and . . . sexy. He bent over and took a towel off a weathered teak chaise longue and began ruffling his hair with it.

"I don't even have a bathing suit," she said.

"If you feel like you have to wear one, I'm sure there's one in the pool

house that would fit you," Matt said. "There are lots of extras for guests."
He hung the towel around his neck and walked toward her.

"Oh, okay," she said. "I guess it could count as part of my training,
since I'm not a very good swimmer."

"That's the spirit," he said. "I'll wait for you. You'll find everything
you need in the pool house."

Ariadne went inside and discovered that the pool house had both men's
and women's bathrooms and dressing rooms. In the women's there were
more than a dozen bathing suits to choose from. She quickly undressed and
found one that fitted, a two-piece with blue and white stripes. Looking at
herself in the mirror before she ventured back to the pool, she took a deep
breath. She thought of the pictures she'd seen of Nikoletta in magazines and
on video and decided that her body compared favorably with her sister's. Before she could give it another thought, she went back out to the pool.

Matt's eyes assessed her appreciatively, she noticed, but he swiftly
averted his gaze. "Good. You found what you needed," he said.

Ariadne went to the shallow end of the pool and dipped a foot in.
"Wow! It is warm, isn't it?"

He nodded. "Practically like a bathtub."

She started down the steps that led down into the pool. "Oh, this feels
so good."

Matt grinned, then went to the steps and followed her into the water.

Ariadne walked in up to her waist, then plunged into the water and
dog-paddled toward the deep end. When she reached it, she turned around
and faced him. "This is so great!" she said. "I don't know why I haven't
done this before."

"Now you can do it anytime."

She shoved off the wall and plunged into the water again, diving under
the surface. Kicking her legs and using long even strokes with her arms,
she swam toward the shallow end. Oblivious to anything but the soothing
water, she hit something with her hands and surfaced, gasping and sput-
tering water.

"You must've had your eyes closed," Matt said, laughing.

"I did," she said. She realized that she was standing directly in front
of him, their bodies practically touching. She looked up at him, and Matt's
eyes met hers.

They were silent for a moment. Then he slowly leaned down and brushed his lips against hers. Ariadne trembled with excitement, and she returned his kiss. His arms encircled her, and he gently pulled her closer to him in the water, his lips on hers, then brushing tenderly against her ears and down her neck. She put her arms around him and held on, her breathing rapid, surges of sensual electricity rushing through her body. It seemed that her body had a life of its own, responding to him of its own accord.

She felt his warm breath on her ear, then his lips gently trailing across her forehead, down each of her cheeks, then back to her lips. They kissed again, more passionately. He parted her lips with his tongue, and Ariadne shivered with pleasure, giving herself up to his exploration, relishing the feel of him. For a long time they kissed and hugged in the water, their arms around each other, until he drew back at last.

"Let's go into the pool house where no one can see us," he said.

She nodded.

He took her hand and led her out of the water and inside the pool house, where he guided her to one of the couches. Ariadne spread out lengthwise, and he lay next to her and began kissing her again. She felt one of his hands on her breasts, and she gasped as he began fondling them gently. He slid the straps from her shoulders, one at a time, then began kissing and licking her nipples. The pleasure was such that she nearly levitated off the couch, and she held him tight, wanting this to never end.

When she felt his hardness against her, she moaned at its strange but erotic power and felt an urgency between her thighs that was heaven-sent. One of her hands trailed down his back to his rounded, muscular ass, and she stroked it in circles, before slipping her hand beneath the tight swimsuit in which it was trapped.

Matt groaned, and his lips found her mouth again. He began kissing her with mounting passion, and one of his hands slid down to the mound between her thighs, brushing against it lightly, teasingly, feeling her heat and dampness. She pushed against his hand, and he responded by easing his hand inside the confines of her bikini bottom, pressing his fingers to her sweet lips.

"Oh, my God, Matt," Ariadne whispered, and began to moan.

He slid her bikini bottom down, and she wriggled out of it as he took off his swimsuit. He sprang free against her, and she reached down and touched him, encircling him with her hand. Matt gasped, then kissed her long and hard before suddenly drawing back.

"Oh, Ariadne," he whispered. "I want you so much. Desperately." He kissed her again, his passion all-consuming.

"I want you, too, Matt," she murmured.

Then slowly he began guiding himself to the anxious, swollen lips between her thighs. He was very gentle, trying to control the impulse to enter her with the thrust his desire demanded.

She felt the swollen head of his manhood inside her. As he tenderly continued entering her, her body accepted and welcomed him there. She grasped his back and held on to him with all her might and started moving with him, the desire to have all of him, to satisfy her own passion and his, overwhelming all else. They moved as one, rhythmically, slowly at first, their pace gradually increasing until they were pounding against each other with wild abandon.

Matt suddenly let out a cry, and his entire body jerked, then tensed, as he came inside her. Ariadne felt herself contract around him as a flood tide of ecstasy swept her up, up, up into a realm of pleasure such as she'd never known existed. Time itself seemed to stand still. She had relished their lovemaking since the first time, but she had not experienced erotic pleasure like this before. It was a feeling of completeness, as if nothing could be added to it to make it more perfect.

Matt exhaled a hot breath against her face and hugged her to him powerfully. He began kissing her face.

"Ariadne," he rasped softly. "Ariadne . . . Ariadne . . . I love you. . . . I love you. . . ."

Ariadne didn't think she would ever forget this moment. It would be etched in her mind with a clarity that would never diminish, she thought. Even the pale, diffuse light from the swimming pool outside that cast its bluish tint into the room would color her memories of this act of love for the rest of her life. All the years of abandonment and loneliness and questioning seemed unimportant now, receding into the past. Their love—for that was what it must be, she thought—displaced those feelings.

"I love you, too, Matt," she finally whispered to him.

When they parted at last, Ariadne reluctantly returned to her room in the house, unafraid and unconcerned of the reactions of anyone there. She felt a strength and a hope that were new and empowering. She should be exhausted, she thought, but her entire being was energized as it never had been before by what she and Matt had discovered together. The future held promise now, and she felt it deep down inside, in a place where no one could take it away.

Chapter Twenty-four

∞

New York City

No construction helmets were necessary this time as Nikoletta toured her favorite place on earth, the almost completed PPHL International Headquarters on West Forty-second Street. In her mind, it was a monument erected to her glory, one that would be a landmark in New York City for decades, if not centuries, to come.

Her considerable entourage included Rik Persoons, the principal architect; his most senior associates; several PPHL senior executives; her personal assistant, Danette Shrager; and Glenn Gund, the interior designer, who had arrived with *his* battalion of minions. The group followed her lead, stopping where she did, showing interest in those things that she did, and staying close to her heels, trying to catch her every word. They all shared certain knowledge: that even at this late stage in the construction process, one single misstep and Nikoletta Papadaki would take great pleasure in seeing a head roll and replacing it with that of someone else. After the arduous process they'd all been through, they wanted the credit for the finished product, and they knew the only way to get it was to be involved until the very end.

After finishing a walk-through of the sixty-seventh floor, where Nikoletta's luxurious suite of offices was nearing readiness, she announced, "Now I wish to tour my triplex apartment."

The majority of the entourage was dismissed, except for Rik Persoons, Danette Shrager, and Glenn Gund. Associates and minions were neither welcomed nor permitted beyond the sixty-seventh floor today.

They took the private keyed elevator to the sixty-eighth floor, the first of the three full floors of living space high above Manhattan. These top three stories of the building that were to be her new digs boasted fifteen-foot ceilings, floor-to-ceiling windows, and thirty thousand square feet of interior space. The terraces on various levels of the apartment would put all others in New York City to shame.

All three floors of the apartment were a hive of activity. Workmen, from plasterers to carpenters, were plowing full speed ahead, and Glenn Gund began rushing around, barking orders, and gesticulating madly as he decided on some last-minute changes. Although he was allowed a certain degree of freedom with the design of the apartment, he always consulted with Nikoletta before making any changes, and those he was demanding today had already been cleared by her.

The workmen grumbled and cursed among themselves, but never within Nikoletta's earshot and seldom within Glenn's. They swore that they'd never worked for two such demanding taskmasters, and hoped that they would never have to take a job that involved either of them again.

Rik Persoons led Nikoletta outside, onto one of the many windswept terraces. "I have news that I think will please you."

"I'm listening."

"Remember how we scheduled the completion of the building for seven weeks from now?"

"Yes?" Nikoletta, guessing what was coming, felt a surge of excitement.

"And remember the weekly bonuses you promised for early completion?" She nodded.

"Well, that's worked wonders with the construction team. The building will be ready for occupancy within three weeks. Maximum."

"You mean . . . it's not too early to plan a grand-opening party?" Nikoletta asked. "Not too soon to get my party planner cracking and sending out the invitations?"

"Not by any means," Rik replied.

"Oh, my God," she swooned. "That will barely give them enough time to get everything ready. I can hear the complaints already. But who cares? This is fantastic news, Rik. This is better . . . oh, my God, this is better than . . . sex!"

Nikoletta was in seventh heaven.

*　　*　　*

"This cuts our time in less than half," Adrian told a fretting Ariadne. "Less than three weeks."

"Does this mean we should call the whole thing off?" she asked.

"Do I detect a note of hope in your question?" he asked.

"No such luck, I'm afraid. I'm into this now. I guess that's the kind of person I am." Ariadne smiled. The increased difficulty of the challenge appealed to her, she discovered.

"But—"

"We'll simply have to cram a lot more learning into a lot less time, won't we?" Ariadne said. *Heaven help me,* she thought. *I actually had an out and didn't take advantage of it.*

Adrian studied her face for a moment. "I think we can do it, Ariadne," he said. "I believe that more now than I ever did before. Let's get busy. I've got a lot of different lessons in business for you today."

"Business I can handle," she said with a sparkle in her eye.

"I've already sent out an information packet to every important magazine and newspaper editor in New York and every major city in the States," Zita Hadad said with pride, displaying the expensively produced folder, complete with recent photographs of the new PPHL headquarters. "And every architecture critic in the country has been sent the packet and been invited, along with some of the more important art critics."

Nikoletta nodded. "Have all the invitations gone out?"

Zita nodded and brushed at her crew-cut black hair. "Yes, by overnight mail, and let me tell you that anybody who's anybody has been sent one. From high society to business leaders, Hollywood stars, celebrity athletes. You name 'em, Niki, and they've got an invitation if they're important." She knocked on the desk with a huge gold ring set with a peridot to emphasize her point. "And I'll guarantee you that ninety percent of them or more will be there because most of 'em owe me and owe me big-time."

"Good," Nikoletta said. She'd been closeted in her office with Lawrence Lowell, the preeminent party planner in New York, as well as most European capitals, and Zita Hadad, the head of the most powerful public relations firm in New York, hearing their reports on the celebration.

"Photographers are going to be there from every publication you can think of," Zita added. "One, because you're giving the party, and two, because they know that everybody who's anybody is not going to miss it. So the publicity factor is going to be *huuuuge*." She threw her hands into the air dramatically, and the big bangle bracelets on her arms clanged against one another.

"And you, Lawrence?" Nikoletta asked. "Do you have everything ready to go?"

"You bet," Lawrence Lowell replied. "I'm pulling out all the stops just like you said, Niki. Everybody in Manhattan is going to know this party is going on unless they're indoors with the curtains drawn." He laughed. "There'll be klieg lights on the Forty-second Street side *and* the West Side Highway, so it'll look like a major movie premiere. Only better. A real red carpet running from the curb of Forty-second all the way into the building, with plenty of cordoned-off space for the press and photographers. They'll be able to shoot away and ask all the questions they want to. It'll be up to the celebrities and their PR people as to whether or not they cooperate, of course, but—"

"I'm aware of all that," Nikoletta said impatiently, "but what about the decor? Have you got that under control? I don't want to hear about thousands of orchids that didn't arrive at the last minute."

"No, no, Niki," he said. "Not to worry. Our Galerie des Glaces is going to be the most beautiful thing anybody's ever seen. Nothing's going to have to be airfreighted from Kathmandu or anything like that. I showed you the drawings, right?"

"Yes, Lawrence," Nikoletta said. "I've seen the drawings a dozen times."

"Well, I've lined up everything, and it's all ready to go. Huge arrangements for the lobby, all the bars, the tables, and so on, along with a zillion potted trees and flowers. The lobby and atrium and all the mezzanines are going to be beautiful. Over sixty crystal chandeliers. I've got the uniforms lined up for the security detail, except for those working incognito, of course. Very dressy and flashy, like the drawings. It's going to be worthy of Versailles. Just like I promised you."

"Yes, but is everything you showed me definitely in place, ready for installation? I don't mean flowers, of course, but everything else? There's going to be *no* last-minute panic?"

"Absolutely not, Niki," Lawrence said, crossing his heart with a hand.

"Okay," she said. "But I'll have your brains for breakfast if there's a screwup. And you'll never get work from anybody *I* know."

"Understood," Lawrence said.

"Now, what about the goody bags?" she asked.

Zita's eyes brightened. "We've gotten *enormous* interest. Like nothing before, I don't think. Cosmetics companies, jewelry firms, luxury purveyors of all kinds—you name it—everybody wants a piece of the action, Niki. So, we're busy sorting through them, deciding exactly what to include in the bags. The women *and* the men are going to leave that party with thousands of dollars' worth of free gifts, thank you, Nikoletta Papadaki. We've already selected fabulous gold compacts studded with tiny diamonds for the ladies and gold cuff links for the men, but that's only the beginning."

A smile crossed Nikoletta's lips. *And it doesn't cost me a penny,* she thought. *All those companies want the free advertising that goes along with giving my guests expensive gifts.*

"Very good, Zita," she said. "Keep me posted. I want to know exactly what's going in those bags."

"I wouldn't think of doing it otherwise," Zita assured her, throwing her bangle-braceleted arms into the air again.

"Okay. Out. Both of you. I've got real work to do," Nikoletta said. "Reports from both of you at the end of the week. Latest."

Sugar Rosebury arrived at Adrian's house with a treasure trove of clothes, shoes, and accessories borrowed from Nikoletta's wardrobe—all for the *Vogue* shoot—and at the sight of the gorgeous display Ariadne's eyes widened with helpless delight. She had never owned anything like the enormously expensive designer items of Nikoletta's, and she couldn't contain her pleasure about such luxury.

"Let's have you try on the shoes first," Sugar told her.

Ariadne obeyed her mentor, and struggled to get into a pair of Nikoletta's shoes. To no avail. They were the tiniest bit too small, but impossible to wear.

"I guess you're not Cinderella after all," Adrian quipped.

"What will we do?" Ariadne asked in a disappointed voice.

Sugar sighed. "The shoes don't pose much of a problem. I can easily get the same shoes or something very similar. They're nearly all either Manolo Blahnik, Jimmy Choo, or Christian Louboutin, and I can get them in New York City." She paused thoughtfully. "Let's see about the clothes right away. I was certain that you would be the identical size, but now I'm not so sure."

She removed a dress from a garment bag. "The problem with these is that they're nearly all couture, so they're fitted to Nikoletta's body and hers alone. A few of them are high-end off-the-rack, but I don't know. . . ." She studied Ariadne's body as if for the first time. "Go try this one on, sweetie," she said, handing her a dress. "Then we'll have a look."

Ariadne disappeared into the bathroom and returned in a few moments, looking downcast. "I can't believe it," she said. "I can't possibly get this zipped up."

"Let me see," Sugar said, although she already had a strong suspicion that Ariadne was about a size larger than Nikoletta. *It's all those damned exercise classes of Nikoletta's,* she thought. *That and the constant dieting.* Ariadne had a beautiful figure, trim but curvaceous in the right places. Nikoletta was more toned, tighter, and almost runway thin.

She attempted closing the zipper on the dress.

"What do you think?" Ariadne asked.

"It's a no go," Sugar said in an irritated voice. "Maybe I could close it, but I'd risk damaging the dress. And that wouldn't do, believe me."

"Is it possible to let them out?" Ariadne asked.

"The problem is, sweetie, there is nothing to let out. Like I said, nearly all of these clothes were made for Nikoletta's body without any excess for letting out allowed."

Ariadne waited. *Now what?* she wondered.

Sugar stood back and thoughtfully studied the way Ariadne looked in the dress, a fingertip poised on her lips. Finally she cleared her throat. "Sweetheart, I know this is the last thing you want to hear. A diuretic will help some, as will a corset, but we really don't have a choice. I'm afraid you'll have to shed about ten or fifteen pounds."

Ariadne's heart sank. *Ten or fifteen pounds! In three weeks? That on top of everything else? Now I won't even be able to eat.* "Okay," she said. "Somehow or other I'll do it."

"That's the spirit," Sugar said. "I suggest the Atkins Diet. Lots of protein and almost no carbs. I know the routine, believe me."

"You really think it'll work?"

"I'm positive. Ten or fifteen pounds off you, and we don't have a problem." She clapped her hands together as if dusting them off. "Now. I'm going off on a VISM, so don't expect me back for a couple of days."

"What's a VISM?" Ariadne asked with curiosity.

"That," Sugar said with a twinkle in her eye, "stands for Very Important Secret Mission. A shoe search. So wish me luck, and off I go."

They exchanged air kisses as Nikoletta would.

"Toodle-oo!" Sugar said, waving a hand. "Be back soon."

Chapter Twenty-five

꩜

Dutchess County, New York

It was after three a.m., and Adrian, unable to sleep, roamed the house. Passing Ariadne's door, he noticed a strip of yellow light beneath it. He knocked quietly, lest she was asleep with the lights on.

"Come in," she murmured.

He stepped inside and saw that she was half sitting up in bed, her hair in disarray. "Are you ill?" he asked.

She shook her head. "Just dizzy, nauseous, and weary from crash dieting and taking crash courses," she joked weakly. "But ill? No."

He gestured to the blueprints and glossy magazine spreads on her bed. "What on earth are you doing at this hour?"

"Becoming acquainted with Nikoletta's office and town house in New York City," she replied.

He took a deep breath, then went to her bedside and gathered up the blueprints.

"What are you doing?"

He balled up the huge sheets of heavy paper. "They're useless now. So are the shelter magazine pictures. Oh, they'll be helpful should someone bring up something about your former office or former apartment, but that's all. With the new headquarters about to be inaugurated, Nikoletta will be moving into the penthouse triplex apartment there, and her new office will be there, of course." He tossed the ball of paper into a wastebasket. "Sorry to have wasted your time studying these, Ariadne.

Someone—me included—should have realized that and gotten the new plans for you."

She shut her eyes and stifled a curse.

He added wryly, "Better you spend your spare time practicing Nikoletta's signature."

She opened her eyes and glared at him. "I have her signature down pat, for your information."

"I know you do," he replied with a smile. "I was only joking."

"Oh," she said, her features amiable again.

"What you should do is to try and get some sleep," Adrian told her. "Tomorrow is another day, and you're going to need all of your energy."

"I will," she promised.

He started to leave, but paused at the door and turned to her. "I've noticed that you and Matt seem to be, uh, seeing a lot of one another," he said in a casual manner.

"Yes," Ariadne said, her tone of voice much like his.

"I hope you . . . well, I hope you know what you're doing."

"Absolutely," she said, a glint in her eyes. "Besides, I am supposed to become Nikoletta, aren't I?"

"Well, yes," he said, momentarily nonplussed by her self-assurance. "But—"

"But nothing," Ariadne said, brushing him off. "If I'm going be involved in this deadly masquerade as my sister, then I'm going to have to get to know a lot about men."

Adrian gazed at her, his features perplexed. *What have we wrought?* "I just hope you'll be . . . careful," he said. "You're not as experienced as—"

"And I *need* experience," Ariadne said with a smile.

Adrian did not want to pursue this any further. "Okay. I'll see you in the morning."

Ariadne congratulated herself when Adrian left the room. She was proud of the love that she and Matt shared, and she wasn't afraid of what Adrian or the others thought. Maybe she wasn't as experienced as Nikoletta, but she knew what she was doing where Matt was concerned; of that, she had no doubts. She would have to tell Matt about this. Adrian or one of the others might say something to him as well, and she hoped that he would be as comfortable with their knowing as she was. They had discussed the issue and had decided not to confront Adrian or any of the others about their affair but not to deny it if asked about it. In the meantime, they'd decided to spend time together when they could.

As she fell asleep, Matt filled her thoughts. Handsome, athletic, quick-witted, mellow, and sweet Matt. She could visualize him in his walking gear, the old but clean jeans or khakis and neat polo shirts, the dusty or muddy hiking boots, depending on the weather. He was comfortable in his own skin.

She missed him tonight, but they had decided that it was best to keep up appearances to some extent. Besides which, they had been getting very little sleep. Ariadne smiled helplessly, thinking about it. When they were together, they found it impossible to resist the urge to make love and talk half the night. She giggled. *Maybe I'm more like Nikoletta than I thought!*

The next week Adrian spent a great deal of time tutoring her, while the others made appearances in the New York City office. There was still so much to learn.

Angelo telephoned from New York City with a most unwelcome piece of news. Adrian and Ariadne both listened to what he had to say. "We're going to have to change our plans."

"Why's that?" Adrian asked.

"Nikoletta is making such a big deal out of the opening of the new headquarters that it's going to be very difficult," Angelo said.

"But I thought that was supposed to make it easier," Ariadne said.

"The problem is this," Angelo went on. "Because Nikoletta has had problems in the past with the people from Mother Earth's Children, she's hired three teams of ex–Secret Service agents to supplement her usual bodyguard contingent. One team for every eight-hour shift. Until the festivities are over, they will follow her everywhere. And I do mean everywhere. They'll be checking out ladies' rooms before she uses them, making certain they're empty, then stationing themselves outside while Nikoletta is inside. I mean, it's going to be as if a head of state were visiting."

Adrian sighed. *As if things aren't difficult enough*, he thought. "Getting around the usual bodyguard contingent is one thing," he said, "but this worries me, Angelo."

"It has me very worried," Angelo agreed. "That's why I called to forewarn you. We're all going to have to be giving a lot of thought to how to work this, taking into consideration all this extra security."

"One advantage is that the new guards won't know Nikoletta like her usual ones," Ariadne brought up. "So it'll be easier to make them think that I'm actually Nikoletta."

"Sharp lady," Adrian said. "That's true, and maybe will prove useful."

"We're going to have to play a lot of this by ear," Angelo said. "There's just no choice. We're going to have to be ready to take advantage of opportunities when and if they arise that night."

"Well," Adrian said, "as you find out more about the schedule of events, keep us up-to-date. Knowing Niki, she's going to allow a few minutes here and there between events to escape the hordes of people and spend time groping her date, whoever he will be."

"Yes," Angelo said thoughtfully. "I'll see what I can find out about the scheduling, that sort of thing. Anyway, I'll keep you apprised of what I find out."

"Talk to you soon," Adrian said, and he hung up the telephone. "You heard him. It's not getting any easier, is it?"

"It doesn't sound as if it is," she agreed.

"The security is something I've been meaning to talk to you about," Adrian said.

"How's that?" she asked.

"You're not used to a constant security detail like Niki is, and it can be a little daunting to find yourself virtually living with a gang of men twenty-four hours a day."

"I've had security here," Ariadne pointed out, "and I haven't had any problems with Matt. In fact, he's been very good company."

"That's different, I'm afraid," Adrian said. "Matt is one person, and he's very discreet, very professional and capable. In your new situation, you're going to have at least four at all times. Some of these guys aren't as experienced as he is or as . . . well . . . some of them don't know how to keep the appropriate distance, if you know what I mean."

"I'm not sure I do," Ariadne said, although she had a good idea.

"Well, Niki is known to have a fling now and then with one of the security men. They're never anything serious, you understand. Just . . .

quickies. Satisfying an itch, you might say. And a lot of the men are more than prepared for that."

"I see," Ariadne said.

"And you're not like that, nor are you used to having them hanging around all the time."

"You know what?" Ariadne asked.

"What?"

"Part of that problem could be solved if you—or I, as Nikoletta—insisted that Matt become the new head of the personal security detail."

Adrian was struck by this terrific idea. "You sometimes surprise me, Ariadne," he said. "That's an excellent suggestion. I wonder why none of us thought of it."

"Well, sometimes the best solutions are right in front of your face, aren't they?"

The next day before lunch, Sugar Rosebury arrived in triumph, accompanied by a wealth of luggage. "There can't be much left in New York City's best shops," she crowed. "But that's not all. I had great success all round."

"What happened?" Ariadne asked.

"Well, first I had a little visit with Nikoletta," Sugar said conspiratorially.

"Yes?"

"And we had a little girl-to-girl chat. You know"—Sugar's smile widened—"I told her that I didn't want to steal her thunder and wear something similar or, God forbid, the very same outfit to the fete as she's planning to wear."

"Do you think the chances of something like that happening are possible?" Ariadne asked in amazement.

"They are so remote," Sugar said, rolling her eyes. "I doubt it would ever happen, even if we do wear the same designers sometimes. But the idea that I would try to avoid stealing any of her thunder appealed to Nikoletta's vanity. Anything that appeals to her vanity always works wonders. So, guess what happened then?"

Ariadne shook her head. "You know I have no idea."

"She showed me her outfit for the opening. Is that a coup?"

"I guess so," Ariadne replied doubtfully.

"Sweetheart, think about it," Sugar said. "Now we know exactly what she's wearing that night, and we can copy it!"

"Ohhhh," Ariadne said with dawning realization. "I can't wait to see." She found she had a growing interest in fashion. It had never seemed important to her before, perhaps because she had never been able to afford to indulge her tastes, but she was discovering that it could be fun.

"Go ahead," Sugar said. "Open these suitcases and take a look."

Ariadne went to the nearest piece of luggage, laid it flat, and flipped open the brass hinges. It was filled with shoe boxes. She glanced at Sugar to make certain that she had permission.

"Oh, for heaven's sake. Go on," Sugar urged her. "They're yours."

"Mine?" Ariadne clasped her hands in disbelieving wonder. "This is like . . . Christmas!"

"Try them on," Sugar said.

Ariadne chose a box and opened it, then donned a single shoe—Christian Louboutin, it said. It was a perfect fit. She studied it closely. Never in her life had she seen such superb craftsmanship, such delicate artistry. And merely for shoes, she couldn't help thinking.

"Now try on those Manolo Blahniks," Sugar commanded. "They're in that black box at the far corner."

Hesitantly Ariadne opened the box and parted the tissue. She let out a gasp as she held up a pair of pointy-toed, backless, stiletto-heeled shoes fashioned of gold-dyed python. Attached to each pair were lengths of very thin gold-dyed ankle straps, also of python.

Ariadne was mind-boggled. "These . . . are shoes?"

"They're not just shoes, sweetie," Sugar corrected her. "They're killer shoes!" She helped Ariadne into them, and showed her how to wrap the ankle straps and secure them.

Again, the fit was perfect, but Ariadne wobbled as she walked across the room in them. Unused to heels, let alone stiletto heels without backs, she discovered that she was going to need practice.

"Now," Sugar announced, "for the *pièce de résistance*." She herself opened another suitcase and lifted out a big flat white box tied with a silk ribbon. She handed it to Ariadne.

Ariadne was almost overwhelmed by the beauty of the package itself and only stared down at it.

"What are you waiting for?" Sugar said. "Open it."

Sitting on the floor, Ariadne carefully began untying the silk ribbon. As she would with a Christmas package, she proceeded slowly, planning to roll up the ribbon neatly to save.

"No, no, no!" Sugar said. "Unwrap it like Nikoletta would. Tear it off like you can't wait to get what's inside."

"But it's such pretty—"

"Tear it," Sugar commanded.

Wincing inside, Ariadne did as she was told, then lifted the lid off the box. She parted the sea of white tissue, and her breath caught in her throat. She lifted out a shoulderless sheath concocted of thick flat lengths of genuine, gold-dyed python stitched together in a chevron pattern. She was speechless.

"It was designed by Cavalli," Sugar said enthusiastically, "and I snagged the last one. Only a few were made, and there were only two left in the whole country. Nikoletta got the one in New York, and there was one on Rodeo Drive in Los Angeles and one in Las Vegas. This one came from Rodeo Drive because the bubbleheaded girl in Las Vegas promised to save me the one she had and send it, then forgot and sold it to some-body else."

"My God!" Ariadne breathed, running her hands over the sheath. "Real snakeskin! Why, it must have cost a king's ransom. And think of all those poor snakes."

"Listen, sweetie," Sugar declared, "the reason God put snakes on this earth was for shoes, handbags, belts, and dresses like this."

"Oh, that's terrible," Ariadne said, although she thought the dress was truly beautiful.

"I'm kidding," Sugar said. "The dress is made of naturally shed skins."

"I see," Ariadne said. "I hadn't thought of that."

"Now, why don't you try it on?" Sugar said. "Let's go upstairs." She took Ariadne's hand and led the way.

It was a struggle. Despite her weight-loss regimen, Ariadne had to hold her breath just to squeeze into it, and although she managed, the dress was obviously too tight.

"Sorry, but you'll have to starve yourself for the next week," Sugar told her. "That and the diuretics should get rid of the excess weight, so no one will be able to tell you and Nikoletta apart." She paused, studying Ariadne. "But you know what?"

"What?" Ariadne asked, still looking at her reflection in the mirror.

"You look smashing, Ariadne," she stated. "And what a sexpot you are!"

"Ohhh!" Ariadne exclaimed. "I . . . I don't know. It exposes so much of my flesh, Sugar," she groaned. "Look at my cleavage!" She gestured in distress at the way the cut of the dress accentuated her bosom.

Sugar was at her most maternal. "Those are natural resources, sweetie," she said gently. "Think of them as God-given gifts. You've got to remember, you're not in the wilds of the Berkshires anymore."

Ariadne looked at herself in the mirror. *Sugar is right*, she realized. *I'm certainly not in Kansas anymore!*

As she continued to study the new person in the mirror, she thought, *What I am involved in is a Byzantine, highly convoluted, and doubtlessly illegal plot*. Surprisingly, she found that she was enjoying it.

Chapter Twenty-six

&

The day had been exhilarating but exhausting. Ariadne had discovered that as beautiful as the clothes, shoes, and accessories were, trying everything on became a grueling exercise after a while. With each change of attire, Sugar had fiddled with her hair and tried different shoes and accessories, determining the best overall look for Ariadne in the various outfits. When they finally finished, they celebrated with a glass of champagne and chitchat.

After dinner, Ariadne walked out to the garden alone, where she strolled among the well-tended perennial beds, inhaling the intoxicating scent that filled the air. It was a commingling of the aromas of many different flowers and herbs, and even the rich earth itself. Sitting down on a weathered teak bench that was still warm from the sun of the day, she luxuriated in the beautiful, peaceful evening. She knew that Matt would join her, and soon she heard his footsteps on the garden path.

He quickly crossed to the bench and sat beside her, taking her hand in his. He kissed her cheek. "You're exhausted, aren't you?"

"I really am," Ariadne replied, "but I wanted to come sit here with you for a while."

"It's a beautiful night, isn't it?" He squeezed her hand in his.

"So quiet and peaceful," Ariadne murmured.

"I think you'd better get to bed," Matt said, brushing a stray tress of hair away from her face. "You can hardly hold your eyes open."

"But—"

"But nothing," Matt said. "Tomorrow's not going to be any easier than today, and as much as I would like to spend some special time with you tonight, I don't think it's a good idea."

Ariadne reluctantly agreed. "You're right. I feel like I could go to sleep here on this bench."

Matt kissed her cheek again. "Come on," he said, standing up, her hand still in his. "Let me walk you back to the house."

Ariadne let him pull her to her feet. He took her in his arms and kissed her, but held her only a moment.

When they reached the house, he relinquished his hold of her hand. "Sleep well," he said.

"What are you doing?" she asked, reluctant to part company.

"The usual," he said. "Just checking on things. Now, off you go, Ariadne." He smiled mischievously. "We'll have a good time tomorrow, so you'll need your energy, won't you?"

She smiled dreamily and nodded. " 'Night."

" 'Night."

He watched her go on into the house, then turned and started his rounds of the property.

Ariadne undressed and got ready for bed. Instead of putting on one of her nightgowns, she slipped one of Matt's T-shirts over her head. It was her newest and most favorite garment to sleep in, and she would gladly substitute it for all of the silk nightgowns and pajamas that Sugar had brought. Getting into bed, she pulled a sheet up over her and switched off the light. There was no point in even trying to read tonight. She could hardly hold her eyes open. She quickly fell into a heavy, dreamless sleep.

The stranger had already done his reconnaissance and knew exactly where to park and conceal his car, where to get into the compound, and where to enter the house. He also knew which bedroom she slept in.

At two a.m. all the lights in the compound had been out for hours. Nevertheless, at the foot of the curving stairwell, he stood stone still in his black cotton tracksuit for a long time, letting his eyes adjust to the darkness, his ears alert to the sound of any movement in the large house.

He could hear nothing but his own breathing.

He knew that the staircase with its old treads and risers was a potential source of noise, and when he took the first step onto it, he placed one rubber-soled track shoe down lightly as close to the wall as possible, testing it for squeaks. When there was no discernible sound, he brought the other leg up and lightly placed his foot on the step, next to the other one, willing the stair to make no sound. The step was cooperative.

He stood stock-still again, but as before could hear nothing other than the sound of his own breathing.

As perspiration began to sheathe his body, he placed a foot on the second step, once again as close to the wall as possible, gradually put his weight on it, then brought the second foot up, placing it lightly beside the other one. So far, so good. Repeating the process, he finally reached the curve in the stairwell without making a sound.

At the curve he paused, resting against the wall. Light from the moon barely penetrated the Palladian-style, second-story window because of the draperies drawn closed across it. Taking a deep breath, he began the long, tedious process again, placing first one shoe, then the other, on the next step.

He was three steps from the top when it happened. As if voicing a complaint, the stair emitted a loud squeak as he placed his shoe on it. The man stopped, sucking in his breath as he did so. His other foot was poised in midair, ready to descend onto the step next to its mate, but he held it there, unmoving, while he listened for any noise in the darkness.

Finally satisfied that he had alerted no one to his presence, he brought the other shoe down, holding his breath as he gradually put his weight on it. There was no protest, and the man quickly took the next step and the next, reaching the top of the stairs. He immediately crossed the landing and placed himself against the hallway wall, his eyes darting around the darkness, searching for anyone who might have heard him.

The house slumbered around him, quiet, still, and unknowing.

He began creeping down the hallway, staying as close to the wall as possible, where there was less likelihood of disturbing loose, noisy floorboards. Pale moonlight from a window at the end of the hall allowed him a dim view of the paintings that hung at intervals along the wall. He bent forward from the waist up so as to avoid them. The dim light also permitted him a view of his goal.

Her bedroom door.

With great patience he inched on. After what seemed an interminable amount of time, he finally reached the door. He drew a Heckler & Koch double-action, semiautomatic pistol fitted with a silencer out of his pocket, holding it pointed at the ceiling, his elbow bent, ready to bring it down to fire. Reaching down with his free hand, he slowly tried the doorknob. It turned smoothly and silently in his hand. The door wasn't locked.

In a single fluid motion, he swung his body around on the ball of his right foot and eased his left foot down onto the floor. He stood squarely in front of the door now, ready to open it. He turned the brass knob again, held it, and slowly pushed it open a few inches, relieved that it hardly made a sound. It was a long way down the hallway and the steps, out the front door and across the lawn, and over the wall and down the road to his car. He didn't want to alert anyone to his presence now.

He put his face to the space between the door and the jamb, his eyes scanning that part of the room within his view. Although the draperies were closed, he could make out the canopied bed in the dim light. And on it, he could detect a figure sheathed by a sheet. His mark: the young woman.

Easing the door open, he crept silently into the room. When he reached the side of the big draped bed, he brought his arm down, aiming the semiautomatic at her sleeping form. Her back was to him, but it didn't matter. One dead-on shot would pierce her back and leave an exit wound the size of a melon.

He pulled back on the trigger, but paused a moment before shooting. Behind him, he thought he heard something, more a disturbance of the air than an actual noise. He started to look, but before he could turn his head all the way around Matt sprang from the doorway, his powerful arms extended, letting out a bellow of fury as he did so.

"Nooooooo." The roar came from deep down inside him, so loud and animallike that the man was momentarily stunned.

Matt was a mere blur in his vision before the assassin felt the weight of Matt's entire body thrown against him, hurling him to the floor. The pistol flew out of his hand, clattering loudly as it skipped across wood. The assassin's head hit a bedside table with a dull thud, overturning it, sending a lamp and clock crashing noisily against the wide pine-board planking, scattering glass.

Before the assassin could move, Matt was on top of him, pinning him with his muscular arms. He heaved against Matt with all his strength, but Matt took the assassin's head in his hands and smashed it against the floor, over and over. When he heard the man moan and felt him slump limply in his hands, Matt let go.

The room was suddenly bathed in light, and Matt jerked around. Ariadne stood at the doorway, her eyes widened in horror as she surveyed the scene. "What—?" she cried.

"I'm not sure yet," Matt rasped, catching his breath. "I think it's safe to say that this man just tried to kill you."

"Oh, my God," Ariadne said. "Are you all right?"

Matt nodded. "I'm fine."

They heard footsteps in the hallway, and Sugar, soon followed by Adrian, stood in the doorway. "What the hell?" Sugar cried. She rushed to Ariadne and put her arms around her.

Adrian stared at Matt. "Who is it?"

Matt shook his head. "I don't know yet," he said. "I'll question him after I've tied him up and gotten him out to the pool house."

"Ariadne, why don't you come with me?" Sugar said.

"No," she replied. "I'm staying here with Matt."

Matt was going to protest, but he saw the determination in her eyes. "Adrian, why don't you take Sugar downstairs? Have a drink or something while we finish up here."

"I don't think—" Sugar began.

"Let's go," Adrian said, taking Sugar's arm. "We're only in the way."

"Well . . . okay," she agreed.

When they had left the room, Matt took Ariadne in his arms. "I could've lost you." He hugged her firmly to him and felt a slight tremor in her body. "Are you sure you're okay?"

She nodded. "Yes, really I am."

"Okay," Matt replied, knowing that she was being very brave. "Do you have some panty hose handy?"

"Panty hose?"

"Yes. I want to tie him up, and I don't want to go downstairs or out to the garage to get some rope."

Ariadne quickly opened a dresser drawer and handed several pairs of panty hose to Matt.

"Now, while I tie him up, see if you can find his gun," Matt told her.

Ariadne looked about the bedroom, and her eyes soon alighted on the pistol. It lay menacingly on the floor against a closet door. She picked it up, examining it as she took it to Matt.

"Careful with that," he said. "Here. Let me have it." With one hand, he held both of the assassin's, reaching for the pistol with his free one. When Ariadne handed it to him, he shoved it between the mattress and the box spring of the bed, concealing it from view.

He began expertly tying up the assassin, rolling him over on his stomach first. He wrapped the panty hose around his wrists several times, securing his hands first. He repeated the process with his feet, but left about six inches of space between them, so he could walk, just barely.

"This will do for the time being," Matt said.

Ariadne, who had been staring at the man, nodded. "I've never seen him before in my life," she said. "At least not that I know of. It's so weird to think that he tried to kill me."

Matt got up off the floor and put his arms around her. "We'll find out who he is," he said. "Not that it's any comfort."

"You saved my life," Ariadne said.

"I guess so," he said, hugging her. He could feel her shaking harder now, and knew that the reality of what had happened was beginning to sink in. He wanted to keep her busy for the time being to help keep her mind off it. He needed to get the assassin out of the bedroom and out to the pool house, where he could question him.

"Can you do me a favor?" he asked.

"Anything."

"Go to my bedroom and get me some clothes. Just pants, shirt, and shoes."

At that moment Ariadne saw that he was wearing only his Jockey shorts. "I didn't even realize . . . ," she murmured. "I'll be right back."

"Thank you."

When she left the room, he searched the man's trousers, looking for identification, but all of his pockets were empty. He untied his track shoes and took them off his feet. Likewise. Nothing hidden in them. *I'll do a complete search once I get him out of here,* Matt decided.

Ariadne returned with his clothes, and he quickly put them on. He took the pistol from its hiding place and shoved it down the back of his jeans at his spine. He looked at Ariadne. "Now, why don't you go downstairs and make us both a drink? I'm going to take him out to the pool house to get some answers out of him."

"I want to stay with you," she said.

"I insist," Matt replied. "I'll have a much better chance of getting information out of him if we're alone. You'll be a distraction for both of us."

"But—"

Matt shook his head. "No buts," he said. "You were just nearly killed, Ariadne, and I'm going to find out who this creep is."

She saw that he was serious and realized, too, that he didn't want her to watch if he had to use force to get answers from the assassin.

"Please go downstairs to the library," Matt said. "I won't be a long time."

"Okay."

When she was gone, he went into the bathroom and filled a glass with water, then went back to the bedroom. He threw some in the man's face, but there was no immediate reaction. He kicked him in the thigh, not hard enough to do him injury, but enough to get a response. Matt heard a moan, then watched as the man opened his eyes and began to struggle against the nylon that bound him tightly.

Matt roughly grabbed his arm. "Get up," he ordered.

The man didn't move, and Matt repeated his command. "Get up. Now. Unless you want me to call the police."

The man did as he was told with Matt's help, gaining purchase on the floor with his bare feet. When he was upright, Matt took him by the arm and led him downstairs and out the front door. He wanted to avoid the others, if possible. He frog-marched him out to the pool house, where he started his interrogation, thankful for once that he'd been trained in a number of methods by the CIA.

They had been sitting in the library for what seemed like hours.

"I can't understand what's taking so long," Sugar said.

"Leave it to Matt," Adrian said. "He knows what he's doing."

"Do you think we should call the police?"

"That's probably not a good idea," Adrian said, "but we'll ask Matt when he comes in. There would be publicity. Articles in the newspaper. That sort of thing. We don't want any questions about anything or anyone. Especially Ariadne."

"Of course not," Sugar agreed.

They heard a door open and close, and Matt came into the library from the direction of the kitchen. Ariadne jumped up off the sofa and rushed to him. "You're okay?"

"Yes," he said. "And you?"

"Worried about you. That's all."

Sugar and Adrian looked at each other, and Sugar nodded as if to confirm what they believed had been going on for some time.

"Let me get you something to drink," Ariadne said. "Wine or something stronger?"

"Wine's good."

"What did you find out?" Adrian asked.

Matt sat down on the sofa, and Ariadne quickly sat beside him, handing him a glass of wine. He took a sip, then set the glass down. "Very little," he said in a guarded voice. "He claims he doesn't know who sent him. Only a voice at the other end of the phone. Payment was a wire from one numbered Swiss account to another."

"Do you believe him?" Adrian asked.

Matt nodded. "Actually, I do. That's the way these things often work. Nobody wants his or *her*," he said with emphasis, "identity known."

"Makes sense," Adrian said. "Did he say whether the caller was male or female?"

"Female, for certain, although that doesn't necessarily mean she was the person who hired him."

"What do you think?" Adrian asked him.

"I think we have to be a lot more careful," Matt said. "Whoever sent him will try again." He took Ariadne's hand in his.

"And the assassin?" Sugar asked.

"He's gone," Matt said.

"Gone?" Ariadne said.

"Think about it," Matt said. "Since calling the police is out of the question, I had no choice, unless I was supposed to off him and get rid of the body. I don't think he'll be back, like I said, but we're going to have to be very careful. Just because whoever it was failed this time . . ."

Ariadne squeezed his hand. *My twin sister's probably trying to have me murdered,* she thought, *and I've never even met her.*

Chapter Twenty-seven

❧

The big night was at hand.

In midtown, Nikoletta was ensconced in her penthouse triplex atop the stunning new PPHL headquarters building that would be inaugurated this evening. Sixty-eight stories below, the red carpet had already been rolled out, and with binoculars she could clearly see it through the floor-to-ceiling windows in her apartment. She could also see up the Hudson River and the West Side of Manhattan past the George Washington Bridge to the Palisades and beyond. When she looked east, she saw past the modern sculptural top of the Condé Nast Building in Times Square, across the entire East Side to Queens, Brooklyn, and Long Island beyond. If she looked south, the missing towers of the World Trade Center, which had once been a lodestar to Manhattanites, immediately came to mind, despite the view of the Verrazano Narrows and Staten Island in the distance.

Putting down her binoculars, she slipped into a pair of flats, threw on a trench coat, and rang for Butch, one of her security guards. "I want to go down to the lobby for a few minutes to see how things are going."

"I'll get some of the men," he replied.

"No," Nikoletta said. "Just you."

"I think—"

"I don't give a damn what you think," Nikoletta said. "Let's go." She took a pair of sunglasses from her purse, slipped them on, and pressed the button for the private elevator that traveled directly to her entrance foyer, before Butch could get it. It opened immediately, and they stepped in.

Descending to the lobby in the high-speed elevator took only a very short time, and after they stepped out, Nikoletta began quickly walking toward the main lobby, with Butch at her side.

Nikoletta stopped to survey the huge space. Thanks to the acres of marble, the clever use of mirrored screens, and over sixty crystal chandeliers made especially for the occasion, Lawrence Lowell, the party planner, and his theatrical set-design wizards had transformed the towering lobby and the vast atrium, with its various mezzanines, from functional architectural spaces into a Galerie des Glaces worthy of Versailles, as he had promised. Nikoletta made a mental note to use Lawrence again and possibly try to talk him into an exclusive contract with PPHL, so that none of her competitors, whether business or social, would have the privilege of using his services.

Everywhere she looked caterers, decorators, and florists, all coordinated by Lawrence, were frenziedly adding last-minute finishing touches. Musicians, from the string quartet to the two dance bands and the DJ, were warming up, testing instruments and electronic equipment. Waiters and waitresses circulated among the round tables, using measuring tapes to make certain the settings were perfectly aligned. Everywhere, everyone was making certain everything was just so.

For Nikoletta had demanded perfection, and she could see that she was receiving it. In abundance, the way she liked it. As she wandered through the vast space unrecognized by all but a few of the army of people readying for the party, she looked out toward Forty-second Street.

Butch followed her gaze. "The police have already cordoned off the two lanes of Forty-second closest to the building," he said, pointing toward the main entrance doors.

"I see," Nikoletta said, gratified that she got such cooperation from New York's Finest.

"Security's going to be extra tight tonight," he went on. "A private security firm is screening all staff as they get here. When the guests arrive, their credentials and invitations will be screened, too. Their invitations warned that everyone would need a picture ID, no exceptions, and the invitations also have a special mark embedded in the paper that can only be read by ultraviolet light."

Nikoletta nodded. She was accustomed to such precautions, especially for large events, but she didn't recall them using the special mark in invitations before. "That sounds like a very good idea."

"They're so easy to copy nowadays," he said. "Crooks can get the same paper and use computers, but they'd be hard put to know about the mark or what it was, much less duplicate it."

"Damn," Nikoletta said under her breath.

"What?"

"I see some of those Mother Earth's Children protesters across the street," she murmured.

"The police are keeping them and all the rubberneckers, even the pedestrians, on the far sidewalk across the street, so I think it'll be all right."

"I wish they could get rid of them altogether."

Butch shrugged. "It's a free country," he said. "But I wouldn't let it worry me too much. They're across several lanes of traffic, cordoned off, and there'll be a big police presence besides our own plainclothes security."

Nikoletta turned back to the lobby for another look-see. It would be crowded with hundreds of important people tonight in their finest apparel and most exquisite jewels. *All for me,* she thought. *Even if they aren't all necessarily my friends or allies, they'll be here.* Her mind wandered to the board of advisers, who were supposed to be both. They would all be here tonight, even though they were scheming against her in what had once been secrecy. Their secret was out, of course, as was hers. They knew it, and she knew it. After the recent failed attempt on the impostor, there was no question that they were working against each other.

The impostor. Will she be here tonight? Nikoletta wondered. *I wouldn't be surprised. She'll surely turn up soon.*

"Let's go," she said to Butch. She quickly headed toward the elevator banks with him at her side. "I don't think any of that scum's going to ruin my party, but I want you to do me one very special favor tonight."

"What's that?" he asked.

"Keep an eye out for anyone who looks like me."

"Looks like you?" he said, staring at her quizzically.

"Yes. And alert the others. I want to know the instant she shows up, if she does."

*   *   *

Despite the small army of guards and guns for hire, Kees Vanmeerendonk had already gained entrance to the building. He wasn't exactly the spitting image of security expert H. Richard Pipe, but some mustache and eyebrow dye had fashioned him into a reasonable enough facsimile. And the various forms of documentation he carried passed muster.

Dressed in the high-level security executive's uniform of a Brooks Brothers suit and silk tie, with an all but invisible earphone planted in one ear and a miniature microphone pinned to his lapel, the fake H. Richard Pipe patrolled the tarted-up lobby of the new PPHL International Headquarters with a show of reassuring professionalism.

He couldn't help but feel a frisson of excitement. Nikoletta Papadaki was here, in this very building, soon to make a sweeping entrance to her own party—

—soon to *die*.

For the first time since his amateurish failed attempt on her life in St. Barth's, he felt a peculiar intimacy with her. The intimacy a hunter felt with his prey, he thought.

Indeed, Nikoletta Papadaki was so close in proximity that Kees Vanmeerendonk could practically smell her. He could also virtually taste the blood that would shortly pump, unchecked, out of her deceptively fragile-looking body.

What a pity she's so beautiful, he thought.

On the other hand, her beauty would make her all the more an appropriate sacrifice to mother earth.

Frans, who still had trouble forcing himself to leave the safe but lonely confines of his downtown loft, had been persuaded to venture uptown for the grand opening of the PPHL headquarters.

"Bianca would've wanted you to, Frans," Nikoletta had told him. "After all, you have to remember that she spent her entire working life at PPHL. She was devoted to the company, and the things we do to try to help people."

Frans, who in reality knew almost nothing about the company and didn't care one way or the other about it, had finally agreed to go, but not only for Bianca. He felt that he owed Nikoletta, even if the sex for him had been no more than a release. An enjoyable release, but not like making love to Bianca.

Now, dressed in white tie and devastatingly handsome, he sprawled across the bed in Nikoletta's room, sipping bourbon, bored as he watched her being pampered. He thought of a thousand places he might be instead, but he knew that he was incapable of enjoying them anyway. What was the use of going someplace if Bianca couldn't go along? The emptiness he had felt after her death remained the only constant in his life.

Nikoletta was not insensitive to his mood, but she thought the best policy regarding Frans was to cajole him into action, especially activity that revolved around her. Dismissing her hair stylist and makeup artist, she stepped into her gold python sheath and turned around.

"Zip me up, darling, will you?" she asked Frans.

He dutifully pushed himself up off the bed and obliged her.

"Now, how about popping the cork on a bottle of champagne, hmmm? I have plenty of time for a celebratory drink or two."

"You're in an awfully good mood," Frans remarked.

"It wouldn't do to arrive too early for my own party, now, would it?" she said. "I mean, that's definitely not the way to make a grand entrance. What do you think, Frans, darling? Hmmm?"

Frans didn't care before, and now he cared less than ever. The bourbon was taking him down. Down to a dark, unhappy place inside that her chirping was beginning to antagonize.

On West Forty-third Street, after being ensnarled in Manhattan gridlock, a black stretch limousine with diplomatic plates finally arrived at the rear garage entrance of the new PPHL International Headquarters. A uniformed security guard with a roster on a clipboard, as well as the candy-striped steel barrier that stretched across the entrance, halted the limousine's progress. The guard on duty went to the driver's window to check him out.

A tinted rear window slid open and Angelo Coveri, smoking a noxious cigar, thrust out his invitation, as well as his PPHL ID. A second guard rushed from the garage and took Angelo's invitation and ID, then leaned down to peruse the second passenger. Angelo partially obscured his view by exhaling a dense cloud of smoke. But through it the guard made out a beautiful young woman with waist-long platinum hair, wearing big sunglasses. She was dressed in a lavish red satin floor-length cape that was pinned together with a massive diamond brooch.

Had the guard had a better view, he might have noticed the gold python shoes she wore, pointy-toed, backless, and held in place with ankle straps. But he didn't have the opportunity, nor would the shoes have meant anything to him.

In rapid-fire Italian, Angelo said something to the platinum-haired woman, and she sighed tiredly in response. She opened a red satin purse and handed him an Italian diplomatic passport. Angelo had borrowed it from a friend at the consulate who had long blond hair, and although she was much older and less glamorous-looking than the woman beside him, he was certain the ruse would work. After all, he was on the board of PPHL. Besides, passport photos never looked flattering. Most of them looked like mug shots.

He handed the passport to the guard, who perused it with a frown, compared it with the blonde in the limousine, then gestured for the other guard to take a look.

Now it's time to pull rank, Angelo thought. Pretending to be fed up with the delay, he brandished his PPHL ID in their faces. "Didn't you see this?" he asked in an irritated voice. "I'm on the board of PPHL, for God's sake, and I don't have all night to sit here."

The guards took a second look at his ID. "Oh, I'm sorry, sir," one of them said.

"I should hope so," Angelo said. "You should be fired for keeping me and the marchesa waiting. If you value your jobs, you won't let this happen again."

"I'm new, sir," the guard said in his defense, "and I—"

"Never mind," Angelo said impatiently. "We have a party to go to."

The guard holding the passport handed it back to him. Then they both stepped aside. One of them pushed the button on an electronic opener, and the steel barrier across the garage entrance lifted. The driver maneuvered the big limousine down into the multistory underground parking garage.

"Whew!" Ariadne exclaimed, releasing a pent-up breath. "That was a close call. For a moment there, I felt like giving myself up."

"There, there," Angelo said. Using a handkerchief, he dabbed perspiration from her forehead.

"Thank you, Angelo," Ariadne said. "I guess my nervousness made me break out in a sweat. Well, that and the wig and the big cape. I feel almost smothered by them."

"Try to relax," he said in a soothing voice.

"Relax!"

"Well, we smuggled you inside, didn't we? The worst is over."

She lowered her sunglasses, and the look she shot him over the rims let him know that they both knew better. Gaining entry into the building was only the first step of many more to come.

As if reading her mind, Angelo said, "Don't think beyond the moment. The immediate moment. We will cross each bridge as we come to it. We can handle that, can't we?"

"Yes." Ariadne nodded. Actually, she wasn't really certain that they could pull it off, but she didn't want to tell Angelo that.

He squeezed her hand and smiled. "That's more like it."

The driver walked around to the rear of the limousine and held the door open for Ariadne. "Marchesa?" he murmured.

Marchesa! she thought. She scoffed. *I'm not only a phony marchesa. I'm a phony Nikoletta, too. God help me, I'm a phony everything!*

The driver helped her out, and she smiled. "Thank you, Marchese," she said.

Matt smiled. "My pleasure, Marchesa."

With Angelo on one arm and the marchese on the other, the marchesa was led into the elevator and up to the party.

Despite the blue wooden barriers, the battery of policemen, and the traffic cops directing motorists, the entire area was madness. Searchlights crisscrossed the sky as at a film premiere, and the new PPHL International Headquarters was awash in floodlights, the latest testament to architectural genius and a worthy addition to the city's skyline. It glowed brighter than any other building in Manhattan.

At street level, the cavalcade of limousines, town cars, and even the occasional taxi spilled out the high-and-mighty, including several former world leaders, powerful politicians, captains of industry, the titled and the talented—members of those parallel and sometimes overlapping universes, the A-lists of both international high society and café society—plus movie stars, recording artists, and various and sundry celebrities. In short, the most select from every sphere of influence were let out directly at the red-carpeted entrance to the new building.

The men were primarily in white tie, although a few chose the less formal black tie, and the women disproved the old adage about the extravagant plumage of the male peacock. Bedecked with jewels, they seemed to float above the carpet, held aloft by billowing gowns of unimaginable lushness, color, and beauty.

Across the street, mere passersby caught up in the crowd, as well as spectators who'd come specifically to see who could be seen, watched enthralled. The fans of the stage, screen, and music luminaries created such hysteria that for much of the time their screams drowned out the chants of the demonstrators from Mother Earth's Children.

High above the hubbub, like a remote goddess atop Mount Olympus, Nikoletta Papadaki welcomed three visitors. Percy, her butler, had admitted them into her futuristic triplex penthouse in the sky.

"Honor," Nikoletta said, "how lovely to see you."

They exchanged air kisses. "Yes," Honor Hurlstone murmured. She wore a smile that seemed to have been set upon her face with cement. She had come out of a sense of duty to the company, but her heart was not in it.

Nikoletta greeted Adrian Single with a hug. "How nice to see you," she said acidly. "You've been spending so much time in the country that it's been a while."

"Well . . . yes," Adrian said.

"But you no doubt met my emissary?" she asked with an arched brow.

"Your . . . emissary?" Adrian paused for a moment, then realized whom she was talking about. *She sent the assassin,* he thought, *and now she's boldly telling me as much.*

"I think so," Adrian said smoothly, "even if only for a minute."

"Too bad you didn't get to spend a lot more time with him," Nikoletta replied with a nasty undertone.

"Hello, darling," Sugar Rosebury said, interrupting them. She exchanged air kisses with Nikoletta. "This is some party you've arranged."

"I hope you have fun," Nikoletta said. "Where are Yves and Angelo? Didn't you come together?"

"No," Sugar said. "But you needn't fear. I spoke to them, and they're definitely coming. They're most likely held up in traffic. Have you seen what it's like down there?"

"Yes," Nikoletta said. She tinkled laughter. "I've been watching with my binoculars." She led them into the vast living room of her penthouse. "Everybody have a seat, please. We'll have a little champagne and caviar. Then if you like, I'll give you the grand tour."

"Oh, I'd love that," Sugar exclaimed, looking about at the futuristic decor. "This is so different from your town house."

"I was getting sick of all that overstuffed English coziness," Nikoletta said. "Besides, it was never really me."

"Frans," Sugar said, seeing him slumped alone in a chair in a far corner of the room. She went to him and gave him a kiss on the cheek, inhaling the reek of bourbon as she did so. "How are you, darling?"

Frans looked up at her with glazed blue eyes. "Fabulous," he said sarcastically. "Can't you tell?"

"Well, it's wonderful to see you out and about," Sugar said.

He nodded.

Oh, dear, Sugar thought. *He's really in bad shape tonight.* She returned to the others, who were taking champagne flutes proffered by a waiter and scooping up caviar on toast points from another. "Frans seems in not very good shape," Sugar said to Nikoletta. "Do you think he ought—?"

"Oh, just ignore him," she replied flippantly. "He's fine. Just sulking as usual."

After a few minutes of small talk, most of it centered on the living room and its decor, Nikoletta proposed a grand tour. "I'll take you myself," she said. "You've got to see what I've done here."

They followed her about the apartment's three enormous floors and its expansive terraces, ooohing and aaaahing at all the appropriate moments. It was a feast to behold, a combination of glass, steel, marble, granite, and onyx—all hard, shiny surfaces, much like Nikoletta herself—but it was softened somewhat by luxuriously soft leathers and silks with a smattering of tropical plants. Orchids bloomed in abundance, and the terraces were magnificently landscaped with trees, shrubs, and flowers, as was the area around the heated pool.

When the tour was over at last, they returned to the living room, where Nikoletta had the waiters ply them with more champagne and beluga caviar.

"Shouldn't we be getting down to the party?" Adrian inquired.

Nikoletta laughed. "And ruin my grand entrance? No, I want everyone gathered there first. Then you and Honor and Sugar will go ahead and be my, well, my honor guard, so to speak. And Angelo and Yves, if they've arrived by then. *Then* Frans will escort me in."

To the sound of trumpets? Sugar was tempted to ask, but stifled the urge.

"And those bodyguards outside your door?" Adrian asked, referring to the ex–Secret Service agents with their tiny earphones and lapel microphones. "Aren't they your honor guard?"

Nikoletta laughed. "Good heavens, no! They're just my Praetorian guard!"

Chapter Twenty-eight

❧

The more Ariadne gazed about the expansive lobby, the more it appeared to her that the number of guests had multiplied exponentially. The noise level of all those voices was like distant surf: white noise that, amazingly enough, rose in that towering space and was somehow magically absorbed, unable to drown out even the performance of Mozart by the first-rate quartet.

She found herself agog. She had been exposed to a lot in the last few weeks, but now she was truly amazed. Humbled. And, yes, thrilled to be part of such an overwhelming spectacle, the likes of which she'd never seen. Never in her life had she been exposed to such luxury and pomp. She was nearly at the point of sensory overload.

She watched streams of new arrivals, each couple's entrance so flawlessly picture-perfect it must surely have been choreographed in advance, she thought, or they were such old hands at attending formal events that practice had indeed bred perfection. There was a veritable typhoon of tycoons, she thought with a laugh, and they wore their wealth as casually as the hand-tailored tailcoats they so often pretended to loathe. The women, she observed—yet further reflections of their financial and social prowess— were like storybook beings who appeared to float above the marble floors as though unhindered by the earthbound rules of lesser mortals.

Even the platoons of formally attired waiters circulating with champagne- and canapé-laden trays seemed not to walk so much as *glide,* as though they were extras performing in some Fred Astaire movie and might, at any moment, break out into song.

Surely, Ariadne thought, *this requires some hidden puppet master, some invisible maestro whose every signal of a magical baton ensures seamless continuity. For without him, how would such masterful coordination ever be possible?*

Then it occurred to her that the hidden puppet master was none other than her twin sister, Nikoletta. She felt her stomach lurch with the thought. *And I am supposed to impersonate this . . . this superbeing?* She doubted that all the training and exposure in the world could ever prepare her for such a formidable task, for it was obvious that Nikoletta was born to stage extravagances like tonight's, and Ariadne realized that she wouldn't even know where to begin.

Despite her awe at the spectacle, judging from the reactions of others at the party, Ariadne fitted right in. In her swirl of floor-length red satin, she didn't realize that she was creating a sensation to which she was blind. She was a flawless ruby strewn among gems of lesser quality, an effect that was unintended.

Angelo Coveri was the most socially gregarious and savvy among his coconspirators. Despite their sophistication, none of them mixed with all strata of society as well as Angelo, nor did any of the others possess the finely tuned social radar that Angelo had acquired. This evening his radar was on full alert, and he was certainly aware of the sensation that Ariadne, the marchesa, and Matt, the marchese, left in their wake. *She couldn't be in better hands than mine,* he thought. That was why he had insisted that he escort her, along with Matt as security. Like a seasoned general in command of a familiar battlefield, he strategically escorted them safely through the potentially lethal minefield, cunningly honing in on the least important and least inquisitive of his vast circle of acquaintances. Thus, he expertly steered them clear of likely trouble spots—the most curious, sharp-eyed, and famously loose-tongued chatterboxes. While Adrian, Yves, or Sugar might have handled some situations adroitly, they would doubtless have become involved in conversation with just the sort of people he was avoiding.

Still, everyone who laid eyes on Ariadne and her handsome young escort—the chest of his tuxedo pinned with elaborate military-looking decorations—was dying to know who the beautiful creature and her husband or boyfriend were, and asked where Angelo found them. To avoid complications, he endlessly repeated what they had agreed upon in advance, introducing Ariadne and Matt not by name but merely as "the marchesa . . . a daughter of an old friend of the family's . . . and her husband, the marchese. . . ."

The sly ruse he invented worked wonders. Ariadne didn't even have to speak, but merely nodded her head in greeting. He apologized to one and all. "The marchesa and marchese have terrible sore throats. Nothing contagious, I am happy to report. It's all the flying they've done recently, they say. Real globe-trotters, these two."

Ariadne would touch her neck, look appropriately apologetic, and smile. Matt would smile and nod. *"Scusi,"* he would murmur. As the elaborate social minuet continued, and Angelo Coveri shepherded her around, Ariadne and Matt didn't once forget his exhortation: to keep on smiling. Which they did, even though Ariadne's teeth were starting to ache.

Platinum wig aside, Sugar Rosebury's artistry at makeup had done the rest. Ariadne didn't resemble Nikoletta in the least, nor would it have occurred to anyone to connect the two. Thus, the mysterious and beautiful marchesa and her marchese convincingly played the part of old family friends of Angelo Coveri's.

While the party downstairs was going splendidly, upstairs in Nikoletta's penthouse, a minor crisis was threatening to foil her best-laid plans. Frans had been sipping bourbon for hours, and he suddenly decided that Nikoletta had not been paying enough attention to him. This, after he'd ignored her all afternoon and the other guests since they'd arrived. As they finally prepared to go downstairs to join the party, Frans balked.

"Go with *them,*" he cried from the long leather couch where he'd most recently slouched. "You obviously don't need *me,* Niki."

Nikoletta couldn't believe such treachery. Frans had always been difficult to handle, but no one had ever refused her at the last moment like this. Then it occurred to her that someone had: Frans. At the birthday party she'd planned for him in East Hampton. The thought infuriated her.

"Oh, for Christ's sake, come on!" she snapped, forgoing use of the more gentle voice she usually employed with him. "Will you get with it?" She stomped a gold python-covered heel on the marble floor.

When he didn't move, she became infuriated. Bending over, she grabbed his arm with both of her hands and physically hauled him off the couch. To keep from falling to the floor, Frans scrambled to his feet. When Niki straightened up, there was the ominous but unmistakable sound of ripping threads.

"*Shit!*" she cried. "Now look at what you've done!"

Shit, Sugar agreed silently with a sinking feeling as she watched.

"I didn't do anything," Frans said recalcitrantly.

Nikoletta ran to the nearest mirror and examined herself by looking over her shoulder. Sugar, too, hurried over to investigate the damage. One look was enough. Sugar shut her eyes and sighed. *We're screwed,* she thought.

"Can your maid sew it back up, you think?" asked Sugar.

"If it were normal fabric," Niki said, "but this being snakeskin—"

Talons extended, Nikoletta whirled around and stalked to the couch, where Frans was once again sprawled. "Look what you've done. You *fuck*!" she shrieked, slapping his face with her hands.

"Me?" he retorted, shrinking back from her slashing nails. "I didn't do a damn thing."

"That's the trouble with you!" she snapped. "Now I have to go change into something else. Goddamn it!"

She looked on the verge of either tears or murder; it was impossible to tell which, Sugar thought. But knowing Nikoletta as well as she did, murder would be the more obvious choice.

"I bought this dress expressly for tonight!"

"Look, Niki. I'm sorry," he said in a pitiful voice.

"Sorry? Sorry is supposed to fix this? Sorry doesn't begin to describe you!"

Sugar, Adrian, and Honor could see that Nikoletta was not going to let him off easily. She was determined to give him a good tongue-lashing before seeing to the dress or changing. They stepped out onto a terrace so as not to listen to the personal battle, complete with Nikoletta's veritable arsenal of filthy words in several languages. All Sugar could think about was that Ariadne was downstairs in the identical dress, beneath the red satin cape. With both twins wearing the same outfit, making the switch would have proved difficult under the best of circumstances. But now, with Nikoletta having to change into something else . . .

Sugar realized that it was vital for Ariadne, Matt, Angelo, and Yves to be forewarned of this latest development. She went back inside and waited for a break in the continuing harangue that Nikoletta had let loose on Frans. Frans was slow to retort, and she saw her chance. "Excuse me, Niki, darling, but don't you think one or two of us should go on downstairs and circulate among the guests?" she suggested.

But Nikoletta was in no mood to be accommodating to anyone. "No!" she responded. "Nobody goes anywhere without me."

"Okay," Sugar said. Then, quickly thinking, she said, "Oh, I need to use the powder room. I'll be right back." Sugar thought she'd have privacy and enough time in the powder room to whip out her cell phone and make some quick calls.

Nikoletta nixed that, too. She grabbed Sugar by the arm and held her tightly. "You'll have to wait. Come with me. I need you to help me decide what to wear."

"But—"

"Come on! We're wasting precious time!"

Sugar could hardly believe her predicament. She saw that Adrian and Honor had come in from the terrace, but it was no use to try to tell Adrian to send a message downstairs. She shot him a glance of helplessness, and he returned it with a puzzled shrug.

Almost all of the guests had arrived, and the lobby and mezzanines were a constantly shifting sea of guests. Not for the first time, Angelo consulted his wristwatch.

"You're getting antsy," Ariadne noted. "Is something wrong that I don't know about?"

"I certainly hope not," Angelo replied. "The thing is, Niki and the others should all have made their appearances long before now. I wonder what could be keeping them."

As if answering him, the cell phone in his pocket vibrated. Angelo was tempted to ignore it, but on second thought he decided he'd better answer it.

It was Sugar. "I'm upstairs in Niki's bathroom, so I have to hurry. Something's come up."

Angelo, barely able to hear Sugar's whisper above the surrounding noise, kept Ariadne, Matt, and himself on the move toward an area where he saw fewer people. "What is it?" he asked, smiling all the while.

Sugar explained the problem.

"I see." Angelo's face became grim, but just as quickly his smile returned. He put his cell phone away.

"What now?" Ariadne asked.

"Oh, just a small snag," he lied. "Nothing of major consequence."

She gave him a challenging look. She had gotten to know him well enough in the last few weeks that she knew he was not being truthful. "Why don't I believe that?"

"You don't have to. All you have to do is keep smiling. You, too, Marchese," he added to Matt.

Matt smiled, but his eyes were scanning the enormous space, ever on the alert for anything amiss.

A half hour had passed, and Nikoletta finally decided on an alternate outfit. Sugar, grateful that she'd been allowed to use Nikoletta's bathroom, was helping her into the black, tan, and white embroidered tank top paired with a full tan silk ball skirt, both from Carolina Herrera. Nikoletta posed in front of a three-sided mirror in her dressing room, moving from left to right, silk rustling, and frowned at herself.

"I'm not sure this is exactly appropriate," she said.

"You look marvelous," Sugar assured her. "It's fabulous with your tan."

Nikoletta pulled a face. "It's not half as dramatic as the Cavalli snakeskin."

Sugar knew it was pointless to argue. How could she, when the other person was always right no matter what the issue? Besides, time was fleeting, and the guests were surely wondering what had happened to their hostess.

Finally Nikoletta let out a sigh. "All right," she said. "We might as well get going. Otherwise, the party will be over before we ever arrive."

The volume of hundreds of voices in the lobby and on the mezzanines dropped to a hush, and the string quartet abruptly segued into appropriately grandiose music, like that used for the triumphant entry of royalty. All attention turned to a glass-sided escalator descending to the main lobby floor. With two ex–Secret Service agents in the lead, followed in turn by Adrian, Honor, and Sugar, Nikoletta Papadaki made her sweeping grand entrance, with Frans following closely behind her. Behind him a contingent of four more security guards, outfitted with discreet earphones and lapel microphones, brought up the rear.

Ariadne set eyes on her twin sister for the first time in her life. She found herself filled with conflicting emotions that she couldn't begin to sort out. A knot formed in her stomach, and gooseflesh joined the tremble that ran up and down her body.

Matt felt her quiver and gave her hand a squeeze. Ariadne squeezed his in return. *Thank God he's here,* she thought.

Concealing her mouth with a gloved hand, Ariadne whispered, "Is that Honor Hurlstone, Angelo? The one in blue?"

"That," Angelo confided in a whisper, "is indeed Honor Hurlstone. Adrian's sister."

Ariadne felt her knees weaken, but she held on to Matt's arm tightly. She could hardly process what she was seeing. She had been curious about her real family. She had wished for this moment—or something like it—for as long as she could remember, but now that it had come, there could be no tearful embrace, no comfort from the arms of her sister being thrown about her in a hug. No words uttered in love, no getting to know each other, making up for all of the years that had gone by. They must remain strangers, for the time being, at least.

"Nikoletta's beautiful, isn't she?" Ariadne murmured at last.

"Oh, yes," Angelo said. "One of the great beauties of this age"—he gave Ariadne an appraising look—"as you are, Ariadne."

She hardly paid his words any mind because her gaze was fixed on the young woman who was her twin.

Nikoletta was greeted and congratulated effusively by throngs of friends and acquaintances and introduced to countless friends of friends. She never grew tired of the compliments and praise lavished on her, especially from the highest and mightiest, including the important architecture critics whose admiration for the building was universal. Any of those among their ranks who had dared make negative remarks about the structure hadn't been invited, so she was assured of nothing but praise. This didn't diminish the glittering success of the night. She allowed herself to be photographed by select members of the press, making certain that Frans was always at her side. He made the perfect accessory, she thought, especially for photographs, since the camera loved him.

As the evening wore on, Frans became increasingly bored, discontent, and withdrawn, eventually refusing to cooperate with Nikoletta, disengaging his hand from hers. He felt as if he'd been in the grip of a tigress and couldn't bear keeping up the pretense of the happy consort. Her harangue about the dress had been more than he could bear. Nikoletta, he decided, had finally shown her true colors. At one point, when she was engrossed in conversation with a contingent of friends from London, Frans slipped away without her noticing and made for the private elevator that took him upstairs to her apartment. He knew the security code that opened the elevator, but had trouble remembering it at first. The bourbon, mixed with champagne at the party, had taken its toll, but then he recalled that he'd written it down. He took his wallet out and found the code on the back of a limousine service's card. He pressed the number in, and the doors opened.

Thank God, he thought. *I'll have some peace at last.*

Honor and Adrian had mingled amiably with the guests and, like Nikoletta, had listened to a constant stream of compliments regarding the new headquarters and the wonderful party. Graciously responding to the praise heaped on Nikoletta, Honor had worn a smile that belied her state of mind all evening.

If only they knew, she thought. But she was well trained for her role. She had played it for many years.

She and Adrian had tried several times to speak to Angelo and the beautiful woman and handsome man with him, but every time they'd approached, Angelo had swept away with the couple.

"I wonder who they are," Honor asked Adrian.

"I don't know, but I hope they're someone special to him. God knows, he needs close friends." He hated lying to her, but for the time being there was no choice. "I think I heard they're Italian friends," Adrian added.

"I'm certain I haven't met them before," Honor said, "and I've met a lot of his friends in Italy."

"I don't recall whether I've met them or not," Adrian said, "but Angelo has a whole different life there, Honor."

"I get the distinct impression that he's avoiding us," she said.

"I doubt it. He's so busy introducing them to people. He'll get to us eventually." Adrian stifled a yawn. He was quickly wearying of the party and its artificial atmosphere. He had always endured Nikoletta's parties more than enjoyed them, and tonight was no exception.

"You're bored to death, aren't you?" Honor chided him. "You've been such a good sport to put up with all this." She felt a tap on her back and turned around. "Oh, Despina!" she cried.

She greeted her old friends from Greece, Despina and David. "You know Adrian, of course."

"Yes, yes."

"It's wonderful to see you," Adrian said. He saw the opportunity he'd been waiting for. "Honor, I'll be back in a few minutes," he said. "I just have to run upstairs for a bit."

"Of course," she said. "Take your time."

"Lovely to see you again," he said to David and Despina.

He left knowing that Honor was in good hands. She genuinely liked Despina and David and wouldn't mind being left with them for a while. He headed straight for the elevator to Nikoletta's apartment, intent on reaching it without having to engage in conversation with anyone else. When he got upstairs, he would take his shoes off, make himself a drink, and relax for a while, away from the forced gaiety of the party.

He pressed in the security code, but the elevator doors didn't open. *That's odd,* he thought. *The elevator should be here, unless someone else has gone up.* He stepped in when it arrived, and reached the apartment very quickly in the high-speed car. In the living room, he went to a heavily stocked drinks table to pour himself a scotch.

If Frans hadn't moved, he wouldn't have noticed him, but the movement out on the terrace caught Adrian's attention. He peered out the window and nearly dropped the glass he'd picked up. Setting it down, he raced to the nearest door to the terrace. Stepping outside, he spoke very calmly, so as not to frighten the young man.

"Frans," he said. "Please get down from there. You might fall."

From atop the parapet that separated the terrace from the sidewalk sixty-eight floors below, Frans turned and looked at him quizzically. A violent gust of wind blew his hair into his face, and he brushed it aside.

"Please, Frans," Adrian said softly. "Please. Get down from there now. You could fall."

"I don't care," Frans said.

"But, Frans, *we* care," Adrian said. "We care about you."

"Nobody cares," Frans cried. "Nobody in the world."

Slowly Adrian came closer to him, trying not to make any sudden movements that would startle Frans. The parapet couldn't be more than eight inches wide, he thought, and even the slightest misstep on Frans's part could send him over the edge.

"Frans, that's not true," Adrian said. "Maybe Nikoletta was nasty because she was angry, but we all love you, Frans." He cringed at the anguished look in the young man's eyes. *What can I do?* he wondered desperately. *What can I say?*

"I know you miss Bianca terribly," he said, trying a slightly different tack. "But she wouldn't have wanted you to do this, Frans. Think of her. Think of Bianca. If something happened to you, she would be heartbroken."

"Bianca's dead!" Frans cried. "Dead!"

"I know, Frans, but she would want you to go on living. Don't you realize that?"

Adrian edged another two steps closer to the wall, hoping he wouldn't alarm Frans.

"She would want you to live to honor her memory," Adrian said. "I loved Bianca, too, and I know she would have wanted that."

Frans emitted a heart-wrenching cry, then began choking. Tears streamed down his face. Lifting both hands, he sobbed into them. Then his body jerked as he began tearing at his hair.

As Adrian hurried another couple of steps toward Frans, his breath caught in his throat. Frans was wobbling on the parapet, losing all control, sobbing so hysterically that he'd apparently forgotten where he was. Or he didn't care.

Just another couple of steps, Adrian thought, *and I can grab—*

Frans suddenly lurched forward and lost his footing. His body started to swing off the parapet into oblivion. Adrian launched forward, thrusting himself toward Frans's legs. He felt his hands on Frans's ankles, and he grasped at them and hung on with every ounce of strength he had.

Frans let out a cry, then fell off the parapet, landing atop Adrian.

Pain jolted through Adrian's shoulder, but he refused to let go. Frans lay inert on top of him, crying but less hysterically. Adrian gradually worked himself out from under, keeping a hold on him all the time, until Frans lay directly on the terrace.

Adrian twisted his head to shake off the pain in his neck and shoulders. "Come on, Frans," he said. "Let's go inside. You and me."

Frans sniffled, then sat up. He threw his arms around Adrian and held on to him tightly, still crying, his chest heaving against Adrian's. Adrian returned the hug, holding him in his arms, and let him cry. *Jesus,* he thought. *This boy really needs help. And he needs to get away from Nikoletta for sure. She must be the worst possible influence on him.*

After the crying had subsided, Adrian patted Frans's back. "Come on," he encouraged him. "Let's go inside now."

Frans nodded, then let Adrian help him to his feet. As an added precaution, Adrian still held on to his arm tightly, not certain that he wouldn't jerk away and try to jump again. But he let himself be guided through the terrace doors and into the living room, where he collapsed on a couch.

Relieved, Adrian walked to the drinks table and poured two scotches. He returned to the couch and offered one to Frans. "Here," he said. "Drink this. It won't solve any of your problems, but it might take the edge off at least."

"Thank you," Frans murmured, taking the drink. He took a sip, then quickly downed the remainder of the drink. The tension in his body was quickly melting, and the wild look in his eyes was rapidly being replaced by a glazed expression, as if he was tuning out reality.

"Want another?" Adrian asked, thinking that at this point another drink would do Frans no harm. In fact, he thought, it was perhaps a way to temporarily sedate him.

"Yes, please," Frans replied.

"Coming up." Adrian replenished the drink, then gave it to him.

"Thank you," Frans repeated, taking the glass. He took a quick sip, then another and another. Setting the drink down on the coffee table, he yanked his tie loose and pulled off his shoes. Heaving a great sigh, he spread out on the couch, listless and silent.

That problem seemed solved, Adrian judged. "I've got to make a quick phone call," he said. "Then I want to talk to you about this. Okay?"

Frans nodded slightly.

Adrian went out to the terrace, where he could watch Frans while he took out his cell phone. He pressed the speed-dial button for Sugar's cell phone. She knew Frans better than anyone here, with the exception of Nikoletta, so he thought he should consult with her about what to do.

Sugar answered on the third ring. "Hello?"

"It's Adrian. I'm upstairs in Niki's apartment. Frans tried to commit suicide, and I'm trying to figure out what the hell to do with him. Tonight of all nights."

"How?" Sugar said. "What did he do?"

"I saw him out on the terrace walking on the parapet."

"Jesus!" Sugar exclaimed. "Is he okay now?"

"He's spread out on a couch in the living room. I gave him a couple of drinks to try to help calm him down. I thought you might be able to talk to him."

"Of course," Sugar said. "Keep him occupied, and I'll be up in a jiffy."

"Thanks, Sugar," Adrian said.

"No problem," she responded, thinking that an ideal opportunity had just presented itself. She was surprised that Adrian didn't realize it himself, but reminded herself he had his hands full with Frans.

Adrian flipped his phone shut and went back into the living room. Frans still lay on the couch, his face turned toward the back of it. He could hear him quietly breathing. Adrian sat sipping his scotch, waiting for Sugar. *I'll let him rest,* he thought. *At least for the time being. But we're going to have to get him out of here soon.* Frans couldn't be around when they carried out their plan.

Richard Pipe stood on one of the mezzanines surveying the throng of people in the lobby. *Sitting ducks, all of them,* he thought. *For all their celebrity, their money, and power, I could blast any of them away in an instant. All of their silks and satins, their fancy jewels and hairdos, and their superior attitudes—they've got no protection from me.* He didn't think he'd ever seen so many of the powerful—and the polluting—assembled in one place before. He discreetly felt the revolver in its shoulder harness beneath his Brooks Brothers suit. He was getting anxious, but opportunities had been nonexistent so far. She'd come down to the party late, then had been constantly surrounded by a sea of sycophants. *Really sickening,* he thought, *the way they suck up to the bitch.*

He couldn't be more than thirty feet away from her, but there was no way he could safely get a shot in now. Not unless he was asking for immediate capture and life behind bars. He didn't want it to go down that way. He was sure the right opportunity would arise. She would eventually have to go to the head, where he could get her by herself or with only a few other chicks around. Or she'd be positioned somewhere near an exit, so he could make a quick getaway. It would happen tonight. He was sure of it. One quick pop would do it. Nikoletta Papadaki's polluted brains would decorate the new PPHL headquarters, just like her toxic waste that seeped into the ground all over the planet.

Sugar had to restrain her excitement. If everything worked out as she hoped it would, their problems were over. First, she decided, she would tell Nikoletta what had happened. She scanned the lobby and mezzanines, and Nikoletta wasn't difficult to spot. A group of rich young Greek scions was gathered in a clump around her.

When Sugar reached the crowd that surrounded Nikoletta, she stretched a hand into the air and waggled it to catch Nikoletta's eye. When she did, Nikoletta immediately snaked her way past her friends to Sugar.

"What's so important?" she asked, knowing that Sugar wouldn't be interrupting her otherwise.

Her hand to Nikoletta's ear, Sugar told her in a hushed voice, "I think you'd better get up to your apartment right away. Frans tried to commit suicide."

"What!"

Sugar nodded. "Yes. Adrian is with him now, but I think it would be helpful if you got up there."

"The selfish bastard!" Nikoletta said. "On a night that's so important to me! First he ruins my dress, and now this! I'll give him a piece of my mind."

No one attempts suicide unless they're in extreme distress, Sugar thought, *but for Niki it's an inconvenience.* "I think he's in pretty bad shape, Niki," Sugar said, "so you might want to go easy on him."

Nikoletta pouted her lips. "I'll go see about him," she said, "but I'll have to hurry back down to the party. Maybe you should come up and . . . oh, I don't know . . . call the doctor or something."

"I'll be there in just a few minutes," Sugar said.

"Hurry," Nikoletta said, then started toward the elevators.

Richard Pipe saw her rushing down the stairs off the mezzanine, and he went after her with a purposeful stride—not too slow, not too fast—that wouldn't attract much attention. When he got downstairs, he saw that she was making a dash for the back of the lobby.

Probably has to take a leak, he thought. *I got her now. Or maybe she's going upstairs to her apartment.*

He didn't dare get too much closer, or she might get on to him. Get suspicious. As he watched, she turned a corner into a small corridor. It led to another elevator bank. He passed by the corridor slowly and saw her enter a code. An elevator door opened immediately and she stepped inside.

She's dead meat now! he thought merrily. *Private elevators with security codes. A small corridor where nobody goes but the handful of people who know the codes. When she comes back downstairs, I can pick her off.*

He could hardly restrain his excitement. He stationed himself across from the small corridor, just out of the range of vision of anyone exiting the car that led to her penthouse. He wouldn't have to wait long because she wouldn't be gone long.

She's a party animal, he thought. *Can't get enough. Especially when she's the star. She'll be back in a flash, and that's when I'll get her.*

From the mezzanine, Sugar searched the crowd for Angelo and Ariadne and Matt, then spotted them toward the back of the lobby. Yves had joined them by now. She quickly worked her way through the crowd.

"Come with me now," she said, taking Angelo's arm.

"What's going on?" he asked.

She leaned in close and told them all.

"Oh, how horrible," Ariadne said.

"Yes, it is," Sugar agreed, "but it gives us the opportunity we've been waiting for."

"Where are we going?" Angelo asked.

"Back there to the freight elevators," Sugar replied.

"But why?"

"Don't you see?" Sugar said. "We're going up to Nikoletta's penthouse. It's the perfect opportunity."

They reached the freight elevator that led up to the penthouse. Sugar pressed in the security code that opened it, and everyone got on. On the way up, Sugar could see that Ariadne looked distressed. She reached over and squeezed her hand. "Sweetheart, everything is going to be all right."

The elevator reached the penthouse and opened onto a service area behind the kitchen.

"Now, all of you wait here," she said. "No one is going to call for the elevator because only a handful of us has the code. I'll be back in a few minutes. After I get rid of Nikoletta's bodyguards, if any of them came up with her."

"We're going to make the switch now?" Ariadne asked in alarm.

"Yes," Sugar replied. "I'm gratified that at least you have the sense to realize what's going on. All of you just stay here until I come and get you."

"But what about—?"

Sugar briefly told them what she planned to do. "Now, no more questions. I'll be back in a minute." She hurried out of the elevator, through the service area, and disappeared.

Sugar reached the entrance foyer that serviced the regular elevator without being seen. In the living room she found Frans still spread out on the couch. Adrian was sitting in a chair talking to Nikoletta, who was perched next to Frans.

Great, she thought when she saw that the bodyguards hadn't come upstairs with Nikoletta.

"How's he feeling?" she asked Adrian in a soft voice. He and Nikoletta looked up at her.

"He's been very quiet," Adrian said.

"So quiet he's hardly said a word to me," Nikoletta added.

"He needs absolute peace and rest now," Sugar said.

"I think you're right," Adrian said.

Sugar whispered to Nikoletta, "I think we should try to get Frans into one of the bedrooms and make him comfortable. What do you think?" She knew that Nikoletta would agree with her if she thought the idea had been hers to begin with.

"I think that's a good idea," Nikoletta said in a hushed reply. "I was going to ask a few special friends up after the party. If he's upstairs, he won't be in the way."

"I think it's a good idea," Adrian said. "Plus, he's resting well enough, and there would be a lot of publicity if we called a doctor now."

Nikoletta nodded, then patted Frans on the shoulder. "Frans? Will you get up and go to a bedroom? I've got to get back to the party, and then friends are going to be coming up here."

He didn't respond, but shifted his shoulder where she had patted it.

Sugar went over to him and leaned down. "Frans, sweetheart. It's Sugar. Let's go to bed. Okay? You need rest, and there's going to be a party here. Come on, sweetheart." She took one of his hands in hers.

Frans groaned, but began sliding his legs off the couch.

Nikoletta quickly stood up, clearing the way.

"You're going to be fine, Frans, sweetheart," Sugar said. "It's not far. Then you can sleep all you want to."

Adrian took one of Frans's hands, and Sugar took the other. Together they helped him to his feet and led him toward the spiral staircase that led upstairs. Nikoletta followed closely behind them. When they finally reached the guest room, Sugar quickly threw back the cover, and they helped him onto the bed. She drew the cover back over him, tucking him in.

"Sleep as long as you want, Frans," she said. "We'll be checking on you, so everything will be all right."

Flipping off the light switch, she closed the door to the room as they left, then went back downstairs to the living room.

"I'll be right back," Sugar said. "I've got to go to the powder room, darling."

"Hurry," Nikoletta said. "I need to get back downstairs to the party."

"In a jiffy." Sugar gave Adrian a significant look, and he nodded slightly, as if he understood. Sugar rushed to the service area, where the freight elevator was located.

"Come on," she said. "Hurry. I've got Niki alone in the living room and nobody else is around but Adrian."

The others stepped off the elevator and followed Sugar back to the living room. Ariadne lagged a bit behind the others. A lump the size of a walnut had lodged in her throat. The switch they had planned for weeks was going to be made now.

She had to become her twin sister.

Chapter Twenty-nine

✥

Nikoletta poured herself a glass of champagne and lit a cigarette while waiting for Sugar. "What's taking her so long?" she asked Adrian.

"Who knows?" Adrian said casually. "She's probably powdering her nose, putting on more lipstick. Whatever."

Nikoletta began pacing back and forth in front of the windows that looked out over the terrace. Looking out at the parapet, she wondered what to do about Frans. She was not in love with him—of that she was certain—but he was the sexiest-looking man she'd ever seen. Major arm candy, and that counted for a lot. Still . . .

She heard footsteps on the marble floor, a lot of them, approaching the living room. *Who the hell?* she wondered. *The bodyguards?* She and Sugar and Adrian had been alone. In the entrance hall Sugar appeared, along with Yves and Angelo, followed by some couple she didn't know. Adrian stood up to greet them.

"Well, well, well," Nikoletta said, "I finally have the pleasure of getting to see some more of my lovely board members. Here to pay your respects, I assume." Her voice was sarcastic. "And who are these people with you?" She gazed at Ariadne and Matt with curiosity.

"We have a little surprise for you," Angelo said, as Yves sat down.

"Oh, I doubt that you could surprise me, Angelo," Nikoletta replied airily. She stubbed out her cigarette in an ashtray.

As they had rehearsed, Ariadne reached up and loosened a couple of pins that helped hold her wig in place, and Angelo slipped it off. Ariadne then took off her sunglasses and slipped out of the red satin cape that enveloped her. Nikoletta's eyes widened in surprise, then narrowed to slits, but she couldn't take her eyes away from Ariadne.

She quickly recovered her composure. "I see you've brought the impostor with you," she said haughtily. "Don't think that I don't know about her."

Then she noticed that Ariadne was wearing the identical snakeskin Cavalli dress that she had planned to wear. "What the—?"

"I think it's time we explained," Adrian said coolly. "This is Ariadne Papadaki, Niki. Your twin sister."

"What?" she exclaimed. She looked at Adrian with disbelief before shifting her gaze back to Ariadne. "You're out of your mind," she snapped. "I don't have a twin sister."

"It's true," Adrian said. "I was there when she was taken away after your birth, so I know it's true."

"You're out of your mind!" Nikoletta screeched, quivering with rage. "I'm the only Papadaki heiress. The only one there is and the only one there'll ever be." Despite her words, she was completely flummoxed. She felt as if she were staring into a mirror.

Ariadne stared back at her speechless. She wished Nikoletta would come to her and embrace her as a sister. But she knew that would not happen. Not tonight. Not ever.

"I assure you that you're wrong," Adrian said. "She is your twin sister, and as such has a right to her share of the Papadaki empire."

"Get her out of here!" Nikoletta screamed. "Get her out of my sight!"

"I don't think so," Adrian said calmly. "We have other plans." He looked over at Matt and nodded.

Matt crossed the room to Nikoletta. Grabbing both of her arms and pulling them behind her, he quickly slipped handcuffs on her.

"You son of a bitch!" Nikoletta cried, struggling against the restraints. "I know what you're doing! I know! You're trying to replace me, aren't you? With her!" She spit the word as if it were poisonous. "Well, it won't work!"

"If you say another word, I'll gag you," Matt said firmly.

"Who the—"

Matt clamped a hand across her mouth tightly. "If gagging you doesn't work, then I'll use chloroform. Understand?"

Nikoletta's eyes had grown wide with alarm, but she nodded.

Matt slowly removed his hand, and she remained silent. The expression on her face, though, was one of utter hatred.

Sugar calmly took a cream-saturated cloth from a plastic bag in her evening purse. In brisk, broad strokes she began wiping away the thick makeup she had applied to Ariadne's face a few hours earlier. As heavy eyebrow pencil, rouge, eye shadow, lipstick, powder, and base makeup began to disappear, Nikoletta's twin began to emerge from beneath her mask.

Nikoletta couldn't help but stare at the woman. The awe that she had felt initially overcame her again. For a moment it was as if time had stopped. Nikoletta and the twin sister she had never known stared at each other. Then Nikoletta's expression contorted once again into an ugly rictus.

"You'll never get away with this," she snarled. *"Never!"*

She focused her attention on Adrian, her eyes burning with intensity. "You traitor!" she cried. "You're responsible for this. I'll kill you for this!"

She began shouting obscenities again, but Matt clamped his hand across her mouth again and held her all but immobile against him.

Ariadne watched the scene in horror. She had felt the same awe Nikoletta had experienced, but Ariadne had also felt a terrible shame wash over her. The reality of what they were about to do to her sister, evil though she was, almost overcame her. Yet when Nikoletta spewed a stream of obscenities, displaying all of the nastiness that she was known for, Ariadne was shocked. She regarded her with a mixture of disgust and sympathy. Her twin was everything they had described and more.

"We'd better get her undressed," Sugar said matter-of-factly. "It's time she put in a final appearance at the party."

Nikoletta made muffled noises against Matt's hand and began to struggle again, her eyes filled with rage. Matt let go of her with one hand and took a plastic bag out of his jacket pocket. Sugar opened it for him, and he pulled out a chloroform-saturated cloth. Releasing the pressure of his hand against her mouth momentarily, he shoved the cloth under Nikoletta's nose, pushing it into her nostrils. She struggled violently for an instant; then her head slumped forward.

Matt released her and gently placed her on the couch. From his jacket pocket he extracted another plastic bag, from which he removed a small plastic case. He held a hypodermic needle and a small alcohol-saturated cotton ball. He took them out of the case, pressed the plunger once to get any air out of the solution, and wiped a place on Nikoletta's arm with the cotton ball. Then he plunged the needle in, pressing all of the fluid into her. When he was finished, he said, "She's going to be out for hours."

"How long, do you think?" Angelo asked.

"Oh, around twelve hours, give or take."

"Will she have any ill effects?" Ariadne asked.

"No, she shouldn't," Matt responded. "It would be very rare if she did, and if so, just a sort of hangover." He retrieved his keys and removed the handcuffs from Nikoletta's wrists.

"Okay, gents," Sugar said. "Make yourselves scarce for a few minutes. Just don't go upstairs where Frans is sleeping."

"I think we ought to wait in the entrance hall," Matt said, "just in case anybody comes up. Just let me get ready." With Adrian's help, he quickly removed the military and other decorations that were pinned to his tuxedo and the two that hung around his neck on large ribbons. Then he slipped off the curly wig on his head and pulled off the mustache glued above his lip. "Ouch. That glue's really strong." He took off the large-framed glasses with clear lenses that he'd worn. "How do I look?"

"Comb your hair," Angelo said.

"And there's some glue from the mustache," Yves said. "You'll have to wash that off."

"Be right back," Matt said. "I'll meet you in the entrance hall."

Sugar and Ariadne began undressing Nikoletta, taking care with the delicate skirt and top. Ariadne felt very strange sensations—indescribable sensations—that threatened to overwhelm her as she helped strip the clothing off her mirror image. *This is someone with whom I was supposed to share my life.* She had to remember that her sister was an evil person, and that she had to right the wrongs that her twin had perpetrated.

When Nikoletta was naked, Ariadne threw her red satin cape over her, carefully tucking her in. Then she began dressing in her sister's clothes, fighting off the creepy feeling that donning each piece gave her.

When she was finished, she turned to Sugar. "What about shoes?" she asked.

"Leave yours on," Sugar replied. "No one will notice because of the floor-length skirt, and even if they do, they'll think that Niki changed shoes for some reason. Now, stand there and let me have a look at you."

Sugar stepped back a few paces and studied Ariadne. She clapped her hands together at last. "You look beautiful, sweetheart," she exclaimed. "If anything, more beautiful than Niki. You have an inner glow that Niki doesn't have, and it shows."

"I . . . I feel so . . ."

Sugar grasped both of Ariadne's hands in her own. "You are doing the right thing. You're doing a noble thing, as unpleasant as it may seem to you now."

Ariadne gave a wobbly smile. "I hope so."

Sugar let go of her hands, then fiddled with a few strands of Ariadne's hair. "Wait just a second," she said. "One more thing."

Sugar took a small silk makeup case out of her evening purse and opened it. She applied a little fresh lipstick to Ariadne's lips, a little blusher to her cheekbones, and, with delicate fingers, a small amount of eye shadow to her lids. She stood back and studied Ariadne's face again. "Perfect," she pronounced. "Wait here while I get the men." Sugar went off toward the entrance hall.

Gazing down at the sleeping body of her twin, Ariadne felt a knot clench in her stomach. The guilt Sugar had mentioned was part of it, but there was so much more twisted up into that knot. The overwhelming sense of loss she felt, knowing that she would never be friends with her twin and that they would probably never even get to know each other was the saddest part, she thought. There would never be anything other than a genetic bond between them.

Sugar hurried back into the living room, the men trailing behind her. "What do you think?" she asked them.

"Perfect," Adrian said. "I could never tell the difference."

"*Bellissima,*" declared Angelo. He approached Ariadne, and she gave him a kiss on the cheek.

"*Grazie,*" Ariadne said. "You've been so wonderful to me."

Tears came into the old man's eyes. "My Bianca is in heaven, and she is smiling because of you coming into my life, *cara.*"

"I can hardly believe it," Yves said with a shake of his head.

Sugar looked at Matt. "Matt? What do you think?"

Matt's eyes traveled up and down Ariadne's elegantly clothed body. "I'll take her," he said.

Everyone laughed.

"That isn't what I meant," Sugar said amiably.

"She'll certainly pass for Nikoletta," he said.

"What do we do about Nikoletta?" Ariadne asked.

"I'm going to take her upstairs to a bedroom," Matt said. He lifted Nikoletta from the couch and carried her upstairs. When he came back down, he joined Ariadne. "We're all set," he said. "Ready?"

"I think so," she said.

"You'll be fine," he told her. In his eyes she saw the confidence that he had in her.

Ariadne turned to address the others. In a loud voice she declared, "It's time to party."

The group got on the elevator, Ariadne leading the way.

When the car reached the lobby, everyone started piling off. Sugar, Adrian, Angelo, and Yves led the way out. As Ariadne and Matt followed, he spotted a security guard stepping directly into their path at the end of the corridor, a hand slipping inside his suit jacket.

Without a moment's hesitation, Matt gave Ariadne a hard shove back toward the elevator, knocking her down. She let out a cry of alarm as she hit the marble floor. Simultaneously, Matt hunkered down to shield Ariadne and whipped out the pistol in his shoulder holster. He took aim at the security guard, who fired off a wild shot before flinging his revolver to the floor and fleeing down the corridor. With all the people, Matt dared not shoot.

He yanked about. "Did you get hit?" he asked frantically, his eyes scanning her body for any indication that she had been.

Ariadne shook her head. "N-no," she said. "I'm okay."

"Take her back upstairs, Angelo," Matt ordered. Then he leaped to his feet and took off in the direction that the security guard had gone. Almost instantly, he saw that it was useless to attempt to find the man in the crowd. Hundreds of people were circulating in the lobby, including dozens of security guards in suits almost identical to the one the shooter had worn. The revolver had been silenced, so the crowd was unaware that anything had even happened. No one was pointing at a man running toward an exit. No one acted as if anything was out of the ordinary.

Retracing his steps, Matt went back to the corridor leading to the elevators. Ariadne, Angelo, and Sugar were in front of the elevator, and Adrian had joined them. One of Sugar's arms was around Ariadne's shoulders.

"I told you to take her back upstairs," Matt said to Angelo.

"She refuses to go," he replied, "and I can't make her."

"Ariadne—" Matt began.

"Nikoletta," she interjected. "And don't forget it."

For a moment he was nonplussed. Then he shook his head, a rueful smile on his lips. "Okay," he said, "but it might not be safe for you to stay down here. That guy may not have been acting alone."

"He's always been alone before," Ariadne replied. "You told me so yourself."

"Tonight might be an exception," Matt said.

"If so, then they are going to have a hard time picking me off once we're in the middle of the crowd," Ariadne said. "So let's make a quick appearance at least, then get out."

"I don't know," Sugar said nervously. "That was a very close call." She pointed to a spot on the wall, at about waist height near the elevator. "Look, Matt. He couldn't have been more than a foot off his mark."

With a grimace Matt inspected the hole Sugar had pointed out. "She's right," he said. "If you hadn't been on the floor, you'd probably be dead."

"But I *was* on the floor," Ariadne said. She smiled. "Thanks to you."

Matt realized that he couldn't argue with her about joining the party. She'd made up her mind, and that was that.

"Okay," he said, shrugging. "Let's go, but let's keep it short."

Ariadne took his arm, and the others followed.

"Did you get a good look at him?" Ariadne asked Matt as they headed down the corridor.

He shook his head. "Not really," he replied. "That's the problem with uniforms. They make everybody look more or less alike." He shook his head in worry. "This is a deadly masquerade, Ariadne."

"I know," she said, "but I feel confident with you."

He squeezed her hand. "Are you ready to go in?"

"Yes." She fixed a smile on her lips. "My first big party. Ever."

"Let's hope it's not the last."

At the party, Ariadne was grateful that her new friends were in constant attendance. She successfully masqueraded as her sister without a hitch. Thanks to Nikoletta's well-known behavior with men, no one asked Ariadne what had happened to Frans. Matt was accepted as her latest in a long series of flings. After an hour the group returned to the penthouse, and Ariadne dismissed her bodyguards.

"After you've left with Nikoletta," Angelo said, "I'll have a talk with Frans. Is that okay?"

Everyone agreed that it was. "You'll have to keep Ariadne out of the way," Matt said. "Frans shouldn't see her. After I've left with her, what if all of you stay on the top floor at the swimming pool until Angelo's gotten Frans out of here?"

"That's fine with me," Angelo said. He looked around the group. "Does that suit everyone? I shouldn't be but a few minutes with him. Then I'll try to get him to leave with me."

Again, everyone agreed. "Call me on your cell when you're leaving," Sugar said. "Then we'll know the coast is clear."

"Okay," Matt said. "Ariadne, you and Sugar had better get Nikoletta ready to leave."

Sugar took Ariadne's hand. "Let's go, sweetheart."

They found Nikoletta as they'd left her, in a deep sleep. Ariadne and Sugar quickly dressed her, cleaned her face of all makeup, and wrapped her head in a scarf. She wouldn't be instantly recognizable by the ambulance attendants as Ariadne's twin. Then they packed a suitcase with casual clothing that would be suitable for her future home.

As Ariadne was forced to handle her sister's inert body, she once again suffered deep pangs of guilt, her mind in turmoil about what she was doing to her own flesh and blood, even though they'd never known each other. She had to repeatedly remind herself that what she was doing was for the greater good.

When they had properly readied Nikoletta, a private ambulance company was called, and its attendants arrived with a stretcher to take her down to the building's garage. Matt would accompany her on the flight to the clinic in Switzerland where she would be confined.

In the entrance hall, he turned to Ariadne. "I'll get back as quickly as possible," he said. "In the meantime, you take care of yourself." He gently brushed her cheek with a kiss.

"I'll miss you," Ariadne said.

"It won't be long."

She nodded. "I hope . . . I hope it goes as well as can be expected."

"Don't worry," Matt replied. "It's going to be okay. I'll get her settled in." He quickly kissed her again, then followed the attendants with the stretcher onto the elevator.

"Wait a minute," Sugar called to them. She hurried into the entrance hall and onto the elevator, where she carefully arranged the sheets in such a way as to virtually hide Nikoletta's face.

As it turned out, the garage was deserted. The attendants slid the stretcher into the back of the ambulance and locked it in place. Then Matt climbed in and sat beside Nikoletta for the ride to Teterboro Airport, where a PPHL jet was waiting to take them to Switzerland.

Upstairs in one of the penthouse guest rooms, Angelo Coveri sat down on the bed next to Frans. He reached over and shook him gently.

"Wh-what?" Frans asked groggily, blinking his eyes.

"Frans. It is Angelo Coveri. Bianca's father."

Frans instantly sat up in bed and looked at him with bleary eyes. "What are you doing here?"

"I came to talk to you, but we only have a minute," Angelo told him. "Why don't you come with me to my house and stay the night there? I have a proposition for you."

Frans listened in disbelief. "What kind of proposition? What are you talking about?"

"You loved Bianca, and she loved you," Angelo said. "I no longer have her, but you are still here. I thought that maybe . . . well, perhaps, first . . ." He struggled to find words. "Bianca loved our place on Lake Como. Maybe you could come there with me for a while and try to get yourself back together again. Giulia, Bianca's old nanny, is still there keeping house for me. You would have good food, a nice place to stay and call home if you like."

"I . . . I don't know," Frans said, taken aback by the old man's offer.

"Why don't you give it a try?" Angelo said. "Maybe you could help me set up some kind of suitable memorial for Bianca." *And maybe it would even help me,* he thought.

"I—I will come," Frans said.

"Good," Angelo said, standing up. "Now, let's get out of this place. We will go to my house tonight. Tomorrow we will fetch whatever you'd like to take to Italy with you and go." He extended a hand to Frans to help him get out of bed.

Frans took the proffered hand and rose to his feet. He was shaky, but he allowed himself to be led downstairs. As they stepped into the elevator, he said, "I am glad to be leaving this snake pit."

"So am I," Angelo said. "We have something in common already, young man. I think this will benefit us both."

Chapter Thirty

~∞~

Château-d'Oex, Switzerland

Nikoletta had carefully applied makeup and fixed her hair, then put on the tightest sweater—without a bra—among the clothes that had been packed for her. Happily she discovered a pair of her favorite low-cut, formfitting jeans in the closet. She looked at her wristwatch. He should be here in less than five minutes. From the minifridge she took out the small half-liter bottle of wine. She was allowed only three glasses a day, she'd been told, and even that might be eliminated, depending on the medication she was placed on and her behavior. The bottle had a screw top—disgusting, she thought—but she unscrewed it and poured herself a glass. She savored its taste, even though it was barely drinkable as far as she was concerned.

The last two days had been the most unbearable in her life. When she had finally come to and realized what had happened, she had flown into a rage of epic proportions. To no avail. No one at the clinic believed that she was truly Nikoletta Papadaki. They accepted what they had been told. She was Ariadne Papadaki, a mentally unstable twin sister the family had long kept sequestered away in secret. The doctors did not find the situation uncommon, especially among families as rich as the Papadakis, who strove to maintain a public image of wealth combined with beauty, physical and mental health, and unstinting service to others.

The doctors at the exclusive Clinique Château-d'Oex who had witnessed their new patient's behavior were accustomed to such outbursts.

After all, they were typical of delusional paranoid schizophrenics like the unfortunate Ariadne Papadaki. The family representative who had accompanied her to the clinic, Matthew Foster, confirmed that such violent rages had become increasingly common. She had given a brilliant performance, the good doctors decided, and her outrageous accusations, incredible though they were, had been beautifully scripted and acted out. That, too, was not an uncommon characteristic of the mentally ill like Ariadne. Initially, in fact, Ariadne had proved her family's case without any prompting whatsoever. Her behavior convinced the doctors that Ariadne was indeed very ill.

It was decided that she would be given a suite on the top floor, the seventh, where she would have a bedroom, sitting room, and bath. The balcony, with its beautiful mountain view, was constructed like a cage, so that she couldn't throw herself off it. The windows were barred, and the mirrors were sheets of highly reflective stainless steel. Should she be determined to injure or kill herself, they agreed that she, like so many others in her sad mental state, would doubtless find a way in her luxurious apartment, but the facilities had been designed to make suicide a less accessible option. She could easily hang herself with the bedsheets, but if she proved bent on suicide, the appropriate drugs would deter her from that.

Nikoletta had quickly realized her dilemma, and after the first few hours had settled down, restraining herself from further outbursts. She would have to behave in a reasonable, "normal" fashion to convince the doctors that what she had said was true. She had been drugged and kidnapped, and her twin sister had taken her place. She realized that she had a difficult road ahead. After all, her twin sister didn't exist, did she? Ariadne had no birth certificate, nothing to prove that she had ever lived, and now *she*—Nikoletta—was Ariadne.

Now she was waiting for Matt Foster to arrive. She was certain that she could get him into her bed and thus on her side. Had any man ever turned her down? No, not unless Frans was considered, and she didn't care to consider Frans. He had been an aberration. A lovesick depressive unworthy of her attention.

There was a soft knock on the door, and Nikoletta got up to answer it. Opening the door, she greeted Matt.

"Hi!" she said perkily. "I'm so glad you came."

"I wanted to see you before I leave anyway," Matt said, not failing to observe her ample breasts. They pressed against the sweater she was wearing, outlining her nipples in bold relief.

"Come in and sit down," Nikoletta said, indicating a chair. "I have some wine."

"No, thanks," Matt replied. He knew that she was allowed only a small amount, and he didn't want to deprive her of that. While the clinic was luxurious, offering various activities for its patients, Nikoletta was going to treasure her modicum of wine, he thought.

"No?" she said. "Well, have it your way. It's not the best anyway." She laughed.

Nikoletta sat down on the couch, curling her legs up under her, and Matt sat in a chair opposite her, across the coffee table.

"Would you like sparkling water?" she asked. "Or soda?"

"No, thanks," Matt replied. She was being awfully civil, he thought, and his guard immediately went up. He knew she was using her charm to entice him.

Nikoletta looked him in the eye. "Are you involved with my sister?"

Matt was startled by her question, but he decided he might as well be honest. "Yes."

Nikoletta nodded. "I thought as much. I'd guess you were hired as her bodyguard, and you made your move when you realized that she was going to be the Papadaki heiress."

Matt felt his face redden, and the muscles in his jaw tensed. "I was hired for security purposes," he replied, "but my involvement with your sister had nothing to do with her being the Papadaki heiress." He was careful not to name Ariadne in case the suite was bugged. After all, Nikoletta was known as Ariadne to the clinic personnel.

"Oh?" Nikoletta made a moue of mock surprise before her expression became harder. "Come on," she said, "you can tell me the truth. I know your type. Don't forget, I've had bodyguards all my life, and I've had more than a few come on to me. They all want your money and will pretend anything to get it."

"Maybe that's been your experience," Matt allowed, "but you're not describing me."

She took a sip of wine, then set the glass down. *I might as well get to the point,* she thought. Rising to her feet, she went to his chair and kneeled down in front of him. Matt arched away as she began stroking his thighs with her hand.

"I could make you very rich," she said. "Richer than you've ever dreamed of."

"I'm not interested in your money," Matt said, "and I'd appreciate it if you take your hands off me and go back to the couch and sit down."

"Oh, don't be a spoilsport," Nikoletta purred. "Nobody would know, Matt. And I figure if you find my sister attractive, surely you must like the way I look, too. We *are* twins, after all."

"You may look like her," Matt said, "but you're not your sister."

Nikoletta quit stroking his thighs and looked up at him with curiosity. "How are we different?" she asked. "I'd like to know why she appeals to you, but I don't."

"I don't have to answer your questions," Matt said.

"No," she agreed, "but couldn't you do me that favor? Think about it, Matt. You've brought me here to this godforsaken place to lock me up. For what? The rest of my life?" She paused. "Don't you think you could answer a simple question for me?"

"Your sister is goodness itself," he said. "She doesn't have a bad bone in her body. She's kind and thoughtful and generous of spirit."

Nikoletta began stroking him again. "I can be very generous," she said with a lascivious smile. "And I can be good, too."

Matt couldn't deny that she looked beautiful—wickedly so—at this moment, and that her hands on his thighs felt . . . well, too good, too stimulating. Suddenly he was furious. With her, but also with himself. "Take your hands off me," he said firmly. "You're not going to get anywhere with me because I'm in love with your sister."

"Are you so sure about that, Matt?" she asked, slowing the movement of her hands but not removing them.

"I'm positive," he said. He took her hands in his and pushed them away, then stood up. "You're a tramp," he said, "only a lot worse. You're greedy, mean, unloving, and just plain evil. I wouldn't find you desirable no matter who you were."

Nikoletta rose to her feet angrily. "You're nothing but a two-bit hustler," she snarled in a low voice. "And you've gotten yourself in over your head. Way in over your head. Just wait! I'll get out of here, and when I do I'll get *you* and I'll get *her*. You haven't seen anything yet! This battle has just begun, and you're both losers."

Matt walked to the door and put his hand on the handle. "I don't want to do battle with you," he said, "but if I have to, *you're* the one who's going to be sorry." He pointed a finger at her. "And don't even think about harming your sister."

"Get out!" she screamed.

"I was just leaving," he said calmly.

Chapter Thirty-one

❧

The entire board of PPHL was gathered around the table in the boardroom of the new headquarters. At its head sat Ariadne, who had called a special meeting.

"I've written a memo, and each of you has a copy in front of you," she said. "I'm not going to read it now or ask you to, but I want you to take it home with you today and read it very carefully. There are going to be some monumental changes at PPHL, in a number of different ways. In our business practices in general and in many more specific ways that are indicated in the memo. If after reading it, any of you disagrees with any part of it, I would ask that you immediately turn in your resignation from the board to me."

The room filled with muffled sounds of surprise. Ariadne looked around the table and cleared her throat before continuing. "For one, PPHL is going to put in place a number of ecofriendly policies. I will order major plant and environment cleanups, improvement of working conditions, more adequate health care, and other policies that some of you may object to. There is no question the bottom line is going to suffer. Profits are inevitably going to drop. But while these changes may be costly to PPHL, they are going to be beneficial to our employees, their immediate workplace environment, and the environment of the world in general. And, I believe, beneficial to PPHL in the long run."

Adrian beamed at her with pride. She was doing a remarkable job, he thought.

"Are there any questions?" Ariadne asked.

"I have just one," Adrian said. He was feeding her the question as they had arranged beforehand. It was a good way, they thought, to get the new guiding principles across to the rest of the board.

"If you don't mind, could you explain what's brought about this reversal in so many of PPHL's policies? This is quite sudden, it seems to me, and I think it is to other board members as well."

Ariadne nodded. "Naturally you would be curious about that," she said. She tapped the paper, indicating its contents. "I've come to realize that a lot of PPHL's policies are creating environmental hazards beyond what I ever imagined. In the last few weeks I've taken the opportunity to visit many of our facilities incognito, and I believe we must—no matter what the costs—change the way we're operating these facilities. I don't condone the violent tactics employed by organizations like Mother Earth's Children, but I think we have a lot to learn from the environmentalists."

With her last comment Ariadne heard shifting chairs and coughs. She had definitely made some of the board members uncomfortable. "As I said earlier, if any one of you doesn't like my new policies after you've read the complete memo, feel free to turn your resignation in. It's this way—*my* way—and no other in the future." She smiled. "Although that's not necessarily a new policy."

There were a few uneasy laughs in the boardroom.

"If there are no further questions, ladies and gentlemen," she said, rising to her feet, "I have a lot to do. We will reconvene exactly a week from today, at which time I will expect your cooperation or your resignation."

Her gaze swept around the table, but there were no raised hands nor did anyone speak. "I will see you next week." She picked up a folder of papers and left the room. She could hear the chatter that immediately started the moment she was out the door, and smiled. *That gave them something to think about,* she thought.

Back in her office, she had hardly sat down before she was joined by Sugar, Adrian, Yves, and Angelo.

"You did a fantastic job," Sugar said.

Angelo patted her shoulder and brushed the top of her head with a kiss. "You're one hell of an angel," he said. "Nothing in the world could make me happier than what you just did in there."

"One hell of an angel," Ariadne repeated with a laugh. "I love that description, Angelo."

"When are you going to let the public relations department release that new information you gave them?" Adrian asked.

"Later this week," Ariadne said. "I'm hoping it will be in the Sunday newspapers and on television and radio news shows over the weekend, too. More coverage that way."

"I don't think you're going to have a problem with coverage, sweetheart," Sugar said as if it was an understatement. "Your donations are going to be front-page news."

"I hope so," Ariadne said. "I've been very careful about choosing which organizations to donate the money to, and I've deliberately made these first few donations really huge ones to generate the maximum amount of publicity. Later on, I'll be donating smaller amounts to worthy organizations here and there."

"It's a very clever ploy," Adrian said. "The whole world is going to know that Nikoletta Papadaki has become an ecosensitive industrialist."

"It's not just a ploy, Adrian," Ariadne said sternly. "I really believe in these organizations and the work that they're doing."

"Another great thing about it is that there are going to be other companies who'll follow your lead," Sugar said.

"Exactly," Ariadne said. "I hope our step forward will be the start of a movement."

Adrian rose to his feet and kissed her cheek. "I've got a lot of work to do, so I'd better get going. You're doing a terrific job, and I think I speak for everyone when I say that."

"Thanks, Adrian."

After work, she went directly upstairs to the penthouse, where Matt was waiting for her. He took her into his arms and kissed her. "I'm so glad to see you," he said, nuzzling her neck.

"And I'm glad to see you, too," she replied. "I'm always glad to see you."

"I thought I would take you out to dinner tonight. We can celebrate the decision we came to about my work," Matt said.

"That would be wonderful."

"Someplace small and quiet, where nobody will know Nikoletta Papadaki."

"Even better," she said with a laugh. "If there is such a place."

"I'm sure there is," Matt said, "if it's inexpensive, unpopular, and not part of a scene."

She leaned back from him. "How did getting set up for your work go?" she asked. "You think the space is going to be okay?"

"It went fine," Matt responded, "and the space is amazing. Why don't we have a glass of wine, and I'll tell you about it? Better yet, why don't we go up there?"

"An excellent suggestion."

"I'll be right back." He let go of her, and Ariadne sat down on a couch and kicked off her shoes, then wiggled her toes. Someday, she thought, she might actually get used to wearing high heels, but not anytime soon.

Matt returned with a bottle of chilled white wine and two glasses. "Ready?"

"Yes." In her bare feet she walked up to the top floor of the triplex with him. There they settled down on a couch in the mammoth glass-enclosed space that Nikoletta had planned to use as a party room.

"Oh, my God," Ariadne exclaimed as she looked about. There were several worktables, some of them displaying maquettes of sculptures that he'd already made or was planning to make, tools of all kinds, racks of different woods and metals, even welder's tanks and torches. Several pieces of sculpture in various stages of completion stood about. "You've done a mountain of work. I can't believe it."

"I had a lot of help with the movers," Matt said. "I could never have done all this myself."

"It's beginning to look like a real artist's studio," she said excitedly.

"It is, isn't it?" Matt put the wine and glasses down on a table, then poured their drinks. He handed her a glass.

"Thank you," Ariadne said.

He slid an arm around her shoulders and kissed her. "Cheers," he said, clinking his glass against hers.

"Cheers."

They both took a sip of wine before Matt turned to her. "You've given me the opportunity I've been looking for, for as long as I can remember, and I'm going to work very hard to prove myself."

"You've already done that, as far as I'm concerned," Ariadne said, "and I think you know that."

"Hearing that from you means the world to me, Ariadne, but I want . . . well, I guess you'd say that I want validation from the outside world."

"You mean the New York art world?"

He nodded. "That's part of it certainly."

"I'm sure it'll happen if you want it to," she said. "I've loved your sculpture from the moment I first set eyes on it at your place in the Berkshires—"

"Our place," he corrected her.

"Hmmm?"

"It's *our* place in the Berkshires now."

"And I love it," she said. "It'll sure be a welcome hideaway." She kissed his cheek. "Anyway, I'm certain a lot of other people are going to love your work, too."

"I hope so because I want to be able to pay my way."

"I know you do."

He set his glass down and waved an arm around. "This means so much to me. You can't imagine." He took her into his arms and hugged her to him. "I love you so much."

Ariadne set her glass down. "I love you, too, Matt."

He kissed her passionately, then drew back. "Why don't we stay in tonight? Do you mind?"

She shook her head. "I'd love that."

"We could order in." He kissed her deeply. "In a while."

"Hmmm, in a while."

"Want to finish your wine in the bedroom?"

"Oh, yes."

Chapter Thirty-two

"What shit!" Kees Vanmeerendonk threw the newspaper across the room, its pages flying apart and leaving a trail across the floor.

"What's wrong?" asked the girl who came out of the bathroom, toweling her short-cropped hair.

"Oh, it's all this crap the newspapers are printing about Nikoletta Papadaki. You'd think she'd turned into the Virgin Mary or something."

"What is it now?"

"Front-page news in the *New York Times* about her latest contribution to an environmental organization," he replied. "The largest they've ever received. Then there's an article in the business section about the change in policies at PPHL. How they're increasing workers' benefits, cleaning up plant sites, all that kind of garbage."

"It must be true," the girl said. "How can they print it if it isn't?"

"You don't understand, Melanie," he told her. "What they're saying may be true, but that doesn't mean that PPHL and Nikoletta Papadaki have really changed course. It only means that she's throwing peanuts at a couple of environmental groups to get publicity about how she and the company have changed. But believe me, they haven't changed one iota. It's all camouflage so that they can continue to pollute and to make things even worse than they are. She's spending a few million dollars to clean up her name, and for her that's chump change."

"Do you really think she'd go to all that trouble?"

Kees slammed a fist on the tabletop, making dishes and silverware jump. A half-empty bottle of wine almost toppled, but he grabbed it before it fell over. "Of course she'd go to that trouble, you idiot," he roared.

His face was red with fury, and Melanie hung her head in shame. She hated herself for angering Kees like this, but she had yet to learn what would set him off. It seemed to her that he was always like a bomb ready to explode, ever since she'd gotten to know him after the meeting in London. "I'm sorry, Kees," she said. "I didn't mean—"

"You never do!" he snapped. "Because you don't think!" he added, pointing at his head with a finger. "I showed you the gossip column in the newspaper about how Nikoletta Papadaki hadn't been seen out and about because of her new 'love,' " he went on, enjoying his tirade, "and you're so stupid that you actually think this man has changed her. What a complete idiot you are!"

"I only meant that—"

"You 'only meant,' " he snarled. "You don't know the first thing about this. Nothing will change her. It's just more camouflage. Don't you see? She hasn't suddenly had a personality change. No! This is all PR. She's trying to make herself and the company look good after the bad publicity they've been getting."

Tears had welled up in Melanie's eyes, and she fought to hold them back as she put on the coveralls she always wore.

Kees sat glaring at her, his fingers beating a steady tattoo on the table-top. "If you're going to cry, Melanie, then get your things and get out of here. And don't come back. I don't need some sniveling wimp in my way."

When she didn't immediately respond, his fury was rekindled. "I suspected from the beginning that you weren't a true believer. You're just a hanger-on, aren't you?"

Melanie's body shook as she cried, and she repeatedly wiped away the tears with the bottom of her T-shirt. Tossing her few possessions into a well-worn backpack, she could hardly wait to get out of the tiny, dark basement apartment.

"So you're packing," he said. "Well, good riddance. I don't need you, and the group doesn't need you. And, believe me, I'm going to tell them. I don't think you can be trusted, and you know what happens to people like you who don't really belong, don't you?"

Melanie heaved the backpack on her shoulders and started toward the door.

"They end up floaters, Melanie. That's what happens to them. And you don't want that happening to you, do you?"

She shook her head.

"So you'll keep your mouth shut, won't you?"

"Yes," she murmured.

Melanie went to the door and unlocked the three dead bolts up and down its length. She didn't look back when she closed the door behind her.

Kees went to the door, locking it behind her. He didn't have to worry about her keys, because he'd never given her a set. Returning to his chair, he picked up the pages of newspaper that he'd thrown down, and placed them on the table. He sat down and brooded, but not about Melanie. She was just another in a long line of acolytes who meant nothing to him.

It was Nikoletta Papadaki who bothered him. Part of PPHL's latest publicity blitz was her seclusion with her new boyfriend. That meant she was staying out of the public eye, making herself a hard target. Since the night of the opening of the new PPHL headquarters, he'd hardly managed to get more than a glimpse of her, even though he'd trailed her almost constantly. Her security had been beefed up, and lately, she seldom left her penthouse atop the new building. When she did, he could detect no pattern in her movements.

Kees smiled. *Just another challenge,* he thought, *because Nikoletta Papadaki will not escape me.* He was certain that she couldn't keep up this new facade much longer. Despite the publicity, she would be out and about. And he would be waiting for her.

He stood up and stretched. In the meantime, he had business to tend to. He would be leaving this basement apartment tonight, moving to another apartment much like it. He began to pack his belongings for the trip to Hell's Kitchen. The apartment was a dump, but it was a mere three blocks from the penthouse in the sky where Nikoletta Papadaki lived. No one else in the New York cell of Mother Earth's Children knew about it, and he'd been saving it for just this sort of occasion. A new countdown had begun. He could feel it in every fiber of his body.

She would be close by, and soon she would be *his*.

Chapter Thirty-three

❦

Weeks passed by, and Ariadne faced test after test, always proving herself capable of running PPHL and impersonating Nikoletta to the outside world. The publicity campaign that centered on PPHL's new business image and Nikoletta Papadaki's personal philanthropy was a great help, but it also created endless fodder for the gossip mills. NIKOLETTA PAPADAKI HAS RELIGIOUS CONVERSION, one tabloid touted, and the same variation on the theme was printed in story after story in various publications. Because Ariadne kept a low profile, the tabloids were forced to use file photographs, and they invariably juxtaposed pictures of Nikoletta in the briefest bikinis along with the articles about her conversion. Ariadne didn't respond to any of them, but remained aloof and pretended no interest.

"Niki's fallen under the spell of a Svengali" went the gist of the confidences exchanged among former friends and acquaintances after repeated calls weren't taken and invitations were turned down. Ariadne quickly discovered that none of the so-called friends and acquaintances were persistent or seemed particularly concerned. Nikoletta was in truth close to no one. She had been surrounded by a host of rich partygoers like herself, and they lost interest when the parties stopped. The telephone quit ringing, and the invitations stopped arriving in the mail. Nikoletta was not especially missed.

The dawning reality of the superficial world in which her twin sister had lived deeply disturbed Ariadne, even though Adrian and the others had tried to prepare her for what to expect. "She won't allow anyone to love her," Adrian had told her. "No one. She doesn't want anyone too close."

"But I thought she had loads of friends," Ariadne replied. "I've seen tons of video footage and pictures from parties all over the world."

Adrian shook his head sadly. "Ariadne, you will quickly discover that her world is almost completely artificial. Those people are brought together because of their money, and they love publicity. Most of them are hungry for the photographers, no matter what they say." He sighed. "It's almost as if they didn't exist unless they saw themselves written up in the gossip columns."

That set Ariadne to thinking about the love her foster parents had given her, both in Greece and Connecticut. And now, with the love that she and Matt shared, she felt a keen compassion toward the sister she'd never known. What if the lack of love had made her the way she was? Maybe, Ariadne decided, she deserved another chance. The guilt she felt over keeping her sister locked away began to eat at her constantly, and she finally decided to broach the subject with Matt.

One Saturday night after making love, she chose to discuss it with him. "I know we've been over and over this," she said, "but I can't put my worries to rest. Nikoletta has been away for several months now, and from what the doctors at the clinic say she's been an angel."

"Of course she has, sweetheart," Matt replied. "She's hoping for a reprieve, so she's on her best behavior."

"Maybe. But could she keep up a front for such a long time? Don't you think that she might have changed?"

Matt shook his head. "That's one of the things I love about you," he replied. "You'll give anybody the benefit of the doubt. But I don't think your sister has changed one iota." He didn't want to discuss the evil he had witnessed during his stint in the CIA, but he firmly believed that some people were born evil, and Nikoletta was one of them.

"She might have," Ariadne said, "and I'll never know unless I go see her for myself."

"But how would you know?" Matt asked. "You don't know her at all."

"I realize that," Ariadne responded, "but what if we made her some kind of offer?" Her fingers began to sketch her ideas as she spoke. "What if we put together a plan that would allow her to live in the outside world? Offered her a huge sum of money to keep quiet?"

Matt shook his head vigorously. "I don't think it would ever work, Ariadne."

"We'll never know unless we try," she replied.

"No."

"I think I'll talk to the advisers about it," she said. "I'd like to see what they think."

"If you say so." Matt kissed her. "I myself certainly wouldn't ask you not to, but I think you're headed for a big disappointment."

"Maybe," she agreed, "but I'll never know unless I try."

Ariadne occupied the seat at the head of the boardroom table that Nikoletta had always sat in. On one side of the table sat Adrian and Honor, who now knew about the switch, and Sugar, and on the other were Angelo and Yves.

"I'm grateful to all of you for responding to my request for a special meeting of the advisers today," she said, "and I wouldn't have troubled you unless I thought it was an urgent matter." She glanced at everyone present and smiled. "I know that some of you feel guilty about keeping my sister locked away in the clinic—"

"I am certainly not one of those individuals," Angelo blurted out.

"I'm well aware of that, Angelo," Ariadne said, holding up a hand to placate him, "and I'm well aware of your reasons for feeling that way. In any case, I personally feel a great responsibility for what has been done to her. In the months since she's been there, the reports from the doctors have been nothing if not glowing—"

"Not in the beginning," Sugar said defiantly. "They said she tried to seduce every male on staff and—"

Ariadne held up a hand again. "Please allow me to finish," she said. "I'll be glad to hear your comments after I'm done."

"Sorry," Sugar said, annoyed.

Ariadne continued. "Since the first couple of weeks of her confinement there, the reports have been very positive. She's even quit claiming that she's Nikoletta Papadaki, the doctors say, although she hasn't said that she's Ariadne. In any case, the doctors believe that she's responded extremely well to their intensive therapy. I know some of you have your doubts about that, but in any case I've thought about this long and hard and am asking for your advice. What I would like to do to put my mind at ease once and for all is go to visit her."

Out of the corner of her eye, she saw Sugar grab Adrian's arm.

"I would like to take a statement with me for her to sign. The statement would be an ironclad agreement in which she would give up all claims to the PPHL empire and promise to live in quiet obscurity for a substantial cash settlement."

The group began talking all at once, and Ariadne asked for their attention. "Please," she said. "One at a time. Angelo?"

"Never!" Angelo Coveri cried, slamming a fist on the table.

"You would be making a terrible mistake," Yves Carre said. "She would never live up to her end of the agreement."

"Even if she signed such an agreement and took the money," Sugar pointed out in an exasperated voice, "how do we know she'll live in quiet obscurity? Niki's never done anything quietly. She wouldn't know how! Where's she going to go? What's she going to do? With the kind of money it would take to buy her off, she'd be so rich she could do anything she pleased."

"You're very well-intentioned," Honor said softly, "but it would never work, Ariadne. Sugar's right. Niki couldn't live quietly. No matter where she went, she would create a stir. Besides, you are twins. A lot of people would immediately recognize her, and some of them might take her side if she decided to break the agreement and go public."

"All of you have good arguments," Adrian said at last. "But we all have the distinct advantage of having known Niki all her life." He opened his arms in a shrug. "We can't stop you if you decide to do this, Ariadne, but I have to agree with everyone else. I don't think this is a wise plan. Even if she was forced to live in disguise in some place like Cape Town and the money was doled out in installments, guaranteeing us some kind of control over her, it would be extremely risky. As much as I hate to say it, Niki is a born troublemaker, and I don't believe she's changed. However," he added, "I'll back you up if you decide to go through with this. If you have to do something to assuage your conscience, and this is what it takes, then do it."

Ariadne felt as if she would burst into tears when he had finished speaking, but she restrained herself. "Thank you," she managed. "I appreciate your vote of confidence."

"If you want me to, I'll go with you," Adrian offered.

"I really appreciate your offer," Ariadne said, "but this is something that I want to do alone. Matt insists on going along because of security."

"Thank God," Adrian said. "You shouldn't even think about taking a trip like this without security, but is he the only security you're going to have?" He was obviously uncomfortable with the idea.

"Matt has it all planned," she replied with a smile. "So I don't think you need to be concerned at all. We'll be taking a company jet with a couple of extra security men on board. Then we'll helicopter to the clinic with them along."

"That ought to do it," Adrian said, "but I still think it's awfully dangerous."

"You know Matt. He wouldn't even think of doing this if he didn't think I was going to be safe."

"Yes, of course. You're right," Adrian replied. "I just have . . . well, an uneasy feeling about it. I guess I'm a little superstitious."

"I think you can put your superstitions to rest," Ariadne said. "Whether Nikoletta is willing to sign or not, I think everything will work out fine. I just have to do this."

Chapter Thirty-four

✺

When Ariadne and Matt along with two security men pulled out of the underground garage at the PPHL headquarters in the early evening, none of them noticed the nondescript old van that eased out from the curb and followed them all the way to the airport in Teterboro, New Jersey. The van driver was careful to keep several vehicles between them at all times. He watched their jet take off a few minutes later, then found out what their flight plan and final destination were with ease: a revolver to the head of the lone man stationed at the PPHL hangar. Afterward, he knocked the man out with a single blow to the head, hauled him into the van, then left the van in a long-term parking lot at JFK Airport. He had just enough time to make a flight to Geneva, where Mother Earth's Children had a cell. From there he could easily reach Château-d'Oex, perhaps even getting there before Nikoletta Papadaki and the three men with her.

Once in the air, he idly wondered why she was going to the tiny Swiss alpine town. *Probably a spa,* he decided. That area of Switzerland was infested with ski resorts and spas for the rich. *Going to hole up with her boy toy for a few days, I bet.* He grinned. *Well, she has a surprise coming to her.*

The chopper landed on the clearly delineated helipad at Clinique Château-d'Oex right on schedule, and Ariadne, Matt, and the two security men quickly debarked. Waiting for them outside the downdraft created by the chopper's rotors were two lab-coated doctors, one male and one female.

"Mr. Foster," the man said, proffering his hand for a shake. "It's a pleasure to see you again. This is my associate, Dr. Weiner."

"Dr. Bernheim. Dr. Weiner," Matt said. "A pleasure. This is Nikoletta Papadaki, of course."

"Yes," Dr. Bernheim said.

"I would never be able to tell you from your sister," Dr. Weiner chimed in.

"That's what everyone says," Ariadne told her.

They walked the short distance to the clinic, chatting about the patient. The building resembled pictures Ariadne had seen of luxurious ski lodges, but she didn't fail to notice the bars that enclosed the balconies that jutted out from each suite. Although it was almost planted out of sight, a high chain-link fence, topped by razor wire, surrounded the perimeter of the beautiful grounds. As they reached the door, Dr. Bernheim turned to her. "I think that you'll be pleased with Ariadne's behavior," he said. "As we've indicated in our reports, she's calmed down considerably, and hasn't given us a single problem. She hasn't even made a single claim to be you, since the first week or two of residency."

Ariadne's face grew pale. It was horrible for her to confront the reality that her sister's true identity had been stripped away and she was herself the impersonator, not her sister. When she could finally reply, she said, "That's wonderful news, Doctor. I can't wait to see for myself."

Inside the clinic, the doctors led them across the polished wood floors to the elevators, and Dr. Bernheim pushed the UP button. "Ariadne, as you know, is on the seventh floor," he said as they waited for the car. "She's expecting you, of course. I hope you'll have a good visit."

"Thank you," Matt said. "I'm sure we will." Holding Ariadne's arm securely, he turned to the security men. "Jessie, stay down here at the entrance door, please, and Luke, you come upstairs with me."

They nodded, but didn't speak.

The elevator car arrived, and Ariadne, Matt, and Luke stepped on. The door whispered closed behind them. Matt took Ariadne's hand in his as they began the ascent to Nikoletta's suite.

The terrain here was rough, and he had to cover a lot of ground on foot, so his vehicle wouldn't be within sight of the clinic. Kees didn't mind. It was what he'd trained for all his life. He crawled forward through the rocks and scrub with his elbows and knees. At a large stone outcropping, he took out his binoculars. Easing up to the top of the stone, he peered through the binoculars toward the clinic.

Slowly moving them from left to right, he first saw some sort of outbuilding, then the main clinic building itself. Continuing to slowly pan the binoculars to his right, he spotted the helicopter. *Goddamn it! They beat me here,* he thought. At the entrance door to the clinic he spied a lone man dressed in a dark suit. One look told him all he needed to know. The man's physique—thick neck, broad shoulders, chest barely contained by his suit—was a dead giveaway. A plainclothes security man. Kees was sure of it. He was one of the two he'd seen in the car with Nikoletta and her new main squeeze. *And I would bet my binoculars that the other one is inside, or wherever she is.*

He swept from left to right again, but saw nothing new, beyond the shadowy movement of people behind windows and the balcony doors. He idly wondered why Nikoletta Papadaki had come to this place. It wasn't a spa, after all, he'd discovered from cell members in Geneva. It was a fancy loony bin for the superrich. *Maybe she has a friend locked up here?* he thought. But it didn't make sense to him. It was out of character for Nikoletta Papadaki to pay a call of this type. *She is the same self-centered, polluting bitch she always was,* he thought.

Well, she was going to pay this time. She had to come back out of the clinic, and when she did, he would have her in his sights. He had the perfect perch behind the stone outcropping and could easily take her with a single shot without moving an inch. He quickly assembled his package from Geneva: an automatic rifle with a telescopic lens. He trained it on the bodyguard. The magnifying power was so good, the goon seemed to be twenty feet away.

Before they reached Nikoletta's door, Matt instructed Luke to wait in the hallway, positioning him between the elevator and Nikoletta's suite. "Keep one eye on the elevator," he said, "and the other one on the door to the suite we're about to enter."

Luke nodded.

Matt wasn't going to give the bodyguard the opportunity to see Nikoletta, if possible. Although Luke and Jessie were recent hires he'd made especially for this trip and had never met Nikoletta before, he didn't want to have to explain anything more than necessary to them. He certainly didn't want word getting out that they had gone to Switzerland to visit Nikoletta Papadaki's twin.

Ariadne and Matt reached the suite, and he softly knocked on the door.

Nikoletta answered it immediately. On her lips was a tentative smile, and her expression was somewhat demure, as if she were shy, perhaps even embarrassed to be receiving guests here at the clinic. "Please, come in," she said politely, opening the door wide and stepping back out of the way.

"H-hello," Ariadne stuttered as she stepped into the suite. Seeing her mirror image on the threshold was a shock, no less so than it had been the first time she'd seen Nikoletta, but if Nikoletta felt anything at the sight of her twin sister, her face didn't register it.

"Have a seat wherever you like," Nikoletta said. "Would you like a glass of wine? I'm afraid it's not very good, but it's drinkable."

"No, thanks," Ariadne said, sitting down on the couch.

"I'll be with you in a moment," Matt said. He slipped a bug-detecting device out of his jacket pocket and began moving about the suite, beginning in the entrance hall, sweeping for any listening devices.

Nikoletta watched him with amusement. "My, my," she said. "Do you think the good doctors want to listen to me talk in my sleep?"

Matt didn't respond, but continued sweeping the rooms, taking his time. After he'd completed the task, he returned to the sitting room from the bedroom, and took a seat next to Ariadne. He took her hand in his. "Clean," he murmured.

"You?" Nikoletta asked, her eyes searching Matt's. "Would you like a glass of wine?"

"No, thanks," he said.

"Mineral water? Anything?"

"No, thanks," they replied in unison.

"Well, if you don't mind, I will," Nikoletta said. She poured herself a glass of wine from the bottle that she'd taken out of the minifridge shortly before they'd arrived, then sat down in a chair across from them, curling her legs up underneath her. Taking a sip of wine, she gazed at them across the rim of the glass, then set the glass down.

"I have to confess that I'm very curious about why you came to visit me," Nikoletta said. "It's been months, and there's been no contact. Of course, I'm sure the doctors keep you posted."

"Yes, they do," Ariadne said. "We are concerned about how you're adapting to living here. I know that it must have taken a lot of adjustment and—"

"I think that's an understatement," Nikoletta broke in. "To tell you the truth, it's felt like what I imagine death would be like, and the feeling hasn't really gone away. I guess I might as well be dead. I no longer have a family. Nothing. Strange as it seems, that's what I miss most. My little family: the advisers. They were really the only family I had after my father died."

She turned her gaze on Ariadne. "Then there's you. I never got to know you at all. Never had the chance to." Nikoletta wanted nothing so much as to assault her sister, to scratch her beautiful face with her nails, to beat her with her fists, to pummel the life out of her, but she knew that she must remain calm and diplomatic. Otherwise, she would jeopardize her chances of getting out of this place. She'd suspected that Ariadne would be guilt-ridden and would come to see her, and in the back of her mind she entertained the possibility that her sister would eventually allow her to leave the clinic.

"I know the feeling well," Ariadne countered, not unsympathetically. "You know how I grew up, snatched from the only family I knew. Never knowing why. Then suddenly I discovered there was you, and believe it or not, I wanted to get to know you." She looked down at her hand, the one Matt was holding, then gazed back up at Nikoletta.

"I didn't know about you until it was too late," Nikoletta responded in a soft voice. "You know, I don't really understand any of this. I always did what the advisers told me to do. Don't you know that? I always did whatever they made me do. Then they turned on me." Her voice broke. "Then they decided to get rid of me, and it was too late to get to know you, the twin I never knew."

Ariadne didn't believe that. She'd seen all the evidence to the contrary, but she decided to let the remark pass. What she wondered about was whether or not Nikoletta really wanted to get to know her. Even if there was the tiniest shred of truth in that, she thought, then perhaps all of this was unnecessary. Perhaps they could be sisters after all.

"I've been misguided," Nikoletta went on, "and I've made some terrible decisions on my own part. I realize that now, and I really regret them." She hung her head, the perfect actress of contrition. "I only wish there was some way I could make up for my mistakes in the past. That's been one wonderful thing about being here. I've had time to think without a lot of interference from other people. That and the therapy have helped me come to know myself better and to actually examine my past behavior. I've come to realize that I have a lot of amends to make, and more than anything else I've come to realize that I have real family I never knew." She paused, looking into Ariadne's eyes. "You." She paused again, then added, "If it's not too late."

Ariadne was nonplussed for a moment. She hadn't expected Nikoletta's seeming warmth, although she'd been warned about her abilities to deceive. She finally cleared her throat and said, "W-we've come here with a proposition for you."

"A proposition? What kind of proposition?" Nikoletta asked, wide-eyed with curiosity.

"I have an agreement," Ariadne said. "I drew it up personally with the help of the advisers." She slipped a folder out the leather carryall she'd brought with her, then opened it and drew out the agreement. "I would like for you to look it over before we discuss it."

Nikoletta began reading the agreement, and as they watched, her facial muscles began to twitch and her flesh began to redden. Even her lips twitched and puckered and finally twisted into an ugly curl. Losing all control, she threw the paper down on the floor and jumped to her feet.

"You bitch!" she snarled, her eyes wild with fury. "I should have known! How dare you come here with an offer like this. I am Nikoletta Papadaki! And don't you forget it! You're a nobody from nowhere. You think that you can waltz in here and try to take what is rightfully mine away from me? You stupid, sniveling upstart! You think you can prove that you're Nikos Papadaki's heir? He was my father, and he left everything to me!" She pointed a trembling finger at her chest, glaring at Ariadne with hatred such as she had never seen before.

"You'll get nothing! Nothing! It's all mine!" she screamed.

As Ariadne watched in horror, Nikoletta grabbed a pack of cigarettes and a lighter, stormed to the balcony door, slid it open with a wild jerk, and went outside.

Matt hugged Ariadne to him as they watched her light a cigarette and puff on it furiously, pacing from one end of the barred balcony to the other. "I think we've seen her true colors at last," he said quietly.

"It's heartbreaking," Ariadne murmured under her voice, her gaze still on her sister. "It's—"

She suddenly started to scream, and Matt turned to follow the direction of her gaze. On the balcony, Nikoletta jerked and slumped to the concrete, dropping the cigarette and knocking over a chair as she fell. It was then that he saw the blood that splattered the sliding glass door.

"Get down!" he said, shoving Ariadne off the couch and to the floor. "Behind the couch!" She did as she was told. Matt scrambled outside on all fours. When he reached Nikoletta, he examined her body, still keeping low to the floor. She lay on her side, her face away from him. A chunk was missing from the back of her head. Rolling her gently onto her back, Matt knew what he would find. A hole in her forehead with hardly a drop of blood leaking out. The point of entry.

There was no reason to feel for a pulse, but he did so anyway. As he knew, there wasn't one. Gazing out through the balcony's bars, his eyes swept the perimeter of the clinic grounds, then beyond the chain-link fence to the woods and road beyond. He didn't see any vehicles on the road that led up to the clinic, and he didn't see anyone on foot, either. No surprise there.

When he stood up, he realized that Ariadne was standing behind him on the balcony. "Get back!" he shouted. He shoved her roughly into the sitting room, causing her to fall.

"Oh, sweetheart," he said. "I'm so sorry. Are you okay?" He helped her back to her feet.

"I'm fine," she said shakily. "Wh-what happened, do you think?"

"A sniper," he replied. "I want you to come with me downstairs. I'm going after whoever it is, and you're going to stay with Luke somewhere in an interior room." He was already dragging her toward the door.

Kees Vanmeerendonk lowered his rifle in shock. *Two of them? There are two of them! What kind of game are these people playing?* He stood stock-still for several moments, gazing up toward the distant balcony. Coming to his senses, he realized that it was too late to try to get off another shot, and he certainly didn't have time to stand around thinking about what he'd seen. He had to get out of there, and fast. Shouldering his rifle, he started rushing downhill through the woods, ignoring the whiplash of pine branches and the heavy scrub. He didn't have time to waste. Two of the Geneva cell members were going to pick him up not far down the road and take him back to safety.

He stumbled headlong over an outcropping of rock, but picked himself up and fled on, asking himself over and over, *What happened back there? Who did I kill?*

In the hallway, Matt called to Luke. "Get the elevator."

On the way down, he said, "I want you to take her to a safe place in the building. Get her out of range."

"What is going—?" Luke began.

"Just do it!"

In the corridor Dr. Bernheim appeared from a doorway with a puzzled expression.

"Your car keys," Matt said.

"What?"

"Give me your car keys. Hurry."

Dr. Bernheim disappeared inside the office, then reappeared, dangling the keys in a hand. "The Range Rover," he said.

"Which way?"

"The quickest way is the stairs, just down there. It's underground."

Matt was already rushing to the entrance doors to the clinic. Jessie was nowhere in sight. He must have heard the shot, Matt thought. He quickly scanned the grounds but saw no sign of him. He darted back inside, down the hallway to the exit sign, and jumped down the stairs, two, three at a time. Rushed through the door that led to the parking area. Matt spotted the big black Range Rover instantly and jumped in. He roared out of the garage and down the drive toward the clinic's gates.

He saw Jessie running down the side of the road, just past a small pedestrian gate next to the big gate for vehicular traffic. The gate was closed, but Matt saw a remote lying on the car seat. Pressing the OPEN button, he watched as the big gate slowly opened. He raced through.

A few feet ahead, he jammed on the brakes and shouted out the window to Jessie, "Did you see anything?"

"Not a damn thing, but I heard a shot. From off to the left of the road, I think." He pointed into the woods with a hand.

"He's got several minutes' lead on us," Matt said. "Get in."

Jessie rounded the front of the SUV and hopped in on the passenger side. "Hit anybody?"

"Killed the patient we were visiting," Matt said.

"Damn. Must've been down in the woods. I didn't see anything. When I heard it, I ran down to that little pedestrian gate. Had to shoot the lock off to get out here, or I'd be on top of him."

"He couldn't have gone far," Matt said, "and this is the only road leading up this way. Watch for him on your side of the road. I'll watch on mine." He slipped his cell phone off his belt, then held it with his driving hand while he punched in a number with the other.

"Karl," he said to the helicopter pilot, "take off now and survey the woods leading downhill from the clinic. We're probably looking for a single man headed downhill. Maybe a vehicle somewhere on down the mountainside. I'm in a black SUV on the road. Call me if you spot any movement or see a vehicle on or near the road."

"Wonder if he heard the shot," Jessie said as Matt laid the cell phone down.

"Had the radio on. I heard the music," Matt replied, trying to keep one eye on the road, the other on the woods.

They heard the helicopter's engine roar into life uphill behind them, and Matt eased up on the gas, restraining himself from driving too fast. The sniper must be on foot. He'd seen no vehicle from the balcony, and even a small ATV with an expert at the wheel would have trouble maneuvering on the mountainous terrain. But he rolled down all the windows in the unlikely event he could hear a telltale motor over the sound of the helicopter engine.

Both sides of the road were lined with thick, uncleared woods, underlaid with rock and brush, and it was difficult to see beyond a few feet into the growth. Hopefully, the young helicopter pilot would serve as their eyes, catching any movement or the glint of metal or other reflective material in the sun. He was overhead now and off to their left, moving very slowly, the *thwack-thwack-thwack* of the rotors drowning out any other sound. The big SUV had hardly gone another fifteen hundred feet before the cell phone bleated.

Matt grabbed it. "Karl?" He shouted to make himself heard over the noise of the helicopter. Its racket came through the open window and over the phone.

"Just ahead of me," Karl shouted back. "A man tearing downhill. About thirty, forty feet into the woods and fifty, sixty feet downhill of you." There was a pause. "He stopped. On a rock outcrop. Watch me. I'm going to hover over the spot."

Matt slammed on the brakes and followed the helicopter with his eyes as it slowly flew downhill. Jessie opened his door and stood half in, half out of the SUV to get a better view of the chopper.

"Let's go," Matt said. "He's stopped." But Jessie was already back in the car, slamming his door shut.

Matt cruised on downhill, then pulled over to the side of the road and killed the engine. He figured he was about parallel to the spot where the chopper was hovering. He and Jessie jumped out at the same time, pulling their revolvers out of their shoulder holsters as they hunched down and scuttled into the woods.

"You head uphill, and I'll go downhill," Matt told him.

Staying hunched down, the two of them split and headed in the general direction of the chopper. The terrain was rough, boulders and scrub beneath the tall conifers that predominated in the landscape. Keeping the helicopter in sight wasn't easy because of the forest canopy of interlaced branches. Matt hadn't gone more than forty feet into the woods when he saw the chopper change position slightly, moving directly toward him. He ran to take cover behind a big pine but stumbled and fell. Picking himself up, he rushed the rest of the way to the tree and plastered himself against it, his body sideways, concealing as much of himself as possible. He slowly peered around one side, then shifted his body and looked around the other. Nothing. Nor could he hear anything above the roar of the chopper, which was almost directly above him now.

Then he heard the unmistakable sound of a rifle report, even above the deafening *thwack-thwack-thwack* of the helicopter. *He has to be close,* he thought. *Real close.* Hunching down, he swerved to his left, gazing into the woods on that side of the tree, but saw no sign of movement. Quickly shifting to his right, he was certain that scrub about fifteen to twenty feet away quivered in place as if it had been hit. The movement wasn't caused by the downdraft from the chopper. Easing into a squat, he watched and waited, his Heckler & Koch ten-shot autopistol ready to fire.

He kept his gaze focused on the spot where he was sure he'd seen movement. *There!*

Another distinct movement in the scrub, a bush swishing back and forth. Matt brought his pistol up to sight, but before he took aim the sniper jumped out of nowhere, headed directly toward him. A blood-curdling scream issued from his mouth. He heard a report and instantly felt the sting of bark and slivers of wood on his forehead and around his eyes.

Momentarily blinded, he hunkered down behind the tree, trying to protect himself until he could see.

Then he heard one shot. Two. Three. The screaming banshee who was lunging toward him was abruptly silenced.

The instant the screaming stopped, he heard a clatter in front of him. His eyes flew open, and he saw the man going down. His rifle was already on the ground, and it was as if he fell in slow motion, knees hitting the ground first, then his right elbow and wrist, and finally his head, landing facedown with a resounding thunk.

Matt looked down at his pistol. Had he fired it?

He heard a noise behind him and jerked around. One of the guards from the clinic had his gun drawn and aimed at the man on the ground. There was a smug smile on the guard's face.

"I got him before he could get you," he said proudly.

Matt felt the barrel of his revolver. It was cool to the touch. He *hadn't* fired.

"You saved my life," he said to the clinic guard.

The guard shrugged. "Doing my job."

Matt crept over to the man on the ground, leaning down and picking up the rifle. He shouldered the rifle, then knelt down beside the man. As with Nikoletta, it was useless to feel for a pulse, but he did so anyway and affirmed what he already knew. The sniper was dead. Rolling him over, he saw two entry wounds, one in the chest and the other in his neck.

Matt took the cell phone off his belt and pressed in Karl's number. "Do you see Jessie?" he yelled into the phone.

"No," Karl responded.

"Go back to the clinic. I'll meet you there. It's over." He flipped the phone shut and replaced it on his belt, then rummaged through the man's pockets to see if he could find any ID. Finally, in a compartment in his small backpack, he discovered a few euros and a driver's license.

Kees Vanmeerendonk. Amsterdam, Netherlands.

Matt expelled a sigh of relief. Unless this was some trick Mother Earth's Children had pulled on them, they had their man. The one who had been arrested in St. Barth's and almost certainly the same man who'd tried to kill Ariadne at the opening of the PPHL headquarters, thinking she was Nikoletta.

Matt rose to his feet, feeling little sense of satisfaction. This death, like so many others he had witnessed, gave him no pleasure. The young man had been a misguided zealot who had killed Nikoletta, but seeing him dead didn't make Matt feel particularly proud. He was only grateful that Ariadne was safe now.

He made his way through the woods, the guard following close behind him. He met Jessie at the SUV on the road. In the distance, he heard the wail of sirens. They piled into the Range Rover, and sped up the hill toward the clinic and Ariadne. He knew that she was going to need whatever comfort he could give her. She had suffered trauma in her past, but she had never confronted cold-blooded murder.

When he arrived at the clinic, Ariadne had gone back upstairs to Nikoletta's suite after Karl had gotten there and told them what had happened. He thanked the young guard again, then went to her. He found her on the balcony, where she sat with her sister's head cradled in her arms, ignoring the blood and gore as if it didn't exist. He squatted down next to her and put his arms around her. Only then did her tears come.

Chapter Thirty-five

◈

It was as if nothing had ever happened that afternoon in Château-d'Oex, Switzerland. There was no mention of the incident in the newspaper there or anywhere else. The exclusive clinic was more than happy to hush up what had happened on its premises, and the local authorities were cooperative. No one claimed the body of Kees Vanmeerendonk, nor did a halfhearted search for relatives or friends by the authorities turn up anyone who professed to know him.

The cremation of Nikoletta Papadaki took place in Switzerland. Ariadne, Matt, and Adrian were in attendance. Afterward, they picked up her ashes and flew to New York on one of PPHL's private jets in order to bypass any inquisitive customs officers on either side of the Atlantic. It was very unlikely that one of the company jets would be searched.

After they arrived in New York, Ariadne called a gathering of the PPHL advisers. The meeting would be held at Adrian's country house on a Saturday afternoon.

It was a clear and sunny day, with a light breeze, the sky a robin's-egg blue, dotted with puffy white clouds. The group gathered in Adrian's library. The simple box containing Nikoletta's ashes rested on the mantelpiece over the fireplace. Adrian served champagne, having sent the caretakers on errands that would keep them away all day. Then he shared the details of Nikoletta's death with Yves, Sugar, and Angelo.

"I don't think there's any need for me to point out that we have to keep this among ourselves," he concluded.

"Of course," Angelo said, more subdued than usual. Even though he hated Nikoletta Papadaki with all his heart, her death reminded him of his beloved Bianca's.

"Who would believe a word of it anyway?" Sugar said.

"Thank you for telling us about it," Yves Carre said. "It's a very sad end to a very unhappy and destructive life, but there were moments . . ." His voice trailed off into silence.

"There were moments when some of us loved her, despite all her faults," Adrian said. "There's no denying that we all hoped that Nikoletta would change. That she would become the woman we put so much hope in." He nodded in the direction of Ariadne. "Now we're very fortunate that the Papadaki legacy is in the best imaginable hands. We know that Ariadne will do everything her father would have wanted her to."

Ariadne held back the tears that threatened to come. She did want to carry on the legacy of her legendary father.

"Now we'll scatter Niki's ashes here in the garden," Adrian said. "Shall we go outside?" Adrian picked up the box containing Nikoletta's remains.

They all went out onto the terrace, then followed Adrian to the entrance to the formal parterre. With everyone watching, he opened the box and flung its contents to the wind. When he was finished, he hugged Ariadne close with his free arm.

"I guess we're finished here," he said. "Let's go."

They all returned to the house quietly.

"Angelo and Yves and I are heading back into the city," Sugar said. She kissed Adrian, then patted Ariadne's cheeks and kissed her. "I love you, sweetheart," she said, then added with a wink, "Everything's going to be fine."

Angelo kissed her on both cheeks. "I'll see you soon, I hope."

"How is Frans doing?" she asked.

"Remarkably well," Angelo replied, his eyes brightening. "He's a different young man. Healthy, robust even! Giulia has fattened him up a bit, so he won't be modeling anytime soon." He chuckled. "But he has no plans to return to modeling anyway. His whole outlook has changed, and that's a blessing. He's helped me start a youth center nearby for the less privileged, and he goes there every day. It's in honor of Bianca."

"You mean there are children in your area who aren't privileged?" Ariadne asked.

He nodded. "It's like I once told Bianca. You hardly have to go much farther than your own back door to find people in need, and even on Lake Como, rich as it is, you only have to go a little ways to find the disadvantaged."

"That's wonderful news about Frans, Angelo," Ariadne said.

"It is wonderful. I can hardly believe it. No one will ever replace Bianca in my heart, but he's become like a son to me. Now I must go. I want to get back there as soon as possible." He kissed her cheek again. *"Arrivederci, cara."*

"Arrivederci, Angelo."

"Stay as long as you want," Adrian said to Ariadne and Matt. "Make this house your own."

"We'll be leaving soon," Ariadne said. "Matt and I have a lot to do."

After everyone had gone, Ariadne and Matt sat back down on the couch in the library together, grateful to be alone. Matt slid an arm around her shoulder and kissed her cheek.

"I'm so glad it's over," Ariadne said.

"Do you feel a sense of closure?"

"Not really." She turned to him. "Do you think we ever do?"

"I don't know," he replied. "Certainly we won't forget. At least a lot of what's happened."

"I can deal with it," she said. "If I can deal with this masquerade, I can deal with anything."

"Maybe rings on our fingers will make a difference," he said.

"We've got plenty of time for that," Ariadne said. "Don't we?"

"Is that a yes?"

Ariadne brushed his cheek with her lips. "Yes," she whispered into his ear.

Acknowledgments

The author would like to acknowledge Alexandre Dumas (*père*) for the inspiration for the plot of *The Secret Heiress*. While I would never pretend to be capable of producing a masterpiece such as *The Man in the Iron Mask*, I found the temptation to play with his classic story—and to make it my own—irresistible.